Kineo Ablaze

by William David Musser

ISBN: 1456541072
ISBN-13: 9781456541071

Library of Congress Control Number: 2011900745

CONTENTS

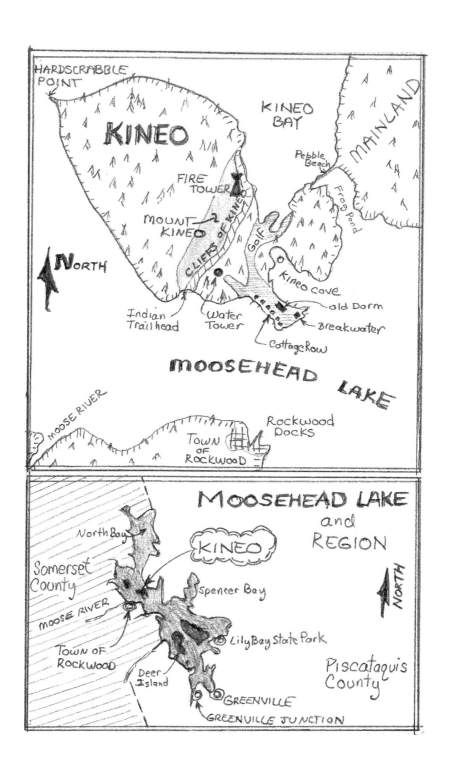

Prologue

Moosehead Lake, 1625

Paddling west along the mouth of Kineo Cove, Kajo heard someone scream out from the shore. It was a cry of distress, a call for help. He had trouble understanding the words; they were slightly different than the Algonquin he had spoken in his youth. Long before he had seen thirty winters pass and headed west, he was fluent in Algonquin, Iroquoian, and English. While trading west of the mighty river that other tribes called the Mississippi, he had learned to speak seven other native languages well enough to trade for the dazzling string of turquoise he wore around his neck.

Kajo saw the canoe-landing area his people called Trout Harvest Point, a place the white invaders would eventually call Sunset Beach. Smoke rose out of the woods in several locations on Kineo. More disturbingly, it was rising up off to the northeast, near Little Mount Kineo. Kajo began to get a sense of the carnage now. The pungent, sickening smell of death by fire was unmistakable everywhere he had traveled. No matter how different people across the world thought they were—usually, how *superior* to those they did not understand—they all shed the same crimson blood. They all smelled just as foul upon death.

Cautiously pulling his canoe ashore, he stepped gingerly out onto the land. His bare feet moved stealthily along the path covered with white pine needles and birch leaves, stepping carefully so that the pine needles muffled the sound of his footsteps. Passing the remains of a small camp, Kajo detected the anguish in a woman's voice in the distance and the sound of feet running toward him. He had no desire to become a part of the madness overtaking this encampment, but could not suppress the anger that was beginning to boil inside him. *You fools! How dare you desecrate the land of the Cow Moose!*

Then suddenly, he saw her, a young mother in flight, heading his way, her child clutched under one arm, its bare feet dangling. The woman's black hair was matted with blood. In her free hand was a scraping tool that normally served to skin beaver hides. Tears made pale tracks down her soot-blackened cheeks. In hot pursuit was an enraged Mohawk warrior, his distinctive black scalplock streaming behind him, his fury fueled by the deep gash that marked the side of his face—evidence of his prey's scraping tool used in self-defense. The gaping wound gushed blood.

The woman rounded the corner, saw Kajo, and squealed in fright, expecting to be trapped. In desperation, she lunged at him with the scraping tool, but the wise shaman anticipated her instinctive reaction and sidestepped the intended assault in one fluid motion. The woman streaked past Kajo, followed by the angry Mohawk who was now almost upon him. The warrior's eyes widened in shock as the older, shorter shaman suddenly appeared in his path, seemingly from nowhere.

Old men are not warriors. It was obvious from Kajo's colorful trinkets and stones that he was not one of the Mohawk's own people. The fierce hunter raised his powerful arm in the air, and a double-bladed hatchet started descending swiftly toward Kajo's head. The shaman didn't flinch as the blade, propelled by the impetus of the hatchet-wielder's rage, swung down at him.

* * *

Rockwood, Maine, in the present

"It sure has, Mrs. Tuttle," the confident voice replied from behind the counter. "Your package from Boston arrived earlier this morning. I'll get it for you."

The elderly woman smiled at the postmaster of Rockwood, a kind man in his fifties the locals called Toonie. He had faithfully worked in the tiny post office for over twenty years. The building was just large enough to accommodate the postal staff needed to serve all of Rockwood, Maine. Toonie didn't mind. He worked best alone. The dozen or so patrons that would visit him this morning were all the company he needed. He enjoyed chatting with his neighbors that came in to mail packages or receive their mail. The residents on the nearby islands had no direct mail-delivery service; so he had plenty of contact with the fine folks of the Moosehead Lake region. Sometimes, the communication lasted fifteen minutes because the locals knew that Toonie always had the latest gossip, serving as the central hub for the exchange of all sorts of personal observations. Such was the life of a small village nestled on the edge of the wilderness. Today was no exception.

Ten minutes later, Mrs. Tuttle strolled out of the Rockwood Post Office, smiling from her pleasant exchanges with the popular postmaster. Toonie watched her leave and waved to her as she looked back from her mud-covered SUV. Behind the vehicle, and across the great lake, the magnificent face of Mt. Kineo served as a picturesque reminder of the symbiotic relationship between the two destinations.

Noticing it was almost noon, Toonie hung the "Out to Lunch" sign on the front door and shuffled back inside. Sliding back behind his desk, he opened the drawer and examined his nine-millimeter. Looking out the window, he saw that no one was in the parking lot; he had a little privacy. Carefully pulling the weapon out of the drawer and sliding the safety off, Toonie raised the firearm and pointed it directly at the face of the ugly man twenty feet to his left.

"Freeze you, mother," he muttered, before slowly squeezing the trigger. The nine-millimeter handgun made a sudden harsh click, but no projectile left the barrel. The postmaster smiled contentedly, knowing that he had expertly eliminated the target once again. The criminal on the Wanted poster was surely a goner, he thought. *If only he would walk into my post office!*

Using a gun rag to wipe the pistol clean with care, Toonie reverently placed it back in his drawer. He sighed, wondering if anything exciting would ever happen in Rockwood. In his twenty years of service as its postmaster and solitary law-enforcement officer, Toonie had fired his weapon in the line of duty only three times: once, to finish off a moose that had been fatally injured by its collision with a truck, and on the other two occasions, to put down deer suffering from grievous injuries after being hit by motorists along the same stretch of road. As Toonie went back to sorting the mail, he could not have known how he would later regret wishing some trouble would wander into his quiet little domain.

PART ONE

Kineo, 1999

1

University of Maine: June 20, 1999

"Sand?" the young graduate student in the second row ventured a guess with little enthusiasm. "How boring."

"Precisely, Miss Walters...sand," responded the immaculately dressed professor.

"In Louisiana, we dig thousands of feet through sand before encountering bedrock." His voice, while dominated by the unmistakable timbre of stuffy academic arrogance, betrayed odd traces of Cajun and the Deep South.

The University of Maine students watched Dr. Les Mongeau shuffle his oxblood loafers across the center of the auditorium. The professor to his right shook his head, noticing how his older colleague enjoyed every moment of center stage as he delivered his over-rehearsed lecture. The deliberate, if meaningless pauses between his comments betrayed overconfidence and lent an unnecessary dramatic thrust to his delivery that was, oftener than not, confusing, rather than interesting. Keenly studying the students' reactions that betrayed confusion, Dr. Wayne realized it was not quite the effect Les was aiming for.

"Rock, Miss Walters, is certainly a more intriguing geologic material. In Maine, we are fortunate to have lots of it." Dr. Mongeau advanced to the next slide. "Here, you see us during our earlier trip this summer, collecting samples from Mt. Kineo."

At the sight of the mountain rising above Moosehead Lake, the students focused their attention on the slides.

Staring over the top of his bifocals and directly into Miss Walters's half-open eyes, Dr. Mongeau raised his voice suddenly. "Throughout most of Maine, a thin crust of sediment from either Quaternary glacial or glacio-marine origins conceals our bedrock material. The lush forests we see today protrude out of soil from this upper veneer layer."

He displayed several representative slides to illustrate his point, then looked searchingly at his students, seeking confirmation that he had captivated them with his dramatic lecturing style and audio-visual aids. Most of them seemed to be simply biding their time till lunch break.

"The most spectacular places in Maine are where the landscape has been created by exposed rugged bedrock, as is visible on the bare mountaintops of Mt. Katahdin, Cadillac Mountain, and Mt. Kineo."

"What time do we leave for Kineo?" a male student-assistant interjected.

"Allow me to finish this segment of my presentation, Mr. Landon!" Mongeau snapped. "Then I'll go over the field-trip agenda for next week."

Sensing that the students needed a break after being saturated with Mongeau's morning topic, "Lithography and Geologic Formations of Central Maine", Dr. Wayne stood up to explain the details of the upcoming trip.

"By all means, Dr. Wayne," his colleague mumbled, retreating from center stage and allowing Max a moment to rejuvenate his audience. Neither a flashy dresser nor a flamboyant lecturer like his colleague, Max Wayne was warm and approachable. The students loved him. Keenly aware of their adoration for his colleague, Dr. Mongeau had to make an effort to restrain the mild sense of resentment it aroused within him. Max presented a disheveled appearance, apparently too busy with his research and academic interests to be bogged down by seemingly mindless and unproductive routines such as shaving every morning or wearing neckties for lectures. He did not consider making his bed every morning a priority and his office was a mess of books, papers, and uncompleted projects.

Max was quite unaware that his rugged good looks and air of intensity appealed to women of all ages. Although his mannerisms were often nerdy and his social graces needed refinement, his cheerful grin could disarm the most determined adversary.

What bothered Les Mongeau most, however, was the fact that his colleague remained quite fit and athletic for an academic. Although a consistently snappy dresser, Les had to squeeze himself into his pleated slacks and freshly pressed oxford button-down shirts, fighting a never-ending battle with his ever-growing girth. With his width fast approaching the measurement that corresponded to his height, Mongeau's clothes had to be tailored to fit his disproportionate frame. He stood only five foot four, whereas Max was tall and lean. During his undergraduate days, Max had been the team captain of his NCAA championship volleyball team where he was known for his wicked spikes. Despite an occasional twinge of petty jealousy, Les admired Max as much as any colleague. The two of them often combined their talents on joint research projects, where solving complex puzzles required fact-gathering from several scientific fields. In the case of that day's lecture, the topics included a blend of geologic and archeological findings.

"Well, ladies and gents," Dr. Wayne began casually, "we had a fun time earlier this summer and gathered much interesting data. But for those of you that were not able to join us, let me set the stage. We set off on this adventurous field trip in several speedy watercraft across the largest lake in Maine."

"Ugh!" groaned Margo.

"Not the old pontoon boats again!" quipped student-assistant Rob Landon.

"Nothing but the best equipment for *our* students, Rob!" laughed Max.

None of the students detected the hint of wariness underlying his cheerful tone as he addressed the younger man.

"Offering the comfort of shredded upholstery, our university pontoon boats will cruise Moosehead Lake once again," Max promised.

"Heck, those boats were fun!" argued another student.

"I hear they opened a new cute shop in Greenville," an attractive blonde undergraduate commented, inviting a few chuckles.

"Why yes, Tonya. You're right," Dr. Wayne allowed. "I presume you mean the new outdoor gear and fly-fishing shop?"

"Why, of course, professor," she teased back.

Julie Walters rolled her eyes at Tonya whose company she found insufferable at times because of her airs, her perfectly manicured nails, and her model-like head of hair.

"We staying at the old dorm again, Dr. Mongeau?" interjected Rob, turning away from Max who made him uneasy.

"Certainly, Mr. Landon," answered the professor, happy to have the question directed at him. Then seizing the opportunity to occupy center stage again, he turned back to the students. "The igneous mountain range that towers over the lake and forms Mt. Kineo abruptly slices the forty-mile-long lake in half, displaying one of the world's most interesting rhyolite formations."

"And Dr. Mongeau," Gary Micnick added, "Doesn't Mt. Kineo look like...a large sperm whale skimming across the surface of Moosehead?"

"Oh Mr. Micnick, really now!" the professor protested. "Do we have to degrade this intriguing igneous formation with such inane descriptions?"

"Actually, Les," Dr. Wayne interjected, "for the early Indians in the area, Mt. Kineo did resemble the back of a huge animal rising from the lake. According to an old Indian legend, the mountain is assumed to be the petrified remains of a monster moose sent to Earth by the Great Spirit to punish men for their sins."

"Really?" quipped Dr. Mongeau, his tone sarcastic.

All the students snickered—except Rob Landon. He was troubled by the secret he'd kept from the professors for several weeks now. He was in possession of a significant artifact from their earlier visit to Kineo. Bringing home what he imagined to be a geologic curiosity had seemed a minor transgression at the time. But the more he researched the possibilities of his findings, the more the object seemed to acquire archeological significance. All the more reason for Dr. Max Wayne to be furious if he found out. *I'd probably be expelled from the program*, Rob reasoned. It was clear that Max did suspect something. Rob wasn't sure just how much he had figured out, but was disturbed by the prospect of his professor finding out all too soon.

* * *

Rockwood, Maine

Jean Pilloud strolled onto the rear upper balcony of his ostentatious, 20,000-square-foot residence—the pride of his twenty-acre estate in Rockwood, Maine. It had taken him three years to complete the construction. But that was before his company had been hit by hard times. He looked out over Moosehead Lake, forty feet below him. The wind at this time of year was so unpredictable. Earlier, the waves had been crashing into his boat landing and whitecaps speckled the horizon. Now the wind had stilled and the black flies were beginning to swarm. At first, he could barely feel one of them biting the back of his neck. The blood-sucking parasites reminded him of so many of his business acquaintances and, more revoltingly—of his family. Stealthily alighting on the back of his neck, the tiny insect began draining the fluids from his flesh so skillfully and surreptitiously as to be barely noticeable at the outset. Then suddenly, Pilloud's nerves snapped to attention with the annoyingly familiar recognition of his skin being violated. The nasty lump its bite left would serve as a daily reminder of the pilfering that had taken place from his wealth of living fluids and tissues. *Yes, black flies and family. Black flies and business associates.* He saw far too many parallels.

A tall, lean man in a black skintight synthetic tee shirt and jeans entered, a drink in each hand, opening the French doors without spilling the contents of either the can of Canadian lager from his employer's native land or the glass of vintage Burgundy from his own. The solemn man on the balcony observed the difficulty with which the other one carried out this tricky maneuver, but made no move to help him. A man of Pilloud's stature expected others to serve him. Smacking the fly from his neck, he watched the other man close the French doors with a nudge of his wrist.

"Très bien," Pilloud said by way of greeting, addressing the other man. "Join me." His words were less invitation than command.

Without uttering a word, the other man handed the wine to his employer. He then took his designated position at the Plexiglas half-wall overlooking the lake and gazed out into the cove.

"I never tire of this view," Pilloud offered.

"You wanted to see me," responded the other man.

"Fine. Right to the point," Pilloud conceded. "Our initiatives did not go as planned last year." He continued to stare into his wine glass. "Last summer was a disaster. You and your men failed to locate the guardian gemstone. I want matters promptly attended to this summer—*professionally.*" Pilloud's expression held menace as he looked up in a deliberate manner, locking eyes with the intimidating mercenary. "This time, you may do whatever is needed to ensure we finish what we started. Go and do what you are paid for!"

"Understood." The tall thin man gulped down the last of his beer, smacked his aluminum can down on the top rail of the Plexiglas, and left the balcony without further comment.

＊ ＊ ＊

"As you can see in this slide, Mt. Kineo offers sheer cliffs of weathering rock overhanging Kineo Bay," Mongeau continued. "Amazingly, the grinding action of glaciers in the past has carved the lake's deepest channel, directly underneath the famous cliff shown in this slide. Here, the lake plunges to a depth of over two hundred and thirty feet!"

"Will we be able to climb the mountain this time?" Julie Walters directed her question specifically at Dr. Wayne.

"Miss Walters," responded Dr. Mongeau, "the crumbly igneous features of this formation are not safe for climbing, even with climbing gear."

"And Julie, most of those routes are a mere five point five to five point eight. Nothing that would interest a climber of your caliber," added Max with his infectious smile.

"Aw! Well, I'll bring my gear anyway this time and show you guys a few moves."

A few male snickers at the unintended innuendo were met with a stern look from Julie. With a pre-emptive snarl, she turned to Gary Micnick, infamous for his chauvinistic humor, and promptly made him swallow back the comment he had been about to let loose.

"Actually, Dr. Wayne," Julie continued, "I know some climbers that do the eastern face and there are, in fact, some five-point-nine to five-point-ten routes. I would like to try a few when we have some free time."

"All right, Julie, bring your gear and show us what you've got."

Max was puzzled by Rob's apparent satisfaction at Julie being granted permission to take her equipment along. "Now, class, my turn," he grinned, turning away from Rob Landon. "The earliest history of man in the Moosehead Lake/Mt. Kineo region is believed to date back to nearly eleven thousand years ago, when the first Paleo-Indians discovered the area. These people were skilled hunters of big game, especially caribou."

Julie's excitement waned as the archeological slides followed, one after the other. While her attention was riveted on the handsome professor at center stage, his words would only be half-absorbed.

"These early hunters," Max went on, "ate bear, moose, and deer, especially during the warmer months. With time, that is, around seven thousand years ago, Indians were living at Kineo, sustained by hunting, gathering, and fishing. Then approximately three thousand years ago, Woodland Indians came from all over North America to harvest the famous Kineo flint."

"Flint?" Dr. Mongeau said with a tone of dissapointment. "Anyone remember what true flint is? Anyone except those that were on Kineo with us last time?" he challenged.

"It's siliceous hornstone—comprised of silicon dioxide," replied an interested geology student in the front row.

"Precisely, sir. Good. Very good. However, despite my colleague's insistence on using the native's colloquial term, there is no flint on Kineo. Flint is a sedimentary rock, as you may recall from your introductory geology classes. Igneous processes formed Mt. Kineo which is entirely volcanic extrusive rock. The rhyolite was born from violent explosions of steam and volcanic ash. It simply displays the mechanical properties of flint. Okay, continue, Dr. Wayne. I got carried away again."

"No, that's fine. We have some new students going this time."

The next slide appeared. Max combed his fingers through his long black hair—an idiosyncrasy that several of the students mimicked in playful jest. From Julie's vantage position in the front row, it was a gesture more significant than a simple nervous habit. That unconscious stroking caused her insides to stir.

"This was during the era of the Red Paint People who were also big-game hunters," Max went on. "And it witnessed substantial movement to Kineo of indigenous peoples who were motivated by their pursuit of the flint, prized because it could be fashioned into tools and weapons for survival."

Dr. Wayne now turned to the students and challenged, "Anyone care to impress me with proof that you've read your lesson this week?"

Gary responded promptly. "Several work areas have been discovered on Kineo. It is believed that the 'injuns' used to collect the best flint and break it into smaller chunks on the island to make tools and weapons. These were actually worked on at nearby camps on the lake, and sometimes used to trade with the other local inebriated 'injuns' for items such as Moosehead lager."

"Very good, Gary. Ten bonus points," applauded Max. "But I believe you'll find the articles you read used the term 'indigenous peoples'. So minus four points for your lack of political sensitivity."

The class burst out laughing and someone from the back row yelled out, "Gary, you suck up!"

Gary stood up and took a bow as the guy behind him began making kissing sounds.

"Moosehead lager? Really now, Mr. Micnick, must we be so…" Dr. Mongeau began to protest.

"Well, Gary, do you wish to finish the lecture now, or is there a question?" Max shook his head at the class.

"Naw! You can finish, Doc. You were doing just fine."

In the back of the auditorium, unnoticed by anyone, sat an older woman with long grayish white hair, quietly observing the proceedings. She was not amused by the exchange of banter in the front of the lecture hall. Nor was she interested in the geology portions of the session. Observing Dr. Wayne with intense curiosity, she thought to herself: *It must be that one…that has something precious of mine. Something ancient. You should not have messed with something you do not understand. It must be returned. Very soon, Dr. Wayne. Very soon.*

2

Three weeks earlier in Tampa, Florida: May 29, 1999

Jennifer Denton felt both excited and sad. It wasn't as though she had never been away from home for the summer, but this time was different. Way different. She sat in the car's back seat, wedged between her nine-year-old younger brother, Brandon, and the box of movies, books, and games the family had brought along for entertainment on their two-and-a-half-day journey to Maine. Through the rear-view window, she watched her home recede into the distance as they drove off.

Brandon was busy playing his Game Boy. The little alien made a pre-programmed squealing noise each time the boy successfully exterminated an extraterrestrial target with his well-honed shooting skills. Tuning out everyone in the car, the "shooter", in contrast, was silent and virtually invisible. Jenny was uncharacteristically quiet, despondent about leaving her best friend, Maria Hernandez, behind and wishing her father was with them.

"Mom! Mom?" the girl finally began.

Laura Denton was not accustomed to sitting in the command chair, the driver's seat of their SUV, on long trips; her husband, David, had assumed that position for so many years. The mother of three was lost in thought, wondering what to do, how far to push, where to stay that night, and how much they could afford.

"Yes, Jenny, what is it?" she replied listlessly, distracted by her many concerns.

"How long will it be till we get there?" her daughter asked.

A long pause ensued. Wondering if she was going to get an answer, Jenny glanced up at the rear-view mirror and caught her mom looking back at her. Laura Denton's lips were pressed tightly together. She did not like to be interrupted when she was deep in contemplation and her expression told Jenny she was going to be lectured to again.

"Honey," she finally responded in her slight southern accent. "I told ya it would be a long trip. Maine's a long drive from Tampa, Jenny, and you'll just have to sit back and find things to do to entertain yourself. Look how quiet and content Brandon is."

Thomas, Laura's first-born, sat in the front seat next to his mother, his MP3 player in his lap, bobbing his head up and down to some uninspired beat from an illegally downloaded song from the Internet.

"Mom…Mom?" Jenny persisted, her mind drifting off and reflecting on the plans she had discussed with Maria this summer. Jenny hadn't wanted to spend her summer in Maine.

"Yes, Jenny. What do you need now?"

"Oh… I was just wondering. Would it be all right to invite Maria to fly up and spend a weekend with us at this new summer house in Maine?"

Laura expelled a long-drawn-out sigh. This was usually not a good sign. The girl wondered if her mother understood how special a friend Maria was for her, the only one that had comforted her when Jenny's father had unexpectedly passed.

"Jenny, we've been over this before," Laura said firmly. "We have a lot to do when we get there. This cottage is over a hundred years old. It'll be a lot of work to restore it so we can open and run it as a bed and breakfast. This will be a fun adventure, sweetie, and a great life experience for all of us. Next year, dear, will be better."

Thomas snickered. Even through his headphones, Jenny's older brother had not failed to acknowledge his sibling's shortcomings. Back to concentrating on her summer concerns, Laura did not notice. Jenny began to tear up as she mumbled to herself, "I wish Daddy were still around!" *He was so creative—making up games for us kids to play in the car on long trips.*

3

Moosehead Lake, Maine, May 29, 1999

Sixteen hundred miles north of Florida, a thirty-foot wooden boat steadily trolled the channel between Rockwood and Kineo. It was a sunny day, sixty-five degrees, with a stiff and constant breeze. The water in Moosehead Lake was no warmer than fifty degrees at the surface and much colder in the depths, where several deep riggings were knifing through the frigid waters. Captain Gus O'Malley stroked his red beard, mottled with gray, frustrated at having to take his boat across the channel without his mate, Jimbo. Not that he wasn't capable of handling the six lines trolling the deep water; it was the lack of company that actually bothered Gus.

The brookies were running deeper than he had expected for this time of year; he considered laying out more line. He had been enticing the brook trout with his favorite lures at depths ranging from thirty to seventy feet, but suspected they were hanging deeper in the channel that guarded the coast of the great cliffs of Kineo. He wanted strikes from either salmon or brookies to verify where the good catch would be, since he had booked several early-season tourists from New Jersey. Such urban visitors often expected a large catch for their day of fishing, or a refund for their wasted efforts. Gus's business was teetering on the brink of bankruptcy, as the fishing in the big lake was no longer what it used to be. *Those damn crawfish!* Their population had exploded in the lakes, the cause, local anglers believed, of the decline in the lake's overall piscine population.

Something was troubling Gus as he let out some line on his deep rigs; his canine teeth had nearly gnawed off the end of the half-chewed stogie dangling from his sun-speckled lips. *Damn you, Jimbo. I'll bet you, Dougie, and Junior stayed out drinking last night till dawn.* He was going to have to talk to that irresponsible young man about his priorities once again.

In the distance, a row of historic cottages along the southwestern lakeshore presented an appealing vista of pastel colors. Each one displayed the characteristic architectural style left over from a glorious age of blossoming tourism that had been a part of the island's past. It seemed to Gus's fanciful imagination that this special island and her towering mountain of volcanic rock, was nestled within Moosehead Lake's nurturing embrace. The wind patterns and water currents, however, behaved erratically from time to time, making flying or boating quite a challenge for the unsuspecting skipper or pilot unfamiliar with this area.

To the south, Kineo was lined with cottages that had successfully resisted the ravages of bitter winter, frequent fires, and gale-force winds. The lake was well known for its rough chop and unpredictable weather—a combination of its fetch length and the effects of the winds skirting around the mountain. Within minutes, the tranquil lake could be whipped into a frenzy with terrifying six-foot swells, and the frigid waters were capable of inducing hypothermia in no time at all. Gus knew this all too well. Swamped by such a gale about twenty years ago, he was lucky enough to have been within fifty yards of the Rockwood shore. Having survived his brush with death on the big lake, the hair-raising experience now inspired, to his secret delight, one of his most thrilling—and highly embellished—tales.

Frustrated with his lack of success and Jimbo's dereliction of duty, Gus didn't even bother to admire the row of historic cottages as he passed them. Two of them had been completely repainted last summer; and now, emerging from the thawing snow drifts that had nearly buried them this winter; the cottages blossomed with color on the peninsula like spring flowers adorning the mountainside. Even if Gus had stopped to take note, he would not have seen the red flicker of light beginning to intensify in the yellow cottage near the end of Kineo Cove—now beyond his range of vision—as he moved west across the glacier-carved channel. Convinced that he simply was not going to meet with success today and annoyed that he had been left to do all this work by himself, Gus steered his boat to the south, away from the channel. He plucked out a fresh cigar from his pocket and wetted the end in his mouth.

"Mm," he murmured, tasting the spicy leaves. He pulled his lighter out from his pocket and flicked the butane into action, producing temporal life for the little flame. He paused, gave off a sort of muffled grunt, and slid the lighter back into his pocket without igniting the rolled leaves. He chewed the end of the cigar, instead, as if it were gum. He had given up smoking long ago. He began setting up his desperate back-up plan—to catch togue if he had to—since catching large fish—*any* fish—was, after all, what made those idiotic tourists happy.

"Ugh!! I hate hooking togue. No sport in that!"

On Kineo, the lone yellow cottage projected a peaceful appearance from the exterior; but inside, a small, strategically lit flame, hovered in remission, like a cancer, ready to spring to life at any moment. This historic fishing cottage had been built in 1897 as an adjunct to the hotel resort that once graced the island and provided jobs to thousands in the Moosehead region. That was long ago. Long before the fire of 1948 had burned the last remnant of the grand hotel down to the ground, leaving in its final resting place a scorched area where the conflagration had produced sufficiently high temperatures to melt and warp an old metal field plough into an unrecognizable version of its former self. And now, half a century later, the old iron carcass still remained. Rusting away in a barren field, it resembled a pathetic tombstone—the only reminder of the last great fire.

This particular two-story cottage, however, was not part of Cottage Row. Constructed a few years earlier at the north end of Kineo Cove, it had provided fishing boats safe harborage from the destructive winds and rough waters. Used primarily as a fishing and hunting cottage, the structure was clearly visible from the Kineo docks, but not from Kineo Pass.

On its first floor, the red glow brightened. The plentiful cleaning supplies, along with old cloths and rags, in its mudroom were just the kind of inflammable items that could, given a chance, be used to ignite a furious reminder to those who meddled where they did not belong.

Approximately two miles away, Gus turned his fishing boat into his private marina and docked. Stumbling over a loosened board on the old dock, he grumbled to himself: Where the hell were those brookies? *Where the hell were the salmon? Not even a blasted togue! Grr! Jimbo, you're going to get an earful from me ten minutes before I kick your ass!* With his patience nearly exhausted, Gus trudged up the wooden stairs of his fishing base camp.

On Kineo, the restored yellow cottage, now inescapably ablaze, disappeared from the island. Its important history had already begun to fade, and its secret began to vanish. Gus would hear about the loss of this historic structure that night at Kate's Bar and Grill on the Moose River. The local patrons would be withdrawn tonight, contemplating the portentous meaning of the latest in a bizarre history of fires on the island. Gus, however, would likely hang out near the out-of-town fishing enthusiasts, oblivious to the significance of that afternoon's events.

* * *

Pastor Davis searched his hymnal for an inspirational hymn that would support his upcoming sermon when, suddenly, he was startled by the shadow of a huge man lurking in the corner next to him. Only one member of the Rockwood Community Church could cast such a large shadow.

"Bear?"

"It's me, Pastor. Sorry to have startled you."

"No, it's...well...you move so quietly and appear so suddenly."

"I'm sorry. I just did not want to disturb you when you were preparing for a sermon."

"No. No, Bear. You are always welcome here, my friend. Come. What troubles you?"

Pastor Davis had grown to respect the huge man. The tiny community church was a sanctuary for Bear, as most of the people on Kineo had not forgiven him for his earlier involvement in certain dubious matters. Of course, that had all happened before he turned his attention to God for higher guidance.

Bear was a virtual giant at nearly six foot seven inches. His intimidating mountain-man physique had been carefully sculpted from years of working the timberlands of Montana, and he bore an uncanny resemblance to Brutus from the old Popeye cartoons, except that his lower half was trimmer. A few locals dared to refer to him as Brutus, but only when they were at least fifty paces beyond the range of his exceptionally sharp hearing. The amusing thing was that despite his immense size and strength, the man was really a peace-loving and sensitive human being.

Having arrived in the region as an "outsider", he was always trying to prove himself. Though rugged and resourceful as an outdoorsman, in the final breakdown, Bear was not a true blood "Maine-iac". Despite living in the northeast for the past ten years, he had not acquired even a trace of the local New England accent. Bear had come to Maine to work timber and had been hired by the great Kokadjo Timber and Paper Company. His shrewd mind and formidable size had caught the attention of the management. Soon, he was one of the owner's favorite henchmen, assisting in negotiating special deals with particularly difficult state agencies and hostile landowners.

Eventually, his skills had placed him at odds with folks in the Moosehead region. Bear had purchased property on Kineo and was in the process of building a home for himself and his trophy wife, Rebecca. Becky was the niece of the Kokadjo Timber and Paper Companies' president—Jean Pilloud. Although the company had made the Pillouds wealthy, it had recently fallen on hard times. Jean Pilloud had now embarked on a different path to reclaim the family's past glory, a depraved path known to none, barring a few insiders.

When Bear was asked by his company to help negotiate on a very controversial issue involving Kineo, his role did not endear him to his neighbors. Despite his instinctive misgivings about acting against their interests, Bear found himself giving in to his employer and his own wife who encouraged him to go ahead. All it required was a little ego building, a significant monetary incentive, and some carefully leaked misinformation to convince the large man to execute his duties as a "team player". Bear only learned about the misinformation after it was too late. Becky had exercised a strong influence on his ultimate decision, since she enjoyed spending the family resources faster than Bear could earn his living through honest means.

The Kokadjo Timber and Paper Company had Bear inform the locals that their intention was to resurrect Kineo's former grandeur with a historic replica of the old hotel of 1884, with all modern amenities. Then an informant inside the company leaked the truth that Pilloud's hidden agenda was to erect a modern-day resort facility on the island; he would allow "accidental" fires to burn down the remaining historic structures. Once the truth was out, the already suspect concept plan was met with fanatical resistance by people from Greenville, Rockwood, and, of course, Kineo.

Bear was never able to escape the ignominy of his involvement in the underhand dealings. Distraught at being singled out by many of the locals as the main culprit in the scandal, he sank into depression and resorted to drinking cases of Moosehead lager. Becky filed for divorce. After a bitter legal battle, funded on Becky's behalf by her uncle, Jean Pilloud, Bear ended up with nothing but their controversial land holdings on Kineo. His ex-wife took all of their worldly possessions and, most importantly, their only son, Jacob. In the last weeks of Bear's now termoiled employment with the Kokadjo Timber and Paper Company, he was involved in a freak accident while visiting one of the neighboring lumber mills. A log slipped from the harness in a lift and crushed his leg. A large insurance settlement from the strange mishap benefited Bear financially, but left him without a position at the Kokadjo Timber and Paper Company.

The accident guided Bear back to God to seek answers. He desperately sought mercy for his involvement in the dubious dealings and for the outcome of the freak accident that had left him with a noticeable limp in his left leg. Bear considered the limp a lifelong reminder from God of what happens if you stray too far from the righteous path.

Thereafter, his newfound monetary blessings were invested frivolously on Kineo—the very island he had apparently betrayed. Now out of the picture by choice, Becky was furious that the accident had occurred after the finalization of their divorce; she would never see a dime of that particular insurance money. But then again, an angry woman of her ilk had other ways to extract her "fair share" when sufficiently motivated. Becky was a beautiful young woman, equipped with a formable arsenal of powerful connections, and she certainly wasn't lacking in motivation.

Ironically, Bear's penitence on Kineo had slowly transformed him into a headstrong Kineo devotee, yearning to preserve its rich history. He had taken a personal vow that the company that had made a clandestine attempt to destroy Kineo and had cast him aside would never succeed in its endeavors. In the end, Bear cared more about Kineo than Becky and her manipulative family. He dedicated his remaining time and resources to Kineo, like a watchful guardian caring for a vulnerable child. Many of the older locals were not quick to dismiss his early transgressions and plenty of snide comments were tossed at him in his presence. Bear seemed content, however, to regard such remarks as part of the atonement for his sins. He channeled his hurt pride and bitter feelings into constructive energy as a faithful member of the Rockwood Community Church, where he had developed a strong admiration for Pastor Davis.

"You still fighting with Rebecca over Jacob?"

"She's an evil bitch, Pastor!"

"Bear! Do not use such language in the house of our Lord."

"I'm sorry, Pastor. You're right. I'm just so mad at her."

"She certainly has lots to worry about if she does not ask for forgiveness, as you have done, but…still… You must practice patience and allow God to help you."

"I know. But she enjoys taunting me. Not letting me see Jacob when I want to and…"

"Bear. Her uncle had great influence with the court and she got the better of the deal. We all know that. Those terms can be amended. But only if you can show the court that you can honor your commitments and become accepted in the community again. Your temper is not an asset when it comes to resolving these problems. Now kneel down with me and pray for strength, son."

"Yes, Pastor. You're right, of course."

* * *

That evening, Gus burst into the Rockwood bar, wearing his usual tan long-sleeved shirt, frayed threadbare at the elbows, under a light, sleeveless sweater. His well-worn slacks were still stained below the knees in the exact places Kate had noticed the previous weekend. Motor oil. His shoes scuffed across a sagging plywood patch in the floor as he rushed over to her. Kate, his greatest friend, the successful restaurateur, and the woman with whom he wished he had taken his relationship further, when he had the chance many years ago. Gus bellowed out a hearty hello to Kate who responded promptly with a sincere inquiry about his day on the lake. Gus grumbled about Jimbo, provided a few excuses for his bad luck, and let out a loud, awkward laugh. Patting Kate affectionately on the shoulder, he reached into his pocket and located the new cigar he had been fantasizing about on the drive over. Gus briefly examined the precious possession between his fingers before sliding onto "his" seat at the bar.

Kate informed him about the fire on Kineo earlier that day, a piece of news that wiped the smile from his face. He paused to reflect on this new development, grunted, and chewed the end of his stogie. Kate turned away to confirm drink orders with Roy, her husband. The latter agreed to watch the bar for a while so that she could join the local patrons engaging in the latest gossip. Kate drifted away from the bar area, ignoring Gus for the remainder of the night. With the destruction of the old Wellington cottage, there were more serious issues to consider.

The beautiful yellow building had hosted several families in past years. Recently, a family from Massachusetts had restored the cottage. The Goldmans would occupy it with their three young children when school was out in July and August. It was now only the end of May. So Dr. and Mrs. Goldman were not due for another month. Aaron Goldman was a respected orthopedic surgeon from Boston. Gossip had it that their restoration had cost around $300,000. The Wellington cottage had been finally converted into their dream vacation home. This year, they had been planning to invite the entire family and friends living nearby to enjoy an entire month with them at the historic cottage. They would, undoubtedly, be devastated by the news about their vacation home.

Already, Bear and his small entourage of followers had assembled in their favorite booth at the back that faced the marina on the river. On Friday nights, Bear would buy drinks for the few people in the area that had forgiven him and scheme about ways to bring tourists back to Kineo. Even Bennington Lomax, normally too sophisticated to mingle with the crustier locals, had made an appearance that evening, elegantly gliding across Kate's floor and quietly slipping into the booth next to Bear's. In times of duress, mainlanders and islanders came together at Kate's bar and united as a community.

Even those who still harbored ill will toward Bear temporarily cast aside those feelings; more pressing concerns were on everyone's minds that night. Although rarely seen in this "blue collar" circle, Bennington would prove to be insightful when discussing the latest mishap on Kineo. At the conclusion of their discussions, he was overheard telling Bear that it might be nice if he called Mrs. Denton in the morning to alert her about the burned cottage before the single mother arrived there with her three eager kids. Fires such as the one that had obliterated the yellow cottage were most unsettling.

Meanwhile, at the bar, Gus had loosened up with a few scotches, found a group of "touries"—the name he used for Moosehead Lake tourists—and embarked on his captivating and highly animated stories. After too many scotches, the clarity of his enunciation blurred, and he began babbling on about the curse of fire on Kineo and how it had exacted revenge on the Wellingtons. Most of the patrons laughed at the strange man's rantings. Some, further away in the bar, mocked him. A few locals, disconnected with the gathering in the back booth area, successfully baited Gus into narrating more tales of mysterious Kineo. Finally, the small gathering became absorbed as they watched this funny man bellow out his infectious chuckle, laughing heartily at his own jokes, lewd innuendos, and perverted gestures. As Gus descended deeper into an inebriated state, he perceived himself to be a more interesting person, with his manner growing more animated and the words flowing thick and fast from his lips. It was the yearning to draw attention to himself that helped him hide the bitter loneliness he wrestled with every time he went home alone to his little fish camp.

Soon, even Gus's most captivating tale of the sunken steamship, *Piscataquis*, and its precious lost cargo could no longer hold the interest of his tiny following. The touries shuffled out the door, filled with enough local folklore to last them for a while. The anglers and fishermen had already left, as they would have to rise early to catch daybreak on the big lake and the local white-water rivers.

Gus swirled his last bit of scotch and, in one gulp, banged it down the hatch. He sighed to himself, realizing that it had been an unrewarding evening. *No one really seemed all that interested in my wisdom tonight*, he lamented. Loneliness spawned bitterness. He had only entertained a few touries. None of his local friends seemed to care he was there. Hiding his disappointment, he rose from the bar stool, slid several crisp twenties onto the bar counter, generously settling far more than his tab, and then departed. No one had appeared interested in his last tale of the night about the strange black sphere that Jimbo and Junior claimed to have found. Unbeknownst to him, a tall tourist in retro black glasses, sitting by the mounted moose head on the back wall, had, in fact, strained to catch the story. None knew who he was, and none cared, for he too had slipped out unobtrusively, virtually unnoticed.

4

May 30, 1999

At 4:45 a.m., while the sun was still rising above the jagged line of eastern white pines on the horizon, a figure descended a winding trail near Little Mt. Kineo. A gray horse with dark, steely eyes and a long black mane carefully picked a path through a patch of unripe blueberries. Other than the horse's breathing and an occasional bird signaling its neighbors that it was time to wake up, the woods were silent.

Riding the horse was an elderly woman with long grayish white hair cascading halfway down her back. Her wary eyes scanned the woods. Her wiry arms were so taut that her sechum tattoo had not lost its shape after all these years. She guided the horse confidently along the steep, poorly defined trail and examined the ground purposefully. She recognized a ravine from which she had last recovered precious relics. Dismounting, she walked over to a fir tree and recognized markings she had etched into its bark only two weeks ago. She had just enough time for a brief search if she were to be on and off Mt. Kineo by 5:15. Even though there were few residents on the island this time of the year, she still preferred to conclude her business on Kineo early and escape to the security of her domicile to the east. *Why risk being seen by an early-morning riser?*

The old woman raked her fingers through the leaf litter and dug down into the soil. The faintness of the predawn light did not deter her. Her eyesight had not deteriorated despite her advanced years. Under her fingers, she felt the shape of a rigid object that she knew was not a weathered piece of the mountain rising above her. She extricated it from the soil and felt the pointed end of the crafted stone carefully. Holding the historic stone up to the faint light of dawn, she smiled at her good fortune at being able to retrieve such a valuable prize in so short a time.

In the space from which the abandoned weapon point had been unearthed, she noticed another lighter-colored object. Digging deeper into the ground, she uncovered the rounded head of a femur bone and gently prodded it out from its resting place. *So many died here—so long ago.* It saddened her to think about the greed-crazed madness that had swept the area. They had never found them all for a proper burial. With too little time left, she would have to return to this spot later. Marking the same tree again with a botanically derived pigment, she remounted Katobaquis and galloped down to the shore of Moosehead Lake.

Within minutes, she had trotted to the isthmus of Kineo and was urging Katobaquis carefully forward. The horse often seemed spooked when approaching Kineo from this direction. Digging his hooves into the rounded cobblestones of Pebble Beach, Katobaquis forged up the sixty-foot-long inclined entrance pathway to Kineo. The pathway, like all pathways here, was a gravel trail, approximately ten feet wide. The more recent inhabitants of Kineo had prohibited motorized vehicles, apart from golf carts, on these "roads". On this particular morning, however, the pathway provided access for only an old horse and his mistress.

Rounding the lower bend, she noticed the old boathouse. She remembered how it served the main shuttle boat, filling the island with white skins. But that was long ago. Now the old timber rafters collapsed a little more into the cove each year. The winters in North Woods Maine were particularly harsh on decaying wooden structures.

Katobaquis continued to advance, following the smell of smoke. The old woman finally traced it to its source. *So it was true. The old Wellington cottage had burned to the ground as well. We are cursed!* Slowly now and silently, she urged Katobaquis up to the charred remains of the old cottage. Razed to the ground though it was, smoke still billowed up from several of the larger smoldering beams.

"The Wellington place, Katobaquis! If only..." she muttered to the horse. "Siding with the English has always had drawbacks. Someone has been messing with sacred grounds again and trouble will come soon...and often."

The horse stood motionless, respectful. Katobaquis followed her instructions with complete confidence. She had raised him since he was a yearling. Patting the horse's mane, she applied just enough pressure to his flanks to have him ease up to what was previously the front door of the old cottage.

"You're a good horse, Katobaquis." She reached into her saddlebag and retrieved the small gray piece of flint she had found earlier that morning. Lifting it up and holding it between her trembling old hands, she chanted a few, barely audible lines. Her ever-keen eyes suddenly became aware of motion in the distance.

"Stay, Katobaquis. We have company this morning after all. We must pay our respects and depart."

She spied a young man down near the docks. Then taking the piece of flint in her hand, she tossed it into the ashes and pulled the reigns on her horse.

Dougie Burelli had just arrived on his own at the Kineo docks to carry out some maintenance work on his ferry shuttle boat. He had not slept well the previous night and was there two hours before his usual time. Sure the fire was a bit unsettling. But his best friend had also been acting very peculiar this week. It disturbed Dougie that Jimbo had not joined him at the pool hall last evening for their Friday night routine of drinking beer and running the table. Even Junior hadn't heard from him. Jimbo was normally very reliable, both as a friend and as an employee. He talked often about how much he appreciated and enjoyed working for Gus. *So why was he skipping out on his friends?* Gus had been furious that Jimbo had not worked the boat the day before. But then again, Jimbo and Junior had both been acting odd recently.

Dougie hadn't had a chance to poke around the Wellington-Goldman cottage and was kind of curious to see the smoky ruins before others awoke. The county fire officials had mandated that all sightseers stay away while the house consumed itself. All they could do was watch it waste away and make sure the fire did not spread. Dougie decided he would finish adding oil to the shuttle boat, then go poke around the site of the fire. He was just starting to lift the hatch cover to the large inboard engine, when he spotted something unusual in the distance—over by the Goldmans' destroyed summer home.

"What the hell?"

He did not know whether to trust his eyes. A figure on a horse was galloping away from the Goldmans'. The light was poor and it was some distance to the smoldering cottage ruins; so, at first, he thought he had seen a moose. Moose were frequently seen at daybreak on Kineo at this time of the year. But the silhouette of the old woman rider was unmistakable and somehow out of place. He closed his eyes. When he looked again, the image was gone. *It must have been my imagination*, he thought.

Turning his attention back to the work at hand, Dougie did not see the horse as it rounded the final corner of the lower cove. Temporarily coming into view and then out of sight again, the rider maintained a steady, quiet retreat. The strange visitor to Kineo this morning was off the island by 5:20 a.m.

* * *

The Dentons' black Ford Explorer continued along Interstate I-95. Mr. Denton had wanted his wife to buy a large silver Chevy Suburban, with all the trimmings, but Laura had other ideas. She was the practical and efficient one in the family. She loved to make lists and find the most cost-effective way to do everything. She had shown her husband David that the numbers could not justify such expenditure at this time and, as usual, her husband had ceded to her sensible rationalizations.

This was the second day of their journey. With such a late start, they had only managed to reach South Carolina the night before. Jenny was reminded more than once by Laura that her procrastinations had much to do with their late departure. Selecting the correct outfits for her summer endeavor was always an important part of Jenny's packing process. She was not able to simply throw clothes in a suitcase like her mother did. Every detail of each single accessory with individual outfits had to be just right. *And there were sooo many potential combinations to make up a cute outfit!* Shoes, in particular, were essential to the overall look. Jenny and her friend, Maria, would spend hours studying Mrs. Hernandez's glamour magazines, especially *Cosmopolitan*, since Laura did not subscribe to such "stereotypic exploitations of a woman's geometry" and engage in "ridiculous waste of family capital".

The Dentons did at least succeed in getting an early jump on the second day. Jenny's stomach was sending signals to her brain that it was time to vocalize her desire to eat breakfast soon. She felt it her duty to communicate these important realizations to her family. Before she could speak, however, Brandon made the first outburst of the day.

"Jennieeee!! You are on *my* side! You *crossed* the line!"

"Geesh, Brandon! You haven't talked to me on this entire trip. And now is that all you have to say to me?" Jenny protested. "You cross my line every time you reach over me to get a new Game Boy stick, so…"

Laura glanced back and snapped immediately. "Jen, keep your hands to yourself. And Brandon, you come up here and sit with me when we stop for breakfast."

And that was that!

That was also when the first of two bizarre phone calls injected an element of suspense into the Dentons' otherwise dull sojourn. Mrs. Denton answered her cell phone, intrigued. It was pretty early in the morning for a call.

"Mom… Who is it?" Jenny inquired.

Laura spoke addressed herself exclusively to the caller. "Oh hello, Bear… Mighty fine, thanks… Yes, we're right on schedule… We'll be there tomorrow in Greenville. I booked with your—Bear? Is everything all right up there?"

"Mom? Is everything okay?" Jenny piped up again.

Listening intently to Bear, Laura did not answer her daughter. There was only silence in the car. Brandon was back to his Game Boy, but Thomas was now looking at his mother's face for signals. He would wait for the appropriate time to ask what was up. Not Jenny. The quiet in the car made her uncomfortably anxious as she observed her mother listening to Bear's obviously disturbing news. She could not stand it any longer.

"Mom?"

"Hush, Jen!" Thomas snapped. "Can't you see she's on the phone?"

Laura glanced over at Thomas and gave him a quick smile, thinking: *Thanks, my young man.* Jenny had heard Laura talk to her older brother about how he had to "step up to the plate" now that Dad was gone. *As a near adult, he needed to take on more responsibility, because she needed a man around to help.* Jenny surmised that Thomas had taken that to mean he could snip at the little sister in the backseat. The rear-view mirror reflected Laura's irritation at Jenny for interrupting her once again. At the same time, the girl strained to hear her mother mutter to Bear a hushed, "Uh huh, I understand." Jenny contemplated her next inquiry, as more information was clearly needed. But somehow, her mother's expression in the mirror settled it. *Okay. Got it. Thank you, everyone,* Jenny thought, *I think I'll wait a while to ask what's going on.*

Once Laura had clicked the cell phone off, the car became strangely quiet. Thomas and Jenny waited for Laura to explain why the man they were meeting in Greenville to show them their new summer home was calling so early in the morning. Sensing the uncomfortable pause in the car, Laura attempted the old deflect-and-run technique at which she was quite skilled. What she told her children next was so interesting they both forgot about Bear's call for over an hour.

"Kids…Tom, Jenny, and Brandon," Laura started. "Brandon, put down your Game Boy for a minute. I want to tell ya more about Kineo."

Thomas chimed in immediately, "Mom, we know how we inherited the old dump when Dad died. But you never explained why Dad had never known his parents owned it in the first place…and…and how come he never spent a summer at their cottage on the island?"

"Yeah Mom," Jenny joined in. "If it's such a fun place to visit, then…"

"Look, guys. Your father isn't around anymore," Laura interrupted. "And neither are his parents there to fill in all the gaps. But I'll tell ya what I do know…and I believe Mr. Pfitzheimer will fill in some of those answers for us when we get there."

"Ya mean, the Bear?" Brandon asked.

"Yes dear…Bear," Laura confirmed. "But right now, I want to tell ya'll about what makes this place so special. This is not a *dump* on some silly island, guys; this is a really special place with an amazing history."

Laura Denton had a way of punctuating her points. Jenny liked the way she threw Thomas a disapproving glance as she repeated the word "dump". Then Laura began telling her kids about the island's history. Thomas refrained from making irreverent remarks, seeing how serious his mother was about this bed-and-breakfast thing. She needed a fresh start. Thomas suspected she needed something outside the daily routine of her meticulously organized and preprogrammed life as a distraction from the pain of being widowed for the past six months. He could sense her hope that the questions looming in the back of her mind about her husband's mysterious family would be finally answered on Kineo. The older Denton children shared the feeling that there was a lot more to the story of how the family had come to inherit the "old dump"—and how their father had died.

"All right, kids. Yes, you heard we own a historic cottage on Kineo, but so what?" Laura began. "Ya know I mentioned to you about the large hotels? Well, imagine an enormous hotel, so fancy and so expensive that only the very wealthy from all over—even from other countries—would come to stay there."

"You mean, like Princess Radziwill?" Jenny burst in.

"Umm…well yes, I suppose, like her… How do you remember her name, Jen?" Laura chuckled.

"Wasn't that the Polish princess that splattered herself all over the rocks of Kineo?" Thomas offered.

"Well, there are books that say she did…uh…jump from the cliff and commit suicide," Laura corrected somewhat awkwardly.

At that, Brandon came alive suddenly. "Oh, cool… You mean she jumped off the mountain near our house?"

"Well, not at our cottage," Laura attempted to clarify.

"Yeahh, Bran," Jenny flew back into the topic. "It was like in nineteen sixteen or something. I read about it in this really cool book Mom has about Kineo. Anyway, as I was saying, Princess Radziwill used to hike up the mountain near our cottage and have picnic lunches. The princess took her mail with her and read it up on the mountain. One day, she got a really mean letter from her boyfriend saying he was dumping her. She had planned to marry the guy in Russia when she got back from Kineo. She was so sad she jumped off the cliff."

"Ooooh, cool!" Brandon perked up. "Did she really, Mom?"

"Well, the local book sorta implies that," Laura answered. "I suppose…or so they say… Heck, I don't know if any of that stuff is…"

"Well, of course she did, Mom!" Jenny completed Laura's response. "It says so in your book right here about Kineo. And I think that's so gloomy. Why did her boyfriend dump her?"

"Geesh, Jenny. You're such a geek!" Thomas offered his opinion.

"Thomas!" Laura snapped, glaring at him.

After a short pause, her son mumbled, "Sorry, Jen." Then he added, "Well, Brandon, Jen hasn't told you the really cool part. Her body was so mangled from the rocks below they had to carry the parts back in picnic baskets."

"Yuck!" Jenny cried out.

"Ohh, cool!" Brandon said, even more engaged in the topic "But who'd ever want to eat from those baskets again?"

"What did they do with her body?" Thomas wondered out loud.

"They buried it over near the...let me seee...the...Breakwater Cottage," Jenny explained, once she had found the page that held that last detail.

"Oh, cooool, Mom!" Brandon blurted out. "Can we go digging for her bones there?"

"Geesh, Brandon!" Thomas laughed, "Go back to geek sleep."

"Look guys, let's get back to my story," Laura said, changing the topic smartly. "Thanks, Jenny, for finding those entertaining facts. The boys were delighted you read out all that morbid detail. But let's concentrate on the less violent history, shall we? Take the hotel, for example. The grand old hotel on Kineo had wonderful dining halls, with fancy furniture and accessories. The guests were able to play tennis and croquet. It even had a bowling alley. Pretty impressive facilities for a hotel at the turn of the century."

"Did anyone kill themselves in the bowling alley, Mom?" Brandon asked.

Laura let out a burst of air. "Oh Brandon, this is going to be long trip for you, isn't it, dear?"

* * *

On Kineo, representatives from the county sheriff's office and the state fire inspection division were back at the Goldman cottage. Something was bothering Bronson Thurman, the state fire inspector from the Offie of State Fire Marshal. It wasn't unusual to have fires in these old cottages. Not with all the old wiring and substandard repairs made over the past eighty years. But still, something about the fire he had witnessed yesterday didn't sit well with him. His sleep was disturbed every time a fire had the despicable signature of an arsonist. Near Bronson, Larry Magleton of the sheriff's department was sifting through the ashes with a shovel. Toonie, the part-time Rockwood law-enforcement officer and postmaster, stood next to him. In the distance, a jogger began to slow down as he approached.

"Look, Larry. If you guys have nothing else for me, I really need to get back to the post office. A lot of people have mail coming in today," Toonie explained.

"Yeah. No problem," Larry said gruffly. "Go tend mail."

Toonie closed his eyes, feeling slighted. He sighed loudly and walked away from the site, passing the jogger. Recognized him as Bennington Lomax, the postmaster greeted him with a friendly morning welcome and headed for his boat. Bennington had just finished his daily jog across the north end of the golf course and was returning to his three-story key lime green cottage located on Cottage Row on the western shoreline. Recognizing one of the two men on the site, he briefly considered jogging the long way round to avoid an encounter, but realized he was pressed for time. He proceeded forward and greeted the county officers investigating the ruins of the former Wellington cottage that had been restored by the Goldman family.

"Such a waste—losing the old Wellington cottage," Bennington offered in his distinct British accent, then fought to catch his breath.

He chose not to look directly at the sheriff, having been involved in an unpleasant situation with him once in the past. Bennington could not recall ever having seen the other gentleman before. He strolled up behind Larry Magleton.

"What are you looking for, Officer?"

"Just routine follow-up, Bennington," the sheriff answered. "No need for alarm."

"I am never alarmed, my good man. But I do confess to an insatiable curiosity."

Bennington looked for confirmation from Bronson, but the latter did not look up. The fire investigator was on the trail of something. His body language reminded Bennington of his old Brittany spaniel trailing the scent of a quail. Always the keen observer, Lomax knew there was more going on here than Larry chose to divulge, but it would have to wait. He had two daughters to pick up at the Rockwood public docks this afternoon, and Dougie was having problems with an oil leak on the Kineo shuttle.

Placing his hand on Larry's shoulder as if they were long-lost buddies, Bennington taunted, "Well, gentleman, I can see Kineo is in capable hands indeed. So do carry on."

Where you headin', *Bennington?*" Larry had suddenly become interested.

"I have two lovely daughters arriving in Rockwood who want to meet up with their charming father."

"I see," responded Larry. "Is Mrs. Lomax going to grace Kineo with her presence this year, *Bennington?*"

Raised in Massachusetts, Larry had inherited a strong New England accent. He had a way of using that accent to exaggerate certain expressions and names that Bennington likened to having a knife twisted into his spleen. The way he emphasized his name "Bennington" was no accident and grated on the nerves. The effect Larry had hoped for was achieved as the speed of Bennington's progress toward the Kineo docks suddenly slackened in mid-stride and his focus was temporarily diverted.

"Hit!" Larry mumbled to himself and smiled.

Now twenty yards from him, Bennington collected himself, looked over his shoulder as he continued to walk away, and responded to the wary sheriff's question. "Well, Sheriff, we can only cross our fingers now, can't we, my good man?"

Then turning away again, he speeded up his pace enough to break into a jog as he preceded toward the Kineo docks where his twenty-four-foot Sea Ray awaited him. The watercraft was a beautiful, sleek inboard outboard, with only 100 hours of engine time. Dougie could be seen in the distance, already at her side, making sure his boss had full tanks.

"A strange man, that Lomax," Larry called over to Bronson.

"What?" the fire investigator raised his head slowly, still entranced by the awkward fall line of the timbers smoldering at his feet.

"Bennington Lomax…you know, the millionaire summer resident. The key lime cottage in the middle of Cottage Row. Runs the shuttle service as a summer hobby. A strange one he is." Larry used his nasal emphasis technique on everybody. He may have been a fair cop in his own right, but his mannerisms did not endear him to many, including Bronson. But that was of little consequence to a driven investigator like Bronson Thurman. Feelings got in the way of results, and he was on the trail of something interesting and potentially sinister. He looked back at Larry and shook his head.

"You know, Larry, you are one strange guy yourself. Now come here. I have something of interest for your highly gifted detective eye."

Using a shovel, Bronson carefully lifted a gold wrist chain off the hot ground near the area where the back left window would have been before the house burned down. The piece of jewelry was barely visible in the scorched grass that was near the house, but not directly in the house footprint. The initials "JWW" were easy to recognize after Bronson had carefully rubbed the soot and dirt off the nameplate.

"An ID bracelet?"

"Exactly! So what do you make of these initials, Detective?"

5

It was afternoon as the Ford Explorer continued north on I-95. Jenny still had plenty of unanswered questions. Brandon was asleep, curled up against the window on his pillow. Thomas still had queries about how his father's family figured in this adventure.

"So after the McMillian Company went bankrupt," Laura told him, "they couldn't continue to finance the reconstruction of the new restaurant and hotel they promised. The grand plans were abandoned. The Breakwater Cottage was the only historic structure that received a lil' attention before the big hopes all fell apart for Kineo. Many investors, like your father's parents, who thought they had purchased a summer paradise became disappointed. There was no shuttle service to the island. No historic steamboat trips from Greenville to Kineo. No restaurants to entice vacationers. Oh—and no access to Kineo across Pebble Beach, since the Timber Company and Kineo residents had failed to see eye to eye since the late forties."

"How come Daddy got the cottage in Maine, Mom?" Jenny asked.

"I don't know for sure. Luck of the draw? Your Grandpa passed away four years ago and Grandma Denton, just last year. I only heard her speak about the cottage once. Each brother was promised one of Grandpa Denton's three properties as inheritance. Your father received the one with the most potential, but certainly the one that needed the most work."

"Maybe 'cuz Dad was so good with fixing things up?" Thomas suggested.

"Who knows?" Laura shrugged. "All I know is your father went up to see the place about a month after his mama passed, and he came back quite excited. He had a vision that we'd all go up there as a family and fix the old cottage up. And have our very own special place to retreat to and..."

Laura's voice trailed off. Jenny could see she was fighting back tears. Her father had been killed in a bizarre accident only three months after her parents had visited Kineo together. To the children's surprise, their father had actually managed to convert Laura to his way of thinking and despite her conservative outlook on life, she too had come back from Maine all excited at the prospect of becoming a summer innkeeper, with her husband retiring early to help her run it.

"Your father's death was...was...darn!" Laura's voice faltered and died away.

Thomas studied his mother's face and thought to himself: *No wonder Mom felt such a compelling urge to bring us all here. We all owe it to Dad to try and give it a go.*

"Mom, are you all right?" he asked tenderly.

"Yes, dear, I am... Thank you for asking," she replied, and then noticed Jenny in the backseat, weeping. "Oh, honey!" Laura exclaimed, directing her compassion toward her only daughter. "It'll be all right once we get up there."

Her phone rang unexpectedly, startling them all. Laura seemed to want to let it ring. After all, the first call had kind of shaken her. Finally, Thomas picked up the phone and handed the intrusive device to her. Laura answered the cell phone for the second time that day, and her reaction to the caller this time proved to be odder than the first.

* * *

Bennington swiftly piloted his Sea Ray across the lake from Kineo to Rockwood and anxiously awaited the arrival of his precious cargo. His heart lit up when he saw them, standing there at the slip, waiting for him. His teenage daughters jumped aboard with their luggage, exchanged hugs with their father, and within five minutes, Bennington had pulled up smoothly against the decrepit wooden bulkheads of the Kineo docks. He cast out his starboard line to Dougie Burelli who was waiting for the Lomax family by their personal slip on the sheltered portion of the cove.

Sitting on the sun deck of the Sea Ray were his two strikingly attractive blond-haired daughters. Tiffany was talking non-stop to her younger sister, Amanda, who simply stared at the dilapidated boathouse across the cove. Tiffany had blossomed, this past year, into a precocious sixteen-year-old with the contours and airs of a woman at least three years older. She was dressed in form-fitting white Capri pants and a bright orange tank top from Lilly. Amanda, just turning thirteen, seemed content to ignore her older sister and father as she fantasized about jumping the wake behind a Ski Nautique. She would have to talk to Dougie immediately about those fun summer activities. He was a free-spirited adventure seeker who had taught her to waterski and kneeboard last summer. This year, he had promised her a lesson in wakeboarding.

Turning away from Tiffany who was admiring herself in the mirror of her cute compact as she chattered away, Amanda spotted Dougie securing the bowline so they could go ashore. He was wrapping the last loop of the rope through the metal cleat as he noticed how young Tiffany had matured since last summer. Bennington noticed the young man staring at Tiffany. Dougie then caught Mr. Lomax watching him and realized this was not a favorable situation; he did not want to jeopardize his job. Witnessing the entire interaction, Amanda smiled, amused at the unspoken dynamics.

"Yo, girls! Good to see ya. Um, did ya have a nice flight?" Dougie asked the girls a bit awkwardly. His eyes had now shifted to the younger, safer target, Amanda

Tiffany permitted herself a smug smile, but chose not to respond. Dougie was quite beneath her.

"Dougie!" Amanda cried out, bolting ahead of Tiffany and allowing the ferry captain to take her hand and escort her off the boat. "We going kneeboarding this summer?"

"Oh, Mandeee, of course! Um…if the boss says it's okay. Heck, in fact, I got access to some wave runners this summer if ya wanna ride upriver and spot moose too?"

"Oh, yes! May I, Father? May I?" Amanda implored.

Bennington would not deny his little angel her request. He never did. He never could. And he did trust Dougie with Amanda, since the young man treated her like the sister he had never had.

"Of course, angel. But let's get you settled first," Bennington suggested. "Dougie, please take the ladies' luggage to the cottage."

"Sure thing, Mr. Lomax," Dougie responded dutifully, picking up the girls' suitcases and carefully loading them on the red golf cart.

The girls sat together on the back cab seat while Bennington sat next to Dougie in the front.

"So, Twerp," Tiffany taunted Amanda, "you going to *flounder* around in the water all summer again with *Doug-lassss* or have some *real* fun with me?" She enjoyed hissing "Doug-lassss" insolently to annoy him.

Amanda carefully selected her words and responded in an undertone to prevent the occupants of the front seat from overhearing her.

Dougie was too disturbed by his early-morning hallucination to care what the girls were saying. He turned to Bennington. "Yo, Mr. Lomax," he said, "I saw suppin' weird this morning."

Bennington glanced over, but said nothing.

"A horse with a rider," Dougie began cautiously. "Dashing across the southwest peninsula near the Goldmans' place early this morning."

"Oh? Do tell, Dougie."

Gauging Bennington's reaction carefully, the young man continued. "A horse with an old woman leaving the ruins of the ol' Wellington cottage."

"Really now? And were you still a bit pickled from last night's billiard-hall endeavors, Douglas?"

"No, sir! Not me!" Dougie protested. "Well, not *last* night," he amended, blushing. "Certainly not this morning."

"And where did this elderly woman escape to?" Bennington inquired, showing increasing interest as the golf cart rounded the bend and approached historic Cottage Row.

"I dunno." Dougie's voice trailed off. "Back toward Mt. Kineo, I think."

"Hmm… Indeed," Bennington replied introspectively.

* * *

"Hello?" Laura asked tentatively.

"I understand you will be joining us on Kineo tomorrow, Mrs. Denton," the older female voice stated in a very refined manner.

"Yes. Who is this, please?"

"Patricia Wellington."

"I don't believe I know ya," Laura said.

"You will... My family is everywhere in the Moosehead region. You'll see." The lady's voice lightened a bit, almost to a chuckle. "I presume Mr. Pfitzheimer informed you that a cottage near yours was destroyed by fire yesterday?"

"Why, yes ma'am... We were informed of that this morning. Those poor Goldmans!"

"My family used to own that place, you know, for many years. It is referred to by the locals as the..."

"The Wellington cottage," Laura supplied, completing the other woman's sentence as a light went on in her head. "Oh yes, I remember reading that somewhere."

"It was time," Patricia Wellington continued. "It was to be expected."

"I don't understand," Laura said.

"You will in time, dear."

"How'd ya get my number?"

"I have my sources, Mrs. Denton. All Wellingtons do."

"I'm sorry? Would you care to explain?"

"I must go now, Mrs. Denton. For the sake of your family, avoid treading on sacred lands."

"I'm sorry, Mrs. Wellington, but you're simply not making sense."

"Goodbye, Mrs. Denton. Be careful."

Laura stared at the cell phone strangely. All three of her children watched her for a while. She finally put her cell phone away.

"Mom, who was that?" Jenny asked.

"A neighbor, Jenny. A very strange neighbor."

"What did she want, Mom?" Jenny persisted. "You acted *weird* again."

"Oh thanks, Jenny, for the compliment." Laura shrugged off the questions with a nervous laugh and begun to wonder whether this trip had been a mistake after all.

Thomas watched his mother's reaction carefully and sat in silence. An hour later, the family stopped for dinner and found a motel room. The next day, they would finally arrive in Maine. Jenny couldn't wait to get on with this adventure. She had had enough of this car ride, of missing her father, and the world ahead certainly was shaping up to be unexpectedly interesting.

6

It was almost three p.m. before the Dentons finally found themselves on the outskirts of Greenville. Laura asked Jenny to awaken Brandon who had drifted into slumber after two hours of Game Boy. Her voice had an optimistic ring to it for the first time since the previous evening's phone calls, as she announced, "Look, kids…down in that valley—Moosehead Lake!"

Being from Florida, the Denton kids were all stunned by the views. Several islands of rock, covered with dark green conifer trees, could be seen in Moosehead Lake, guarding the entrance to Greenville. The lake itself was vast and picturesque. Greenville was a quaint little town on the lake's southern edge, with lots of appealing shops dotting it. Jenny begged her mother to stop so they could get some memorable souvenirs for her bedroom. Laura replied that they didn't have time to add to Jenny's "trinket collection". She had a *real* surprise in mind for all of them.

Driving along the main street, the Dentons passed Black Frog, a local restaurant on the lake's southern shore. Laura promised her brood she would treat them to an enjoyable dinner there that week, including fun ice-cream drinks. A little further down the road, she pulled into Kraft's Air Service.

"Why are we stopping here?" Thomas asked, his gaze affixed to the Maine Gazetteer map book. "Isn't Rockwood another twenty minutes around the bend?"

"Very good! You read the maps well, my young navigator," Laura saluted her son. "I told ya I had a neat surprise for ya'all. Something we wouldn't normally stop to do."

Strolling up to the Denton Explorer was a young, good-looking man with a slight build. He wore his hair short and was clean-shaven. He also had a deep dimple in his chin that widened when he smiled. Jenny noticed his black flight jacket and the embroidered logo on his pocket that read: "Kraft's Air Service". The Dentons watched the young man walk up to their truck and bend down, looking in through the driver's window. Expecting someone to greet her, Laura rolled her window down.

"Hello. I'm Matt Kowalski," said the young man. "You must be Laura Denton?"

"Nice to meet ya, Matt. Yes, I'm Laura and this is my family. My kids—Thomas, Jenny, and Brandon in the back."

Matt gave the kids a big, toothy smile, displaying perfect teeth that were paid for out of state. He was a newcomer to the area. His dimple was so large it mesmerized Jenny as he spoke to Laura.

"Well, you're right on time. I have my plane ready and it's perfect flying weather today."

"Are you going on a flight, Mom?" Thomas inquired.

"We *all* are," she explained.

In the water, tied up to the dock, was a striking blue and white floatplane. The Dentons walked up to it. Thomas stroked his hand along the aluminum wing tip

"Are we really going up in this, Mom?" Brandon asked

"Uh huh. Thought it might be a fun reward for the long drive to first show ya'll our summer home from the air," Laura explained.

Matt laughed, seeing the excited younger passengers, then turned and noticed a tall figure appearing from the hangar.

"Laura Denton?" said the huge creature as he approached. "I'm Bear."

Laura's eyes widened noticeably as she came face to face with Bear for the first time.

"Oh, my! I had no idea you were so…"

"Handsome? Intelligent-looking? Ha!" he barked out.

"Huge!" Laura offered.

"Well, why do you think they call me Bear?" he laughed out loud, looking at Laura and Jenny. "So, I see you met Matt. He may look young, Mrs. Denton, but I assure you he is the best darn pilot in these parts. I'm glad you're flying with him."

Bear turned to Matt. "You fly them around Kineo. Fly over their cottage. Under the cliffs and over the breakwater. Be sure to point out all the landmarks to Mrs. Denton. I have to get supplies in Greenville, and I'll meet you guys at the Rockwood Marina at say…two, to introduce you to Chuck. You can decide if you like the used boat I found for your family. Chuck will give you a fair price. Then I'll introduce you to Dougie who will shuttle you to Kineo to see your cottage."

Bear had all the answers. He was a take-charge type of man. Matt appeared to like him quite a bit. Laura did not seem to know how to respond to Bear at first. He was friendly, yet intimidating. He wore new blue jeans that were a trace too short and a long-sleeved flannel plaid shirt. Jenny studied her mother's reaction to this bearded giant who resembled both a lumberjack and a grizzly bear.

It was hard to predict how Laura would act around men she was meeting for the first time. She was always polite, but often very distant. She chose her words carefully and spoke slowly, and a trace of southern Louisiana was always discernible in her voice. There were times when her accent would slip into a more noticeable drawl. This often happened when she needed a positive response from a difficult man. David used to call it "laying on the southern charm". Jenny noticed that when Bear took charge of the schedule, Laura slid into her native Louisiana accent. *Does Mom think Bear is a difficult man*, she wondered.

Bear stood and watched momma bear escort her cubs onto the floatplane, one at a time. Matt was there with a hand for each of the customers. Bear watched each Denton board the plane. He dwelled on Laura the longest. She was not a flashy dresser; a pretty woman, who didn't exploit her potential. She wore no make-up. Not even lipstick. Her hair was neatly combed and pulled back into a scrunchie with a floral pattern, but that was about as exciting as her uninspired wardrobe got. She wore neat, classic-looking jeans that Bear seemed to notice when they stretched tightly across her rear while she was ducking down to enter the plane through the tiny side door. Laura had a shapely figure hidden under her oversized oxford yellow shirt, but rarely used her blessings to her advantage.

Jenny had heard her mother tell her lady friends that "a woman should be judged on her sensible decisions in life, not on the curves of her body". Despite her views about a blatant display of femininity, she had occasionally reminded her husband that she was capable of turning a head or two. Jenny remembered the day, last year, when her parents had gone out on their anniversary. Laura had come down the stairs in a long, slinky dress that showed off her plentiful curves; her husband had stood looking up at her, speechless.

Laura had slowly and deliberately moved her heavily painted lips and taunted him, "What's a matter, handsome? Haven't seen me wearin' my war paint in a while? Take my arm, ya lucky warrior!"

Since their father's passing, Laura had had little opportunity to apply her "war paint". Jenny felt so awful for her mother. But looking at her now in the floatplane, waving kindly to Bear for providing assistance, she looked beautiful. Her smile said it all. Laura was with her cubs, about to treat them to their first Kineo adventure. Brandon clapped in approval as Matt revved up the plane's single Pratt and Whitney engine nestled squarely in the nose. The two aluminum pontoons slapped at the stout, but manageable chop, and the old de Havilland rose above Moosehead Lake, heading north to Kineo.

* * *

In Greenville, Bear purchased all the supplies needed to complete the snowmobile and the golf cart shed he was building on Kineo. Loading the roofing materials onto his fiberglass tri-hull at the dock, Bear noticed Gus pulling up with his Boston Whaler. Normally at this distance, Gus would be spouting off loud, obnoxious insults like a vulgar celebrity announcing his arrival for all landward to hear. Today, however, he wore a solemn look on his weathered face, highlighted by a deep crease etched into his upper brow. In one fluid motion, the old captain skillfully maneuvered his boat up to the dock, where he threw his bowline to Bear.

"Things all right, Gus?" the big man asked in all sincerity, wrapping a figure-eight loop around the aluminum ears of the cleat.

Gus did not look up. He snatched up his duffle bag and grunted.

"Jimbo still missing?" Bear continued cautiously.

Plucking his stogie out from his mouth, Gus looked up at the other man, squinting at the sun blazing into his eyes.

"Yeah. Foolish son of a bitch! I swear I'm going to bust his chops when he…" Gus hesitated and turned away from the sun.

Normally quick to respond, Bear was astute when it came to people's feelings. "You're worried about him, aren't you, Gus?"

"Oh, hell! Man, it isn't like him. Nobody has seen the kid."

"I'll keep an eye out for him, Gus. In the meantime, do you need some help with those customers this week? I have a few young guys working with me that might be able to fill in for Jimbo, if you like."

Gus was touched by Bear's compassion. After all, he himself had been one of the locals who had ostracized the huge man for his association with Big Timber in the area. Over the past year, he had come to revise his opinion. He believed that Bear had been too hastily judged. Gus found himself feeling guilty, once again, for not being more sympathetic to the other man during that period of turmoil. He grimaced to himself, hating to be caught in a moment of visible weakness. "Nah! Don't think I'll need help." Gus planted his cigar back into his mouth, a gesture which signaled to Bear that the conversation was over.

"Yeah. Okay, Gus. But the offer stands if you need it."

Gus strolled into town while Bear generously tipped the young man from the lumber store who had helped him load the supplies onto his boat. Lifting his crippled leg gingerly over the rail, he hobbled over to the control console. Studying his watch, he knew the heavy load would delay his travel time. He set off toward Kineo, knowing it would take forty minutes to reach Rockwood.

* * *

"Mommy! Oh, cooool… Look at the big island!" Brandon yelled out.

"That's Moose Island, Brandon, and the one below us is Deer Island," explained Matt. "You'll have to try out the big rope swing on the island's south side. You can get thirty feet of air!"

"Whoah!" Thomas gushed. "We have to go do that, Mom!"

Laura could barely hear her older son over the drone of the engines, but smiled at him and his rare display of enthusiasm.

"Is that our island over there?" Brandon inquired sheepishly from the side window, pointing to a large mass of rock rising out of the lake.

"Oh my gosh, Mommy!" Jenny cried out, "is that it?"

Laura turned to Matt and gave him a proud smile as Brandon turned to his mother for confirmation as well. In front of the plane, the impressive vertical rock face of Mt. Kineo guarded the rolling slopes of birch, white pine, spruce, and maple. Two peninsulas protruded away from Kineo's sheer wall, anchoring the southern approach and forming two inspiring coves. On the southwest peninsula, the Dentons saw a few buildings and the tight-cropped grass of the historic golf course.

"The mountain, Mommy! A really big mountain!" Brandon pointed out

"Yes, dear. I see it," Laura responded calmly, holding back the feeling of jubilation that was rising steadily within her as they approached.

"What do you say we fly right over your place, Mrs. Denton?" suggested Matt

"Please, Matt. I'm not old enough to be your mother, so call me Laura."

"Fine. Laura," corrected Matt with another toothy smile.

"Whoah! What's that five-story building?" Thomas interrupted.

"That, Thomas, is the old dorm where the hotel employees slept. And everyone? Can you hear me okay through your headsets?"

A row of seven cottages became the focus of attention along the peninsula's western shore as the Dentons flew past the five-story white dormitory. Everyone acknowledged with a "Yeah!" or "Yes!" as Matt dropped his plane a bit lower and began to point to a three-story cottage with a black shingled roof and blue shingled sides.

"Is that our cottage, Mommy?" Jenny asked.

"That's the one, dear."

Matt circled the row again as Jenny and her brothers admired the old structure from about 500 feet above Moosehead Lake. The peninsula that supported Cottage Row also provided the two fairways of a scenic golf course surrounded by water. A thin row of birch trees formed the backdrop of the cottages along the southwest shore, but the front doors opened out onto the eighth hole of the historic golf course. The old dormitory rested on the opposite bank, out of place in the landscape, like an abandoned warehouse. Its windows were boarded up, and the fire-escape platforms were rusted and dilapidated.

"Look, everyone!" Thomas demanded. "At the old dormitory...what is that?"

Matt chuckled out loud as they all stared at the strange sight below. It looked like a black cloud swirling out from the building. *Tiny black particles? A small tornado?* Jenny was confused. Looking back over their shoulders, nobody said a word until Thomas ventured, "Birds?"

"Very good, Thomas. Chimney swifts, actually. They normally gather later near sunset. We are lucky to see them this early," Matt continued. "Maybe my plane spooked them."

"Reminds me of the old Hitchcock movie, *The Birds*," Laura offered.

The plane moved away from Cottage Row and began to fly in the direction of the great talus pile on the mountain's western edge.

"Those crazy birds do that often at this time of year," Matt explained to the Dentons. "All of a sudden, you see them swarm together like a cloud of locusts and swirl in circles over the old chimney. Then one lead bird plunges into the chimney, and they all follow. It's quite remarkable to see."

"What are low cusses?" Brandon asked.

"Kinda like grasshoppers, Brandon," Laura responded.

The little boy's eyes were already anticipating the next surprise ahead of them. The plane flew out over the large talus pile, which extended from the top of a jagged rock formation and all the way down to the old carriage trail along the water's edge. The broken chunks of rhyolite provided the type of scrambling opportunity that the boys would, undoubtedly, enjoy soon enough.

The plane banked left and tipped its wing to show the Dentons the coast of Rockwood to the west. Matt explained that Rockwood was the last civilized outpost before heading into Maine's wilderness to the north and northwest.

"You don't want to take a boat up to the northern part of the lake without someone knowing where you are," Matt warned.

Then the plane made a slow, gradual arc around the island's north side, revealing its gentle, tree-lined slopes. Unlike the other faces of Mt. Kineo that provided spectacular views of precarious cliffs, the north side looked deceptively harmless. The forest below simply started at the water's edge at Hardscrabble Point and climbed up the north slopes like a long, rounded ramp. The floatplane banked again, this time to the right. Matt informed his passengers that they were about to see the mountain's eastern edge—the most impressive view of the island.

Suddenly, it became clear to the Dentons why this was the climax of the sightseeing venture. The cliffs on the east side were nearly sheer. In one place, the mountain actually undercut itself, creating a concave dimple in its side.

"Tight, Mom!" From inside the plane, both Thomas and Brandon's voices rang out almost simultaneously, much to their handsome pilot's delight.

Laura herself was beaming at the discovery of what a huge hit this little splurge on her part had been with her weary brood from Florida.

* * *

Bear had nearly reached Kineo when he saw the floatplane bank overhead and tip its wings to him. The plane's color and the visible call letters confirmed that the Dentons had completed their tour and had been dropped off at the Rockwood Marina on the Moose River. Bear waved to Matt as he leveled his plane and headed back to Greenville. *Matt was a good kid*, he thought to himself. *Shame his dad has been such an ass!*

Bear squinted into the sun and watched the plane fade off to the south. As he dropped his waving hand to his side, he remembered how he too had wanted to be a pilot once, but had never quite got around to completing his flight training. Well, of course there was that one little incident down in Portland with his flight trainer, where Bear had clipped the trees coming in too low, *but by gosh! The damage to the aircraft had not been that bad.*

Bear had hoped to go with the Dentons to the Rockwood Marina to help them purchase a fine used boat. He didn't have time, however, as he had to unload his supplies on Kineo. He felt a strong, uninexplicable compulsion to help Laura and her children. Maybe it had something to do with him losing his own family through a nasty divorce.

Bear scanned the horizon to the west, with one last concern on his mind. It was after five p.m.—the last shuttle of the day had completed its run already. Dougie rounded off his day by taking Bennington's shuttle up to the Moosehead Marina for some simple adjustments. Fortunately, the timing worked in the Dentons' favor. They could hitch a ride back to Kineo on the fully operating shuttle with Dougie. The young man was always responsible, and Bear normally didn't worry about such things. But with Laura and her family counting on that ride, he felt an obligation to worry anyhow.

There she is, Bear said to himself. *The* Penobscot. *Way to go, Dougie! Right on schedule.* The shuttle boat, *Penobscot*, cruised toward the mouth of the Moose River to pick up the Dentons and moved quickly out of the range of Bear's watchful eyes.

* * *

Moosehead Lake Marina, Rockwood

"Thank you, Chuck. This whaler will do fine to get us around for now. Later this summer, we plan to purchase a pontoon boat to get our guests around," Laura said. "Another used boat, of course, presuming things go well this summer."

"No problem, Mrs. Denton," Chuck replied, "This little whaler I am selling you is a very safe boat. Fast enough to get you around too. The previous owner took fine care of it." Then with a clever smile, he added, "My um...son had it!"

Thomas was already running his hands up and down the whaler's sides as Laura finished writing the check in favor of Chuck Danzten, owner of the Moosehead Marina.

Jenny cried out, "Mom! Is this really gonna be *our* boat?"

"Yes, sweetie, it will be. They have to do some maintenance first."

"Can I drive it, Mom. Can I?" Jenny pleaded.

"Be real!" Thomas interrupted his sister, making an annoyed face at her.

"Mrs. Denton, you need to be careful now." Chuck took over. "This is a very safe boat for kids. Virtually unsinkable, actually. But the lake itself can be very unpredictable. This boat will get you from the marina and back to your home or to the Rockwood docks quick enough, but this is *not* the right size of craft for touring the lake or getting far away from the shore. If you get caught in a large squall out there or try to cross in large waves and..." Chuck paused and looked at the kids with concern. "Look, lady. This isn't a little Florida lake, is all I am saying. Ya know?"

"I'm aware of how easily one can get hypothermia, Mr. Dantzen. We'll be *very* careful," Laura assured him with a disarming smile and her rarely used feminine voice that caught so many men by surprise when strategically unleashed. Her timing was, as always, impeccable, and Chuck's concerned scowl melted into a half-grin. He turned and clapped his hands to get the attention of one of his employees.

"Mrs. Denton will be by first thing in the morning to pick up the whaler," he explained to his worker. "I want all those throttle cables replaced *today!*"

Laura thanked the marina's owner, gathered her kids together, and strolled casually to the floating docks. The weather was beautiful this early evening, and in every direction you looked, you could see colorful boats, floatplanes, and friendly folks swarming around on their way back from an enjoyable day on the lake. It seemed like paradise to the Dentons.

"If only..." Laura sighed. The thought of how this had been her husband's dream and the fact that *she* was experiencing it now with their kids struck a bittersweet chord in her heart. She began to feel emotions rumbling inside as she stared off at Mt. Kineo.

Suddenly, a strange-looking boat pulled up to the dock and a small young man—no, a kid, Laura wasn't sure—piloting the vessel approached. The boat's captain was a rather short male with a very stalky build and long blonde hair. He had the smooth face of a kid, but a man's physique.

"Yo! Any of you guys the Dentons?" the shuttle driver called out.

Jenny cried out with excitement, "Hey! You must be Dougie. Is that your boat?"

Brandon and Thomas crowded to the dock now, watching the large wooden boat bump slowly into the dock. The smell of diesel fuel filled the air. Dougie wore a bandana around his long blonde hair that was tied into a ponytail in the back. His captain apparel consisted of cut-off jeans, Teva sandals, and a tank-top shirt with the rock group, Metallica, half faded across his chest. His large shoulder muscles protruded from the shirt with significant definition. It was clear to Thomas that this was a guy who could lift weight well and above his mere 160 pounds.

"Yo, yo, and yo to all. Come aboard *Penobscot*," Dougie said in welcome.

* * *

Lily Bay, Moosehead Lake; May 31, 1999; six p.m.

The Johnsons approached a small, heavily treed island on the east side of Laker Point—a very treacherous area in Mathews Cove near the State Park and within Lily Bay that boaters tended to avoid, because one could easily lose a prop in these shallow, rock-infested waters. Mr. Johnson, however, liked seeking out remote areas to enjoy sunset with his family.

He spotted a group of small rock islands with a few trees sprouting from them and pointed them out to his wife "What say ye, my love?"

"Looks like a splendid place to enjoy the special treats I brought along for our *favorite* son," she agreed.

"I'm your *only* son, Mom," the young boy corrected her.

"Well then, Michael, my first mate, grab the bow line and let's tie up to that big rock over..."

Mr. Johnson's words were choked off as he suddenly identified a large mass half-floating in the water and half-entangled in the rocks ahead. His wife and son were bewildered at the sight ahead of them. As the boat drifted closer, Mrs. Johnson gasped. Michael dropped his bowline in the water, and his father quickly killed the idling engines. There would be no picnic at sunset, after all.

7

"Kewl beans, Dougie! This boat…is it yours?" Jennifer asked.

"Naw," he replied. "It's the boss man's, ya know? Bennington's shuttle, lil'lady."

It was still sunny, but the wind had picked up significantly in the past hour. Thomas admired the way the large bow of the open-hulled boat cut through the whitecaps with ease. The wind whipped the cold clear water back across the passengers, much to Jenny's delight. Although his smile wasn't as intense as his energetic sister's, Thomas was clearly enjoying this experience as well. Brandon seemed to withdraw a bit and cuddled against his mother for warmth. Content with her successful day, Laura let the water splash against her face.

"This boat was actually the lifeboat for a World War Two destroyer," Dougie offered

"No way!" Thomas responded with immediate interest.

"'Fraid so, dude. In fact, she saw action in the Pacific."

Laura and Jenny observed Thomas affectionately stroking the wooden gunnels outside. To his mother, it seemed like a strange gesture until she remembered how her husband had been a war history buff. Thomas and his father used to stay up late, watching the History Channel and reading stories of the Great War. David Denton's father had served in the Navy in World War II.

"Hope ya dudes like to kneeboard and wakeboard, 'cuz we're going to have some great rides this summer," Dougie promised, moving onto his favorite subject.

The ride to the Kineo docks was busy with chatter. Dougie had a way with kids. He was probably nearing thirty, Laura surmised, and filled with foolish youthful energy and optimism. Neither one's age nor gender mattered to Dougie. He saw life as an endless opportunity for adventure. His ferry-captain job was simply a means to scrape by until the off days, when his life centered around snowmobile racing and snowboarding in the winter; rock climbing and scuba diving in the summer; and, of course, wakeboarding, whenever and wherever he could.

The twelve-minute ride to the docks at Kineo went quickly as the Dentons bonded with Dougie. Then they spotted Bear's unmistakable silhouette; it was as if General Patton were directing the bustle of traffic at Kineo's docks.

* * *

In a small stone dwelling nestled in the side of a rocky outcropping adjoining Spencer Mountain, a very old woman with black tattoos marking her arms sat at her table, admiring a collection of stones and minerals. She picked up a highly polished stone that had been worked meticulously into a perfect sphere.

"This big beauty," she cackled to her chocolate Lab who was sprawled on the floor, "must be returned this evening. No guardian stone should be apart from its cradle for more than a couple of hours. The spirit of Kajo will be upset."

The old dog was used to the lonely lady's ramblings, but still looked up at her with the unconditional admiration only a canine could have for its mistress.

"Horrible misfortunes for those that disrespect Kineo," the woman muttered.

The Lab continued to listen to his elderly owner without lifting his head off his paws, cocking an eye in her direction and wagging his tail occasionally in acknowledgement.

The gemstone was three inches in diameter and glowed with a pinkish hue. She wondered why the Trader had given the Abenaki the pretty pink sphere while her own people had received the black one. It was now her responsibility to protect the guardian spheres and the special place where they resided. Although she had deep respect for the ancestors each gemstone represented, she was very old now and finding it exceedingly difficult to perform her duties. It was so dark in the cramped tunnels and in the inner chamber. She could not see in the dark like she used to only ten years ago.

She would have to find a suitable descendant to train in the ways of the Kineo guardians before she turned eighty-five. That only provided another year, assuming she lasted that long. There used to be nine guardians—three for each gemstone. Now, there were only three remaining guardians in all—one guardian for each sphere. And with one crucial sphere missing for so many years, the other guardians had all but lost faith in their future. The poor Abenaki guardian wasn't ambulatory anymore despite being ten years younger than her. The youth that should have been helping them had grown apathetic to the traditional ways of their ancestors. Most had either completely lost their way or been assimilated. She was disheartened, realizing how many had lost their appreciation of tradition and the history that had once made them all a proud and productive people.

The guardian of the purple guardian gemstone was still mobile; but he too had become inactive as a groundskeeper of the inner chamber. He now lived so far away that he had only visited Kineo a couple of times last year. He had told the old woman when he saw her last summer that a rockslide had blocked a portion of his designated entranceway, and it was nearly impossible to administer to the needs of the inner chamber. She wondered if he had created the rockslide so he would have an excuse to drop his lifelong duties as a guardian. She stared out the window and recalled the last thing he had said to her…

"You silly old woman!" he had scolded her. *"Nobody still believes in the old legend of the Trader and the Circle of Unity. The sphere on my side must be buried under heavy rock. Just let it be. Just let the spirit of Kajo rest."*

"There are some, my dear friend, that still believe," she had chastised him crossly. *"We are too dispersed as peoples. There's so little we can do since our sphere was stolen long before my watch. But damn you…you old fool! You know what troubles continue to curse us all since the black sphere was lost!"*

"Yes, I know. That's when the fires began again, and I suppose, it might explain what happened to all of our peoples. Clearly, those that displaced us are consumed by a curse, but…it's been so many years now…we will never find it! Give up, woman. We've lost all we once had. What does it matter now anyway?"

"Oh, you old fool! It does matter," she grumbled. But then she realized that they had had the same argument many times and it hadn't changed things. *"So now that it's buried in there—you're merely going to leave it?"*

"Why not?" he had said, shrugging his tired shoulders. *"The old rock walls crumbled down and now part of the tunnel is exposed. Someone will find his way in now. And what difference does it make? You need to move with the times. You don't even have a TV set!"*

With time, the guardian of the purple sphere had become increasingly indifferent, but not the old woman—the guardian of the black sphere. The *missing* black guardian stone! Surely, her persistence in keeping the inner chamber safe from tresspassers, grave robbers, and artifact collectors should count for something? Maybe keeping the other spheres safe would help mitigate the recklessness of the previous guardians that had allowed the sphere to be lost on *their* watch. There would have been many more fires, diseases, and other unimaginable disasters if she and the others before her had not worked so hard to honor the rituals handed down to her by former guardians. She looked at the pink Abenaki sphere, remembering how she had heard about her ancestors despising *those* people. But she had no choice. She had been appointed the guardian. She continued to polish the beautiful gemstone and derived solace from the knowledge that the misdeeds of her people were being absolved by her own symbolic actions.

Luckily, her horse, Katobaquis, could still negotiate the trails easily enough and it only took twenty minutes to find the chamber once she had reached the clandestine entrance of the "flint people". She would make her journey at dusk, mindful of any early-season tourist who might be wandering in the area. At this time of the year, however, hardly anyone ascended Mt. Kineo at dusk. She could not risk being seen. The secret trail she had followed over the years approached Mt. Kineo through the impenetrable wall of fir trees on the north face. It was so far off the beaten track that no one had ever seen her go in or come out. It was a trail that had been used by her father, her grandfather, and her great-grandmother before her—all former guardians of the black sphere.

She let out a deep breath and looked at the chocolate Lab on the floor by her feet. "Guardians of *what* black sphere?" she sighed.

The sphere had always been missing. In fact, she had never actually seen it. It had been lost way back, about the time she was born. *Maybe it didn't really exist*, she thought. *No! I can't think that way! Such thoughts are heresy.* No. She had seen the resting cradle where it was meant to be perched. There were several pedestals with cradles surrounding the outer walls of the inner mining chamber. Only three of the pedestals were meant to support the three guardian stones in a particular arrangement. When all three were resting in the correct cradles, you could use the location of the spheres to determine the precise location of the most sacred grounds in the chamber. She had held the other spheres in her own hands. Her faith was very strong. She had the remaining proof of the great legend of Kajo in her hands right now.

She finished polishing the pink sphere, placed it reverentially in a deerskin cloth, then set it aside in a leather saddlebag that she would use to return it. She picked up a grayish point of rhyolite that she had collected this week and examined it. The arrowhead was in excellent shape. Something that Dr. Wayne and the other white invaders would consider museum quality. *Bastards! What are we, some extinct species?*

This particular specimen, however, was certainly not destined to be under the care of some ambivalent white curator. This precious reminder of her nearly vanished culture was not to become another symbol of another race they had so callously exterminated. *They would never understand. Their kind never did. Whites have always been arrogant. They have no idea what they are doing. All those that disturb the sacred grounds of Kineo anger the spirit of the Cow Moose and will be cursed. And if anyone disturbs Kajo's burial site—will deal with me!*

✳ ✳ ✳

Mr. Johnson recognized the bloated mass in the water as the corpse of a drowned man. It wore a light fishing vest and appeared to have been burned. He yelled for Michael to hold the boat still while he jumped into the cold water. Grasping the vest by its strap, Mr. Johnson pulled the corpse close and noticed that it was charred, almost beyond recognition; it was also stiff from rigor mortis. Other parts of the unfortunate victim's body were distended and pale. The contrast of black burned flesh and swollen white flesh was sickening, and he found himself overcome by nausea.

Mr. Johnson spun around and stumbled back to the boat. Grabbing the rail to get his balance, he took several deep breaths. The body had been entangled in the rocks and exposed to the elements long enough to give off a putrid odor that made Michael cover his nose. Mrs. Johnson insisted that they leave immediately and report their discovery to the authorities.

Traumatized by what they had stumbled upon, the Johnsons sped to shore.

8

"Be sure, ladies and gentlemen, that you have everything you need before leaving the boats," Dr. Mongeau insisted.

"Checked and rechecked, Professor," responded Rob Landon, his first-year student-assistant.

"Wonderful, Rob," Mongeau said with approval before turning to Max. "This was a great idea. Combining the geology and archeology departments this summer could help both of us have a breakthrough in our research."

"Look at that mountain, Les," Max said to Dr. Mongeau. "Can you imagine what the Red Paint People must have thought, seeing it from this angle?"

"Yes, Dr. Wayne. I suspect they were quite stirred, just as I am this moment," agreed Dr. Mongeau. "Now Rob, make sure all this geologic gear gets unloaded from the boats and is protected, in case it rains tonight."

Rob and five other graduate students formed a human chain and carefully began unloading the supplies and equipment needed for their two-week stay on Kineo. Off in the distance, the sky grew gray and angry. Sure enough, an early summer squall was working its way up from the Greenville area and would be pelting them soon with cold, stinging rain. The students began to move the equipment faster from the pontoon platforms to the docks.

The university had rented an entire floor of the old hotel dormitory from the current owner who was slowly refurbishing it. The first floor had been successfully remodeled to make it just about ready for overnight rental. The basement, with its plentiful counter space and concrete floors, lent itself perfectly for sorting artifacts, minerals, and other academic collectibles of interest. The university had rented the entire basement and first floor for two weeks at a very reasonable rate. It was only fifty yards from the Kineo docks to the dormitory and the two professors walked ahead to unlock the double doors to the basement floor.

"Good Lord, Les!" Max exclaimed. "One of my students just came from the upper part of the cove. He noticed the charred remains of one of the old historic cottages."

"Yes Max," Les began. "Back in Greenville, I heard that one of the historic fishing cottages had mysteriously burned down this week."

"Not another one! What is it with Kineo?" Max asked. "I don't know how much you know about the history of this island, Les, but as an archeologist and anthropologist, I'm obviously fascinated with history. I've read up on Kineo history extending beyond the point where the indigenous peoples were chased away."

As Les fumbled with the dormitory keys to the basement, a brand new red golf cart ripped around the corner. The sound of the tires spraying gravel and the cackle of feminine laughter made everyone turn in that direction. The cart contained two young passengers with long, flowing blonde hair. Both wore oodles of make-up. The girl driving the cart was crowded into tight-fitting white Capri pants and a bright orange tank top. She appeared old enough to Rob as she approached the college boys, flashing a flirtatious smile.

Rob found himself waving to her without thinking as they passed him, and the younger passenger yelled out, "Her name…is Tiffany!"

The driver grabbed Amanda, placed her in a sudden headlock, and continued to speed on down the gravel road.

"Jailbait, stupid!" Gary warned Rob and punched him in the shoulder. Rob turned red in the face as Julie scowled at him.

"She's probably only seventeen, Rob!"

Looking back at this whole incident, Les shook his head and grumbled. "Juvenile distractions! Just what we need!"

Max laughed at him. "Come on, Professor, it's summer. Don't you remember the summers when *you* were young?"

Suddenly, Les found the right key and the large wooden door to the historic building opened. "Spare me the recollections of your wanton youth, my friend," he said. "Instead, I beg you to share your knowledge of Kineo with your weary colleague, while I open things up in here."

Max grinned at him, and then explained how the departure of the Native Americans in the area was followed by a flourishing lumber industry that created a unique tourist destination linked by steamships and rail. In eighteen forty, Kineo became privately owned property when John Bradbury purchased it for only three hundred and fifty dollars—about thirty cents an acre. The first building on Kineo was a tavern. The island developed a small causeway to gain access to it from the east making it popular with the logging men in the area that were using the lake to move lumber. Shortly thereafter the first large hotel was constructed.

Max pointed through the open window to Kineo's southwest peninsula. Not much stood there today to attest to the facts he eagerly presented. "Kineo became very popular—primarily because of successful hunting and fishing opportunities," he continued. "But the Kineo hotel burned down in eighteen seventy and another was constructed in its place."

Les finished packing his pipe, lit the tobacco, and inhaled deeply. Several students had climbed up to the first floor carrying supplies and equipment. With his focus still on Max, Dr. Mongeau directed them with a quick dismissive motion of the hand to the back room.

Max continued to explain how the high demand for hotel rooms, required that an annex to the hotel be constructed along with a winter cottage. However, this fanciful expanded hotel also burned down.

"The demand for this island was staggering, Les. We're talking unique vacation opportunities in the heartland of Maine's best hunting and fishing region. They were eager to rebuild the resort again. In the early eighteen eighties, an even grander hotel was constructed while they were still hauling out the charred remains of the previous one. The grand opening of this third hotel took place around…" Max paused and squinted, hoping to jog his memory. "Um…seems to me it was…July of eighteen eighty-four."

Julie Walters had just finished unloading her armful of supplies and was massaging her sore arms, with her youthful bottom resting against the counter near Dr. Wayne, in an attempt to be included without directly intruding on Dr. Mongeau.

Noticing the young lady encroach upon their scholarly discussion, Dr. Mongeau winced.

"Ever notice how pelicans sit around the pilings as the fishing boats come in, Max?" Les asked.

Puzzled by the comment, his younger colleague looked at him oddly.

"Well, Max, I guess you haven't spent a lot of time in Louisiana. Our state bird, you know, *Pelecanus occidentalis*," Les continued. "Brown pelicans sit there with their bottoms resting on the pilings, watching the fisherman clean their daily catches. Lazily awaiting a tidbit of flesh to be thrown to them instead of forging for food themselves."

While certain that Les had found this strange analogy profoundly meangingful in some way, Max had not yet grasped what the heck it was. Julie sensed that the tone of the conversation had shifted awkwardly since her arrival; she was beginning to realize she was not welcome.

"Miss Walters," Les said, directing his attention to the attractive young grad student. "I believe you will find that the coolers have plenty of lunch supplies. Why don't you go find Margo in the adjacent room, and see about getting dinner ready for everyone, since you appear to be without responsibility at this moment?"

Julie lifted her bottom slowly from the counter, sighed, spun on her heels quickly, and hurried away. As she passed Rob Landon, she mimicked Les's stuffy voice. "*Miss Walters, why don't you and the other female serving wench cater to the needs of the great Mongeau?* Sexist asshole!"

In the other room, Les grinned slightly. "Now that the pelican has flown from the piling, my dear friend, please continue. I'm curious. What was happening in the little town across the lake from here during that boom in development?"

Max gave up trying to understand the pelican thing. Such was the way with Dr. Mongeau and his strange moods. He continued to explain how the Town of Rockwood prospered as Kineo grew. The people of Rockwood were awestruck as they watched the island develop. They finished building the Mount Kineo House in the early nineteen hundreds; a behemoth of a resort hotel that could accommodate over five hundred guests. Postcards from the resort boasted of dream vacations with plentiful fishing and sights to see. The guests were treated to spacious dining facilities and a golf course with spectacular views of the cliffs of Mt. Kineo. The resort eventually even provided tennis courts, a bowling alley, billiard tables, a croquet ground, and private parlors.

Julie, Rob, Gary and Margo came into the room carrying sodas in their hands and offered them to the professors. Dr. Wayne thanked the ladies with a gracious, appreciative smile. Les simply popped the soda can top and nodded. Margo, a geology student that had an interest in history, observed that she had heard about relics of the great hotels still surfacing on the island; she hoped to discover some in her spare time. Dr. Wayne gave her a genial smile and offered to join her on that quest.

Max explained to them how the southern shores of Kineo and the southwest peninsula, in particular, had eventually ended up resembling a small city, equipped with general stores, a marina, and housing for the employees as well as the guests. Dignitaries from around the world visited Kineo. The students and Dr. Mongeau followed Max out onto the golf lawn accessible through the dormitory's back door and looked out onto the vast open space. All that grandeur was gone now. Only traces of the past were left standing. And, of course, Cottage Row. The deserted buildings at dusk gave Margo an eerie feeling.

"What happened to Kineo?" she asked. "I mean, I know they had fires and all, but they kept rebuilding the place, didn't they?"

"Yeah, so why is it now so deserted?" Rob inquired.

"Well…" Max paused, collecting his thoughts. "Steamships, canoes, and railroad were the modes of transportation in that era. But by the nineteen thirties, people were clamoring for the independence to travel and explore at will. That privilege became available to them with the advent and sudden popularity of the gas-powered automobile."

"Yeah," added Gary Micnick. "Kineo also declined when the Maine Central Railroad eliminated its Kineo branch. My grandfather used to work for them in the mid-nineteen thirties."

"Well, get this," added Max in a mysterious tone. "The grand hotel was sold again near the beginning of World War Two. During the demolition, the huge wooden structure inexplicably caught fire again. The residents of Kineo were astonished to watch another key building burn to the ground."

Dr. Mongeau stared at Max, remembering how the sight of the ruins of the old fishing cottage earlier had disturbed him in the same way. He pointed to a raised mound of dirt a few yards to the south.

"Isn't this where the hotel annex used to be?"

"Right, Les. The annex was the only major structure, besides our dormitory, standing after the last of the great fires. It remained unused during the tough economic times until the Great War, when a series of sales and grand plans by outside investors began."

"Obviously, none ever came to fruition," Les concluded.

"Apparently not. The annex was allowed to fall into ruin and was finally demolished in the nineteen nineties."

Max turned to the students. "There you have it guys. Look around," he challenged. "A few ancillary historic summer cottages constructed in the early nineteen hundreds. Behind us are the remains of the old boiler room, and across Kineo Cove, you can see the fallen timbers of the old boathouse."

"Hey, don't forget *our* place here, man!" burst in Gary.

"Righto Gary," Max replied. "This dilapidated shell of the five-story dormitory is our new home—at least for two weeks. Now organize your gear; we have some ancient artifacts to uncover in the morning."

* * *

Laura had just finished showing her kids around their new summer home. While it was a bit disheartening to see how much work it needed, the children glowed with excitement at the old cottage's amazing potential. Though some of its rooms were in shambles, others were in reasonable shape and the Dentons would be able to sleep comfortably in them once a few beds had been replaced. The old storm windows were jagged with broken glass and thick with cobwebs. Dust enveloped everything. Yet, there was so much to explore.

Consumed by curiosity, Brandon and Jenny roamed the house. Tired from another day of simply being a teenager, Thomas threw himself down on an old couch in the sitting room, causing an explosion of dust that slowly settled all over him and prompted from him a rapid succession of uncontrolled sneezes.

"Okay," he said out loud, after catching his breath. "Lesson Numero Uno. When Mom says no jumping on the couch in *this* home, obey the rules."

From across the golf course, he could see people unload technical gear and carry it into the old dorm building. It looked like there were about ten people going in and out. He had assumed the building was abandoned. After all, it had "No trespassing" signs plastered over the exterior walls and all of the windows on the top three stories were completely sealed off. Laura had forbidden them to go inside. The building was dangerous and in need of significant repairs. But apparently, the first two floors had been repaired to some extent and the bottom floor was being rented.

Brandon entered the sitting room, grinning widely from his great adventure of having explored every corner of the old cottage. He paused to follow the direction of Thomas's gaze.

"Oh no, Thomas!" he exclaimed. "We got to go warn those people about the birds!"

"Naw, Bran," Thomas laughed. "It's fine. Let's tell Mom, though. We got early-season neighbors."

9

June 1, 1999

Laura was still overwhelmed by the previous day's experiences. Long car rides. Strange phone calls. Plane rides. Boat rides. Haggling over the price of the first family boat. And then to finally see her new summer cottage and come to terms with all the work it actually required. Somehow, in planning this ambitious summer quest, she had failed to anticipate the amount of labor it would ultimately demand.

A fresh start was needed. That morning, she was going to meet the local handy man, Rix Kraft. The younger brother of Bob Kraft who owned the air service that had provided the Dentons the previous day's flyover of Kineo, Rix was to meet Laura at eight sharp to discuss the renovation of the house. After a hot, refreshing shower, Laura slipped into fresh clothes and opened her bedroom window. She looked out at the lake below and felt the cool breeze caress her face. She was now ready to attack the new day and whatever adventures were in store for her.

The boys were still fast asleep when Rix showed up at the door at nine a.m. Being late by a mere hour was considered "early" on Kineo. Jenny shot out of bed like a bullet, chattering excitedly about all the things she wished to do. Her energy level was amazing and Laura had actually coaxed her daughter into cleaning an entire bathroom by herself before Rix's arrival.

"Mrs. Denton?" Rix ventured, each step creaking under his weight as he walked up to the front porch. "I am Richard Kraft, but folks around here just call me Rix."

Rix stood no more than five feet ten and carried over two hundred pounds on his frame. He looked sleepy and his skin was weathered from too many years working in the sun. At fifty, he gave the impression of being a much older man. Despite his worn and torn persona, his gray-blue eyes radiated a kindness which immediately put Laura at ease.

"I'm afraid, Mr. Kraft, I may have bitten off a little more than I can chew here," she confessed, offering her hand in a polite handshake. "I'm not all that experienced in refurbishing homes."

Laura's smile seemed vulnerable, and oddly in contrast with her handshake that was anything but frail. Rix immediately took a liking to her. Jenny burst out onto the wooden front porch, letting the screen door slam back against the house with a loud crash. There was an immediate scowl on Laura's face as her eyes met her daughter's.

"Well, it appears the first thing on my list is to get you a new spring for your screen door," Rix noted out loud. He walked over the deck of the porch and pointed out where the latticework and decking needed replacing, but Laura suggested that those could wait till next year. He needed to see the interior first.

The fireplace and living room were actually in pretty good condition, but the kitchen was a disaster. Worse, the wiring and plumbing throughout the cottage had to be replaced immediately.

"Mrs. Denton?"

"Laura please, Rix," she corrected.

"Laura," he amended. "The wiring in this place is a mess. You have wiring from every electrical era. Many of these wires are dangerously frayed. It's easy to imagine a fire starting here."

"Oh dear!" she gasped. "Ya think that's what started the fire at the Wellingtons' place?"

Rix paused, started to speak, then turned, instead, to face the fireplace, mumbling a comment about the quality of the historic brickwork.

"Rix? Do you think faulty wiring had anything to do with the fire at the old Wellington place?" Laura persisted, her voice betraying her rising concern.

Rix seemed to contemplate the question, searching for the right thing to say. "I dunno, Mrs. Denton," he finally managed. "I doubt it. The Goldmans had the entire place rewired. All the electrical stuff was new. But let's concentrate on *your* place here. Your wiring is a hazard and I insist we fix it first, before turning our attention to any cosmetic concerns you might have."

It seemed like very prudent advice to Laura, if it weren't for her feeling that he had left something unsaid. But she feared pushing her luck; there was not another handyman in the Kineo area if Rix up and left.

"Your plumbing also needs work," Rix went on. "It's amazing you didn't have a leak when we repressurized your house from the winterizing. Normally, leaks spring where the old metal pipe joints burst or the lines from the ice expand in areas where the house has settled and the drain lines are no longer able to drain out by gravity."

Laura had no idea what that meant, but she nodded knowledgeably and followed him to the next room.

"Mom, does that mean our pipes are gonna burst?" Jenny asked. "Won't water go all over the place?"

"Not if Mr. Kraft fixes it, dear."

"I need to check your basement," Rix stated.

"We have a basement?" Jenny burst out excitedly. "We never see no basements in Florida!"

"*Any*, Jenny," Laura corrected.

"Huh?"

"We don't see *any*…Jenny," Laura repeated.

"Whatever, Mom! Geesh! Can't we go see this basement now?" she pleaded.

"It's all right, Laura. Let her come and take a look." Rix smiled warmly. "If it isn't safe, I'll let you both know."

The door to the basement was in an awkward location, but the confident manner in which Rix made his way to the back hallway, where the old basement door was hidden, suggested he had been there before. Moving aside an old card table and some boxes, he exposed the door. Laura made a note to herself to ask him later how he had known *exactly* where to find this strangely located door, when she herself hadn't even known the place had a basement. The door was old, and when it was pushed open, the hinges let out a moan that had an unpleasant pitch. The sound of metal ripping metal echoed in the narrow and dark stairwell as Rix forced the door all the way open. There was a peculiar odor that moved up the stairwell to greet them. It was part musty and part something no longer alive. Cobwebs licked their faces as Rix groped for a light switch, but the old bulbs would not spring to life.

Pulling out his flashlight, Rix guided them carefully down the stairs, hugging the wall for support. Each step creaked, giving away the fact that the staircase, constructed in 1906, had never been replaced. Reaching the bottom more quickly than she had expected, Laura realized that the basement ceiling was not high enough to allow a person to stand erect, unless he were only a bit over five feet tall.

"Some basement," she mumbled softly, her disappointment evident.

"There's not much headroom," Rix warned. "This basement is shallow because the cottage does not sit up high enough from the lake level to allow deep excavation. Watch your head, pretty lady," he smiled, turning to Jenny.

Both mother and daughter turned to see whom Rix was referring to, but he seemed to be lavishing his attentions on Jenny. Rix had noticed how quiet she had become as she walked down the stairs and wondered if she found the stairway spooky.

"You doing all right, Jenny?" he asked gently.

"Sure, Mr. Kraft. I'm the *brave* one!" she replied confidently. Then as she looked past the beam of his flashlight, Jenny gasped and froze suddenly. "*What's that?*" she cried out.

* * *

In the sheriff's office in Greenville, Larry Magleton sat back in the chair behind his desk and studied his revolver. It was so many years ago that he had been forced to use the damn thing. And he *had* acted properly in an unavoidable situation, with his partner in imminent danger. Instantaneously, and without passion, as he had been trained to do. Yet, in that instinctual moment, his life had changed irrevocably. And he had been banished to serve here, in the middle of nowhere. *Damn!* He studied his revolver with something close to hatred. *Some people just have all the hard luck.*

The sudden clamor of the ringing telephone shattered his reverie. Reaching quickly to silence the unwelcome intrusion, he picked up the receiver.

"Yeah, Magleton here." Larry paused. "Last night?...Yes I heard. Do you know who he is? ...Okay, fine. I'll be there in an hour. Get the coroner there now! I expect his opinion upon my arrival."

As Larry snatched up his coat, Bronson Thurman walked into the office.

"Headin' out? Toonie and I want to talk to you about the Goldman cottage fire."

"Not a good time, Bronson. They found a drowned stiff up on the eastern shore near the State Park last night. Gotta go."

As Larry rushed out of the office and opened his patrol car door, he looked back at Bronson who was staring at the small ID chain he had found at the Wellington/Goldman cottage fire. *Why was Toonie, a deputy with Somerset County, calling a state fire examiner,* wondered Piscataquis County Sheriff Larry Magleton. He suddenly stopped and yelled back at Bronson.

"Hey…Bronson," he said hesitantly. "I know this is sheriff business and all, but if you want to talk to me, you can ride along. It may not be a bad idea to have you come along."

"Oh?" the other man replied, taking a few steps toward the patrol car.

"Yeah. Seems the stiff has bad burns on much of his body."

Bronson quickened his pace. Larry had the passenger door open by the time the other man arrived.

"But you said it was a drowning, didn't you?" the fire investigator quizzed, sliding into the car.

"I know," Larry grumbled, as the vehicle sped away.

* * *

The Denton boys awoke and pulled their boots on over their wool hiking socks. Laura had given permission for her older son to take the younger one on a hike up the Indian Trail to climb the fire tower. They had packed a meal of fruit, granola bars, and cookies, and a small fruit drink the night before. Now that he was fully awake, Thomas was particularly anxious to get going. The floatplane flight over the talus pile and along the cliffs of Kineo had stirred his imagination; he was raring to climb the mountain. Even Brandon was in a state of high excitement.

Thomas looked around for his mother or Jenny, but could find neither. He scribbled a quick note and left it on the kitchen refrigerator, letting his mother know where they were going. Jumping into the white golf cart that Bear had loaned them until their own was delivered, the boys set out on their first expedition. As the cart rambled along the golf course toward Mt. Kineo, the boys saw a handful of graduate students sifting through soil in a small wooden box along the path.

Ever the most inquisitive Denton offspring, Thomas stopped the cart, looked over the students' shoulders for a moment, then asked carefully, "Whatcha looking for?"

Gary Micnick replied mischievously, "Aw, nothing special, kid…just *gold!*"

"Really?" asked Brandon.

The two male grad students laughed.

"Naw, kidding, little dude. We're looking for native artifacts."

Having no idea what an artifact was, Brandon accepted the answer and urged Thomas to drive on. *These big kids were rude*, Brandon thought, *and boring. We have a mountain to explore.* Thomas smiled at the students and released the brake. The cart raced forward, moving as fast as the governor would allow—which was only about twelve miles an hour. Thomas considered the trouble that he would get into if he removed the governor from the carburetor. Then he smirked and decided against it—*at least for the moment.*

The golf cart path slowly turned from worn grass to gravel. The historic Carriage Trail on the mountain's west side was flanked by Moosehead Lake on the left and lush deciduous forest carpeting the foothill toe slopes of Mt. Kineo immediately to their right. The aspen leaves swayed in the early morning sunlight to the rhythm of the wind gusting from the huge lake. They passed the large talus pile of crushed rhyolite and Brandon released a squeal of delight.

"Thomas, we have to climb that ginormous rock pile! Can we?"

"Later, lil' bro," Thomas answered. "That pile alone will take several hours. We have a really cool hike around the corner to do first."

Parking the cart at the end of the Carriage Trail, the boys continued on foot along the edge of the lake, as the sheer walls of granitic rock began to crowd them on the right. In one location, the glacial scouring of the igneous mass formed a large slab of volcanic rock that was nearly as smooth as glass. Brandon drew his fingers across it and skipped merrily along the path.

Shortly, they spotted the historic Indian Trail and began the strenuous ascent. The boys soon found that it was more than just a hike, as scrambling on all fours became mandatory for both of them. Thomas had to stop several times for his younger brother to catch up, as the steep, rugged trail was more than his shorter legs could handle. Soon, they had reached one of the many spectacular vantage points 600 feet above the lake. The boys stopped to catch their breath and looked out over the golf course. Thomas recognized their cottage to the south.

As they ate a quick snack, the boys watched some of the grad students assemble on Sunset Beach by the Breakwater Cottage. They appeared to be looking for something in the field next to the lake. Another group of students was heading on foot up a trail toward Mt. Kineo. *Apparently, that group is going to be joining us,* thought Thomas. *I wonder what they're up to?*

"C'mon, Brandon," he urged. "Before it gets too crowded up here, let's make it to the top."

The boys picked up their daypacks and enthusiastically continued climbing the Indian Trail.

* * *

"Wha'd ya see, Jenny?" Rix asked.

"Over there!" the little girl pointed, her hands noticeably trembling as she snuggled tight against Laura's hip for comfort. "Something moving in the shadows."

"Oh, you just saw a bat," Rix reassured her. "We have lots of bats."

"Nooo! It wasn't flying. It was big!" she insisted.

"Mr. Kraft, did you see it? Laura asked impatiently. "You're there with the flashlight."

"Well, no. I was looking back at you when she cried out," he explained. "So Jenny, you saw an animal then? How large?"

"Big! Like you!" Jenny explained, panic in her voice. "And it ran into the corner of the back wall!"

"You mean like a bear?" Rix suggested, crouching down and moving along under the very low ceiling toward the corner.

"Nooo!" Jenny sounded frustrated, unable to describe what she had seen. "It was running on two feet!"

"Okay. You two stay there. I'll check it out," Rix offered.

Stumbling along in the dark with his small flashlight, Rix Kraft cracked his head on a pipe suspended from a floor joist. He blurted out something unintelligible that likely was unrepeatable. Clearing cobwebs from his path and pulling old plywood sheets away from a brick support column, he found a large hole penetrating the brick foundation. It was around the corner, out of the Dentons' sight, as mother and daughter still huddled near the staircase.

"Everything fine, Mr. Kraft?" Laura inquired, concern discernible in her voice.

"Fine, Laura. Just give me another second to make sure there is nothing here to worry your sweet daughter," he said with a trace of anxiety.

Ducking through the hole, Rix found a small area under the house that was not part of the original basement. Yet, it shared two of the cottage's support walls, while the other two sides were bare earth held up by old, musty railroad timbers and fairly recent plywood. Considering how flimsy its structure was, the small chamber had likely been created in a hurry. Its purpose was apparently to allow excavation without long-term utility being addressed.

A creepy feeling began to descend over Rix. He scanned the chamber with his flashlight. On the floor lay a shovel and a pickaxe that looked recently used. Fresh earth had been uncovered and the smell of soil and stove fuel were noticeable in this tiny confined area. On the ground near the pickaxe was a small wooden stool with a Coleman backpacking lantern. On the table were a few pieces of rhyolite that had been worked like flint and what looked to be bone.

Rix's skin crawled as a dark, suppressed memory from his childhood flashed before him. *Rats! The old Indian woman and the gravesite! What was it the old woman used to rant on about? She would point to a tattoo on her arm that displayed a circle with three lines radiating out from the center. Then she would mumble something about disturbing the gravesites of her ancestors.*

Now that his eyes had fully adjusted to the dark, Rix noticed a small beam of light. He moved to the side of the excavation where the old timbers were holding back the soil near the ground surface and found a plywood cover with a handle. Pulling it outward exposed a tiny escapeway to the outside of the cottage. The passageway exited directly into the steep bank of Moosehead Lake. The plywood was disguised with brush and leaves attached to the door. The opening was not part of the service yard around the cottage but within the thick stand of aspen, cornus, birch saplings, and revetment rocks used to stablize the outer bank between the cottages and the lake. *Dear God*, he thought to himself. *This exit area is only yards from the back of the cottage and yet it is completely concealed...as if someone wanted to access the excavation site next to the basement unseen. This cottage has sat dormant for years. Nobody would have noticed at all. Until now. Whoever was using this excavation site would surely not appreciate the Dentons' sudden arrival.*

"Oh rats! What am I thinking?" Rix shook his head. *This is just a silly hole dug out by local kids to create a fort. There's nothing here to indicate anything else. So they found some old Indian points. Flint. Who hasn't on Kineo? Ha!*

He laughed at himself, feeling foolish for his loss of confidence. Even at fifty, a man can get spooked crawling around in the dark. *Still, no need to worry the Dentons. I'll cover up the access and warn the local kids to stay away from the cottage, since it is now occupied.* Rix had an idea whose kids would make such a fort. The hole and chamber would be sealed and shored up safely. Then all would be fine. Rix decided to get back to the Dentons and start his renovations. Shored up by a new resolve about his plans, he stumbled through the hole in the brick wall back into the basement.

"Well Laura," he called back. "There's no animal under here, but I did find a hole in your foundation that's not structurally safe. I'll fix it, but you should keep your kids out of here until I do. It would be best to get Jenny upstairs. I recommend keeping this interesting discovery from your curious boys until I have a chance to shore it up and close it off properly."

Fully aware of her sons' inquisitiveness, Laura recognized sensible advice when she heard it. She herded Jenny upstairs.

"You're the expert, Mr. Kraft," Laura said as she climbed up the stairs. "Why don't you complete your investigation of our basement wiring and plumbing? We'll talk more later. I need to see if my boys got up and started their hike."

Rix waved his flashlight and went back to inspecting the basement by himself. Outside, crawling between the rocks of the outer revetment through the aspen saplings was a thin, lanky man wearing black retro glasses. Grumbling to himself for nearly being discovered, he inched his way down the steep slope to his kayak. The man removed the aspen branches covering his concealed kayak and escaped into Moosehead Lake.

* * *

It took only an hour and a half to reach the top of Mt. Kineo despite the boys stopping and gazing out over each of the cliff overlooks. Brandon found an outcropping of rocks that looked liked the crusted face of an old man with a hat. Since the trail was called the Indian Trail, Thomas told his brother that the face was that of Chief Seminola and proceeded with an elaborate tale of confused Indian facts. Brandon eventually realized his older brother was messing with him. He punched Thomas on the shoulder. Deriving great satisfaction from this response, the older boy told his brother that the Seminole Indians lived in Florida. Following which he called Brandon a goof for believing him. As a result, the rock outcropping would henceforth be known to the Dentons as the "Chief's Head". Thomas promised Brandon that if they had time, he would allow him to scramble out onto the Chief's Head and gaze out over the lake.

Once the boys had made the very top of Kineo, the old fire tower awaited them. The rusty steel structure had a series of spiral stairs that wound their way up above the conifers, providing the only unobstructed panoramic view of the entire lake. Thomas scrambled to the top, his shoes making an echoing "ping" sound, as each foot smacked a steel rung, while Brandon carefully picked his way up. The open view through the metal rungs to the rocks below was a bit more frightening than the boy had imagined from the ground, now far below him. The hair on his arms stood up as if static electricity had zapped him. At the top, the boys viewed all of Moosehead Lake. Greenville was barely visible to the south. Rockwood and the marina were close to them as they scanned the west by the mouth of the Moosehead River. Thomas was very good with maps. He explained the nearby mountaintops, rivers, and towns to Brandon.

"I love this island!" proclaimed the younger boy.

"It isn't technically an island, Brandon," Thomas corrected him, "but I'm not sure why. Maybe we can ask one of the college students to explain it to us on the way back."

"Those college kids were mean to us earlier," grumbled Brandon. "Specially that red-haired guy."

"Naw," laughed Thomas. "They were just teasing us. Older kids do that."

Brandon looked up and smiled at his older brother. For a jerk, he was often a pretty cool big brother. Then Brandon suddenly stood up and pointed to the southeast shoreline. There were flashing lights in the distance that he had not noticed earlier. To the southeast, the boys could see the lights of a police patrol boat and emergency vehicles along the shore. The excitement of an emergency made the boys hasten their departure. They packed up their things and started back down. Maybe their mother would let them pick up their Boston whaler and go for a joy ride and see what the excitement below was all about.

10

Lily Bay State Park

"So watcha got, Harris?" bellowed Larry Magleton as he slammed the door and joined the investigation underway. A female deputy with the sheriff's office strode up to Magleton's vehicle and began the rundown.

"A young male, dead. Drowned two, maybe three days ago. Burns on half of his body. Grisly thing to see actually, sir. Those people over there are the Johnsons. They're the unfortunate ones who came up upon the body at dusk last night while boating."

"Did it occur in the State Park? Are we sure it's our jurisdiction?"

"Yeah," the deputy responded. "We checked it out with the State Park. It occurred outside their boundary in the bay. It's our problem, but the Park Rangers are being very helpful. Think they're worried about tourist perception of a murder *within* the park. They'd rather it were written up as a Piscataquis County event."

"Protect the local economy. Whatever—got it. Do we have an identity yet?" Larry barked out.

"Yes," Deputy Harris replied. "His wallet has an ID. His name was James West."

"Hmm. Name's familiar. James, you say?" Larry repeated. "Let me see the photos."

"I took these images last night." Deputy Harris noted. "Took a while to extricate him from the rocks."

"James West. Jim West. Hmm?" Larry muttered, walking past the various investigators and emergency response personnel. Looking down and pulling back the cover, he recognized the face. "Jimbo."

Bronson grimaced as he saw the photos of the half-burned and bloated victim. "You knew him?" he mumbled, stepping back.

"Yeah. He used to come into town quite a bit. From Rockwood. He was ol' Gus O'Malley's first mate and a friend of Dougie's, the guy who runs the Kineo shuttle service. They reported him missing."

"Hmm. Do you know what his middle name was?" asked Bronson.

"No. Everyone called him Jimbo."

Deputy Harris shook her head as well.

Looking out into the small crowd of investigators, Larry inquired as to whether anyone had known him locally. A few acknowledged that they had seen him around or knew who he was, but no one had known him well enough to be aware of his middle name. In fact, no one had even known that the name given on his driver's license was James West. He was simply Jimbo. Certainly, his friend, Dougie, would know. Or Gus.

"Well, Larry, I'd run it through records," suggested Bronson.

"Of course. What's up? You have some theory forming, *Fireman?*"

Bronson was amazed at how annoying Larry could be. He sighed and paused. Then he said, "Well, let's just say that I suspect his middle name begins with a 'W', Sheriff." Bronson extended his hand and allowed the ID chain he had found at the scene of the Goldman fire to uncoil and drop to its full length. The chain caught on his thumb and the plate dangled out in front of Larry's face. The three initials were clearly visible.

"JWW."

"Hm," grunted Larry. "I see. Well, Deputy Harris—you inform the next of kin?"

"Yes, sir. I will let Gus and Dougie know as well."

"I need to go to the county morgue and examine the burns and talk to the coroner. Things are looking a bit suspicious now, aren't they?"

Larry did not respond. He simply grunted and walked back to his vehicle. He wondered how much of Bronson's intuition was related to Toonie's tip. *Why hadn't Toonie called him?* The Moosehead region had been a perfect retreat for Larry Magleton. No murders, rapes or other unspeakable deeds were ever inflicted on his residents here. He did not miss the barbarians he had hunted in the big cities of Massachusetts. Suddenly, he felt disgust. Sheriff Larry Magleton felt an eerie premonition that the violent life he had left behind was about to catch up with him and disrupt his peaceful existence in the Moosehead Lake region.

* * *

Thomas and Brandon knew their mother would certainly be expecting them to return for lunch. The boys had eaten all of their daypack goods and were off the fire tower, scrambling down a ragged section of trail with exposed rhyolite. The boys had made it back to the Chief's Head formation, when Brandon begged his older brother to let him climb out and look over the lake. Keeping his earlier promise, Thomas guided him along a narrow path through a thicket of mountain blueberries out to the craggy and weathered pinnacle. As they approached, they could hear voices. It was one of the professors and two of his students. They were looking through small hand lenses at the rocks that made up the formation.

Thomas heard the only woman in the group mention something about how the microcrystalline quartz in this rock was more prevalent than in the specimens back at the talus pile. The professor looked up as the boys approached.

"Hi!" Thomas greeted the academics. "Do you mind if we see what you guys are up to?"

"Not at all young man," replied Dr. Mongeau affably. "Curiosity is the foundation of science."

Thomas walked out to the ledge and watched the students study the various minerals in a freshly broken piece of rhyolite. Less interested in the mineral examination, Brandon scrambled up to the top of the Chief's Head and sat basking in the sun. The young woman walked over to Thomas and offered him a piece of Mt. Kineo that she had just cracked open with a crack hammer.

"Isn't it fascinating?" The student showed Thomas a freshly broken piece of rhyolite through her hand lens. "The natives call this flint, but it's really a granitic rock. Granite grows under the earth where it cools slowly. This rock was exposed to the air quickly because of volcanic activity. The rock is glassy with microscopic crystals. We call it rhyolite. The whitish micro-crystal looks like feldspar. I'll verify that with the professor. These slightly larger, clear crystals are the mineral quartz made of SiO_2. But look here!"

Thomas was fascinated by the girl's enthusiasm, or maybe the fact that she was a *girl*.

"The rock in my right hand is *real* flint that I brought with me for comparison," the student continued. "A chalcedony variety of quartz, also chemically composed of SiO_2 but with a compact micro-crystalline granular texture."

Thomas enjoyed the attention he was getting from the older girl—young woman—grad student—even though most of what she was talking about went way over his head. She seemed so excited about the little crystals under her hand lens that Thomas figured they must be some exciting geological discovery. The stone's intimidating angles and sharp edges were actually what interested him. It was dark gray and jagged and had the kind of very sharp edge that would make any boy stop and drag it across his palm to see if it would cut skin. The enthusiastic graduate student, Julie Walters, saw the young boy's fascination with the rhyolite edges and realized this teenager would probably prefer a topic with a different twist.

"Can't you just see an early pioneer on this peninsula using a shard of flint like this as a knife to skin a deer?" the student asked, pleased with her choice of words.

Thomas responded with a shy smile as he felt the blade begin to open his skin. Then he stopped and looked up, catching a glimpse of her auburn hair blowing into her face from the stiff wind swirling around on top of the Chief's Head. Her use of the word "peninsula" bothered him, as he watched her brush her hair out of her eyes with interest.

Julie explained that Mt. Kineo sat on the spectacular landmass often referred to as "Kineo Island", although it was, technically, a peninsula. The confusion occurred because the narrow isthmus on the eastern shore provided a connection between the island and the mainland.

"If you were on the fire tower earlier, gentlemen," added Dr. Mongeau, "you would have seen the narrow connection dividing Frog Pond from Kineo Bay."

The Denton boys looked over in the direction the professor indicated and remembered seeing the straight causeway.

"The isthmus was artificially raised and graded to provide vehicular access to this large landmass we stand upon," the professor continued. "They connected the tiny rock-outcrop islands in the northern section of Frog Pond on what was probably a natural breakwater of very shallow water. My colleague, Dr. Wayne, tells me that early man had no problem crossing this row of low obstacles and shallow water. This debate is all academic, of course. Today, Kineo is physically a peninsula, but acts functionally as an island. The vehicular path that remains today has been deliberately blocked by boulders because of legal entanglements between the islanders and the timber company that owns the mainland side of the connection."

"I see. Kineo acts as an island, because the only way to get here now is by boat," Thomas reaffirmed. "So Pebble Beach is really an *isthmus*."

"Right. And we have seen pictures from the late eighteen hundreds referring to the isthmus as Pebble Beach."

"Don't sweat the difference, honey," laughed Julie. "We too usually refer to Kineo as 'the island'. It eliminates confusion between descriptions of the southwest peninsula where your family's cottage stands."

Suddenly, Dr. Mongeau looked at his watch and noted that it was time for Julie and Rob to move along and collect more samples. The boys thanked the professor and his students for their friendly explanations and waved goodbye. Brandon agreed with Thomas that the college kids and their professor weren't so bad after all. The boys raced down the Indian Trail, invigorated with all they had seen and learned on this wonderful island.

* * *

Bennington Lomax and his daughters stopped by the yellow cottage on their ride to the Kineo docks. The red stretch golf cart slid to a stop and Bennington jumped out of the driver's seat. Laura was just outside on the front step, with Jenny thanking Rix for his walk-through of the cottage.

"I'll get started on the electrical on Wednesday. I'll do the plumbing next week," Rix promised. "I'll return in the morning to finish shoring up that hole in the basement to make things safe."

"Mr. Kraft. Good evening," smiled Bennington, as he walked majestically up the walkway.

"How did those improvements hold up during the winter?" Rix asked him.

"Most satisfactory," the other man replied in his distinguished English accent. "Your craftsmanship is indisputable."

Rix smiled at the compliment and looked back at Laura, hoping she had heard the testimonial. Not that he had much competition in the area, but still, a man had his pride. He waved to all and set off to take his boat back to Greenville Junction where he lived.

Laura watched the stately man walk toward her. Bennington was around five foot eleven and weighed no more than 180 pounds. His black hair was peppered with gray and his meticulously groomed sideburns were completely gray. Yet, he looked far younger than his forty-eight years. Bennington's skin was smooth and free of wrinkles. He strolled up the stairs with an elegance that was unlike any man's she had ever seen. He wore pleated khaki pants with a white button-down oxford cloth shirt and a blue sweater was casually flung over his shoulder. He wore leather cordovan loafers without socks.

In the golf cart waited two young girls. One looked bored and indifferent. The other was smiling and cocked like a trigger, ready to explode out of the golf cart when commanded.

"Bennington Lomax," the regal man announced, extending his hand to Laura.

"Jenny Denton," answered Jennifer Denton, before her mother could even open her mouth. "And this is my mother, Laura."

"Why, thank you, Jenny. I couldn't have introduced myself without you." Laura's eyes twinkled at Bennington and then at Jenny. "Pleased to meet you, Bennington."

"Are those your daughters?" Jenny inquired exuberantly.

"Indeed," Bennington answered. "Girls?"

Amanda bolted from the cart like a hunting dog commanded to fetch. She had been eager to finally meet another girl her own age. Tiffany, the seemingly bored sibling, remained in the cart, arms crossed, and looked out, unamused, at the whole "welcome your new neighbors" routine. The adults introduced the girls. Sure enough, Amanda and Jenny were the same age. Tiffany, nearly seventeen, had no interest in meeting someone Amanda's age. She slowly unwrapped her legs and arms that were wound up so noticeably tight that she appeared to be in restraints and ceremoniously slithered down from the golf cart, as if readying herself for a grand entrance.

"Where is Mr. Denton?" Bennington asked politely, noticing the wedding ring on Laura's finger.

"I'm afraid he's no longer with us, Bennington." Laura's tone remained steady and assured. But her reply was a little too matter-of-fact, and Bennington surmised there was more to this story than was appropriate for him to inquire about at this time.

"I love your outfit, Amanda," bubbled Jenny. "Where did you get those beautiful shorts?"

The other girl blushed and simply thanked Jenny. Tiffany now strolled up the stairs with a sway in her hips and tossed her long wavy blonde hair with her fingers. Waiting for the precise moment when all eyes were upon her, the Lomax Princess finally made her presence known.

"Those shorts were purchased in Italy, Jennifer—an exclusive label, Cannoloni, that Mum favors. I doubt *you* would be familiar with the designer."

Laura's cheerful smile faltered. *This little bitch is trouble*, she thought. She watched Tiffany pose next to the porch rail, staring out through her Gucci sunglasses.

"I like your blouse, Jenny," Amanda offered as a conciliatory gesture.

"Thank you, Amanda. It was a birthday present from my mom," Jenny explained. "Roxy is my favorite."

"Common, but cute," mumbled Tiffany, barely audible.

It appeared to her that only Laura picked up the words. Or at least she was the only person whose body stiffened when she uttered them. Bennington appeared distracted and detached from the initial clothing-related banter. He explained that he was going to the airport to pick up his wife. Laura could see that Jenny was hitting it off with the sweeter younger daughter, Amanda. But she was wary about the older brat. Sizing up the situation quickly, Laura thought out a plan which she initiated with a polite offer.

"The girls are welcome to stay here and help me bake cookies while you go pick your wife up at the airport, Bennington. If that's fine?"

"Can we, Father?" Amanda asked.

Bennington considered the request for a moment as Tiffany rolled her eyes heavenward under her $400 sunglasses. Then he agreed to let the girls stay. His decision brought a cheer from Jenny and a big smile from Amanda. Tiffany walked away, announcing that she would keep her father company on the ride to the airport, and then insisted that they set off immediately. Laura grinned imperceptibly, having been aware of the outcome long before it had played itself out.

"We don't want to keep dear Mummy waiting now, Daddy...do we?"

Bennington smiled at Laura who assured him that it was all right to have Amanda stay until he got back after dinner. The two girls raced upstairs to play in Jenny's still dilapidated room. Laura watched as the odd pair of father and daughter drove off in their well-polished red cart, Tiffany looking smugly over her shoulder to toss her a forced smile. Laura thought to herself how interesting this island adventure was promising to be. The socio-economic backgrounds of the folks she had met so far were very diverse. Then she retreated to her cottage to continue with her chore of throwing out old items.

* * *

Brandon was slow to get to the golf cart; his little legs had had quite enough adventure for one day. Thomas sat in the EZ Go cart, impatiently waiting for his brother. They had been out longer than their mother would have liked, and Thomas was not keen on being hauled up for it. He slammed the pedal to the floor, disengaging the parking brake, and headed for their cottage. They sped around the corner of the rock cliffs and beyond the talus pile along the old Carriage Trail. Dashing across the par three fairway, Brandon pointed at a moose splashing about in the nearby water hazard. Startled by the cart, the large animal bounded out of the water toward them, then suddenly jerked to the left and took immediate refuge in the nearby woods. The boys' eyes widened in surprise, looking as enormous as half-dollars. Thomas gave Brandon a high five as they raced up the hill and turned onto the gravel road along Cottage Row.

Amanda and Jenny asked Laura if she minded them exploring the area along the lake's shoreline. Laura warned them to stay away from the university students if they saw them.

"Look from a distance and don't be a pest," she instructed Jenny.

As the two girls headed out of the cottage, skipping and laughing on their way to Sunset Beach, where their curiosity would be whetted by the activities of a small group of people with large wooden stands and equipment, Laura watched her little girl and wondered if she had been right in letting her go unsupervised, knowing Jenny would be unable to contain her enthusiasm around the visitors.

But before she could call her daughter back, she was distracted by the sound of a golf cart speeding down toward her from the north. Finally, her boys were back. Thomas came to a sudden halt right in front of the porch. Dust spewed from underneath the cart, and the wind seized the loose particles and whirled them around for a brief second before carrying them off toward the cottage

"Oops!" said Thomas, a worrisome grin on his face, as the cloud of dust floated over Laura's head. "Sorry, Mom."

His mother looked at her watch, and then fixed him with a disapproving stare. Unaware of the unspoken communications around him, Brandon jumped off the cart, ran up to his mother, grabbed her, and gave her a big hug.

"Mommy!" he said excitedly. "I had the most coolest time with Thomas. We saw a moose, climbed a big tower, climbed big rocks, and saw an Indian chief's head. And we learned about rock knives and met these neat college kids!"

"Whoa!" Laura stopped him. "Slow down, mister. I want to hear all about it. But first, you boys need to eat the lunch I made for you over an hour ago!"

"Yo, Mom! I'll eat whatever you made and more," Thomas announced, giving his mother a peck on her right cheek.

The three left for the kitchen, while Jenny and Amanda began charming their way into the hearts of one very kind professor and six students on Sunset Beach.

* * *

"So did they see you?" the man with the distinctly Canadian accent inquired.

"*Non.* I was too quick for them," came the confident reply.

"You are paid far too much to be so careless," said the portly man, walking up to the man in black glasses. "I can't have the Denton widow becoming suspicious. We have a schedule to keep and I am not a man who tolerates falling behind."

"Understood," Pierre nodded respectfully. "But all else is going well. I don't need to return to that site—it wasn't there."

"To be safe, we begin the second part of our operation," Pilloud announced.

"Your orders will be carried out," the Frenchman said. "I will take Boxer to assist me on that job in the morning."

"Then our conversation is over." The portly man squashed his cigar in the nearby ashtray, then turned and walked out of his opulent study.

11

Greenville Junction

Later that evening, Bob Kraft was working on tuning his engine. The floatplane had not been running smoothly this week, and he had another plane out of service, with a faulty wing strut being replaced. He looked down from the ladder at his brother, Rix, who was just entering the hangar.

"Well, look who's in town!" laughed the older brother. "Thought you were busy in Rockwood today."

"I was," Rix answered sheepishly. "I was working on the old yellow cottage on Kineo. A very nice family moved in there. They need a lot of help."

Bob took his cap off, exposing his bald head. "Uh huh, I'll bet *she* does!" he grinned.

"What?" Rix said to his brother "What's that smart-ass grin for?"

"I hear she has back!" Bob tested the waters before turning his head back to his wrench and began working a spark plug out of its socket.

"Who?"

"She's *too young*—for a fat...old...man like you anyway," Bob taunted.

"Okay, okay," Rix stammered, his tone becoming testy. "What'd you hear?"

"Matt gave the Dentons a plane ride earlier, *Richard*, so...all's well. Now settle down," Bob calmed him. "I'm just messin' with my lil' bro."

"Oh...ha!" Rix chuckled. "Yeah, Matt's the best young pilot I've ever seen fly for you. So what did young Matt say about the Dentons?"

"Just that they were a nice family, and the widowed mother was mid-to-late thirties, had a pretty fine-looking frame." Bob looked down at Rix. "Hell. I'm fifty-five. Too old, too fat, and way too happily married. But *you*, my brother...you are only too old and too fat!"

"Don't go there, Bobby. Not today," Rix's voice trailed off. "I'm not in the mood, okay?"

"Touchy, aren't we, sweet cheeks?" Bob baited him again and put the wrench down. He climbed down the ladder and stood next to Rix. "So what's eating the handyman anyway?"

"Sorry, Bob. It isn't you. It's me," Rix explained. "I saw something disturbing today. Remember when we were kids, and that old Indian spooked us over near Spencer Mountain?"

"Hell yeah, I remember! She appeared outta' nowhere. Said all that crap about the Kineo residents disturbing native burial sites and about a curse on Kineo and fires."

"Exactly," Rix continued. "I thought she was some sort of witch or something."

"Yeah. You didn't sleep a wink for a week after that," Bob reminded him.

"But do you remember all the strange things that happened that summer, with the fires and that old man who died mysteriously?"

"I'll never forget that summer," Bob answered solemnly. "The old Indian woman said it happened because the whites kept messing around with ancestral burial sites near Spencer Mountain and on Kineo."

"What was that really weird warning she gave us?" Rix tried to remember.

"How could ya forget, lil' brother? She said a white princess had lost the black stone of the Mohawk while tresspassin' on Kajo's sacred mountain. Somethin' about a fire curse that'd plague all the white invaders and their ancestors."

"Right. And if we ever stumbled across it, we were to return it to her immediately or else be watching our possessions burn for the rest of our lives. She was one spooky old woman!"

"So what brought all of this on?"

"I found an excavation site that looked a lot like the one we found that summer over by Spencer Mountain. I mean there were flint scrapers and arrowheads and bones. But this one was under the Denton cottage," continued Rix. "It was probably just some stupid kids messing around while the cottage was abandoned. You know, like making a fort or something. Anyway, it just had that same feeling...you know?"

"Hey, Rix, I don't want to sound superstitious, but if I were you, I'd just do my work and get out there."

Rix knew exactly what his brother meant. After working on Kineo for years, he had developed a sixth sense about things. Especially when buildings were burning down on Kineo. He had already decided he would finish boarding off the hole in the basement and get back to working upstairs as quickly as possible.

* * *

Laura had been fully debriefed on her boys' adventures and noted that the sun was getting a bit low in the sky. She wanted to round up all her children before dark and encourage them to help her with some of the indoor projects she had lined up to restore their cottage. Her ambitious goal was to have actual tenants renting the old cottage this year and generate some tangible income to offset the outrageous expenses that she foresaw on the horizon. Laura's sense of accounting was flawless and her calculations were precise—down to the last penny. It was this attention to detail in the matter of the family's daily bookkeeping that had been the source of disagreements in a marriage that was otherwise entirely harmonious. Now her thoughts were focused on Jenny, as she wondered if her daughter was not being a pest to the group of college students.

Laura approached her boys who were busy painting the living room walls, as instructed. "C'mon, guys," she said, "we better go see what's going on down on Sunset Beach."

Both jumped at the chance of having a few moments away from the smell of brand new paint. Laura and her sons walked down the gravel road along Cottage Row. Brandon walked slowly alongside his mother, while Thomas, seeing the gathering of academics down by Sunset Beach, quickened his pace. He was feeling that same stirring he had experienced earlier. There was something about field investigations and science that had an adventurous appeal for the teenager.

In the distance, Thomas spotted Jenny and Amanda. They were standing next to a wooden frame with a sifter and many large buckets. A tall man in his mid-thirties stood next to the girls, laughing and holding up a small object. A sandy-haired grad student carried away another pail full of sifted earth from underneath the wooden table, and another student dutifully poured an unsifted earthload into the center of the box for close examination.

Laura took in the scene as well, but her perceptions were less focused on the mechanics of the operation and more on the interpersonal dynamics. The man was rugged and good-looking. He wore a pair of Levis with a noticeable hole in the left knee and a green and black plaid cotton long-sleeved shirt that was only partially tucked into his jeans. The man appeared to be the person in charge. Jenny had evidently charmed her way into his favor. Laura stopped and watched him explain the significance of a piece of pottery found in the soil. Jenny appeared to hang on to every word of his explanation. He was so animated in his description that Amanda was also paying close attention.

"Oh girls, you must realize," Dr. Wayne explained, "that Paleo-Indian artifacts are very scarce. They are three to five *thousand* years old in this area."

Amanda wasn't sure exactly what that meant. But it was evident that the object that had surfaced in the sifter had captured the undivided attention of all these college students. Another grad student had abandoned his post, where his day's effort had yielded nothing but worn glass fragments, remnants of the more recent period in Kineo history, when many hotel guests had broken bottles along the beach. The excitement at this wooden table, however, was for all to enjoy.

"These artifacts that you two girls found are *very* important." Dr. Wayne said warmly. "We've been studying similar ones from nearby sites and we've reconstructed the lives of these fascinating people. These artifacts collectively indicate that their users traveled by water and hunted big game."

The girls giggled as the somewhat eccentric professor stretched out his arms to indicate *how* big the game was. Thomas stepped up to the table and said hello to everyone. Jenny immediately took credit for the "big find" and the professor winked surreptitiously at her brother, urging him silently to refrain from ruining his sister's sense of achievement by demanding further evidence. Thomas caught on straight away and Dr. Wayne offered him his hand.

"You must be the *renowned* Thomas Denton," Max said.

Thomas rocked back on his heels and looked surprised. The college students laughed.

"Oh, don't be surprised," Margo said. "Surely, you're used to your little sister talking about her big brother."

"Yuppers," agreed Dr. Wayne. "We've heard *all* about you, Brandon, and the most *amazing* mother on the planet," he continued.

"Oh, no!" Thomas laughed. "Sounds like you got an earful from Jenny."

"Aw, be assured that it was all positive comments about you, Thomas!" Max smiled reassuringly, turning to the woman who was slowly making her presence felt as she came up behind her son.

"Max Wayne," the professor introduced himself. "And you must be the *amazing* Laura Denton."

Laura met his gaze, her expression curious, her smile bashful. The man was full of energy and life, but not in an offensive way. Self-assured, yet somehow restrained and in control. She couldn't help but wonder, though, what mischief lay hidden behind those crystal blue eyes that presented such a stark contrast to his dark—nearly black—hair. She found herself staring into his eyes a little longer than was comfortable for her.

Before she could reply, Jenny filled the awkward void. "Yeah! That's my mom, Professor Max."

"Professor Max!" exclaimed Laura, turning with disapproval to her daughter. "I believe you should address him as *Doctor* Wayne, Jenny."

"Oh gosh, no, Mrs. Denton!" the professor protested. "Doctors are people who wear lab coats at work, not jeans. Doctors are *old* men with impressive academic tenure like my colleague, Dr. Mongeau. And heck, the Professor Max thing is…kind of cute anyway. So please, will you call me Max?"

"Well, I suppose I can do that…Max…if you promise to call me Laura."

Max offered his hand to her in formal acknowledgement of the understanding and said, "Deal, Laura."

Margo watched them with curiosity. When Laura felt Max's fingers firmly grip her own, a sudden rush of nervous anxiety that she had not felt in a long time went through her. It was a sensation that caused her some uneasiness, because she was still grieving for her dead husband. It simply was too early, she felt, to move beyond her pain to something positive and joyful. *At least, not yet.* Withdrawing her hand first, Laura allowed the professor's fingers to slide across her own as they separated. She walked away, her cheeks flushed, and diverted her attention, asking Jenny to show her what they had found that was so exciting. To Thomas and Laura, the artifact simply looked like a broken piece of clay.

Jenny looked at Amanda and rolled her eyes, which made the other girl laugh.

"Geesh, Mom, don't ya get it?" Jenny ribbed her. "Explain it to her, Professor Max."

"I'd be honored to do so," Max said with a bow to the girls. "This fragment, although tiny and seemingly unimportant, is actually part of a ceremonial pot used during the burial rites of the Red Paint People. These Indians, Kineo's early inhabitants, were so named because of the red ochre found in their excavated graves."

"Mom! There were actual gravesites of the Red Paint People near the Mount Kineo Hotel!" Jenny announced.

"Now Jenny, let's not tell *too* many people that, like we agreed, okay?" warned Max suddenly, his tone more protective.

"Seriously?" Thomas inquired with wide-eyed interest.

"Yes," answered one of the grad students, pointing over toward the bulkheads and the Breakwater Cottage. "Right here on the Kineo peninsula."

"Sadly," interjected Max, "these ancient graves were virtually destroyed years ago, when tennis courts were constructed right over there for hotel guests. The surviving artifacts from the graves were displayed at the hotel for many years. Others were taken away."

"To Boston and the Peabody Museum," added Margo. "We saw them last year."

Beginning to clue in to certain implications of this adult discussion, Brandon started wondering about the dead bodies. He tapped Max on the shoulder. The professor smiled at the small child and leaned down to catch his question so that the others wouldn't overhear. The boy's voice was so low even Laura could not decipher the words.

"Nooo, little guy, have no worries," Max reassured Brandon.

Laura could not help but admire the professor's easy way with her kids. In fact, looking at his students, she realized that he could hold everyone's interest, regardless of age. She caught herself wondering why a man of such phenomenal charm wore no wedding ring.

"What happened to the Red Paint People, Dr. Wayne?" Thomas inquired.

"They left the area or died out—we are not quite sure, Thomas. As far as we know, there was a period during which the island was uninhabited. It was not until about a thousand years ago that modern tribes came to the region."

"Ya mean like Seminole Injins?" asked Brandon.

"Oh no, Brandon," Max chuckled. "The Seminoles were a renegade band of disorganized indigenous peoples and freed slaves throughout Florida. They appeared much later in history."

The professor explained that it was generally believed that most of the Indians in Maine were Algonquins who had migrated south from Canada. The geographic areas where the Indians lived determined particular tribes. Some of the tribes that frequented the Moosehead region included the Kennebecs, Piscataquis, Penobscot, and Saint Francis. But the indigenous peoples who played the most significant role had come later.

"The rush to harvest the finest flint in the northeast caused a lot of ugliness between the modern tribes," continued the professor, "and marked the start of many years of trouble for the land known as Kineo."

* * *

Later that evening, Laura washed the dishes with Thomas and Amanda's help. The young girl had turned out to be very sweet and helpful. A little pretentious like her family, but by no means a difficult guest. In fact, she herself had offered to help with the dishes. Laura sensed that Amanda needed a role model for a mother and was not getting all the maternal nurturing she craved. *Meeting Mrs. Lomax might prove to be interesting,* Laura thought to herself as she talked to Amanda and formed an impression of the Lomax family.

Around nine p.m., Bennington knocked on the Dentons' door. Both girls had tired of waiting up and were fast asleep on the family-room couch. Brandon was asleep in the boys' room and only Thomas was still up with his mother. Bennington knocked lightly again and poked his head in the screened door. Laura immediately noticed the look of concern on his face. His English accent was more pronounced than earlier in the day as he asked her how Amanda had been as their guest. Softly awakening her from the couch, Laura inquired as to how Mrs. Lomax was feeling after her flight.

"I'm afraid we've had a difficult night, Mrs. Denton," Bennington replied. "Forgive me for my tardiness. My shuttle captain and hired help, Dougie, were not waiting for us with my boat to shuttle us to Kineo. It seems they was pulled away on a rather disturbing matter involving the sheriff's department."

Laura debated whether she should ask further questions, but decided to let Lomax divulge only as much as he felt appropriate.

"Father?" Amanda mumbled as she awoke from her sleep. "Is everything all right with Dougie?"

"I know he was taking you kneeboarding in the morning, precious," he answered. "I think we may have to reschedule."

"Father, what's happened?" she asked, concerned.

"It appears they found his best friend, Jimbo, last night," he answered cautiously. "There was a dreadful accident. Dougie is helping the authorities sort things out."

"I heard Bear say Gus was worried about his missing first mate," Thomas stated matter-of-factly. "I think Jimbo is his name."

"Indeed, Thomas." Bennington looked at him and then at Laura. "Gus is a bit gruff in manner, as you will learn in time. But he means well and is going to be very hurt by this. He does not move as well as he used to and needs help on his boat. This will impact charter fishing on the lake. It's neither good for the tourists nor for rental property in the area."

"Oh, the poor man," Laura commiserated.

"I would allow Dougie to assist him for a few days, but I need him to run the Kineo shuttle service."

"Does he need a first mate?" Thomas asked suddenly. "I mean someone to work with the bait and rigging?"

"You know something about salmon fishing, Thomas?" Bennington looked surprised.

"Well, not deep-lake fishing," the boy clarified. "But Dad and I went fishing a lot in Florida. I know how to catch a bass and skin a catfish! Heck, I could help for a few days while he finds a replacement."

Laura contemplated her son's kind suggestion and was proud of him for having offered his services so freely. He had been pleading with her to allow him to take on part-time work to earn some money so he could start saving up for a car. *But damn*, she thought, *I want him to help around the cottage this summer. He's so big and strong, and with his father gone...he's now the man of the house*, she reflected.

"Look, Thomas. I think it's wonderful that you'd offer to help him, but we need to discuss for how long, because I need your help too, dear."

"I know, Mom," Thomas assured her. "It'd only be for a little while till Gus found a permanent first mate."

"Well, I'd be glad to introduce you to Gus and see what you all think after that," concluded Bennington, and the conversation turned back to Mrs. Lomax.

"I guess the strain was a bit much for Mrs. Lomax?" Laura inquired.

"Quite!" Bennington replied. "She insisted I drive her straight home and immediately retired for the evening. She does not take sudden surprises in her stride and well…" his voice trailed off.

"I understand, Bennington" Laura assured him. "I'm sure it was a very stressful day for her. We'll let her rest and catch up with her tomorrow."

"Yes, that would be splendid," Bennington agreed. "She'll be anxious to meet your family. Thank you for having Amanda over."

"She was a wonderful guest. The girls played nicely all day and had some interesting adventures. I'm sure she'll tell ya about them in the morning."

Amanda gave Laura the warmest smile and said goodnight. As the Lomaxes walked back to their cottage nearby, Thomas ran up the stairs to ready himself for bed. Tomorrow looked to be another eventful day.

Laura, on the other hand, simply stood in the family room for a few more minutes, starring out into the darkness of the front porch. She stepped outside onto the porch and looked at the billions of summer stars over the golf course. They had looked so beautiful to her the previous night. But not tonight. She felt crushed by the burden of responsibility and emotions rushed through her. Things just didn't seem to be right and she wondered why she was forced to face this all alone. *Kineo…are you going to be my dream vacation site or a nightmare?*

12

Kineo, One Week Later; June 8, 1999

During the following days, projects seemed to fall into place around Kineo. Rix covered up the lower excavation next to the basement and placed fresh bricks into the hole in the wall. He made significant strides in plumbing the cottage and all the dangerous wiring was successfully replaced for the Dentons. Rix and Laura were fast becoming friends, and she served him a hearty lunch every day. Other summer residents began to arrive on Kineo.

Mrs. Lomax was in classic form one week after her arrival. Her less-than-grandiose entrance to her lovely little cottage on Kineo, along with all the melancholy exhibited by her family over this "Jim Bob" character, had been too much for her. Not that she didn't feel somewhat sorry for the "poor bastard"—getting burned and drowned would certainly ruin anyone's day—but mostly, she hated to see Dougie depressed. After all, the young man hadn't disappointed her nearly as much as other hired help had. She had to acknowledge that he was someone who helped her family in many ways—as servant, bellhop, errand boy, Amanda's ski instructor, and whatever role Bennington insisted that he assume. *Oh yes, the boat-shuttle thing.* Fact was, there was a paid servant like Dougie at each of the Lomax family retreats. Frankly, it was hard enough to keep up with each of their trivial personal lives, let alone that of their friends too. Yes, that "Jim Bob" character's untimely death had simply rained on her parade last week.

Pushing back thoughts of the unpleasant episode involving her return to Kineo, Mrs. Lomax began concentrating on the more important tasks at hand. These included remodeling the master bedroom suite to accommodate a larger closet for her clothes; and trips to Dover-Foxcroft and Greenville for brief shopping sprees. For longer, more involved shopping endeavors, Boston and New York City were not out of reach; they served well for a weekend splurge. Tiffany was sure to follow on those trips, whereas Amanda was more interested in staying on Kineo with her friends. Especially now. A week had gone by since that appalling night when Dougie had learned of Jimbo's fate. The young man had returned to serving the Lomaxes, and seemed, more than ever, compelled to get out on the lake to play.

Dougie knocked on the door, then stepped off the front porch of the Lomax cottage and seated himself on a white Adirondack chair basking in the morning sunlight. The early summer annuals he had helped Mrs. Lomax plant were blooming already. He often did such chores for her after he had finished his duties as Bennington's primary shuttle captain. He waited patiently for the door to open, knowing that at this hour, it could be a few minutes before someone allowed him access or came out to greet him.

Normally Bennington or Amanda would greet Dougie at the door. So he was a little surprised when the diminutive five-foot-two Pricilla Lomax stepped out to instruct him about the chores he was to take on. With a thick gold chain draped over her tight turquoise sweater and her diamond earrings sparkling in the morning sunlight, Mrs. Lomax was a sight to behold. It amazed Dougie that such a small woman with such a quiet voice could be so demanding. Pricilla Lomax was quite a bit younger than her husband. Her cosmetically enhanced face, heavily sculpted blonde hair, and surgically improved figure constituted the trophy-like "prize" that Bennington had apparently sought in his hasty quest of a second wife. Dougie watched her sway her tiny hips up to the flower planter, and he couldn't help but think that despite her exceptional looks, she was still, at the end of the day, a manipulative bitch.

"Dougie darling," she slowly enunciated in her detectable Brooklyn accent, "have you watered my flowers today? I want the plants to explode with blossoms."

Dougie stood up. "Yes, Mrs. Lomax," he replied, "I have. What projects do you have for me this afternoon? I have the day off as the shuttle captain—Chester's duty today." He grinned. "I promised I would take Amanda out boarding on the lake."

"Yes, I know," she said in a manner that hinted at some resentment. "She talks about you and these water activities quite a lot. I guess without Jim Bob, you need another…"

"His name was Jimbo!" he snarled.

The look on Dougie's face cut through her words like a chainsaw. He looked as if he would explode, but controlled himself in time. He needed this job and he was not going to blow it over this bitch, because he rarely had to deal with her anyway. Mrs. Lomax didn't seem to mind his tone as she went on about how Amanda was far more interested in water play than in the *normal* activities in which a young lady should participate.

"I'll take Amanda along with me, Mrs. Lomax, 'cause she's a great kid, and she's fun. She's a good little athlete too. She'd love to have her mother watch her sometime."

Pricilla Lomax let out an impatient sigh and looked at her diamond watch, as if to let Dougie know that her time was precious and his impertinent comments were simply wasting it.

"Fine! Take her. Have fun!" she snapped back with a dismissive wave of her perfectly manicured hand. "But have her back in two hours. I need some help from you in my bedroom today," she ordered in her characteristically quiet, yet demanding way.

"Pardon?" Dougie replied uneasily.

"We begin remodeling my bedroom closet, remember?" she said. "There is much to move out of there before the carpenter arrives tomorrow."

"Okay, Mrs. Lomax. Thank you." Then he walked past her to go inside and let Amanda know she could go wakeboarding with him.

* * *

During their first week on Kineo, Brandon took up a new hobby. A hobby not normally adopted by an introspective nine-year-old, but then again, Kineo was not a normal summer refuge. The golf course on the island was thought to be the second-oldest constructed in New England—from around 1880, which added to the appeal of the great hotels that once boasted their presence on Kineo. The greens and tees were a modern-day golfer's nightmare. The fairways were very narrow, bumpy, and laden with numerous pits caused by ice scouring the ground during the merciless winters. The putting greens were equally challenging. Tiny chips of Mt. Kineo rhyolite worked their way up through them, causing unexpected deflections in rather routine putts.

Over the years, the greens keepers had attempted to restore the course to its original splendor. Unfortunately, visiting tourists simply did not bring their clubs across the white-caps of Moosehead Lake often enough to generate the type of revenue needed to complete the restoration efforts. Still, many loyal golfers from New England continued their annual summer pilgrimage to the Kineo course. Disregarding the challenging conditions, these purists simply enjoyed the spectacular views surrounding the unique course and soaked up the history that enveloped all of Kineo.

"Ready to go out and smack the dimples off some balls?" barked out Bear.

"Yeah! Let's go!" Brandon cried out and waved goodbye to his mother.

Laura walked to the porch rail, leaned over, and smiled at Bear. "Bear? You sure you want to take him *again* this week?" she asked.

"Aw, shoot, Laura! He's a great kid. He's banging the ball!" Bear high-fived Brandon and smiled back at the boy's mother. "We'll just play one round of nine."

Bear had become enamored with Brandon. *Or was it Laura?* Maybe both. Truth was, Bear didn't get to see his own kid much anymore, and Brandon somehow reminded him of what he expected his little cub to be like in a few more years. Plus, Bear loved golf. He used to be a very good golfer before his disabling injury. He was said to clobber a driver 400 yards. Now with his crippled leg, driving the golf cart and giving little Brandon lessons were activities more in line for him.

"Think we'll see that crazy old moose on the course today, Bear?" Brandon asked with enthusiasm.

"Never can tell, Bran," Bear bellowed out. Despite the sound of the cart speeding forward, his impeccable hearing could discern the voice of Jenny joining Laura on the porch to yell out a good-luck wish to both "boys".

* * *

"I'm sorry, sir. We're just not interested," the older woman said.

"I know, madam. I really hate to be so persistent. I do hope I'm not being a pest," continued the polite young man with the peculiar accent. "It's just that…well, the place holds some significance for me…" The man's voice trailed off.

She had never met the man before, but he certainly sounded sincere enough and pleasant on the telephone. "Thing is, my husband really doesn't want to sell," she explained. "We're retired and where else would we go during the summer? Our only child died a few years back and we don't even have grandchildren."

"Oh, I am sorry, madam," the man said, sounding very sympathetic. "I understand only too well. That old cottage was a place where my grandfather spent so many summers. I have these old postcards from nineteen hundred and seven to nineteen hundred and fifteen which he wrote to my father, describing all the fun he and my grandmother had had fishing and playing golf on Kineo. They always stayed in the cottages. My parents then made it a part of their family tradition and spent summers on the island as well."

"Oh, I didn't realize all of that," she said, softening.

"Since the forties," he sighed, "there just hasn't been a good run of luck for Kineo. My parents stayed at the annex when it was open in the sixties and up until…well heck, until things *really* declined."

He paused, but the elderly lady on the other end of the line remained quiet. *She had always been polite*, he thought to himself, even though this was his *fourth* call to the Remingtons. He preferred to talk to Mrs. Remington, because her husband—the old codger—was difficult to negotiate with.

"Well, anyway," he continued, sensing he had finally broken through her defenses, "I know it's appraised at three twenty. Last time we spoke, I offered to buy it for four."

She took a deep breath, knowing that the persistent young man was about to raise the price again, and she would have to tell Mr. Remington. Her husband would once again lose his temper over the discussion. Mr. Remington was not a lot of fun to be around when he was angry. Certainly another 20,000 or so would not change her husband's mind, although she wasn't opposed to selling the cottage at 400,000. *Oh my, no!* That was well above the value of the old structure and the extra money could go toward traveling in Europe—something she'd wanted to do before she died. Mr. Remington had never allowed her to pursue the idea of overseas travel. He would scold her, "I waz in dah army ovah dare. T'was no big deal."

Damn. For how many years would both of them remain mobile, thought Mrs. Remington.

"Okay, Mrs. Remington. I'll let you go and won't bother you again," the man continued, "But…I know this will sound foolish…but…I'll pay you six fifty."

Mrs. Remington didn't quite let that sink in and the man just let the air become still on both ends of the phone. Then he provided a little hook to seal the deal.

"Recently, I inherited a large sum of money," he said, talking faster. "I know this cottage isn't worth six hundred and fifty thousand in the market place, and the world will call me crazy. But I have the money and I want to revive precious memories for my family on Kineo while we are all young. I plan to help get things going on the island and make it a family place again. But if you absolutely don't want to sell…I'll finish my negotiations with the other cottage…"

"What other cottage?" she asked, suddenly interested.

"Oh, I'm sorry. I shouldn't have…" His voice trailed off. "Look. I was asked to keep that confidential. My mistake. One of your neighbors wants out 'cause of all the fires. Is willing to sell for four fifty. Thing is…I don't want *that* cottage. I have always dreamed of owning the light blue one on the hill. The one shown on my grandfather's postcards to my father. *Yours*.

"Who? Who?" she stammered, "Which neighbor is..."

"I'm afraid I promised not to divulge that, madam, you understand...but anyway...let me know. You have my number. I can close on the other cottage by the end of the week if you two remain uninterested in selling. I'd rather seed *your* dream to travel over Europe... as you fulfill my dream to have my kids experience Kineo in this cottage. Goodbye, Mrs. Remington, and have a pleasant afternoon."

"Wait!" she burst out. "I think I can work things out with Mr. Remington."

* * *

On the cliffs of Kineo, Professors Wayne and Mongeau were delivering a joint lecture explaining the significance of the natural resources influencing the development of culture and trade between the many native peoples that lived in the region. As always, whenever Dr. Wayne announced that his students would be involved in archeological digs, Jenny was in attendance. Having found out from him about their only dig scheduled "up the big rock they call Kineo", she was not going to miss it.

"'Fraid so, Rob," replied Dr. Wayne. "Remember, we leave in two days to go back to university life."

"Yeah, but you get to come back in a few weeks," Margo teased Rob, "so stop your crying, you big baby!"

"Okay, guys and gals, let's get focused on the topic at hand," Max began. "As these modern Indians moved into the Moosehead region, they began settling in locations around Moosehead Lake, including Seboomook, Northeast Carry, Indian Hill in Greenville, Birch Point in Rockwood, and here on Kineo."

Jenny loved the way Dr. Wayne dramatically pointed in the direction of the various settlements he discussed. Perched 700 feet above Moosehead Lake, they all had a panoramic view of the places he pointed to on the horizon.

"Early Indians from several tribes continued to be drawn to this region because of Mt. Kineo and the famous supply of flint."

Max noted that his colleague had noticed his technical slip; Les's face had flushed red. It was difficult for the younger man to retain a formal classroom manner while instructing his students in so magnificent and laid back a setting as Kineo. He would try, however, as he held Les in great regard as both professor and friend.

"The Indians traveled great distances," Max Wayne continued. "to obtain the stone essential for their arrowheads, spearheads, and other weapons. In fact, the *rhyolite's* unique physical properties allow scientists to trace the trade of Mt. Kineo flint across much of the eastern United States and Canada."

Thomas, who had just finished assisting Captain Gus O'Malley stow away gear this morning, raced up the mountain by himself to join the crowd on the summit. Running the Indian Trail every other morning to get in shape before school started in fall, he had shaved ten minutes off his time from two days ago, but was quite winded as he reached the group.

Pausing in the back with Jenny, he clutched his knees, his back bent. He was breathing hard and sweat dripped from his nose.

"Have…uhh…have I…uhh," Thomas gasped out. "missed much?"

"Hey, Thomas!" Jenny beamed, giving her brother a quick hug. "Ooooh, gross! You're all sweaty."

"No, duh," Thomas gasped, closing his eyes as he pinched the pain in his side.

"They haven't started digging yet," his sister continued sweetly.

Thomas could only nod in reply. They watched intently, hoping the dig would begin soon. Dr. Wayne gave him a quick nod of acknowledgement, but didn't miss a beat as he proceeded with his teaching.

"In general, the Indians of that period had a difficult life. But their interactions with each other were typically peaceful until the Mohawk came to the region for flint."

"Oh good," Thomas whispered to his sister, "now things are going to get interesting."

"As trading partners with the local Abenaki, the Mohawk were not affable." Dr. Wayne circled the students and bounced a piece of flint in his right hand. "In fact, they were bitter enemies of the Abenaki and countless battles were fought between these two groups in the woods surrounding Moosehead Lake."

Max noticed the interest in Thomas's eyes and tossed the flint at him. The boy caught it in his hand. The professor grinned before turning to Rob Landon and asking him a few questions to gauge whether the students were following him but noticed he has disappeared somewhere.

✳ ✳ ✳

"Mrs. Denton. I'll be brief. They burned my family's cottage down—what you may know as the Goldman cottage by Kineo Cove. *They* will soon own the blue cottage on top of the hill. *They* will seek yours next."

The lady's voice on the phone was familiar—an older woman, calm, collected, and wise.

Laura ventured an intelligent guess. "Patricia Wellington?"

"Yes," replied the other woman, betraying no emotion. "I've warned you. But now you have to make choices. Tough choices. Protect your children, sell it."

There was something stone-cold sobering about the tone of her voice. Laura felt a chill streak up her spine and the hair stand up on the back of her arms and neck.

"Your husband was given similar advice when he was up here."

"You knew my husband David?"

"Not really. I knew his parents."

"Look, Mrs. Wellington…" Laura started.

"I must go now, Mrs. Denton. Goodbye."

"No! Please wait…"

And just as she had, the last time, Patricia Wellington ended the conversation. Laura put the phone back in its cradle. She poured herself a glass of cabernet, swirled it, and took a sip. She then walked over to the couch and sat down. *Dang, that woman is strange*, she reflected. Her nerves calmed quickly as she realized it was likely dementia or the early signs of Alzheimer's disease. Laura had heard that Mrs. Wellington was getting on in years. *Seventy-five*, she thought Bear had mentioned. When he got back with Brandon, she would sit him down and have a few words with him. He would surely shed some light on this strange lady and on whatever she was trying to tell Laura.

13

Bear crushed the ball off the tee and it looked like it had gone 360 yards! The course was challenging for long ball hitters. There was fairway and out of bounds. Nothing in between. You had to hit the ball true down the center. A little hitter like Brandon could be off by fifteen degrees and the ball would stay in bounds. For Bear, however, a 300-yard drive had to be within a few degrees of center to land in bounds. There was no rough to forgive even the slightest slice or hook. Half of the time, Bear would crunch the ball out of bounds. The safe play then would have been to use a shorter club, but he liked to crush a golf ball and see it disappear.

Brandon was still gushing at him for landing his herculean drive on the middle of the fairway. With a respectable chip up to the green and a one putt, he birdied the hole. His handicap would be quite impressive if he ever learned to keep more drives in the fairway. Bear limped back to the cart and got in on the passenger side

"Why don't *you* drive, lil' fella?" he asked Brandon.

"Really?" The boy chirped excitedly, hopping into the driver's seat.

"Yup. Really," Bear answered. "My leg is kind of hurting and I think I'll just sit here and coach you from the cart, lil' man. Now get out there and crunch one the way I just showed ya. Your mama wants you home soon. This is gonna have to be the last hole for me."

Brandon didn't care if they played seven holes or seventeen; he was just happy to be out there chasing the ball around. Getting up out of the driver's seat, he smiled proudly at Bear and grabbed the driver that the man had modified to fit the boy's small stature.

"Keep your head down and swing smoothly through the ball, son," advised the gentle giant from the golf cart.

Brandon reared back with a mighty backswing, envisioning the long drive he had witnessed on the last hole, and then rocked forward with a loud grunt. The ball exploded off the tee and straight into the water.

* * *

The sun was beginning to dip low in the sky, prompting the professors to decide on hiking off the great rock before it became too dark to see. All of the teams gathered their equipment and samples together. A roll call by Dr. Mongeau to ensure that all the students were accounted for verified what Max had already surmised, that —that Rob Landon was missing. Having remembered seeing him minutes ago, just around the last outcroppings, Max offered to go find Rob. Dr. Mongeau complained that his back hurt and he was ready to get down. He began the descent, followed by their herd of students carrying their fruitful day's collection of geologic samples.

Hurrying over to the spot where he had last seen Rob, Max noticed someone ducking down off the trail into a valley depression that was one of the upstream discharge areas feeding the winter ice falls. This was off the beaten track and excluded from Dr. Mongeau's agenda. In fact, the undergrowth was so dense it made little sense for Rob to be there. *Oh well, of course*, thought Max, *maybe he needed to relieve himself.* Instead of yelling out, "Hey, Rob!"—his first impulse—Max hesitated, watching the tall student climb through the underbrush and out to a rocky outcropping.

Unaware of being observed, Rob was staring intently at the small but heavy object in his hands—a large sphere with a brilliant lavender hue. As Max stepped off the rocky perch from where he had been observing the student, Rob suddenly sensed someone approach and hastily stuffed the sphere into his camera bag.

Max strolled casually down the beaten path of Vaccinium which his student had taken earlier and pushed his way through the dead lower branches of the small conifers. The younger man heard the crunch of feet trampling forest litter and began climbing down off the rock outcropping.

"Rob?" Max called out, "That you, Rob?"

"Yeah, Prof. Over here."

"There you are," Max said, his voice so even that Rob's rapidly beating heart began to steady. "Time to get off the rock."

"Fine."

"What did you find?"

"You know…just some rocks…" Rob laughed a bit nervously. He had the look of a kid that had just got busted taking the last cookie and was waiting to see how his mom would react.

"Kinda far out from the rest of the group…don't ya think?" Max probed.

"Yeah. But once you get past the conifer thicket, there's a killer view from the cliffs out there."

"Do tell," Max said, his tone a trifle skeptical.

Rob's heart began to beat faster. He was sure the other man could see his pulse racing in his neck. He wondered if Max had caught him examining the exquisite amethyst treasure he had uncovered from its most improbable resting place. The highly polished and perfectly spherical gemstone was something he knew he had to show Dr. Mongeau—and planned to in the morning—but not just yet. It was too soon. He had just found the incredible site where some sort of recent rockslide had uncovered an apparently man-made passageway along the side of the mountain. Something this special would lure all the other students into visiting the site. They would trample the area and remove things. It was the most amazing find of Rob's life and it surely had some archeological significance. No natural caves were formed in rhyolite. So the tunnel he had uncovered was evidently created by historic man who had placed tons of broken stone by hand at wedged angles between the two narrow walls of a cleft in the mountain. *Everyone will descend into the buried tunnels*, Rob thought, continuing to brood. *Once they take possession of the sphere, the university will claim credit for the find. HIS find! No one will remember that Rob Landon had found it first!*

These thoughts had been nagging at him from the time he found the spherical mineral stone nearly an hour ago. If it had archeological significance, he would have to share it with Dr. Wayne and all of his eager-beaver students too. *No harm in studying it in private for a day or two. Nah, no harm. Then why am I feeling guilty—and acting sneaky?* Watching the fading sunlight beam through the glassy purple quartz in his hand had been a mesmerizing experience. Amethyst was not to be found in this part of Maine. The sedimentary geologic processes necessary to form it were absent in this volcanic rock. *Then how the hell...*

That would all have to wait. Rob had to get off the mountain now as it was nearing dark, and negotiating the Indian Trail was tricky enough in daylight. Carrying equipment and samples at night involved the risk of taking a bad fall or breaking an ankle. The two men would take the safer route down—the Bridal Trail.

"Enough of the view, Doc. We better get down before dark," Rob finally suggested, walking past Dr. Wayne. Then abruptly, he changed the subject. "So...you going to play in our volleyball match tomorrow?"

Max decided not to comment on the young man's odd behavior. "Yeah Rob," he replied, rolling with the change in topic. "I hear you got game. You've certainly got height... We'll see if you got heart."

"I hear you were quite the player a long time ago...back when you were in college, Prof," baited Rob.

"Wasn't all that long ago, Rob. We'll see tomorrow, won't we?"

"Rock Jocks versus the Grave Robbers, right?"

The young man's tone bothered Max. This was not the Rob he knew. He wondered what exactly the student had been doing up there—away from the rest of the group—for so long.

"Yeah Rob," he said, "Dr. Mongeau's geology students versus my archeology students."

The underlying tone in his own voice had also changed from casual to guarded. Rob realized that his favorite professor had grown suspicious of his activities on Kineo. The dynamics of their relationship had shifted irreversibly since his discovery of the amethyst sphere.

* * *

Gus sat on the edge of his bed as darkness began to descend. The older Denton boy had proved to be a pleasant surprise. How quickly he had picked up the skill of deep-water trolling! When Bennington had first suggested his name as a temporary replacement for Jimbo, Gus had laughed disdainfully.

"Look at the kid, Bennington," he'd barked out. "Jesus, man! He's a walking bone bag. How the hell's he gonna do the heavies? And he's too quiet to work the touries!"

Waving him off and shaking his head from side to side to indicate a definitive "no way", Gus had turned to walk away from Bennington and Thomas. Lomax had frowned at the stubborn old man and given Thomas a reassuring look. Then pointing his finger at the crusty old boat captain, he had said to Thomas, "Go!"

"Heck, Captain O'Malley," The boy had called out after the retreating figure. "I may not be a man and all, but shoot, I can handle a fish or two! I brought in some big largemouth with my dad and won a bass tournament in my age group in Kissimmee last year. Heck, I think I'd be a good first mate, and you *need* the help. What do you have to lose?"

Gus O'Malley laughed now, thinking back to the day the bony kid had shown the guts to defend himself like that. The kid had proved himself too. Thomas certainly had the ability and was a natural on the water. Shame he couldn't stay on all summer and help. Gus had promised Mrs. Denton that he'd only use Thomas for a week or two until he found full-time help.

He pulled out a cigar from his drawer and a picked up a shot glass. Pouring himself a strong drink, he began chewing on the end of a fresh Cuban cigar.

"Aw, what the hell!" Gus barked out. Picking up a pack of matches, he struck a light. Having given up smoking altogether a year ago, it had been a very long time since he had actually smoked a cigar. The doctors had warned him that his three packs of cigarettes and six cigars a day were killing him. One day, he simply had not lighted up—and hadn't since. Gus still retained a few vices, however. He would still suck on a cigar all day long, tasting tobacco leaves in his mouth; and he drank more than his fair share.

Losing Jimbo, though, had rocked his lonely world. The lit match started igniting the dry leaves. Gus began to draw oxygen through the leaves until the end of the cigar burned red.

"Hell, it ain't like I inhale or nothing," he mumbled to no one. Then he swallowed a large cloud of smoke and tasted the tobacco. His mouth immediately began to water to replace the loss of moisture brought on by the smoke. He spat into a cup and mused at how cigar smoke desiccated the inside of his mouth and made him salivate uncontrollably. The scotch he drank further sucked moisture from his mouth, and his glands began to work overtime to fight the combined effect of the drugs.

Suspicious death, they say. Hmm? Gus lay back in his bed. It began to rain outside, and he could hear the pinging of the water as it ricocheted off of his metal roof. *Such a soothing sound to sleep to.* A few more shots of the lovely amber liquid and he would be warmed to the core.

What the hell did the sheriff mean when he said 'suspicious death'? Why was Jimbo found burned? How could that fire investigator from Piscataquis County think Jimbo had anything to do with the fire at the old Wellington place? None of it made sense. However, what really bothered Gus was the fact that Jimbo had been AWOL the day of the fire. *Had Jimbo been in the Wellington/Goldman cottage?* Gus recalled that he had acted strangely the night before. Jimbo had drunk heavily enough to pass out and bunk with Gus instead of heading out with his buddies. Dougie and the other guys seemed to be as clueless as Gus on the matter.

Sheriff Larry Magleton had asked Gus to check if Jimbo had left anything behind that would shed light on their investigation. Gus had checked the boat and the room Jimbo had slept in. There were no clues. Nothing left on the floor. No notes on the nightstand. Nothing found on the boat. Just a lot of questions. *Why did Sheriff Magleton want to know about Jimbo's scuba- diving experience? Could his little diving job on the side with the Pillouds have anything to do with this? He was hanging out with Junior and I never liked that kid! Ugh! Too many questions.*

Gus took another deep drag from the cigar and let the smoke out in small, deliberate bursts. Each burst released a separate white cloud of toxins that floated toward the ceiling fan where it was quickly captured in a swirl and dispersed.

The rain smacked the roof harder. Gus was feeling lousy. He got up and walked into the spare room where Jimbo had last rested. *Poor bastard.* Rainwater was hitting the roof so hard now it was deafening, and a constant bead of water dripped through a small hole in it, pelting the little nightstand next to the bed.

"Damn it! I thought I had that leak fixed!"

Gus stumbled over to the table and noticed rainwater dripping down the tabletop and into the drawer. He opened it to see if there was anything of value being damaged. His eyes fell on a bandana wrapped around something the size of a baseball.

"What the hell is this?" Gus mumbled, beginning to unwrap the heavy spherical object.

A large black sphere fell out of the bandana and dropped onto the bed. *Ahhh. So here it is!* Gus thought. *I remember overhearing you talk about this.* Gus picked it up, amazed at how heavy and perfectly round it was. At least three inches in diameter and brightly polished, it was made of some sort of stone or mineral and looked like black glass, the solid black of the eight ball on a billiard table. He held this beautiful rock in his hand and thought, *Where the hell did this come from? Jimbo?*

He could not figure out what it was or how it could be tied to Jimbo's strange behavior. Then he wondered if it was some sort of valuable gemstone. *Had the young man been smuggling gemstones? Was he a thief? Oh, Jimbo. I know I didn't pay you much, but it was all I had. You were like a son to me.* Giving in to his drunken stupor, the old fishing guide began to weep again.

He had hit the bottle hard this evening and on an empty stomach. His head hurt. His heart hurt. The room began to spin, and he had to sit down on the guest bed and place both feet on the floor. As he heard the drumming of the rain above, he realized that he had a mystery to solve. *No need to tell that arrogant Sheriff Magleton about this strange black sphere. Nor that suspicious fireman from the state. Hell, what if Jimbo was dealing with things that were unlawful? He was helping the Pillouds on the side, after all.*

Gus cursed out loud. He looked out the window at the whitecaps on the lake and thought about Jimbo. *He was a good boy. He's dead now, but he deserves to be remembered favorably. Those county boys would surely crucify him and what purpose would that serve? He's dead anyway. Let it be. Let it be.* The sound of the rain hammered everything into submission and drowned out his thoughts. Gus passed out on the bed that Jimbo had last slept in.

14

Busy wrapping up their initial fieldwork on Kineo, the university students would return in a few weeks to complete their summer investigation. The day was unusually sunny for the start of summer and not as breezy as it had been in the past two days. Moosehead Lake was calm and the ride back on the pontoon boats would not splash the students with the icy water the way the ride over had. The gear was stored on the boats, and all that remained before their return to the University of Maine was the interdepartmental volleyball challenge between the Rock Jocks and the Grave Robbers. The islanders had developed quite a fascination for the students and their two professors. Word had spread quickly that the volleyball match was about to get underway.

The faculty and the students had started a tradition a year ago, with the easy victory of the Grave Robbers riding on the back of the very talented Max Wayne—a former college standout. This year would be different. Dr. Mongeau had more student talent than last year; it included Margo, who had been starting setter in her high-school days, and the skyscraper-shaped graduate student Rob Landon."

Of above average height for a boy his age, Thomas loved to play volleyball. He and Jenny had run over to the Lomax place to see if Amanda and Tiffany wanted to tag along. Jenny and Amanda had then gathered friends and neighbors on the island to watch the collegiate gladiators do battle on the lake shore. Tiffany surprised Thomas by eagerly accepting the invitation to accompany them. The opportunity to sway her royal tail in front of the older college boys was more fun than she could resist, and she had dressed the part, wearing bright lime green shorts that aptly redefined the meaning of "short" and a tight orange tube top with a white blouse conservatively draped around her. As soon as she was out of her father's range of vision, the white blouse was flung off, and Thomas found himself wondering why his eyes automatically drifted to "that rich girl with the bad attitude."

The match was already in progress, and Rob had just successfully blocked a gentlemanly spike attempt by Dr. Wayne. Some friendly trash talk ensued. Dr. Wayne seemed genuinely unaware of the score, and was playing for fun. He was about to serve the ball when Laura came strolling up with Bear and Brandon who had both just finished another round of golf.

"C'mon, Professor, drill it!" Julie Walters hollered from the sidelines. Max noticed Laura approach with Bear and sit gracefully on the grass with the other cheering spectators. She was wearing jeans that fit her nicely and a pale yellow blouse that was tied in a knot right at her belly button.

Max seemed to lose focus. Sensing all of the spectators' eyes upon him, he hesitated releasing his serve. With the lingering image of Laura in his thoughts, he gathered himself, but ended up slamming his serve into the net. He looked over toward her and she gave him an encouraging smile. Bear smirked. The game ended with a score of fifteen-twelve in favor of the underdog team—Rock Jocks. The most humbling aspect of the loss to the Grave Diggers, however, was the fact that Dr. Mongeau even played in the game. The pompous, overweight academic had only cost his team five points off unforced errors!

But that was the warm-up match. The second one would be for keeps. Bragging rights were based on the best of three. Dr. Mongeau knew that and decided to sit out the second game. Rob only allowed his very best players in the line-up this time. Dr. Wayne continued to play lightheartedly. He substituted students in and out, letting each one play and have fun. *It was for fun after all, wasn't it?* Max considered the match for a moment.

With a second game score of ten-three and the Rock Jocks on top once again, things began heating up. Rob spiked a ball into the face of one of Dr. Wayne's most popular female students. Blood dripped from Tonya's nose onto her white tee shirt that read, "TODAY'S TRASH PILE: TOMORROW'S TREASURE." Her tee shirt began turning crimson inch by inch, till the cartoon of the garbage dump was no longer discernible. The injury temporarily halted play. Dr. Mongeau scolded Rob, whose brief and unconving apology included a suggestion that it was time to get over the nosebleed and see what the archeologists really had this year.

"Look...I'm sorry I hit Tonya in the face, but let's get on with it," Rob said.

His teammate, Margo, was too furious to even look at him. Max finished dabbing the blood from Tonya's nose as she assured him with a determined grin that she was fine. Then looking into her favorite professor's crystal blue eyes, she said, "I had no business being out there. Time for me to sit and watch before something worse happens—like a broken nail."

Max smiled back at her as she prodded him. "Now get in there and finish this, will ya?"

The onlookers became silent when he stood up and abruptly faced Rob. He pulled his shirt off and flung it on the ground, causing it to land near Laura and Bear's feet. Max may have resembled a nerdy academic, but there was nothing nerdy about his upper torso. He still sported the remnants of what must have been a very well-defined six-pack in his day and his shoulders and triceps were well muscled. Two of the Grave Diggers' players had also decided to sit out and let only the four best players remain in the game. These four quickly assembled into the classic diamond formation.

Rob pointed at his two weakest players who immediately left the court. Each team fielded one lady and three men. The young woman in Max's backcourt received the first serve by the Rock Jocks, and she bumped the ball skillfully to the setter. Everyone on Kineo knew where the set was going. Both Rob and another geology student simultaneously hurled themselves upward to block the spike from Max, but it was too late. Max exploded off the ground and his hand belted a ferocious spike right down the baseline. The ball continued to roll all the way down to the lake. The crowd murmured and the ring of people backed up a few steps, as competitive play had obviously commenced. Within minutes, the score had closed to eleven-thirteen and Max took his turn behind the serving line.

"Service!" he yelled out. "One, three."

He looked up into the air, threw the ball ten feet above him, and timed his jump perfectly. It appeared to Laura as if he hung in the air for six minutes, possibly more. She caught herself admiring his bare chest and nicely sculpted muscles and suddenly felt herself blush. The ball punched from his palm and cut the edge of the net, dropping and landing right in front an overwhelmed Margo.

Thomas smiled at his mother thinking: *Man, this guy has some game!* Disinterested in volleyball, Amanda and Jenny were off talking girl talk. Much to Bennington's displeasure, Tiffany was flirting with one of the sidelined college students. The twenty-one-year-old college junior was still trying to convince himself that the hot blond chick was at least eighteen or nineteen, even though Tonya, still dabbing blood from her nose, whispered from behind him, "Still too young, dipstick!"

Several more driving serves left the Rock Jocks floundering and bickering between their players as to who should have attempted to dive and dig out the last few serves.

"Game point," Max announced and then launched a floater to the back corner which the opposing team was more than content to watch sailing out of bounds. Unfortunately, the professor had placed a wicked spin on the ball, and it curved at the last minute and hit the rope for the come-from-behind game winner. The crowd burst into catcalls and cheers.

After a short recess and Gatorade, the two teams reassembled for the final match. To Laura's surprise, the Grave Robbers returned with their standard six-man rotation, with her son, Thomas, playing and Max sitting out. Apparently, with the point clearly being made to the Rock Jocks in the last game, that Max was more interested in allowing everyone at the event to have some fun. All of his team was going to play in the last match. Max slid his shirt back on and ventured over to Bear and Laura. Even Tonya rotated back into play. Everyone had a fun time in the last match, especially Thomas. The Rock Jocks edged out the Grave Robbers fifteen-twelve. At the end, everyone demonstrated sportsmanship and high-fived each other. Max was the first to jump to his feet and congratulate the geologists.

"Good match, Rob," he said hiding what he was thinking.

"Sorry, Professor," started Rob. "I guess...I was getting a bit too serious out there."

"Yup. You could say you were being an ass," Max said, stone-cold serious.

Rob's jaw hung and he seemed uncomfortable as students from both teams crowded around the two of them.

"Heck Rob," Max continued. "In fact... I felt you Rock Jocks were taking us for *granite!*" Then he flashed one of his characteristic smart-ass grins and everyone laughed.

"How *gneiss* of you to notice," chuckled Dr. Mongeau, paving the way for a whole round of sophomoric geology jokes erupted.

Everyone laughed and some hugged. There was something in this entire exchange that struck Laura as curious. The camaraderie was apparent enough, but so was some odd—barely below the surface—tension. In the end, Max gave away the match, letting her son and the less athletic students play. It was mesmerizing watching this young animated professor with his on-and-off intensity, followed by his relaxed southern Californian manner. Laura felt a stirring inside that made her very uncomfortable. Thank goodness he was leaving tomorrow! Bear broke through her reverie by asking her some mundane question.

Many students shook hands or hugged favorite residents before departing for their pontoon boats. Max looked back over his shoulder in the direction where he had last seen Bear and Laura, but she was no longer there. He let out a sigh and wondered when he might see her again.

* * *

Later that afternoon, Thomas was surprised to see Tiffany still hanging with him, Jenny, and Amanda. *Maybe even a snot like her needed friends?* She sure did smell nice. *Must be some fancy perfume from Paris*, he quipped to himself. And he found himself staring at her long golden hair that bounced playfully in the breeze.

"Ever seen the old water tower, Tommy Boy?" Tiffany asked in a surprisingly inviting manner.

"Oooo, I love the tower," Jenny cut in. "Amanda showed it to me yesterday."

Tiffany shot her one of those "back off" looks as she turned the corners of her lips into a threatening snarl. Jenny's eager expression faded and she sauntered back to the comforting presence of her friend, Amanda. The latter shook her head slowly and whispered something to Jenny that made both girls giggle.

"Did I tell you that Maria, my friend in Tampa, is coming to visit next week?" Jenny asked.

"Uh, yeah!" Amanda laughed. "Like about three times now."

She smiled at the other girl, deciding not to be jealous. Jenny could not help being— Jenny. "I can't wait to meet her, Jen."

The unlikely quartet proceeded up the inclined path that meandered above the golf course to the base of Mt. Kineo. Around the corner stood a large wooden structure that looked like a wooden pickle barrel balanced on a stone foundation. Jenny immediately saw a world of endless possibilities and summoned Amanda to help her climb the backside of the tower.

This wooden structure had once served the island as its main water reservoir, supplying to all the cottages and hotels and accessory structures. It sat perched between aspen and maple trees next to the cliff face, approximately 200 feet above the lake. The water had long been drained from the structure. Jenny climbed the rusted steel ladder which swayed precariously, making her feel a bit queasy. A fall from the top of the ladder into the wooden barrel would be quite hazardous, if not fatal.

Meanwhile, Tiffany had persuaded Thomas to explore the structure's "underworld" with her. He had climbed through the rock doorway into the belly of the abandoned water tower. It was dark in the lower foundation and dozens of aluminum beer cans littered the room.

"Do you like beer, Thomas?" Tiffany taunted suddenly.

As he turned around to respond, he felt the tip of his nose accidentally brush against her silky hair. Maneuvering in near complete darkness, she had entered close behind him.

"Um, pardon?" he replied, embarrassed, feeling acid devour his stomach from the inside out.

"Oh, I guess the older Denton boy stays clear of such trouble," Tiffany said in a condescending voice that somehow managed to sound sultry.

Thomas bit his lip. He wanted to say something, but his vocal chords would not obey the commands from his brain, as if they had been severed deep down in his throat. Or maybe his throat had simply been swallowed by his stomach, which was bouncing back and forth between his kneecaps and his chin. Suddenly, he felt a soft hand slide right over his. It made him jump.

"Ouch!" he cried out, as his head crunched against the rocks making up the roof of the structure. "Oh, man!"

"Oh my Gawd!" Tiffany laughed out loud, instinctively covering her mouth with her hand like her mom had taught her to (even in the dark, a sophisticated lady's mouth was supposed to be pressed shut in laughter). "Thomas you are hilarious! Haven't you *ever* been with a…"

Before she could finish her question, Brandon and Bear came bounding through the opening in the rock foundation.

"Hey guys, what are you two up to?" Bear asked squinting into the dark water-tower basement.

"Brandon! Glad you found us," blurted out Thomas. "I promised to take you boulder climbing today on the southeast wall."

"Yup!" his younger brother replied. "And Bear brung me up to find ya."

Tiffany climbed out of the rock enclosure with sudden urgency and reminded Amanda that it was time to return to their summer cottage. The younger girl pleaded with her to be allowed to remain, but Big Sis insisted, citing their father's strict instructions to be home in an hour. Tiffany glanced down at her Rolex.

"We certainly do not want to displease Daddy now, Mandy," she snipped.

"I'll see that these young ladies make it back to their cottage safely, Thomas," Bear offered. "You take Brandon and your sister on that journey you promised."

Glad to have his stomach functioning normally again, Thomas felt an obligation to be civil with his siblings. There was a new gentleness in his attitude to his sister and little brother and he was even somewhat relieved to be alone with them. Even Jenny's non-stop mouth, firing off endless questions, failed to bother him. She, for her part, was finding her brother's unusual behavior refreshing. Thomas felt more alive than he had all year, having escaped the adolescent torture earlier; yet, he somehow, felt more adult than ever before. An audacious adventure seemed appropriate under the circumstances, and he asked his siblings if they would like to venture off-trail to see what was on the northeast face of the Kineo cliffs. There were no paths on that side of the woods, since no one had ever explored that direction.

"YES!" replied Brandon and Jenny in unison, and they were off. Thomas assumed point and his younger brother merrily accepted the tail position.

* * *

"Whatcha sayin', Bronson?"

"What I've been saying from the first time we saw the charred ruins of the Goldman cottage—arson."

"Okay, fine." Sheriff Magleton looked away. "What's the connection with this Jimbo guy? Christ! The kid was burned to hell and then drowned?"

"I had to track down his birth certificate 'cause no one locally knew his full name, and the 'JWW' initials were eating at me," explained Bronson Thurman. "But I can smell foul play a mile away, Larry."

"Fine. What evah!" the sheriff's voice was particularly nasal as the fire inspector walked over, picked up the ID chain, and dropped it on Larry's desk with a dramatic "clunk".

"James Wellington West."

"Huh?"

"Jimbo," Bronson continued. "James *Wellington* West."

"Well, hell's bells!" Larry Magleton stammered. "You mean as in...? Did you say *Wellington?*"

"You got it!"

"Related?"

"Very."

"But the Goldman cottage used to be owned by..."

"The Wellingtons," Bronson answered. "Uh huh. His grandmother."

"Okay, fine. Let's go through this again, Bronson, but take me through it nice and slow. I want to understand everything you learned."

15

Thomas pulled aside the branches from the young aspens and maples so that Jenny, who was following him, would not get scratched. The path he had chosen was rugged and certainly not used by any living creature, other than an occasional white-tailed deer or porcupine.

"So what did Tiffany say to you down in the stone place, Thomas?" Jenny inquired.

"Nothing," he said gruffly.

"Huh?" repeated Jenny.

"*Nothing*, Jen!" Thomas cut her off at the pass. "Look, there are some rocks ahead we have to scramble over. Are you up to it?"

"Ya mean, I can go boulder climbing with you and Bran?" she asked excitedly.

"Yeah, sure. Just follow me."

Thomas led his brother and sister out of the densely wooded maples, oaks, and aspens into a sunny clearing that was part of the upper boulder field and far behind the talus pile. The elevation was several hundred feet above the lake at the foot of the eastern cliffs.

Brandon got excited when he saw the enormous boulder field and began scrabbling over the broken chunks of rhyolite. Some of the boulders were over forty feet in diameter and had interesting passageways and tunnels underneath them. Jenny felt more comfortable crawling under the rocks and in the tunnels, whereas Brandon loved to climb up and over the rocks.

"There's got to be a way up there," Thomas mumbled. "There has to be some sort of fissure between the cliffs. Probably in one of the three winter ice falls." He remembered Dr. Mongeau instructing his students: *Where there is flowing water and time, mountains erode the softer minerals. In places where such erosion has occurred, you often find passages.*

"What are you looking for, Thomas?" Jenny persisted. "Thomas?"

"Another way up, Jen," her older brother answered patiently. "Got to be another way up besides the Indian Trail and the North Trail."

"What?" Jenny repeated. "Why do you want to find a new way up, Thomas?"

It was nearing the time to head back to the cottage. Laura needed additional help from her child-labor pool, as Bear referred to them. Thomas finally conceded that there was probably no other way up, or else someone would have found it by now and some evidence of a trail would have been visible. He halted the expedition and began to round up his brother and sister who were still dashing in and out of the boulders like two marmot cubs.

Then he noticed a suspicious fold in the side of the mountain that was flush against the toe of the cliff. The fold was so well hidden by trees that you had to be right up against it to even see it. Thomas inspected the ground and saw no footprints or trash. Only fox, marten, fisher, and porcupine poop everywhere.

He edged closer to the mountain wall. He looked around the fold in the rocks and his heart began to race as he found what he had been seeking.

* * *

"Why would I want to sell our cottage? We just inherited it."

A long pause.

"I don't understand," Laura said to the slightly accented voice on the telephone. "Sure we could use the additional money, but that isn't the point—we didn't start restoring this place to make—"

"Perhaps, in time, you will reconsider," the voice said, cutting her short. His comment hung in the air for a few seconds. "Well…sorry for disturbing you, Mrs. Denton. You have our number. Good day."

Although his voice sounded polite, interrupting her in mid-sentence had been rude. A *southern* gentleman would not be so presumptuous and forthright with a lady, she judged. *And that accent? French? Yet, somehow different.* Laura had picked up some French when her dad was stationed in Europe for a year.

Her father had been relocated many times while serving his country as a career officer in the Navy. Laura was pleased when he stopped traveling and was stationed in Pensacola, Florida, as an instructor at the local base. She and had moved to Louisiana with her mother when the latter left her father. Laura had lived in a small town near the heart of Cajun country. It was here that she had been exposed to a distinctly different dialect born from French descendants long ago. Laura had attended college in Louisiana and become a "Rajun Cajun". She had studied French her sophomore year, but graduated with a degree in business administration, specializing in accounting.

Reflecting on the "voice" she had heard on the other end of the phone, Laura surmised from its owner's enunciation, refined and well rehearsed though it was, that French, rather than English, was his primary language. But the dialect his accent hinted at bore no resemblance at all either to the French she was familiar with from her early European encounters, or to the southern dialect that had developed a life of its own in the swamplands of the Deep South. Laura concluded that the accent she had heard was distinctly North American—Canadian French, to be precise—although the name the caller had given her sounded unmistakably English.

This summer was turning out to be quite an experience for her. It was, in fact, helping Laura to assuage the lingering pain of losing her soul mate. Keeping busy with new challenges was medicine one couldn't purchase from a pharmacy. Her kids were having the time of their lives. Her husband's vision about this place had been sound. If only he had lived to see the way his family was learning to love it. It was, after all, *his* dream.

The Denton cottage was almost ready for patrons. Rix Kraft had performed miracles in the main dining room where Laura intended to serve breakfasts. She had been reading up on ways to elegantly present fruit and other breakfast items for her guests. She had already received her box of chocolate cordials to place on her guests' pillows at night and after dinner liquors.

The tiny post office in Rockwood had left a message at the cottage earlier. Toonie had personally called Laura to let her know the package had finally arrived and was there, ready for pick-up. Rockwood was such a small town that the postmaster—and lone Somerset Sherriff Department representative—knew everyone on a first-name basis. It was these little things about rural New England that warmed her inner core. Laura had nearly forgotten the characteristically considerate way people behaved in smaller towns. She had missed the personalized service when her family moved to the Tampa area and adopted suburban life.

Of the four rentable rooms in the cottage, only two were still in need of repair and decoration. The other two had been satisfactorily made over and were ready for rent. Two would have to do. She needed to initiate the business side to this life-altering endeavor to see how *she* would do as a B & B hostess. July would be the summer's peak rental season. Completing the renovation of the bedrooms she and her children were to use at night would also have to wait. She needed immediate revenue. Rix hadto be paid. Her husband's life insurance would not last forever.

The previous night, Laura had been given a potential break. Jenny had called Maria Hernandez in Tampa and talked to her best friend for nearly an hour. Before she hung up, Maria's mother, Ana, had asked to speak with Laura to inquire about how things were going. By the end of the conversation, Mr. and Mrs. Hernandez had volunteered to fly up and be the first "guests" at the Denton's B & B. Laura had welcomed their visit, but insisted that they were not to pay. Roberto Hernandez had argued otherwise. Laura had understood the benefit of having her friends provide her a trial run.

Jenny had nearly cried with excitement when she learned of Maria's impending visit. Laura herself had nearly cried with worry, wondering if she and Rix would have the place ready in time. She had so much else to be anxious about, now that the strange phone call she had just received was stored in her memory file cabinet under Weird Phone Call Number Four; Kineo Summer Number One.

* * *

"Hey, Brandon! Did I tell you Maria was coming to visit next weekend?"

"Geesh, only like ten times now!" Jenny's younger brother scoffed.

"Hey, you guys! C'mere quick!" The excitement in Thomas's voice instantly aroused the curiosity of his younger siblings. Thomas was Mister Ice—rarely betraying much emotion or giving way to sentimentality. Since their father's death, he had taken the role of the "little man of the house" a bit too seriously at times. This summer seemed to have reminded him that the joys of childhood were not perhaps something to squander away too quickly.

"Look!" Thomas commanded. "A potential route up the southeast face."

"Up there?" Jenny inquired in a thoroughly disapproving tone.

"Oh, coool! Can we?" was Brandon's response, coming from the other end of the spectrum.

"Carefully...maybe," Thomas replied as he examined the wall with his hands. "Well, not too far up the wall. This gets technical real fast. Mom would kill me if any of us got hurt. Brandon, you go first, but do exactly what I say and do *not* climb any higher than I tell you to. I want to be right behind you to help you with your footing, if need be."

"I'm not going up there, guys—no way!" warned Jenny.

"You don't have to," Thomas assured her. "Just sit here and do *not* distract us while we are climbing. Okay?"

Brandon started up the rock face slowly. The heavily weathered igneous rock over much of Mt. Kineo's face was dangerous, but here, in this location, the geologic processes of scouring and splitting had formed an inviting vertical passageway before them. The wall was pitched at a nearly vertical angle, but a small ice-heaved chimney had formed, with a series of six-inch vertical steps that acted like a stone ladder.

The width of the steps, however—two to five inches, at best—was not suitable for accommodating all feet. Although the most fearless and agile climber in the family, Brandon could barely secure a firm hold on the smaller steps, even with his tiny hiking boots, and supported himself by grasping the walls with his fingers for a better grip. This was of increasing concern to Thomas, who knew that climbing *up* was always easier than climbing *down*. He felt his stomach muscles tighten, as if Tiffany were around to try and take his hand again.

At about fifteen feet above the ground, the rock steps began to give way to broken chunks of rock that could be easily scrambled over. Thomas was right behind Brandon, every step of the way. This part of the route was no longer technically difficult and his stomach settled again as he relaxed a little.

"Be careful, boys!" Jenny called up, the fear in her voice obvious to Thomas who began to re-evaluate the whole exercise, now that they had climbed to an elevation that would be hazardous if either of them slipped.

"Mommy wouldn't like this, Tom!" Jenny warned.

"Hush, Jenny, please!" Thomas snapped back, as Brandon kept climbing.

Thomas was distracted now, looking down at Jenny, half-irritated at her for opening her mouth and half-grateful for reminding him to think like an adult. He gauged the distance from his sister and contemplated calling Brandon back, but "Spiderman" was moving up the face with no apparent fear. He was traversing an area that was no longer an easy scramble, but required complex bouldering techniques.

"Crap! Brandon, stop!" Thomas cried out.

His younger brother was now forty feet up the wall, while he himself was way below at an elevation of twenty-five feet. With a hand sheltering her eyes from the glare, Jenny was pleading out loud for Thomas to *please* get her little brother down. A large rock, dislodged from underneath Brandon's hiking boot, skipped over the side of the small ledge where the boy had perched himself. The chunk of rock made an increasingly fearsome noise as it bounced down. Thomas looked up, saw the rock heading his way, and ducked in time, turning to watch it fly down past him.

"Stand back, Jenny!" he yelled out, as the rock careened off the wall once more, gaining an ominous momentum. The little girl was already up and running back for cover. The rock landed with a dull thud, burying itself in the soil at the very spot where Jenny had been standing. Thomas's face turned white at the thought of what could have happened to his sister. He suddenly felt nauseated.

"Brandon, do NOT move a muscle. Do you hear me?" Thomas sounded like his father. The younger boy was unaffected by all the commotion far below him.

"Thomas! Thomas! What's this? You've got to see this. C'mere!"

"What?" His brother asked huffily, angrier at himself than at Brandon "Are you *nuts?*"

"This is *cool!*" Brandon exclaimed. "There's some sort of painting on the rocks here!"

Still trembling with fear after his own narrow escape and Jenny's, Thomas tried to digest what he had just heard.

"What are you babbling about?" he snapped.

"Painting…in red…and brown. Someone painted up here on the rocks," Brandon explained.

"Wha…what…what do you see?"

"C'mere! I wanna show ya!"

Thomas looked up to where his brother was perched, then looked down. He suddenly felt both excited and scared. *Can I make it up there? If he can, so can I. Heck! But he hasn't tried getting down—what if he gets stuck? I need to stay below him, in case I have to help him down. Dang it!* Thomas considered how his father might have handled the situation and took a deep breath to calm himself.

"I see four brown lines and three…red circles…and…some things that look like… bird's feet and…"

"Don't go up there, Thomas!" Jenny cried, and her older brother recognized in her quivering voice a note that suggested she was near emotional collapse. "Get him down now!" she demanded.

Thomas thought long and hard about his next move. Then his mind turned inward and he realized what he had to do and summoned the courage to act. Skillfully pulling himself up the steeper face above him, he studied his every move swiftly and intently. He memorized every step he took and every handhold he chose, but stopped short of the ledge that Brandon was sitting on. Down below, he could hear Jenny sobbing uncontrollably now. She was blubbering something about Daddy being dead and that she didn't want to lose her brothers too. In that single defining moment, Thomas grew a year older. When he spoke up, he suddenly sounded like his father.

"Jenny," he said deliberately and calmly. "It's all right. We're fine. We're not falling and I ain't planning on dying. I'm bringing our little brother down now. You just sit there and let *me* do this."

At the reassuring tone in his voice, his sister stopped wailing instantly. She sat down obediently and watched her big brother responding to the crisis far above her, hoping he knew what he was doing.

Inside, Thomas was thinking the same thing.

"Oh my God, Brandon!" he exclaimed. "That looks like cave paintings. Only, there's no cave." He stopped and stared at the fascinating images painted on the rocks until they had become etched in his memory as part of this amazing and stressful day. "Okay, look," he finally said. "We really need to get down now. We'll discuss the images on the rocks later. You must climb down back the way you came up."

Brandon got down on his belly and rotated his little legs over the edge of the rock ledge, discovering that it was a whole lot scarier going down than it had been going up. He could not feel his way down to the step he had set foot on while going up and over the ledge, and he could not see below him to locate it.

"Keep trying, Brandon," Thomas urged. "To your left. No, your left. No! YOUR LEFT!"

Suddenly, the younger boy started to cry. "Stop yelling at me! I can't find a place for my foot!"

"Okay, okay… Sorry," Thomas comforted him and the exasperation in his voice faded. "Slide your left foot… No. Stop, Bran. Your *other* left foot… There ya go. There ya go… Okay, another few inches…little more…little more… Now STOP!"

Brandon followed his brother's instructions carefully.

"Now take the weight off your hands, Bran, and lower yourself. Your foot is only three inches from a foothold. I know you can't see it, but it's there. This is the step you used to get up."

"I can't," the younger boy whined. "I can't! I don't see it."

"You can't see it, Bran, but the steps are there. Trust me. You can do it."

"I can't," he whimpered again.

Thomas could see that he was losing Brandon quickly. If his brother became petrified with fear, this could get ugly pretty fast. Thomas had seen a grown woman get vertigo while descending the fire tower last week. It had taken two adults to slowly guide her trembling body down the ladder. *Think. Think. Think.* He remembered the time his dad had helped him off a ledge in the Grand Canyon when he was only twelve and scared to death.

"Bran…" he said softly.

"Yeahh," Brandon replied, panic in his voice.

"Take a deep breath… Again… Take another deep breath. Now you know that painting you found? That's probably some archeological treasure, an Indian painting from a *long* time ago, and you discovered it. I'll bet if we call Dr. Wayne at the university, he'll wanna come back to see it. They might even name this whole rock cliff after *you*!"

"Reaa-ally?" Brandon asked, a pinprick of hope surfacing from his terror-struck voice.

"I'm sure of it! You might be famous. But first, you have to put that left foot down a few inches. Okay, bud?"

"I'm scared."

"I know you are, Bran, but you can do it. C'mon now, let's do this so we can call Dr. Wayne and tell him what you discovered."

Brandon simply nodded and slowly shifted some weight off his arms. He would have had to anyway, because muscle fatigue was quickly setting in, and the build-up of lactic acid would soon make his decision for him. His foot suddenly struck the step and the boy sighed with relief.

"My arms are tired," he informed Thomas.

"I know, big guy. C'mon, just follow my instructions and climb back down to here. Then I can help you better by placing your foot in the steps for you. One step at a time."

Jenny expelled a huge sigh of relief when Brandon finally joined up with Thomas who was about thirty-two feet above her. It took about five more minutes for the two boys to complete their careful descent. Jenny grabbed Brandon the instant he set foot on safe ground and hugged him.

"Ya know, Jenny...I'm gonna be famous?" Brandon's paralyzing fear had been swiftly replaced by his excitement over the discovery. "Thomas said I'm gonna be famous."

Jenny smiled because he was finally down safely. They both looked over at Thomas, both hoping to discuss the Indian painting with him, but he was leaning over a downed tree behind them, clutching his stomach, and wretching uncontrollably.

PART TWO

Kineo in the 1600s

16

Kineo Island, 1646

It is believed that the first outsiders "discovered" Kineo in the mid-1600s. Gabriel Druilletes, a Jesuit priest, had traveled up the Kennebec River in 1646 on his way to Canada. Some accounts claim he was the first white man to view the impressive face of Mt. Kineo projecting out of Moosehead Lake. Druillete's encounter with the peace-loving Abenaki Indians from the region's Norridgewock area was reported to be friendly. This was not the case in other areas of North America, where European "invaders" were pushing further and further westward into the heartland of "their" new colony. Soon, war would break out across the territory, triggered by the complex interactions between dozens of native cultures and a half-dozen European peoples.

The French and the English, along with the Spaniards, had been arriving in the New World since the 1500s, driven by the will to conquer its untamed frontiers. The period between 1611 and 1626 was marked by the arrival of the Dutch, and in 1638, Swedish settlers colonized the Delaware River area. The first settlement in Maine was established by English colonizers in 1625, only forty years after their pioneering brethren had arrived in America.

The French settled primarily in Canada and in the far northeast. The Spaniards conquered Mexico and Florida, while the English and other Europeans settlers traveled west from the east coast, covering the territory that lay essentially between Massachusetts and South Carolina. The Native Americans were driven back in every direction as the European invaders brought guns and worse—deadly diseases, to which the indigeous peoples had no immunity. Smallpox, influenza, diphtheria, and measles ultimately succeeded in wiping out more of them than all the wars they would be embroiled in.

At the time of Gabriel Druillete's travels through the Kineo area, the region boasted of abundant natural resources, including lumber and game. The first white man had settled in Maine not twenty-one years earlier and had yet to expand into the heartland. Some stories of the exploits of these white invaders occasionally made it to the Abenaki, but they had their own concerns to deal with, as other native tribes were gradually being pushed into their region and competing for the same limited resources.

This was the beginning of a very tumultuous time in Native American history. Earlier, so few native peoples had been living in the area that the various "nations" and tribes that came into contact with each other were usually able to quickly settle disagreements. The weaker group simply moved to another area. Before the arrival of Christopher Columbus, there had probably been no more than seven million Native Americans scattered all over America (including Alaska). Today, New York City alone, as one single population center, contains more than eight million people. Thus, the density of all of the Indian tribes together in America was historically of little significance.

By 1890, the Native American population in the entire country had plummeted to a low of 400,000—equivalent to the approximate population of Tulsa, Oklahoma, in the year 2000. In the New England area, most of the native "nations" contained only about 40,000 to 60,000 people, scattered over a large territory (now known as "states"). Today, America consists of hundreds of such population centers. The state of California alone has over fifty cities that contain over 100,000 people.

But in the early 1600s, the trouble brewing around the Moosehead region was still a few hundred miles off and a couple of decades away. Indians from various tribes and nations in the area were largely free to camp, visit, or harvest flint from Kineo without fear of reprisal. The many lakes, rivers, and streams in the area provided not only water to drink and cook with, but also a means of transportation between their various encampments.

The early white explorers in the Moosehead Lake area saw, by and large, peace-loving Indians working in harmony. Little did the Jesuit priest foresee that the destiny of Kineo had already been predetermined a mere thirteen years before his sojourn in the region. There was no sign of the horrific violence and bloodshed that would ravage Kineo in the early 1600s. Nor would Druilletes learn of the lone shaman responsible for rescuing the Moosehead region from escalating violence between the rival tribes. All the Jesuit priest was able to witness was the remarkable outcome of the shaman's thoughtful actions that would establish a state of peaceful co-existence between the various tribes, little knowing that this extraordinary man would be referred to by the natives of the era by a most ordinary name: "Kajo the Trader".

17

Moosehead Region and Kineo, 1633

It had been many years since the trader, Kojoweemis, returned to the land of moose and Penobscot. In his native language, the term "penobscot" meant a "place of rocks". Centuries later, the whites would butcher this honorable term and use it to describe one of "their" rivers in a land they would later call Maine.

He had survived more than fifty cycles of the four seasons as far as he could remember—as if the actual number really mattered—and come across a great many interesting peoples, places, animals, and landscapes. There may have been no wiser human on the North American landmass than he—not that he cared about such fulsome praise.

He was a nomad. Everywhere he journeyed, the inhabitants instantly gravitated to him because of his unassuming nature, his flamboyant display of precious stones and jewelry, and his animal pelts from faraway lands. His wise suggestions often eluded the grasp of the average native person. Having escaped from the jaws of death countless times, he no longer feared it. In fact, he welcomed it, having developed a strong belief in a spiritual afterlife.

People called him a shaman. The concept amused him. Unlike other medicine men he had encountered in his travels, the things he did with plants and animals were neither magical nor spiritual. He simply used the inherent properties of their inner life force; nothing to mock at or ridicule; nothing to fear or be awestruck by. Certain berries, when fermented, simply made you laugh; others cured you of illness; a few gave you strength before combat and heightened your alertness; others made you sleepy. Some pigments used to adorn the face signified it was time for you to take a mate; others conveyed the message to your enemy that you were prepared to die for your people.

With time came knowledge and experience that others would revere as wisdom. Being a nomad had some amazing benefits for Kojoweemis, as he slowly assembled the sum of everybody's discoveries. Every innovation, every seemingly magical display, every medicinal herb was just a *trade* away. To acquire new knowledge, all he had to do was be willing to part with the right merchandise at the right time.

But it had not always been so easy for him. As he steadied his canoe on his journey up the Moosehead Lake, with the cliffs of Kineo in the distance, memories of his life began to overwhelm him.

* * *

Born in the year the Europeans called 1580, Kojoweemis the Trader was the second child of an Abenaki family of Penobscot in the Moosehead Lake region. While the Penobscot on Moosehead Lake were known as Moosehead Lake Indians, they were simply part of a geographic division of the Eastern Abenaki. Kojoweemis's family lived in the village of Kenduskeag. Owing to his diminutive stature, the village, and even the boy's father, shunned him. Unlike his older, stronger brother, he had been born premature. Tiny and weak, he was teased and ridiculed by the other children. He would never grow up to be a great warrior, hunter, or husband.

When he turned seven, his disgruntled family moved to the area he had been partly named after—Kokadjoweemgwasebemis or Kettle Mountain. They had relatives living there in a smaller, more intimate group of Abenaki and hoped that a smaller group comprising many relatives would be more open to accepting Kojoweemis. Although this small band of Indians did, in fact, accept him, the boy continued to be sensitive to parental rejection and had to endure a daily round of belittling from his brother. The realization that he would never be accepted burdened his heart till he could not stand the grief any longer. At the age of thirteen, he slipped off into the woods during a frightening storm, set off in a canoe, and ended up in Moosehead Lake. Willing the great lake to overturn his canoe and drown him, he stopped paddling. Then something remarkable happened.

His beleaguered canoe came across the great spirit of the moose. Kineo? He had heard of the great rock spirit, but had never actually seen it. Because of his puny size and overly protective mother, Kojoweemis had not been allowed to travel with the other boys when the elders took the young hunters on their first overnight trip. The name Kineo simply meant "a place with a high bluff", but the elders had taught him that the mountain meant much more. Awed and inspired by the site of the big rock jutting out of Moosehead Lake, Kojoweemis no longer felt that his life was meaningless.

He remembered the traditional tale of how this mountain had originally been an ancient mother moose. The Cow Moose, now long dead, had left the rock behind as the legacy of her past existence. A mighty Indian hunter had fought ferociously until this queen of the moose tribe was slain. The calf of the queen moose was killed somewhere among the islands in Penobscot Bay (aptly named, since that bay was full of tiny rock islands).

Staring up at Mt. Kineo, he felt a chill settle over him and shuddered. The form of the moose was so obvious to him—it was just as the elders had described. The poor Cow Moose looked out from her reclining position, with the precipitous side of the mountain presenting the outline of her head.

How could the great hunter have killed such a mighty moose? And then it struck him. If a mere hunter could tame the ferocity of a protective mother moose that large, anything and everything was ultimately vulnerable. Everything died. Life was a struggle. Even a towering physical frame could not prevent one from surrendering to the inevitability of death. The Cow Moose was huge indeed, but in the end, she and her calf had been slain. Now she burst out of the great lake as the most inspiring image Kojoweemis had ever seen in his short and pathetic life. Kineo spoke to him that day and the spirit of the slain mother moose nestled in his soul. He would never be afraid again. He would never consider himself insignificant because he was small. He would travel the land and find the worldly inspirations that had been kept from him by those who had predetermined that he couldn't accomplish anything important because of his diminutive stature.

Later that day, he constructed a small shelter for the night, gathered blueberries, and killed a small rabbit. Walking along the shore, he stumbled upon a small group of Indians camped there. They also appeared to be Kennebec—Eastern Abenaki Indians—and spoke a version of the Algonquin language he too had been raised to speak.

The men and women were making a canoe. Kojoweemis decided that he would learn to build a canoe and then set out in search of adventure. He was ashamed of his given name which, in its full form, meant "Little Kettle". Not Big Kettle, but Little Kettle—always little. And the "weemis" part sounded like it was designed to ridicule a tiny child. So the older boys pronounced the last part of his name as "weeeeeee-missss weeeee-missssss". In the instant that he encountered the band of Kennebec Abenaki Indians, he abandoned his past forever and abbreviated his name to "Kajo".

The curious Indians had no idea what this name meant, but looking at his small frame and exposed ribcage, they assumed he was lost, hungry, and delirious. Feeling sorry for the small boy, they gestured for him to eat with them and later, to help construct canoes. They had no idea how old Kajo was and figured him to be much younger than he actually was. The boy tossed the rabbit down on the ground in a gesture that indicated that he wished to "trade" his game for the security of their company, and to learn the skills that went into canoe-making. The Indians laughed approvingly at the oddly mature gesture, and adopted him immediately. They showed him the kind of respect he had never known previously. Covered in spruce-bark and cornel, Kajo assembled his first canoe.

He was amazed at how many types of wood they used to construct a canoe: red maple, willow, aspen, and spruce. He gathered some white spruce roots to use as binding straps, but the Kennebec Indians showed him how black spruce was superior, because it did not split as readily. Another canoe-making craftsman named Coosuwacket showed him how the winter bark (stripped from the trees before the sap flowed in May) was harder, and much better material than summer bark.

Early every morning, Kajo would rise and return with some game to "trade" with the men who were teaching him how to complete his canoe. He made necklaces with simple wooden beads that he traded with the ladies for certain foods. At first, the game for the men was rabbit. But by the time his canoe was completed, he had successfully hunted and exchanged beaver, otter, sable, partridge, and several ducks. At first, the beads were simple, soft conifer carvings, but later, he adorned the ladies with stone, bone, and intricately carved maple and oak. Kajo rapidly learned to hunt, make unique jewelry, and construct a sturdy canoe.

Belonging to the Norridgewock area, the men from this band rewarded the young boy with a present on the day he took his canoe out on its maiden voyage. Kajo and the original four Kennebec men who had found him paddled over to Kineo. The five of them stowed their canoes, and then hiked the steep cliff-edge trail that ascended the great Cow Moose.

Kajo strained to keep up with the older, more physically fit men, as they scrambled up the rugged trail. As he neared the summit, his breathing became uncontrollably rapid and he felt the spirit of the Mother Moose rise inside him. The men gathered a slick, smooth stone material and showed it to Kajo. It was generally slate-colored, with white specks. When the rocks were broken, the material turned a whitish color. Each blow produced a circular fracture with a ragged cutting edge. The men made a primitive knife from the material and gave it to the boy. This "Kineo knife" had such a sharp blade that Kajo learned to slice in half a green aspen branch, one inch thick, without even bending the latter.

The next day, he warmly embraced the four craftsmen and gave them each a gift—a fine pelt of rabbit fur worked into the shape of a cold-weather footwear liner. The men smiled as they saw their young companion set out in his canoe for the last time. And they each wondered if, or when, they would ever see him again.

* * *

The memories rushing through the wise shaman's mind began to fade as his birch-bark canoe came around Farm Island. Forty years ago, he had first climbed the petrified remains of the Cow Moose and marveled over the unique stone that cut so easily. Thirteen years from this day, the French Jesuit would meet the friendly camp of Abenakis from Norridgewock. On this particular day, however, things were not peaceful. Off in the distance, Kajo the Trader could see smoke billowing up ahead.

This is not good, he thought. During his travels, he had learned to recognize lightning-borne fires brought down to the earth as a gift by ancestral spirits. The patterns he saw ahead of him now bore the unmistakable signature of man's malevolent intentions—death and destruction. He had witnessed before the type of ignorance that caused peace-loving people to turn hostile, the kind of people who would tease and abuse a scrawny kid (as he had once been). *How many times have I seen a mighty hunter squash a harmless spider because the sight of it offended him? Did it really make him feel superior?*

Every time Kajo returned to the region where he was born, and more importantly, to the island where he had been *reborn*, he was amazed at how easily the memories flowed. Neither time nor the constant acquisition of worldly wisdom could erase the pain he still harbored, but shared with no one. Kajo returned to Kineo every decade and paid homage to the great Cow Moose that had stirred his imagination and changed his life into its current nomadic shaman existence. The spirits of Kineo summoned him now once again. It did not matter where he was trading in the world; he would answer the cry of the Cow Moose and return home.

Kajo continued on his way, until he could see the cliffs of Kineo from his canoe. Inside his canoe were amazing items that he had collected from people belonging to faraway places. It had been almost ten years to the day since he last traded with the Abenaki Indians on Kineo. He assumed, of course, that the Abenaki were still there. The Iroquois had moved into the area and the relations between the groups were confusing. The Iroquois was a confederation of Indians made up of five distinct sub-nations or tribes. These sub-groups included the Cayuga, Mohawk, Oneida, Onondaga, and Seneca.

Although the Mohawk would ultimately become the most famous of the Iroquois tribes, in many ways, they were quite different from the others in the confederation. As a result, the "people of the flint" kept to themselves and only associated with the other Iroquois in times of war or when trading. The Mohawk, in particular, sought the Kineo flint as a prized material for their weapons. They competed for the resources of Kineo and developed a disdain for the Abenaki.

Kajo approached one of the coves on Kineo and continued to observe the smoke billowing out above the treetops at several locations on the island.

"Iroquois," he muttered to himself. He could sense what was going on long before his suspicions were actually confirmed. Paddling along the edge of the cove, Kajo began to recall what he had learned about the Iroquois during his travels:

The Iroquois call themselves Haudenosaune—"people of the long house". All of the sub-nations speak Iroquian. The languages of individual tribes are closely related and, although not identical, mutually intelligible.

Kajo remembered he had heard of another camp of Iroquois settled in the area with, primarily, members of the Onondago tribe. Well liked by the nation's other tribes of the nation, the Onondago were considered the "people of the hills" and "keepers of the fire". Kajo had traded with these people before. He remembered that two separate Iroquois camps had eventually evolved in the area. One camp, always maintained by the keepers of the fire, had members of various Iroquois tribes openly coming and going. The loners of the nation—the Mohawk—maintained the other camp. Kajo had not had particularly pleasant trade experiences with these unpredictable people.

He paddled west along the mouth of Kineo Cove, where he had heard someone scream out from the shoreline.

The smoke continued to rise out of the woods at several locations on Kineo. More disturbingly, he could see smoke rising up off to the northeast near Little Kineo. Kajo began to see the carnage now and detect the smell of death.

Cautiously pulling his canoe ashore, he stepped gingerly out onto the shore. Noticing the tiny rounded pebbles on the shore, he made his way over some roots to skirt around the stones likely to give his presence away if he stepped on them.

In the distance, he could hear the anguish of a woman's voice and the sound of feet running toward him. He had no desire to become part of whatever madness was overtaking this encampment, but he could not suppress the anger beginning to boil inside him. *You fools! How dare you desecrate the land of the Cow Moose!*

Then he saw a young mother fleeing with her child. The woman's black hair was matted with dried blood as she ran toward Kajo. Close behind in hot pursuit, his distinctive black scalplock of hair streaming behind him, was one angry Mohawk warrior with a deep gash down the side of his face.

The woman rounded the corner, saw Kajo, and squealed in fright, expecting to be ambushed from both sides. She lunged at him in a quick, defensive move, but the wise shaman anticipated her reaction and sidestepped the intended assault in one fluid motion. The woman streaked past Kajo, followed by the angry Mohawk who was now almost upon him. The fierce hunter raised his powerful arm in the air and a double-bladed hatchet started descending toward Kajo's head. The shaman did not flinch as the blade came down.

* * *

The white man was busy discovering North America. In the Moosehead Lake region, however, he had not yet made his inevitable impact. By the year 1890, however, many Native Americans would succumb to genocide, war, starvation, enslavement, and of course, disease, leaving no more than 400,000 survivors through all of America. In 1633, however, the Indians on Kineo were still blissfully ignorant of what their future held. Their time to experience the trauma of colonial expansionism would follow soon enough. Besides the havoc wrought by the arrival of the white invaders, the combination of greed and limited resources would eventually cause one group to exploit another. No single group of people on the planet ever remains "king of the hill" for too long.

Most of the northeast region, up through what is now called Canada, was broadly organized by the Iroquois group of Indians. Hiawatha and Deganawidah had formed an Iroquois Confederation for peace in the early and mid-1400s. Relatively harmonious relationships would prevail for sometime thereafter. Now 150 years later, there was instability once again in the nations. With the white man plunging deeper into North America, the Native Americans found themselves pushed out of their homelands.

As the Indians migrated to new areas, an imbalance between the nations was created. Once-plentiful natural resources were steadily depleted. Even the mountain known as Kineo, a place of spiritual enlightenment, would arouse envy and cause turmoil. Indians from many different tribes were traveling to the big Cow Moose to harvest her magnificent flint for their tools and weapons. As their workers moved in and out of the camps, game and other resources, once found in abundance, declined. The concept of land ownership once exclusive to the European invaders began to infect the native peoples' way of thinking; and the white man's plague—the diseases he brought in and passed on to the original settlers—may well have been a symptom of the overcrowding that resulted.

The Abenaki Indians, followed by the Iroquois, accumulated the greatest number of people in the Moosehead region during this time. Each group eventually set up permanent encampments on Kineo. But now a new tribe of Iroquois—the Mohawk—had arrived in the region, and the Abenaki, in particular, did not take kindly to the additional competition. Eventually, the three groups of Indians resolved their differences amicably by agreeing to let the Abenaki control the southwest peninsula up to the foot of the great mountain. The general Iroquois camp, managed primarily by the Onondago, used Kineo's eastern wooded hilly side, right up to the chain of connecting islands that is now called Pebble Beach, while the Mohawk camped on the other side of the mountain to the north of the island near what is today called Hardscrabble Point. This suited the Mohawk fine, as they preferred to be on their own. They created several carefully concealed paths that led up through the thick aspen, birch, maple, and conifer woods to the high rhyolite cliffs above.

This arrangement worked for many years, and tensions eased. Having to travel a longer distance to the prime flint harvesting sites, however, the Mohawk generally felt excluded. Consequently, they barred other peoples from using *their* side of the island. The Abenaki had very little forest on their side of the mountain and could no longer hunt game close to their camps. This forced them to hunt on the other side of the lake and have the game canoed to their workers on Kineo. Meanwhile, the other Iroquois associated with the Onondago, the keepers of the fire, attempted to stay out of the squabbles that broke out from time to time between the two, more fractious tribes. They made frequent concessions to both sides, attemping to stay neutral and keep the peace.

As a result of the influx of numerous peoples from the region to harvest the renowned mineral on Kineo, the natural resources were rapidly depleted, leading to tensions among the Onondago Iroquois as well. Wherever he traveled, the wise shaman, Kajo, had seen the same kind of behavior patterns emerge in native peoples—the Creek, Pequot, Sioux, Arapaho, Hopi, and others. *Place enough men together in a confined space and it is inevitable. Eventually, man exposes his darker, destructive side in any culture, regardless of where it has evolved.*

* * *

The large hatchet in the Mohawk warrior's hand was fitted with twin blades made from the glassy fracture of Kineo flint. These were wrapped securely around a strong maple branch with a twine made from spruce roots and vine. Had the Mohawk's strong grip not relaxed so abruptly, releasing his weapon before it found its mark, Kajo's skull would have been split wide open. The Mohawk warrior looked down in stunned disbelief as the tip of the shaman's obsidian black spear sliced through his chest, piercing his heart in a fatal thrust. Flung from the Mohawk's hand, the lethal hatchet circumscribed three revolutions in the air before embedding itself deep in the bark of a white pine nearby.

The terrified Abenaki mother stumbled, dropping her skinning tool in order to cradle her son protectively in her arms and shield him from possible injury as she fell. With great determination, she wrapped her child in her arms and rolled as she hit the ground, taking the full impact of the fall on her shoulders and back. When her bruised body had come to rest, she was facing the spot where she had encountered the two hostile warriors. With the breath knocked out of her, she struggled to overcome her sense of helplessness. She was semiconscious as her son crawled out of her arms and her body started going numb. Astonishingly, the small boy was unharmed. Her eyes tried desperately to focus on the blurred image of a small man approaching her. She was beyond being frightened at this point and ready to resign herself to whatever fate the small warrior had in store for her. *If only her son were spared.*

The little warrior cautiously walked up to the dazed woman and held out his hand. Reluctantly, she took it. Kajo helped her up into a sitting position, then gathered her son, and placed him gently on her lap. His smile was endearing and went well with his graying hair. Kajo took the leather container draped around his shoulder and sprinkled cold water on the woman's face and hair. Suddenly, she recognized the turquoise jewelry and the garnet-studded bands. She had heard of this man from the elders. Despite his diminutive stature, she realized she was in the presence of a great man, a medicine man whose strength was mighty and whose wisdom remained unsurpassed. She knew of this man, known to many as Kajo the Trader.

18

On the other side of Kineo, the fires continued to rage, and the tribes were engaged in hand-to-hand combat. The Mohawk had taken the Abenaki completely by surprise. The Onondago Iroquois camp had tried to nip the conflict in the bud by sending on a group of their leaders in an attempt to dissuade their sister tribe from following through with the attack on their neighbors. What, they wondered, would ensue if their Mohawk "allies" were allowed to prevail in this conflict? *Might the reclusive Mohawk then decide the island wasn't big enough for the two of them? Besides, the Abenaki—despite their differences in culture and language—had been peaceful neighbors for many years.* The mixed Iroquois presence on the island was not large enough, however, to challenge the size and strength of the angry Mohawk. Even though the various tribes were similar, there were still too many factions involved to obtain a consensus on how to respond to the crisis. There were not even enough Onondago to deal with the Mohawk alone. In the past few weeks, the latter had amassed a formidable group of skilled warriors.

The fires were the only way. A small band of Onondago Iroquois snuck around the mountain's rear where strong prevailing winds were blowing in their favor. Setting fire to several dry wooded slopes where the Kineo winds were creating an updraft, the Ondondago Iroquois quickly managed to whip up a lethal defense. As the Mohawk had the Abenaki retreating into Moosehead Lake, the "keepers of the fire" created curtains of flames to cut off the advance routes and the potential flanking lanes the Mohawk might use. The Iroquois were not about to harm their sister tribe, but the fires, they calculated, might discourage them from continuing their campaign of violence against the neighboring Abenaki. Many of the Mohawk combatants began to look back toward their camp, worrying about the fate of their women and children.

Unfortunately, the wind-fed fires spread out of control and began to either burn or threaten to burn all of the camps on Kineo. A few remaining Abenaki warriors counter-attacked one of the Iroquois camps, believing that they had set the fires in support of the Mohawk offensive against the speakers of the Algonquin language. The counterattack, however, was too little too late. In the end, the island found itself locked in a bitter stalemate between the three groups, with much of its territory ablaze. With the Mohawk successfully convincing the Abenaki that the Iroquois camp had deliberately set the Abenaki encampment on fire, the vicious circle of mistrust was completed, and no one group could proclaim itself the victor.

Surveying the ruin as he explored Kineo the next morning, Kajo wept. He had witnessed such senseless brutality before, but not on quite so catastrophic a scale as in his own back-yard. *Such a waste! Such ignorance!* What infuriated and wounded him most was the instinctive awareness that the areas occupied by these selfish tribes, like the many others Kajo had visited, were mere years away from being invaded by the white man. The wise shaman knew that these disorganized groups of people would be slaughtered all over again. Some would lose their identity through cultural assimilation. Others would succumb to diseases that even his great shamanic skills and medicinal herbs could not cure. Most terrifying, however, was the death that awaited them in the form of advanced weapons that could fire small balls of lead over great distances.

Even Kajo in his great wisdom would fail to foresee the ludicrous nature of the alliances that were about to be formed or the extent of the violence that would eventually be unleashed. Just forty-two years later, in the area known today as New York, the Mohawk would ally with the white colonists of Plymouth in a war against the British, later called the King Phillips War. The resulting hostilities would end up wiping out approximately forty percent of southern New England's Native American population and quash forever any effective native resistance to colonial territorial expansion.

Looking up at the cliffs of Kineo, Kajo sighed. Nature and the spirit world were as one, but the spirit of Kineo would never speak to the Europeans in the way the spirit of the slain Mother Moose had spoken to him forty years earlier. Now, after rescuing the Abenaki mother and her son from the angry Mohawk, he heard her spirit speak to him once again. The Cow Moose had not been able to prevent the great hunter from slaying her calf and her, but Kajo had prevented the strong Mohawk warrior from slaying the innocent Abenaki mother and her son. Finding a sense of purpose deep within his troubled soul, he felt renewed. Kajo now knew why he had been drawn back to Kineo. *The spirit of the Cow Moose had summoned his help.*

He looked up into the rock face and heard the Cow Moose speak to him once again. Kajo listened intently and his mission became clear to him: he would first have to revive the spirit of the Cow Moose in the hearts of the three groups of Indians engaged in hostilities on Kineo; he would then persuade them to share the resources of Kineo guarded by her great spirit. After his mission had been accomplished, he would travel through New England and try to bind the various disorganized and unmotivated indigenous peoples in a common purpose before it was too late.

The grateful Abenaki woman Kajo had rescued found him the following morning, seized his hand, and insisted that he accompany her to the smoldering remains of the encampment to which she had belonged. By now, the battle was over and all warring factions had retreated to nurse their wounds. The desperate Abenaki surrounded the exhausted mother, listened to the tale of her rescue, and welcomed her saviour into their midst. The woman then summoned the few living elders to join them, look upon the stranger's face, and discover what she already knew—that this was the medicine man known as "the Trader".

The oldest of the surviving leaders approached Kajo and examined his flamboyant jewelry and odd garments from faraway lands. *It was him!* One elder stepped forward and looked directly into his eyes. Another elder's face lit up in joyous recognition. They all embraced Kajo and cheered loudly.

"Kajo! It *is* you!" the oldest of the elders cried in relief. "It has been far too many moons since our paths crossed, my friend. But you are always welcome here among your own."

"It has been ten seasons of the opening of the maple buds," the shaman replied without emotion. "No more. No less."

"It is sad that you must appear in such dark times for our people. But we welcome any words of wisdom you may have that will help put an end to this madness," the old man said, looking at Kajo for guidance.

"I have no words of wisdom that will ever stop man's cruelty to his brothers, my friend," the shaman replied. "Liberation from such madness comes from the heart, not the mind, and only after freeing oneself from the superstitions promulgated by ignorance."

Still weary from their narrow escape, the assembled Indians were unable to grasp the import of the strange shaman's words. No matter. For him to have returned *now*, of all times, was, by no means, a coincidence. The spirit of the Cow Moose had sent him to make peace among the troubled Abenaki people.

"I have herbs I will bring up from my canoe that will assist the healing. I will teach you new uses of mountain cinquefoil, bunch-berry, and cornus," the shaman promised as all listened intently. "Then we will make amends with our brothers on the east face."

* * *

Kajo captivated all who listened to him. Having witnessed much in his short life, he carried himself with an air of boundless knowledge. Some of the younger Kineo Indians had heard of the Trader, but were skeptical about his abilities, since they had neither seen nor tested him. They crowded around him now and asked him to sit with them and tell them of his adventures. They would see for themselves if he were truly a gifted shaman. The concept of a shaman was alien to the Abenaki. They had simply been told that his curative powers had been acquired from trading in faraway lands and with faraway peoples.

"You talk of strangers from across the large water body that arrive on mammoth canoes and carry sticks that spit flames," a warrior observed skeptically.

"I have seen such men and even learned to talk to them in their language," replied Kajo.

"Is it true that their wooden sticks can throw a stone with enough force to knock a bear down?" another young flint miner probed.

"Yes, my brother," the shaman answered. "The object those sticks hurl is not a stone, but a very heavy substance they call lead and fashion from liquid rock."

The assembled men turned, looked at each other, and laughed.

"I must first warn you of their fire stick—what the white man calls a gun." Kajo frowned, realizing there was much to teach these innocent tribesmen and very little time to do it in. He wondered how much longer they could evade contact with the European invaders. "Have not some of you seen the white man?"

"I have," replied an older warrior. "But that was when I hunted far to the east. I heard their guns' mighty thunder—but I was too far away to witness the power of the fire stick."

"Well then, my brothers, let me tell you about my first encounter with the white invaders in the area south of here known as Massachusetts," Kajo began.

All of the Abenaki sat down around his feet and listened.

"The white man set down roots in our land years ago. He simply has not expanded this far into our territory yet," Kajo explained. "As you know, I have lived a good life roaming my brothers' lands in search of trade. I join up with other roaming bands of Abenaki from time to time. On one such occasion, I accidentally met up with a very interesting character named Samoset. That is how I learned English—the invader's language."

"What is English?" asked the young man to his left.

The shaman laughed and began speaking to the Abenaki in that foreign language which sounded very strange to them all. They laughed loudly and attempted to mimic the words that Kajo uttered, but none could manage to. More laughter ensued. They asked the shaman to translate what he had just said. Then Kajo became serious and told them of his first encounter with the white man and the amazing story of Samoset.

19

During the early 1620s, most of the native peoples of America were organized into confederacies with lesser sachems under the authority of a Grand Sachem. The English often referred to the Grand Sachems as "kings". In reality, there was nothing regal about the position. Such leaders had limited authority and invited little respect compared to European royalty.

Samoset was a Pemaquid sachem leader of the Abaneki. He had traveled south to the area that is present-day Massachusetts from his home (the land that is now called Maine) in pursuit of game. Having had several brief encounters with the English during the past three years, he had actually learned to speak some of the colonizers' language. In early spring, Samoset had come across English colonizers settled in Plymouth. With the advantage of knowing a bit of their language, while they remained ignorant of his native tongue, he had strolled confidently into their settlement and startled the pilgrims by greeting them with, "Hello Englishmen."

Kajo, who had met Samoset while trading, had become friends with him. For the past four weeks, he had been traveling with him, but had chosen to stay back at their camp when Samoset marched into Plymouth. The shaman was suspicious of these strange white men and their loud wooden sticks that could heave fire and rock at animals and kill them in their tracks. Samoset, however, was unafraid. He had stayed the night in Plymouth with the English and left the next morning. By the end of the week, Kajo had begun accompanying the other man on his visits to the English pilgrims and engaged in very interesting and satisfying trade.

Despite his diminutive size, Kajo had become a respectable hunter by developing the ability to move stealthily in the woods and use his alertness and cunning to his advantage. His understanding of animal behavior was the most fine-tuned of any hunter that Samoset had encountered; he thus, found his traveling companion quite intriguing.

The two men watched Squanto, another Native American, take on the key role of intermediary between the pilgrims and the Wampanoag Indians—a tribe to which he himself belonged—in the Massachusetts area. The two Abenaki drifters debated about expanding their involvement further, reluctant to get caught up in the tensions between the native people of Massachusetts and the white invaders who lived in the area. Kajo was preparing to trade in areas much further to the west. But first, he was keen to meet Massasoit, the Grand Sachem of the Wampanoag, who was expertly developing statesmanship abilities with the newcomers who appeared to be good neighbors. Samoset persuaded Squanto to introduce Kajo to this influential Wampanoag and the shaman decided to stay another week. He was learning so much from these three fascinating native men who had strongly influenced the early history of colonial America. Kajo stayed up many nights talking to them and absorbing wisdom. Soon, his English would be as fluent as that of any of the other Indian translators in the region.

Then in March 1621, Samoset, the unlikely Abenaki leader, and Massasoit, the "grand king" of the Wampanoag, headed into Plymouth and established a treaty of friendship with the English colonizers. This important alliance gave the white newcomers permission to occupy approximately 12,000 acres around the Plymouth settlement. For Massasoit, this concession was not a matter of undue concern. After all, his people shared resources with native peoples from other nations and tribes. Land was not something you "owned"; it was something you shared and respected.

The discrepancy between the European concept of territorial ownership and the native notion of sharing land soon became very obvious to Massasoit, as his Wampanoag people began perishing from rampant epidemics. Soon the tribe's population in the region had dwindled to almost nothing. Massasoit would never understand that the microscopic germs the white invaders had brought in their wake were more effective in exterminating his people than the fire sticks he had learned to fear.

In addition, the "grand king" of the Wampanoag regarded the pilgrims as peace-loving, but inept. They didn't hunt or fish well and would certainly have starved, if it were not for the usefulness of their fire sticks and the generous assistance provided by the friendly natives. The Wampanoag continued to cohabitate in a spirit of cooperation with their pilgrim neighbors. The latter were so grateful to them that during autumn, they invited Massasoit and his Wampanoag guests to celebrate their first harvest with them.

Kajo bade his friends farewell in Plymouth after warily participating in the first Thanksgiving in America. As he headed west by himself, he looked back over his shoulder and wondered to himself: *My brothers, Samoset and Massasoit, have extended their hand in a long-term friendship. I only hope they have not unwittingly allowed a pack of sleeping wolves to take up their abode in their home.*

20

Kineo, 1633

The assembly of Abenaki was captivated by Kajo's story of his encounter with the white invaders in Massachusetts. But questions from the battle-worn Kineo Abenaki soon followed.

"What happened to the Wampanoag?" one of the warriors asked.

"I did not remain to find out, my brother," the shaman answered. "I hear they all got along for years. Things have gone terribly wrong since then. I learned much about the Wampanoag during that period of my life. They speak Algonquin in a dialect similar to ours. I also continued learning English, and developed an understanding of the white settlers. I learned to trade with them, as they had very valuable and interesting things. But I never learned to trust them."

"Massasoit trusted them?"

"Wholeheartedly, until death," Kajo laughed. "But that's a story we will save for another day, my brother."

* * *

A week later, under Kajo's leadership, the Iroquois and Abenaki were working together again. Every night, the surviving elders of each of the three tribes listened to the Trader speak. The shaman was ready to fulfill his destiny. He packed an animal-skin container with items to trade with the Mohawk Iroquois and some peace offerings from both the Onondago Iroquois and the Abenaki. He awoke early the next morning to have a serious discussion with the senior surviving elders of each Indian group.

The Mohawk had taken over the higher land on Kineo with the most challenging terrain. They believed that *they* had been chosen in life to be "cliff walkers" and prided themselves on having absolutely no fear of heights. Strategically, holding the high ground had proven to be a military advantage over those tribes attempting to hold the lower elevations. Being comfortable with heights was, in fact, a part of Mohawk culture. Many years later, surviving Mohawk Indians would be employed to construct skyscrapers in the development of New York City, because they were absolutely fearless about walking out on steel beams suspended high above the city.

The leader of the surviving Mohawk was a forty-year-old warrior whose chest was adorned with tattoos. He remembered the Trader from the latter's two visits to Kineo—the first, twenty years back and the second, a decade ago. He knew Kajo to be a fair and honorable man who was not tied down by his loyalty to a particular tribe. Both the shaman's keen insight and potent medicines would benefit his people. Kajo thus regained the trust of the Mohawk and brokered many deals. The Mohawk were ready to sit at the Table of Peace with the other two Indian groups and arrive at an amicable solution that would allow all to share the resources of Kineo.

The primary obstacle to the process was the Mohawk's recent discovery of a superior grade of flint in a remote location accessed from the top of Mt. Kineo. When broken, the flint had extremely sharp edges that could, with little effort, be turned into weapons-grade arrowheads and spears. Cutting and skinning tools could be produced in half the time it had taken earlier. The discovery was so exciting that the Mohawk's desire to keep the mineral a secret from the other two tribes, along with the rapidly dwindling resources in the area, would lead to the series of events that eventually culminated in their violent attempt to drive the others from Kineo. The Mohawk shamefully admitted to Kajo what the shaman had already surmised. *Greed*. The elder asked a young boy to describe how he had stumbled upon "the great discovery". The boy hesitated at first. Then, with a little encouragement, he stepped forward proudly.

"I was out looking to harvest more flint for my people and accidentally stumbled upon a hidden crevasse in the mountain," he began.

The passage was over the edge of a very narrow ledge on Kineo's east face. He had seen an unusual feature in the wall—a deep fissure—about ninety feet below the spot where he was standing. To access it, he had had to crawl across a very treacherous ledge and then scale down the cliff side.

"If he had fallen, we would never have found him," one of the Mohawk added.

"I am a fearless Mohawk," the boy proclaimed proudly. "No cliff frightens me!"

He went on to explain how he had eventually shimmied through a small crack in the wall that led to a very narrow passage. He had entered it and soon come upon a large chamber that was part of a limestone and sandstone formation below the volcanic rhyolite. The high-grade rhyolite continued to weather and fall from the ceiling and sides of the chamber.

"I found the flint in this chamber which was strewn with the bones of dead people."

"Only a Mohawk would find such a dangerous entrance," mused Kajo, much to the tribe's delight. "But now it is time to share this special place with all those who inhabit Kineo."

The Mohawk elders looked at each other, then nodded in agreement. The tribe immediately took Kajo to see the hidden chamber. The shaman climbed up the mountain, inviting the two seniormost elders from each tribe, along with the two seniormost Mohawk elders—a man and a woman—to a very special meeting in the Kineo chamber just before dark. The Mohawk would lead the other elders to the chamber, but Kajo had much preparation to do and hurried back to his canoe and camp for supplies.

An hour before sunset, the two Mohawk gathered the others and led them to the chamber as agreed upon. Kajo worked with the young boy that had discovered the chamber entrance to provide some branch ladders and safety lines from nearby trees so that access to the main tunnel would be less harrowing for the six elders.

Soon, the shaman was inside the chamber and sitting by the small fire he had lit in anticipation of the arrival of the chosen delegates. The smoke vented upward through the many fissures that ventilated the space he occupied. He began to see how the many angular rocks in the chamber and nearby fissures could be used to conceal the entire area. Large chunks of broken rhyolite could be used to create tunnels in and out of this special area so it would not be visible from the lake below.

As he contemplated an ingenious plan for construction, Kajo's thoughts were interrupted by the arrival of the first Mohawk elders, followed by the other guests. He nodded at the two visitors, remembering how pleased he had been with them for willingly sharing their people's discovery of the high-grade flint and the remains of ancestral harvesters, still intact, within the main chamber.

"My brothers," Kajo said on a note that contained a sudden serious warning to all. "The Abenaki and other tribes had harvested flint from this mountain long before the Mohawk migrated to this region. Those old bones you just saw are certainly those of native people who lived around here long before any of us even knew of the riches of Kineo. Its resources are for *all* native people and must be shared."

After an hour of listening to the shaman's inspirational wisdom, all the elders agreed to share this newly discovered harvesting site with those living at lower elevations. Each group would take turns improving the site so that it could be accessed in a manner that reduced the risk of death or injury. Timber and rock would be used to completely conceal the chamber so that it was invisible from the top saddle above. Each group would begin clearing the site around the entrance and make it more accessible to workers. The harvested stones and flint would be lowered to the working camps, where distribution and trading would take place, away from Kineo.

The Trader knew that the spirit of the Mother Moose had cursed Mt. Kineo as punishment for the madness that had recently been unleashed. At his request, a warrior would be chosen from each tribe to guard the entrance to the fissure at all times. Each sentry, thus appointed, took an oath before the elders and Kajo to honor the spirit of the Cow Moose and ensure that no avaricious outsider or delinquents among their own people further desecrated the rich mountain and its plentiful resources, even if it meant defending the site with his life. The bones of the ancestral harvesters would be properly laid to rest within stone walls built inside the chamber. An important ceremony was performed to honor their contribution to the early workings of the mining chamber.

Inside the chamber, a stone table was placed in the middle of the room. On it rested a large, shiny metallic ore of pure copper provided by Kajo from one of his trading excursions west of the Great River.

Three unique entranceways were selected for the construction of tunnels. These would be created either by stacking large rocks of rhyolite at wedged angles or combining that process with excavation by hand through the crumbly granitic rock fissures. Kajo described the kind of tools they would eventually be able to obtain from the white invaders through trade and use them in camouflaging the tunnels and ceilings from prospective invaders.

Within two months of the meeting, the basic layout had been satisfactorily completed, although the process to fine-tune the rough structure would continue for another hundred years. Ice expanding through the ages had loosened the rock sufficiently for fifty strong warriors from all of the participating tribes to be required to remove the initial rock obstacle during several weeks of backbreaking labor. These unique passageways all led to the central chamber to which each tribe had access through its own unique tunnel made with broken angular slabs of heavy rhyolite and covered in mud and native plants so that they blended seamlessly into the mountainside. These entrances resembled the interiors of caverns from the inside; from the outside, they were ingeniously camouflaged with the natural resources available and seemed an integral part of the Kineo landscape.

Smaller "tables" built from layered sheets of rhyolite were stacked just inside the entrance to each tribe's tunnel. In the middle of the topmost slab was an area about the size of a man's fist. This was carved and rounded to support a sphere with a three-inch diameter. Each tribe retained its separate harvesting schedule and the three-inch sphere would symbolize their entrance to harvest the main mining chamber from their unique location. The mined flint would then be distributed to their peoples in whatever manner each tribe felt appropriate.

Finally, after three full months of preparing the tunnels and setting up the chamber for all the tribes to use, Kajo assembled the six elders once again in the main chamber and sat them down around a fire he had lit in the middle. The shaman explained that he would soon provide to each group a rough-cut stone of precious material. Each tribe would craft their designated stone and work it skillfully for months until it was a perfect sphere of the precise diameter provided by Kajo. The model was a perfectly spherical, with a diameter of nearly three inches, carved from the mineral apatite that the shaman had brought along with him from his travels.

Kajo held up the strange white sphere of polished apatite and showed it to them. The elders were amazed at the beauty of this smooth white rock and several moved forward to examine it. Others were compelled to rub their hands over it. The shaman smiled at them.

"Polish each rough stone this smooth and reflect on what has been lost. Consider what the Cow Moose lost. Forgive. Share. Craft these three polished spheres to remind future generations of the anger that ripped Kineo apart, and how you all banded together to set things right again."

Kajo stood and looked at each of the men in the chamber.

"My brothers, the curse on Kineo is a very powerful one. Patience, trust, and fairness are characteristics you must hold dear to share its resources with your brothers. Dishonesty, envy, and greed will disrupt the balance."

"What balance, shaman?" the matriarch of the Mohawk inquired.

"The unity of your three tribes," Kajo explained. "When one of you dies, the rest grieve. Every member of each tribe pays respect to his fallen brothers. You are all bound together now by the spirit of the Kineo Cow Moose.

"Finish working and polishing your gem spheres together. When you all agree they are complete, place each of your polished spheres to rest in its guardian stone cradle. And when each is safely placed, your tribes may begin to enjoy the blessings of Kineo provided by the spirit of the Cow Moose."

"But that could take many months!" the other Mohawk protested.

"Yes, many months," concurred one of the Abenaki elders.

"True, my brothers," continued Kajo. "It will require time to heal the wounds of your madness. But in time, your blessings will be restored."

The six elders sat quietly, wrestling with the words of the great shaman. Some understood the message. Others did not.

An Onondago Iroquois elder finally broke the silence and asked Kajo to explain the curse.

"Those who dare desecrate the mountain of the fallen Cow Moose and her calf will know," Kajo responded firmly.

"Yes, shaman. But what *are* those consequences?" the male Mohawk asked

Kajo walked over to the small fire lit in the center of the chamber. He stuck a dead spruce branch into the fire and waited for the wood to ignite.

"Remember how many of you lost wives, children, friends, and warriors, when Kineo was ablaze with your battles?"

He then walked carefully over to a deerskin he had laid out, covering something in the dark corner of the chamber. All eyes followed his every move.

"The curse of Kineo my brothers…is *fire!*"

Kajo spoke with the indomitable voice of a father warning his children, as he plunged the ignited spruce stick dramatically into the side of the deerskin. Immediately, the hide caught fire, and its ghostly image illuminated the gathering. Under the animal pelt, loud pops and cracks sounded, as some material foreign to the elders began to ignite. White-hot sparks shot off in every direction, and the sounds and explosions sent all of the tribe representatives running for cover. None had ever seen "such powerful magic as this" before.

Kajo stood there, unafraid, while the primitive fireworks display continued all around him. The mixture of charcoal, sulfur, glycerine, and other substances acquired during his trading out west performed exactly has he had expected.

One by one, the frightened Indians crept back to their seats around the chamber fire, realizing that Kajo had not run from the alarming combustion of the deerskin and that *he* was in control of this angry fire display before them. The miniature explosions that were erupting from the remains of the charred deerskin were startling and loud. Finally, Kajo pointed out to the entrance tunnel that faced Moosehead Lake and asked, "Do you not hear the Mother Moose and her calf calling you, my brothers?"

The chamber, secure in the belly of Mt. Kineo, became so quiet you could hear the men breathe. In the distance, the eerie call of a loon echoed through a primitive ventilation shaft connecting the inner chamber to the face of Kineo. As each man watched the ashes left by the charred deerskin fall to the chamber floor, the *hoo-hoooo* melancholy call of the loon continued to resonate somewhere far below. Although the cry of the loon was common on the lake, its timing had a chilling effect on the small gathering. It seemed to be a warning song, with special lyrics for each man and the lone Mohawk woman. They got up and crawled out to the open ledge overlooking Moosehead Lake, far below, to listen intently to the loon's cry. Seconds later, a lone wolf howled briefly somewhere off in the distance.

The elders looked back and forth at one another and finally the highly adorned Mohawk warrior-elder turned to the nearest Abenaki and decreed, "I am not one to ignore the warning cry of a lone wolf, nor turn my back on the melancholy cries from Moosehead Lake below."

An Onondago Iroquois added, "We will not allow the desecration of the spirit island—Kineo. I hear the calling of the slain Cow Moose and her calf. I will stand by my brothers, as the shaman has shown us the path!"

The eldest Abenaki stood and held out his arm. The Iroquois and Mohawk clasped arms with him in the traditional manner, confirming their unity. The others then all stood up and united as Kineo brothers. Now that the group was in full agreement, Kajo had fulfilled his destiny. It was time now to distribute the rough-cut spheres, then load his canoe with Kineo flint that would certainly bring him some excellent trade in his next adventure.

"My brothers," Kajo said to them. "You have heard the calling of Kineo in your hearts. The time is now. Come receive your guardian stone." Then he reached into a basket and changed the history of Kineo forever.

21

Kineo, 1643 and 1653

The Trader visited Kineo only twice more in his lifetime and was happy to see the unified tribes still actively at work. The tunnels were complete and impossible to detect, unless you were standing in one of their entranceways. During his last visit, he had noticed how new pressures were being brought to bear on the area from needless wars ravaging the region around New England. The relationship between the three tribes had continued to improve and their combative impulses had been replaced by cooperation and understanding. The resources of Kineo were once again being harmoniously shared among the native peoples in the Moosehead area.

Eventually, all the Iroquois—Mohawk and Onondago—would move their camps from Kineo as trust between the tribes flourished. There was not enough game and other materials needed to sustain so many tool-finishing camps. Therefore, the other two tribes elected to finish their materials at nearby locations. Onondago, Mohawk, and Abenaki could pass freely through each other's territory. By 1640, all Abenaki camps had been abandoned, except the lone camp the Jesuit priest Gabriel Druilletes had come upon as he passed through Kineo on his way to French-controlled Canada. The rapid approach of the white man with his lethal fire sticks and his blatant disregard for the local concept of sharing resources would soon become a matter of grave concern among the three native groups.

With the passing of the years, each generation would hand down to their children the legend of the Cow Moose and how the great hunter had killed her and her calf. Each child was familiarized with the terrible war being waged on Kineo. Surviving grandparents provided living testimony to the anguish of watching the raging fires set by neighboring tribes destroy their camps. No lesson was complete without discussions of the inherent evil of greed.

In the declining years of his life, Kajo chose to return to Kineo to die. When he finally passed, the three tribes honored the fallen shaman with the longest ceremony the region had ever known, then buried his remains in a special tomb inside the inner mining chamber, thus transforming it into a very sacred place.

The guardians of each tribe accepted their responsibility as the stewards of Kineo's sacred burial grounds and its great flint resource. Dereliction of their duties could invite the unimaginable curse of fire upon their own people. The legend of Kajo, the medicine man/shaman/drifter/trader would live on for hundreds of years.

Eventually, the expansion of the white invaders into their territory began in earnest. The native people soon noticed that the white man's building structures were prone to burning down. It was obvious that spreading as he was over the land like a pestilence, recklessly consuming everything in sight, the foreign aggressor was aggravating the spirit of the Cow

Moose and the curse of fire was being unleashed. Most of the Native Indians moved out of the Moosehead Lake region and off Kineo to safer locations. Except for the six faithful guardians of Kineo who would remain in hiding in the immediate area, sworn to protect with their dying breath the secrets of Kineo.

22

From U.S. Naval Records

On October 9, 1861, an iron-clad gunboat was launched from Portland, Maine, and commissioned at the Boston Navy Yard on February 8, 1862. One hundred and fifty-eight feet long and named, according to official naval records, after "a mountain peak in central Maine", the new gunboat, *Kineo*, was commanded by Lt. George M. Ransom. Slated for Admiral Farragut's West Gulf Blockading Squadron, the *Kineo* saw action in the War Between the States while assisting the Union Forces in their preparation for the conquest of New Orleans. On April 18, 1862, the mortar flotilla opened steady fire on Fort Jackson and St. Philip and continued the bombardment until the Union ships had braved a heavy Confederate cannonade as they dashed by the forts six days later. The *Kineo* was welcomed to duty with a barrage of artillery from Confederate guns and was struck several times as she ran the gauntlet with the other ships in the division, commanded by Union Captain Bailey. On April 27, she captured five Confederate sailboats below New Orleans.

In the ensuing months, *Kineo* patrolled the Mississippi, exchanging fire from time to time with shore batteries. She reached sight of Vicksburg on May 19 and engaged Southern batteries at Grand Gulf a week later. On August 6, along with *Sumter*, *Cayuga*, and *Katahdin*, she helped repel a Confederate attack on the Union garrison at Baton Rouge, enabling the Union Navy to maintain its blockade of the important Red River supply line. *Kineo* shelled a guerrilla camp on the 9th and fired over the city on the 20th to keep an approaching Confederate force at bay. On August 28, *Kineo* captured and destroyed several small boats.

Gunboats were essential to protect Union steamboats from attacks by flying batteries and roving snipers. *Kineo* efficiently performed this duty during the months when the Union Navy and Army fought to take Vicksburg. As the campaign to clear the Mississippi approached its climax, Admiral Farragut decided to move up the river to a position where he could intercept Southern supplies from the West at the mouth of the Red River. Powerful batteries at Port Hudson, La., barred his way, but the admiral was undaunted. He lashed gunboats to his deep-water ships to shield them from gunfire and assist them in navigating the tricky waters of the Mississippi River. *Kineo* was paired with the ship, *Monongahela*, for the dash on the nights of March 13 and 14th. Heavy and deadly accurate fire rained down on the Union ships, which prevented all but the flagship, *Hartford*, and her consort, *Albatross*, from passing the fort. A shot disabled *Monongahela*'s rudder, causing her to run aground, along with *Kineo*. The stubborn crew of the gunboat worked herself free and then pulled *Monongahela* off, guiding her as they drifted downstream, out of the range of fire.

After this engagement, *Kineo* resumed her varied but vital duties in the lower river and remained at the task until after the fall of Vicksburg. She left the Mississippi on August 16 and reached Baltimore on the 25th for repairs. Back in top trim, *Kineo* left the Delaware Capes on February 29, 1864, transporting a Union Army major on special duty, and rejoined the West Gulf Blockading Squadron at New Orleans on March 17. It was assigned to blockade duty off the Texas coast. Five days later, the crew of *Kineo* boarded the British schooner, *Sting Ray May*, but the blockade runner's crew overcame the Kineo's veteran sailors, then ran the schooner aground. The schooner crew then turned the Union sailors from *Kineo* over to Confederate troops unfolding a series of clandestine events that would change the destiny of the place that inspired the gunboat's name. Those events, off the coast of Louisiana, were, however, unknown to those that would prepare the aforementioned official Naval Records.

23

May 23, 1864

"The gold must be relocated quietly before it's noticed missing."

"We counted three hundred bars at four hundred troy ounces each."

"How much weight?"

"About twenty-seven and half pounds a bar. More than four tons to move."

"We must avoid detection by the Army of Northern Aggression."

"But how? They're approaching rapidly from positions captured along the Mississippi."

"We must find a ship near the river and move it quickly."

"We have no access to such a boat and even if we did, how would we get it past the Union blockade?"

"A problem, indeed, Lieutenant, but perhaps not...not...if we commission the use of a Union boat."

"What the hell!"

"Consider the irony. They would never expect one of their own insignificant gunboats to be loaded with Confederate reserves."

"But we don't have a Union gunboat."

"We have a crew."

"You mean the sailors and the army officer that the *Sting Ray* turned over to us?"

"You're starting to see now..."

"But how? We would need a traitor. Someone willing to turn against his own."

"In every army or navy, Lieutenant, there are always those who weigh their moral values against ther financial opportunities."

"You mean every man can be bought?"

"Not quite. Every man has a price. The key is to identify the crew member, preferably an officer, whose price we can afford."

"And how do we do that?"

"Ha! I'm a fine judge of character...or lack thereof, Lieutenant. After all, did I not discover you? You were an easy turn. You helped me confiscate our local treasury right underneath the noses of our own officers."

"That's different Captain. The Confederacy is gonna lose this war and my home was left in ruins. Should I not benefit from a little gain for fighting the northerners? But you, sir? Don't *you* feel a bit guilty conspiring with the enemy?"

"Enemy? Ha, ha ha... In life, there are but potential business partners and competitors. Come, Lieutenant. Let me demonstrate how to identify a business partner among the captured Union sailors."

* * *

Of the original four men that knew about the confiscated Confederate treasury stolen during the final collapse of the rebel forces, only one man wore a blue uniform. All the other three wore gray coats. Rivalries and greed among the four men would lead to the death by gunfire of one "business partner" and the unexplained disappearance of another. The remaining two men—until recently, officers of opposing armies at war who had, each in their own sordid manner, found a way to eliminate one of the original partners—subsequently concealed the Confederate gold reserve. Naturally, with neither trusting nor liking the other, the partnership between the two survivors was becoming more burdensome, as every waking moment of the day required constant vigilance. They both acted as if they believed that neither of them was responsible for the deaths of their other partners. Being intelligent men, however, the lone Union officer and his surviving Confederate counterpart each hid his share of the gold.

The plan was to wait for the war to be over, allowing the dust to settle in the wake of the confusion that prevailed after the capture of the Confederate town where the secret gold reserve had been stored. Most of the southern officers in the area that had known of the gold were now dead, and their northern counterparts were unaware of its existence. Or, at least, that was the abiding hope. If the authorities holding the reins of power at the time lost track of the records of the missing reserve, they were home free.

The Confederate officer became impatient waiting for the Union major to make his move. He could not wait indefinitely and needed cash. He tried to sell a bar of gold at a highly discounted price to an unscrupulous local dealer. He was reported and fatally shot by the authorities during their attempt to apprehend him. The United States marshals contacted officials in Washington. The accountants realized that there was more missing from the gold reserve and began to search for it around the dead lieutenant's last known whereabouts. His dying confession that a Union officer had made off with half of the gold was deemed lacking in credibility and disregarded. The authorities believed at the time he had hidden the other half and that they had found all that there was to find.

The surviving man who knew very well where the remaining 150 bars of Confederate gold reserve had been relocated was the former officer of the Union Army, Major Louis Pilloud. Pilloud was being transported on special assignment by the gunboat, *Kineo*, to the Mississippi to join Union forces, when the crew of the British schooner seized the gunboat and its crew. Since he was a ranking Union Army officer on board a naval operation that he was not part of, he held no particular loyalties to the captured Union sailors.

Major Pilloud was a descendant of French colonists in North America. The Pillouds were now spread out in the northeast, living primarily in Canada, Maine, and Vermont. Pilloud lived in Vermont and had volunteered to fight against the rebellious armies of the southern states because he believed he could amass a great deal of wealth by claiming the spoils of war from the southerners. Louis was promoted swiftly through the ranks of the Union Army because of his guile in battle and would make major within the next month.

Major Pilloud cleverly hid his portion of the gold reserve and let it lie for several more years until he was sure that all efforts to investigate the lost reserve had ended. He then employed a small group of retired soldiers, loyal to him and his brother, to retrieve the valuable load. The 150 remaining bars weighed around 4,200 pounds. They slowly moved the gold north in an effort to relocate the wealth to Canada. Federal officials, however, had been looking for Pilloud's younger brother who had set a notorious record of unpunished crimes and carried a price on his head. They caught up with the Pillouds in Maine. To ensure that the law officials did not accidentally stumble upon their stolen loot, Pilloud temporarily halted their journey into Canadian territory and hid his cache of gold in a remote location in the southwest mountains of Maine. When Federal marshals caught up with the group in the fall of 1869, Pilloud reluctantly turned over his brother's dead body—slain by his own gun. The marshals found nothing else, but honored the terms of the bounty offered on Pilloud's brother and paid his sibling for turning him over to them. They remained suspicious of him and his entourage, however.

With the brutally cold winter months rapidly approaching and the authorities too close for comfort, Pilloud decided to wait before moving the stolen Confederate gold out of Maine. The authorities, for their part, continued to keep Pilloud and his men under surveillance for over a year.

Finally, by September 12, 1871, Pilloud and his loyal band had set up meticulous plans. It was decided that the spoils of war could now be moved out from their hidden location in the mountains of southwest Maine and up into Canada where the major's other partners were waiting. The clandestine shipments arrived in the town of Greenville by two separate horse-drawn wagons—each dispatched with seventy-five bars from a different location. The carts were labeled, "building supplies for the Kineo Hotel project", and loaded onto a steamship in Greenville at 9:30 p.m. The shipment was to be transported sixty miles northward up Moosehead Lake to the Northwest Cove—a remote area on the lake that was rarely traversed. Here the shipment was to be unloaded by seven French Canadian workers and three English assistants and guided by one Iroquois confidant to an undisclosed location in the north woods of Maine. From there, a very secluded route through the wild North Country would allow the disreputable band of thieves to enter Canada. The entire plot had been planned well in advance.

"Did you get the *alternate* crates on the boat?"

"Done."

"You make the exchange later. The weather is getting rough. Let's move it!"

"Yes sir, Major Pilloud. But do you think it wise to pull the *Piscataquis* out of dock at this hour?"

"Look, you idiot. We don't want to attract undue attention to our activities now, do we?"

"No sir, I understand that. But don't you think there's something suspicious about a steamship pulling out of dock this late at night?"

"We can't use the roads beyond here. It's rained all week and they're in poor condition for our wagons. Once we get beyond Kineo, we reach the last outpost of civilization, where some curious onlooker might stumble onto the contents we are actually moving. We can get back to wagon roads once we make the north woods. Our Canadian friends will join us, help divide the load, and escort us through the North Country."

"I'm aware of that, sir. But what about the risk of taking the steamship that far up the lake? There are a lot of obstacles in the water to contend with, Major."

"We'll be fine. I have hired a skipper with a good understanding of the lake."

"And what about suspicious activity being witnessed by locals in Greenville?"

"There are only a few commercial shops down near the docks. Look around you. All the shops are closed at this hour. Don't worry. Besides, once we drop this shipment off with our partners, it won't matter what someone thinks about the *Piscataquis* embarking on a nocturnal voyage. It'll be too late. The goods will be on *our* side of the border by tomorrow afternoon."

"Fine, Major. But look, with the winds being so gusty and all, I was thinking…"

"Enough! I don't pay you to think. Get this boat moving now! I have contacts waiting and deception in mind. You know how I get near the hour of betrayal!"

The journey to the Northwest Cove began uneventfully. The skipper had traveled the entire length of the lake so many times in his life, he knew the location of every obstacle—even at night. Piloting the ship in the dark was no bother to this longtime Maine captain. The cut of money he had been promised to take the *Piscataquis* on the clandestine outing was more than adequate to alleviate any misgivings he might normally have entertained about the shipment of—whatever it was, now securely in the hold—to the Northwest Cove. Keeping his curiosity in check and practicing discretion in such matters was his business.

The ship steamed past Rockwood and Kineo as soundlessly as possible. Major Pilloud could feel the hairs on his neck stand up as he passed the mysterious mountain, silhouetted against the dark skyline by a rather luminous moon. It was the very mountain that his smuggling gunboat had been named after. *So there it is,* he thought, *Mt. Kineo.* He thought back to the day the Confederate officers had isolated him, interrogated him, and then accurately assessed his virtues. It was not hard to persuade him to make a pact with the devil and help in smuggling their gold reserve out of Mississippi. It was no more difficult than when he had betrayed his first partner and snagged his share of the gold.

There was something very sinister about the mountain rising out of the water that night. Pilloud felt as if some unknown spirit were watching them pass by from high up on the mountain…perhaps passing judgment upon him and his crew. He shook off his momentary lapse of common sense, realizing that he had allowed his nerves to get the better of him. Looking back toward the Rockwood shoreline, he regained his focus and concentrated on meeting his shipment schedule.

Nobody appeared to be out and about on the immense lake. Not only was it late, but a storm was whipping up from the northeast. The fetch length in the North Bay from the Northeast Cove to Rockwood was nearly twenty miles and gale force winds began to push up a stack of waves that proved to be both inconvenient for navigation and advantageous in terms of maintaining their cover. The pelting rain and crackling thunder above would certainly discourage potential witnesses from being outdoors. The steamship rocked back and forth in the swells of the main channel and traveled the length of the lake at a far more sedate speed than Pilloud would have wanted. Spitting venom at this unexpected turn of events, he roundly abused the crew. Suddenly, as they neared a small cove, a signal light was observed near the shore. A large candle lantern swung back and forth, indicating the meeting spot. Bounding recklessly through the two-foot waves of the semi-protected cove was a lone canoe. Rowed by one man, it began surfing through the whitecaps toward the steamship. The captain, however, was puzzled. This was not the Northwest Cove. *Hadn't Pilloud said the guide was going to meet them at the Northwest Cove?*

"There he is!" Pilloud barked, spotting the Iroquois guide paddling toward the *Piscataquis*. Amazed by this act of both madness and bravery, the crew watched the Indian guide plunge his canoe through the whitecaps, riding the waves expertly toward the steamship. Without the protection the cove offered, the canoe would surely have capsized. Pilloud felt a strange chill surge down his spine as the evening started to seem too familiar to him—in a way reminding him of the dreadful night when the crew of the gunboat, *Kineo*, had boarded the *Sting Ray*, only to be overtaken by those unruly British sailors.

The disturbing feeling of déjà vu passed as Pilloud reassured himself that while the *Sting Ray* had been a large vessel filled with untrustworthy foreigners, this was simply a harmless Indian guide in a very non-threatening canoe, struggling to meet his obligation in a dangerous storm. Pilloud mocked himself for being so jumpy.

"Ya damn fool Indian!" he yelled out. "Hurry up!"

"Major Pilloud, shall I instruct the crew to guard the perimeter?"

"What for, you idiot?" Pilloud admonished his companion. "Can't you see the crew is busy tending ship in shallow waters and bothersome waves?"

"Sir. I do. In fact, that's what troubles me. Don't you think it strange that your Indian guide is approaching us from the *protected* side of the cove while we are getting beaten around here in the rough water surrounded by rocks?"

"Major Pilloud?" the skipper hollered down from the bridge. "Are you sure this is *your* Indian?"

"Yes, who else would it be?" replied the major, irritated. Then turning to his companion, he asked, "You get the load redistributed and the other hidden behind the bulkhead?"

"Almost done sir, but…"

"There are other concerns?"

"Well frankly, yes, Major," he continued. "I think the captain should move the ship around where the waters are less…"

"Damn it, man! Enough! Don't you understand that the cove is too shallow over there for us to proceed?" Pilloud was furious with his subordinate once again. "Have your men bring the cargo up to the main deck. I want out of this damn storm."

"Yes sir," grumbled his defeated second-in-command as he slipped past the major and down the hatch. No use arguing with Pilloud, but he was going to climb up to the skipper's bridge and verify that this was the correct location. It did not seem to him that they had traveled but a few miles from Mt. Kineo and were nowhere near the Northwest Cove. *Something was not right.* The inclement weather seemed to have the major rattled tonight. He would instruct the men, as ordered, but then seek out the skipper. Something was very wrong.

Despite the pelting rain, the Iroquois guide was now in clear view of the starboard gunnel. He looked up and waved to Major Pilloud. On the port side of the vessel, several men dressed in deerskin hooked the port gunnel and quietly climbed up the side of the ship. Three Iroquois braves lightly scampered over the port rail as the major stared at the Iroquois guide in his canoe on the other side of the ship. Pilloud began to develop an unsettling feeling in his gut once again. Something his ever-cautious deputy commander had just warned him about began to haunt him. Once again, his confidence began to wane.

The skipper yelled down from the bridge once again, "Major...you know that crazy Indian guide of yours doesn't know his directions very well. This is *not* the Northwest Cove, you know? We're still ten to fifteen miles south!"

Suddenly, realization struck Pilloud hard. He was far too intelligent a man to be so careless. He turned sharply to one of the crew and ordered him to go stand watch on the ship's port side. His mind flashed back to the fateful moment on *Kineo*, seven years earlier, when he and his crew had been overtaken by the British. *No! That's impossible!* The crewmate the major had ordered to the ship's port side was never heard from again. For the second time in his career, Pilloud's boat was forcibly overtaken. This time, however, the boarding party was not as civilized as the British.

24

September 12, 1883

It was the fall of 1883—twelve years after the burning and sinking of the steamship, *Piscataquis*, and over two centuries since Kajo the Trader had died and been laid to rest in the central mining chamber on Kineo. The English had now staked a claim to the north woods of Maine and declared it "their territory". Most surviving indigenous peoples had been driven out of their historic lands and Kineo was now devoid of its native inhabitants. The French had claimed the land now called Quebec. It had been little more than a hundred years since the neo-native white man proclaimed independence from his English-speaking brethren who had sent pilgrims to this land in the first place. The latter called the land they now ruled the United States of America.

Greenville was still a relatively new town, populated by subsequent generations of the first white European settlers on the shores of Moosehead Lake. Although living conditions were tough, the opportunities were endless. The first and second grand hotels on Kineo had burned to the ground and been replaced by the third, even grander hotel only a year ago. Its ceremonious opening had been scheduled for the following year. Meanwhile, the timber industry was flourishing, sending billions of logs down the lake to various mills. Steamships still dominated the lake during that period.

The great feud between the northern and southern states had come to an end only eighteen years earlier, leaving a horrific death toll in its wake. Ironically, the Native Americans had come to understand that one of the most compelling reasons for the white man slaughtering his own kind was his perceived right to "own" black men. The very concept was repugnant to the small band of ancestral Native Americans still monitoring the guardian stones of Kineo. The guardian of the black sphere thought to himself: *At least the white men are killing each other, instead of our brothers.*

Summarizing his interpretation of recent history with the other guardians that would listen to him, he said, "First, the European whites come from across the water to steal our territory and fight many wars, killing most of the native peoples. The various European white tribes kill each other to control our lands. Then the white colonizers win the war against the white British and claim our land as theirs. The southern whites enslave the black-skinned Indians from Africa and insist that the land is theirs, only to have their northern white brothers go to war with them to ensure the unity of the nation. These whites I will never understand!"

With the white invaders' increasing activity on Kineo, it was becoming harder to ensure protection both for Kajo's sacred burial grounds and for the area's flint reserves. The beautiful guardian spheres acted as an inspirational reminder to the six guardians of Kineo that the curse of fire was never far away. The need to mine flint, however, had run its course, as most of the compliant Indians had been assimilated into the white man's society. They had access to guns to hunt with as long as they remained compliant and non-threatening.

Ironically, the guardians themselves had no idea what the small band of renegade Iroquois had hidden in the now abandoned central mining chamber and believed they were protecting Kajo's burial site, along with some weapons-grade flint. They had little idea that they were also protecting the secret hiding place of another sought-after treasure in the quest of which the descendants of Major Pilloud would waste another hundred odd years.

PART THREE

Kineo, Present

25

June 18, 1999

Rix was working hard to complete the improvements to the Dentons' bed and breakfast before the day was over. The Hernandez family had just made their trial run for Laura and helped identify a number of problems that still needed to be taken care of. With guests already booked in two of the four bedrooms, she was finally on the verge of realizing her dream. The first guests would be arriving that day on the shuttle at four-thirty p.m.. The cottage had been thoroughly cleaned and the old windows were sparkling. In the process, Laura had seen more spiders than she had encountered in her entire life. You could, she had discovered, vacuum away all the pesky spiderwebs cluttering the windows in the cottage in the morning and by noon, they would be back. All the beds had been made up with brand new sheets and the specially designed emblem of the Denton B&B was embossed on each of the small, fragrant soaps provided. Now that the place was ready for her first paying guests, Laura sat back and took a deep breath. She looked over her hard work with pride, even as the butterflies began to flutter in her stomach. She wished her husband had lived to see this moment.

"All right, kids," she said, as they gathered in the now immaculately clean living-room area. "I want ya'll out of here so the place stays clean till our guests arrive."

"I can't wait to greet them, Mother!" Jenny declared.

"Right," Laura said, studying her childrens' faces one by one. "That reminds me. Before you go, let's be sure ya'll have got it covered."

"Geesh, Mom, not again! We got it," protested Thomas. "You want me home by three-thirty to make sure the golf cart has gas and to be at the dock by four p.m., in case Dougie brings 'em early. Take their luggage up to Room Three and be sure to smile."

"Good, Thomas. Now Jenny and Brandon, when do ya'll have to be home and what are your duties?"

Brandon responded dutifully, but Jenny was distracted and did not answer. The young girl was beginning to drive her family crazy, because Maria had just left with her family and she missed her close friend already. The Lomaxes had also left Kineo for a few days to celebrate Tiffany's seventeenth birthday. So there was no Amanda to play with. Bennington and Dougie had both returned to Kineo that morning, but all of the Lomax ladies would stay over in Manhattan for a while longer. Jenny and Laura missed Amanda a lot. Tiffany, not so much. The older Lomax girl had found many interesting activities at home that better suited her. As a result, she was less keen on returning to Kineo. Being seventeen, blonde, shapely, and wealthy, with an urge to bound around with reckless abandon, had made Tiffany quite popular with certain crowds. *Undesirable* crowds, thought Laura. If the teenager didn't show up till August, that would be just fine with her.

The Denton children left the cottage for a while so their mother could sit back on the porch for a few minutes, sip her Chardonnay, and collect her thoughts before one last pass through the rooms to make sure they were perfect for her guests. Brandon accompanied Jenny to go find other Kineo kids to play with. Thomas, on the other hand, took out the notebook he had stowed under his bed with great care and pulled out a sketch. He jumped into the family golf cart and sped down to the large talus pile on the west side of the mountain.

Hiking up the talus pile for fifteen minutes, Thomas found a large boulder, sat down on it, and began studying the sketch. The paper contained notes on the weird painting he and Brandon had discovered only nine days ago while bouldering the southeast wall. He had been so frightened by the difficulties his younger brother had faced during his attempt to climb down that he had decided not to tell anyone where they had been. Both his siblings had agreed with him. Of course Jenny *had* to tell Maria when she was visiting. *But at least Mom hadn't found out*, thought Thomas. At least he hoped not.

He had drawn a picture of the odd paintings they had found on the wall so that he would not forget what he had seen. Now facing that same wall again, he looked up at the paintings, then down at his drawing again. Then he began tracing the image with his finger and closed his eyes, trying to make sure he had correctly recorded every detail. He did not have time to climb the wall right now, but could make out enough of the images from the ground to jog his memory. In the paintings, there were three men in a canoe. Below it were four parallel lines etched into the mountain wall and highlighted with a reddish paint. At the end of those lines were three short lines that spread out like feet. *That was it*, he realized. *They were two pairs of birds' legs.*

Over the bird's feet designs was a stranger symbol painted in a brownish color. It was a circle, with three lines emanating out from the center. These lines were precisely spaced so that you could draw a perfect equilateral triangle between them. At the end of each line was a small circle. *A ring? Some sort of sphere.* Thomas had no idea what the paintings meant. The markings were quite faded and probably very old. When Dr. Wayne and his students returned to Kineo, Thomas would have him study the sketch. Till then, it was best to keep it hisself. If they found out, the local kids might disturb the place, and it was likely a historic site that should be protected for study. Dr. Wayne had taught the Denton kids to be respectful of archeological finds, and Thomas had developed great respect for the professor.

* * *

The tall, lanky man dressed in black approached Jean Pilloud. In his hand was a report. Pilloud snatched the document from him and began reading it without even acknowledging the other's presence. After a few moments, he looked up, rubbed his chin, walked to the French doors, and stepped out. Then spinning around, he looked at Pierre who was still standing in the large living room of his employer's mansion, holding a brief case full of meticulously arranged files.

"You performed well, Pierre," Pilloud finally conceded, breaking the silence. "This is very good indeed. Come join me for a brandy. It's on the bar. Pour us both one."

Pierre silently complied. *As a well-trained man handling complicated matters should*, thought Pilloud, watching him step out onto the balcony carrying two glasses filled with an amber fluid.

"I never finished telling you how I came to know about the lost Confederate reserve hidden on Kineo, did I Pierre?"

"Non Monsieur," the other man replied, his tone neither curious nor indifferent. It was a terse response, but a polite one that promised a patient hearing. Pierre knew his role and was paid handsomely to stay within its parameters.

"Well, as you may remember, I told you how my great-great-grandfather had served in the American civil war," Pilloud went on, needing no response from the other man who simply sipped his brandy and stared out over the lake. "He was a major in the Union forces. Was fortunate enough to be the only surviving officer of a nasty little incident during which a sizable amount of Confederate gold was discovered while the town that had been seized was being looted and torched. The unexpected loot was subsequently appropriated and transported secretly by a small group of men loyal to my grandfather and hidden in safe Union territory."

Pierre took another sip of brandy, but said nothing, admiring the fury of the whitecaps on Moosehead Lake.

"Enlisting the help of a few trusted colleagues, the major had the gold moved. It remained hidden until the war ended. There was an extensive search for missing assets by both sides. Major Pilloud waited patiently for the situation to stabilize. He continued moving his share of that loot north, closer to home, and succeeded in regrouping the gold in two locations in southern Maine.

"The major reunited his accomplices one night in Greenville. He was close to finally smuggling the gold into Canada. However, he made the mistake of trusting those damn Iroquois in the area. The major's men had the entire load in the steamship, *Piscataquis*, when they were double-crossed just northwest of Kineo. Only my great-great-grandfather survived the slaughter that night, although he was seriously wounded by those heathens, assumed to be dead, and left in the water."

As Pilloud sloshed a large amount of brandy around in his mouth, Pierre continued to gaze intently out at the lake. Then he spoke softly and without emotion.

"I wondered why you paid so many people to locate that sunken steamship."

"And when we finally found it," Pilloud continued, "we dsicovered no gold on board. Burned by those savages, the damn ship had sunk. While the vessel was under attack and his men were engaged in a short, but fierce skirmish, the captain had turned it away from the cove and was heading back into the lake. He had locked the door to the bridge, but the Iroquois broke it down and killed him as well. Then they set the ship ablaze and it sank that night."

"It was no easy task for the scuba divers to find," Pierre offered.

"That local kid you hired, Pierre... Jimbo, was it? Yes, Jimbo. He was foolish enough to tell us he had found that sphere at the Goldman cottage."

"Stupid local. He was so sure there would be treasure on that old steamship."

"Oui, Pierre. He was very disappointed. So when he found the sphere later that week, his hope was rekindled."

"And the missing sphere is the clue you needed to solve the puzzle about where the Iroquois hid your family's gold?"

"Indeed it was, Pierre. How ironic! We searched the bottom of Moosehead Lake for nearly three years and when we finally found the sunken steamship—nothing! Then one of our divers—a local kid, of all people—finds the missing clue we needed and it was right here, all along, on Kineo. We are close now to solving this puzzle. I can feel it!"

* * *

Back at the cottage, Laura finished her glass of wine and got back to work. She found a few windows that had not been properly cleaned.

"Brandon, ugh!" she grumbled, noticing the careless vertical streaks left by her son's attempts to clean the early-twentieth-century rippled glass windows.

"My fault... This is what happens when you delegate work to a nine-year-old!"

Laura was interrupted by the sound of knocking at the cottage door. She could hear Rix Kraft calling up the stairs in his thick New England accent.

"Laura...? Laura, you there?"

"Be right down, Rix!" she yelled down the stairwell, heading over to pick up the check she had written to square his account. She checked her hair in the mirror and noticed that she looked more like a cleaning maid than the elegant, but down-to-earth bed-and-breakfast owner that she now fancied herself. *Ugh! Oh well. At least it's just Rix at the door*, she thought, gliding confidently down the creaky old wooden staircase.

Even in a worn-out tee shirt and faded jeans, her hair pulled back in a ponytail, Laura presented a picture that made Rix suddenly feel inadequate. She handed him the check with a radiant smile.

"You did a superb job, Rix. My guests will certainly be impressed with the molding and paneling restoration. Are ya sure I don't owe ya more?"

"Naw shucks, Laura... We're good," he replied, evidently embarrassed.

"No, seriously. This can't possibly cover all you've done."

"Look, Laura. Just get this place up and running and don't sell out. That's all I want, okay?"

Something in the way he'd said, "Sell out," gave too much away. Laura sensed there was more to his words than he'd intended to reveal. The smile on Rix's face faded as he too realized it. This pleasant discussion was about to take a sudden detour that he wished he hadn't accidentally initiated. *Why do I always say the wrong thing at the wrong time when I'm around attractive women*, he asked himself in exasperation.

"Rix?" Laura's tone was assertive and the look she threw him encapsulated every bit of her determination, along with her innate feminine appeal. She had a way of sending out those dual signals to a man whenever she needed in order to extract a prompt response. "Have a seat, Mister."

Rix complied, feeling a bit foolish at how easily his knees had buckled when she issued her command.

"I'm not selling this cottage," Laura told him. "You know that. What d'ya know that I should know?"

Rix looked at the floor and refused to speak. She gave him a few moments before repeating herself.

"Rix?"

"Damn, Laura!" He looked her in the eye and shook his head. "We all know *they* are trying to buy up the row again. With all the strange stuff happening lately, no one would blame you if you sold out."

"Well, this gal ain't sellin', Mistah," Laura declared, her most pronounced Deep South accent coming to the fore. "And what 'strange stuff', in particular, are you talking about?"

"You remember the day I found that disturbed area in your basement?"

Laura had put aside her memory of that creepy episode. She had had too much to worry about. The unpleasant incident came back to her now. Looking into Rix's eyes, she recognized something else there. Something she hadn't noticed before—fear. *But fear of what?*

"Rix, tell me now!"

Laura listened intently as he told her about the time, many years ago, when he and his brother, Bob, had encountered the elderly Indian woman.

"A witch?" Laura said skeptically.

"No, no... Well, not really. An *Indian* woman with strange..." Rix faltered. "Heck, Laura, this is hard. I know this sounds strange, but just trust me on this—she was one creepy old woman. She spoke with a wisdom that's hard to explain and she knew about things. The fires on Kineo. The flint. She spoke of strange warnings and how the graves of her ancestors had been disturbed by white invaders and how the 'unity of the circle' had been broken and... some angry spirit of the fallen mother moose and..."

"Go on," Laura urged. "I fail to see how your experiences as a kid could have anything to do with me and my cottage now."

"Laura, I saw some things in your basement that day that gave me the creeps. I didn't put it all together then, but the more I thought about the items and the old lady..." He paused and looked at his feet again. "Look, Laura. I think your cottage was constructed on the ruins of an old Indian settlement and there may be an Indian burial site in your side yard."

"Why are you telling me all this crazy stuff *now*, Rix?" Laura asked, annoyance starting to surface. "You know I have guests coming in soon!"

"Yes, I know. I'm sorry." Rix sighed and took a deep breath. "Laura, you know about the death of Gus's first mate—Jimbo?"

"Well, of course! Who doesn't? Rix, what's your point?"

"He may have been the one digging around in your basement."

"What? Why? You said it was local kids making a fort. Didn't you say that?" Laura's voice now held anger.

"Yes, yes. I did, Laura. I wasn't sure then. It might have been kids then. At least I thought so." Rix looked out the door. Reaching into his pocket, he took out a pack of cigarettes, and started to pull one out from it. Laura's gaze was sharp as it bored into his eyes. He immediately got the message and fumbled to put the pack back in his shirt pocket.

"Sorry. I don't know what I was thinking," Rix said in a hushed voice, then looked back at Laura who was still shaking her head.

"Rix?"

Her gaze was so intent that he felt shackled to her sofa by steel chains. Suddenly, he wanted to jump up, but couldn't.

"What's changed to make you think it was Jimbo?" Laura asked him.

"Something he said to me a few weeks before he disappeared. Jimbo used to assist me on job sites sometimes. I had done a lot of the work on the Goldmans' cottage earlier, as you know. Jimbo helped me with that work. Good with a hammer and saw. Actually, he was pretty talented. The Goldmans had me restore the old Wellington place. We were replacing old maple planks in the flooring in the kitchen. Jimbo saw something odd through the floor joists. He dropped my good leather-wrap-handled hammer though the floor joists and said he needed to go under the crawl space to fetch it. I had my hands full and didn't bother to see what he had discovered. After a few minutes, I heard him below, all excited about finding some bizarre black sphere. The incident meant nothing to me at the time. But when I read in the newspaper that Jimbo had been a Wellington descendant, it came back to me. Then yesterday, I ran into Bronson Thurman in Greenville. I asked him how Larry was doing figuring out the reason behind Jimbo's death."

"In your exchange of information, something else clicked, did it?" Laura ventured a guess.

"Right," Rix continued. "The strange fire. The strange way Jimbo died. I don't know, Laura. This is probably all sounding crazy to you, but...I really like you and your family. I just want you to be careful."

"What are you afraid of? Tell me, Rix... You suspect more than you've let on."

Rix sighed. "Yeah, this is the weirdest part, Laura. I was talking to Dougie last week. He was Jimbo's best friend. We were sitting at Kate's tavern on the river and had had one too many drinks. Stories were flowing from our tongues. He told me that he had seen the ghost-like figure of an old Indian woman on a horse at the Wellington place the morning after it burned down. When he described her, I felt a chill down my spine. I swear it's the same woman that scared the bajeesus out of me and Bobby when we were kids."

"So did he really see an old woman on a horse, or are all of you Kineo locals going loco?" She attempted a half-smile, but Rix found no humor in the topic.

"Bobby reminded me of something else that the old Indian witch had said to us as kids."

"Go on, Rix," Laura encouraged softly.

"She said if we ever stumbled onto a black sphere, we should remember that it belonged to the Mohawk and had to be returned. I think that Jimbo found their black sphere hidden under the flooring of the old Wellington place. Who knows how long it had been there?

The Goldmans certainly had no idea. I think Jimbo felt it was his to keep, since he was a Wellington heir."

"And where do you suppose he hid this black thing?"

"*Sphere*, Laura," he corrected. "A black sphere!" Turning his face to look toward the back closet, where the stairs headed down to the Denton basement, he laid the rest of his suspicions on the table.

"Maybe it was hidden in the basement of *your* cottage!"

"Why there?"

"Because no one had been living here for a long time," Rix explained. "Your cottage sat idle for years. And he was collecting other old Indian artifacts. Arrowheads. Implements. Pottery. All safe, until *your* family inherited this place and came up here this summer. He must have moved it before you guys got here. There's more. I saw something else I didn't like when I entered the little chamber beside your foundation wall."

"Wonderful, Rix. Now what?"

"It seemed more like...like...the excavation he was doing into the side of the bank was part of an old Indian burial area."

Laura closed her eyes, trying to take in all she had heard and decide how much was true and how much was just folklore related by a superstitious local hanyman. *Why now*, She thought. *Who needs this crap only two hours before my first guests arrive?*

Laura knew that Dr. Wayne would be back on Kineo soon. Perhaps he could make some sense out of all of this. *Maybe I should give him a call,* she thought.

"You will think I am mad, Laura. But I want to reopen that hole in your basement."

"What?" she blurted out. "Are you crazy?"

＊ ＊ ＊

The Denton children were all back in time to shower and get down to the boat docks. Dougie was depositing a boatload of tourists on Kineo. Thomas and Jenny went up to the shuttle, and the boy quickly decided which of the passengers were the Dentons' B & B guests from Philadelphia. Most of Dougie's passengers had on hiking shorts or golf attire, but two others were wearing long, smart slacks and carried lots of luggage.

"Hi! I'm Jenny. So nice to meet you," the little girl said, nearly jumping onto the boat to greet their guests before Dougie could even give them a hand off the shuttle.

Thomas pulled Jenny back carefully and whispered, "Wait!" to her.

"I'm Thomas and this is my sister, Jenny," he said. "We'll take your bags and give ya a ride to the Denton bed and breakfast."

"You must be Dr. Pembroke and his wife, Jill," Jenny added. "We are *soooo* pleased to have you stay with us!"

Her innocent smile and enthusiasm immediately melted Jill Pembroke's heart, although her husband was a bit overwhelmed by all the sudden attention. Dougie loaded the luggage into the Dentons' golf cart and winked at the siblings.

"Well, Dr. and Mrs. Pembroke, enjoy your stay. You'll find the Dentons to be very hospitable hosts."

Dr. Pembroke slipped a handsome tip into Dougie's hand, and the latter returned to the shuttle. Thomas proudly escorted the first two "paying" guests to their cottage. Jenny launched into a chatty narration about Kineo's fascinating past as they drove their golf cart by the historic buildings at the dock and along Cottage Row.

26

University of Maine; July 1, 1999

Inside Room 212, Rob Landon finished examining the sphere. It had been a few weeks now since he had removed the unusual gem-quality object from the tunnel. He felt relieved that Dr. Wayne had not interrogated him at length about his explorations on the Kineo summit. Rob had no idea what he had in his possession—he just knew it was something very, very special. He had wanted to show it to Dr. Mongeau the very day he had found it, but something about the sphere held him in thrall. Some of it was even clear, like glass. Perfectly spherical in shape, flawlessly polished, and with a faint resemblance to a huge billiard ball in strange hues of purple, violet, and white, it was the most amazing gemstone he had ever seen, the most significant find of his life. But then, he hadn't found it just anywhere.

Rob had followed a spectacular vein of recrystallized quartz, that had filled the fracture transecting a large rhyolitic formation he was studying, to its termination at the base of a wall with a small crevasse. His prying tools had uncovered some loosely packed organic debris that he had easily cleared away to get a better look at the insertion area of the recrystallized zone. It was then that he had made his startling discovery. Several rocks had recently tumbled away in a rockslide and exposed a narrow passageway that had been blocked with large cobblestone-sized chunks of rhyolite. Digging through the mysteriously concealed entrance with his geologic pick and crack hammer, Rob had managed to unearth a sheer face of chalcedony containing an ancient painting on its smoothest surface. It looked like two bird's feet and a peculiar symbol in brown paint—a circle with three lines radiating outward. At the ends of the "arms" were spheres—almost like hands on a three-armed man.

Rob was sure he had stumbled onto something of immense archeological significance and considered returning to the site with Dr. Wayne. Something powerful, however, had drawn him back to the tiny crawl space like iron to a magnet. He was not sure whether it was his own scientific curiosity or something more. Rob was compelled to duck his head under the sharp rocks and worm his way into the tunnel, clearing rocks and debris out of the way. It took nearly thirty minutes for him to advance approximately thirty feet into the dark tunnel. Then he came upon a partially excavated tunnel, with barely enough room to actually stand up and walk. It was dim inside, but Rob had a small LCD light on his key chain and depressed it to life, so he continued to follow the tunnel a little further until it opened into a chamber inside the rock's fracture zone. Rob realized he was inside the bowels of Mt. Kineo, surrounded by walls of rock that had been erected by man.

Had he been carrying enough light to illuminate the chamber, he would have gasped. For without knowing it, he had stopped precariously close to a fracture in the rhyolite that dropped down like an abyss in front of him. His attention was focused, rather, on a large pile of rocks guarding the tiny tunnel he had just crawled through. Rob was about to toss some of the stones aside to make his excursion easier when something about the backlit image blocking his way made him pause. It seemed strangely out of place. He flashed his LCD at the dark image that looked like a small column of rocks. *A marker of some kind*, Rob thought to himself. He felt the rocks and noticed that they were flat and had been stacked in a manner that suggested the handiwork of man. The spacing was not random at all.

Reaching up to feel the top of the uppermost rock on the slab, his hand brushed against a hard cold stone of such smooth texture it disoriented him. Picking it up from its stand, he saw that it was a sphere, about three inches in diameter. Wedged into the cramped space, he tried to examine it in the beam of his small LCD light. It was too difficult to see anything. He was sure, however, that this round object was something of great archeological value. He slowly turned himself around in the mouth of the chamber, barely missing the steep ledge that could have snatched his life away from him, and crawled back the way he had come.

His reverie was suddenly interrupted by the abrupt ringtone of the phone on his desk.

"Yeah, Tonya. There'll be plenty of room for one more bag," Rob told the very sexy young voice on the other end of the phone. A voice so enticing that a young grad student might actually derive pleasure from listening to it, were he not so distracted.

"Just bring it to the vans in the morning, Tonya. I'll make room... Yup. Okay. Gotta go now. 'Bye."

Setting the phone down, Rob lifted the gem-sphere into his hands once again. The object had obsessed him day and night since he discovered it. In fact, he'd performed many tests on the sphere. It was made of simple silicon dioxide. Quartz, he mused. *Just simple quartz.* Well, not quite so simple—it had impurities of iron and other trace metals within it that gave it that beautiful purple hue characteristic of amethyst. That was the thing that intrigued him most. Amethyst was a relatively hard mineral that formed in large hexagonal crystals. It did not form spheres three inches in diameter. *Heck*, Rob thought, *if it had been a softer purple mineral like fluorite, it would be so much easier to give it this shape. But it wasn't fluorite. How long ago had it been shaped by someone? How did early Native Americans find and polish such an enormous crystal like that into a perfect sphere? And why?* Its gem-like quality was quite remarkable.

Rob was aware that there were no known findings of amethyst in the immediate Kineo area. It might have been imported from sites in eastern Canada. The parent rock the sphere was shaped from had to be huge! Rob recalled that amethyst was given a seven out of ten on the hardness scale, with diamonds being ten and talc being only one. As a child, he had had a polishing stone tumbler. He remembered how long it had taken to tumble a stone into a smooth shape from a harder mineral. *How had someone tumbled this amethyst into a three-inch sphere? And how had he crafted it, before the advent of tumblers, into a shape that was so perfectly round and smooth?*

* * *

"I'm telling you, Larry, I can crack this case. I'm coming close."

"What do you want me to do?" the other man complained. "I can't just give orders to have my staff…"

"Damn it! What more do you need?" argued Bronson. "I proved to you it was arson. I proved to you that Jimbo was involved. I linked Jimbo to the Wellington family. And you even admit that Gus appears to be hiding something. And what about *this?*"

Bronson tossed a manila folder down on Larry's desk. The folder clunked down on the desk and some photos slid out. One was a black and white picture of Jimbo and an attractive young woman that did not look like she belonged with a local like him.

"I don't have time for your drama, Bronson. I need details!"

"Connect the dots!" said the other man impatiently. "Look at the photos and connect the facts."

Sheriff Larry Magleton studied the photos.

"So what? Some woman walks up to a truck. No laws broken there, from what I remember of the law."

"That isn't just any woman, Larry. Look closely, man!" Bronson was staring intently at the sheriff. "That's the Pilloud woman…Jean Pilloud's niece, Rebecca."

"And…?" Larry prompted.

"After that shady development fiasco with Bear Pfitzheimer and Rebecca's father, no one—and I mean *no* one—would want to be seen with a Pilloud. Especially not one of our local residents like Jimbo."

"Look Bronson," Larry chastised. "You're not a damn detective. You're a fire inspector with the county. I appreciate your help, but enough! This is my job. Let it alone, will ya? And stay away from the Pillouds. Ya hear me?"

With that, Larry opened the door. Bronson shook his head and walked out. The sheriff was stubborn, with sluggish, if not poor instincts. He was too wrapped up in layers of detailed analysis to see the overall picture unfolding in front of him. Bronson worked off intuition. He flew by the seat of his pants, but was certainly closing in on something. He was going to dig deeper into the Pillouds' affairs. He was sure there was more to the connection between Jimbo and Becky than met the eye.

The photos he had uncovered of the two were disturbing. A security camera, installed a week earlier at the new bank in Greenville, had captured them together. No bank in the area had ever had such a camera until this summer—no wonder neither party was aware they were being filmed.

The film recorded Becky pulling up in her black Lincoln Navigator with her son, Jacob, secured firmly in his car seat in the back. She left her vehicle and flipped back her designer shades on to the top of her dyed black hair. She wore black leather pants and a tight sweater. Gold chains were draped around her neck. Becky walked into the bank and withdrew a large sum of money. She methodically stuffed the crisp new twenties into a sealing envelope and walked nonchalantly toward a beat-up old Chevy pick-up in the parking lot. Jimbo's pick-up.

The security camera showed the driver's window of the Chevy slowly roll down. A puff of smoke rose out of the window and dissipated above the truck. Bronson found the incongruity captured by the tape unsettling: Becky, a wealthy aristocrat decked out in fine jewelry, walking purposefully to a deadbeat vehicle with a poor fishing mate for a driver—a local loser, from her snobbish perspective.

If that image wasn't incongruous enough, the recorded frames capturing Becky tossing the envelope stuffed with twenties in through the open truck window certainly caught one's attention. The exchange was quick and furtive, taking place at the back of the bank parking lot where nobody was around to witness it. And it certainly would have gone unnoticed, had it not been for Phillip Brinkman—the bank security consultant who was still adjusting the angles of the cameras that week and checking the frames carefully. Luckily for Bronson, Phil knew the fire inspector from a recent fire at a local bank and he realized that these frames were suspicious and inquired to him if he should report them to a supervisor.

The last frame showed the Chevy pick-up driving past the tiny security camera mounted on the side of the bank. Jimbo's window was still down as it passed the camera. The young man looked out the window and flicked his spent cigarette onto the parking lot below. The image of his face was unmistakable. When the newspaper ran the article of the strange burning/drowning victim, the photo of Jimbo's face had not registered immediately with Phillip. It was only a week later that he made the connection and called Bronson for advice. His spirit of inquiry invigorated by the security frames, the state fire inspector found himself moving in a new investigative direction. Aware of Larry's skepticism about his efforts, Bronson waited till he had amassed more proof. He was closing in on something big. He could feel it. Call it intuition. Bronson knew he would have to work around Larry.

* * *

"It's a lot of hard work, Gus," Kate said. "You never get a break when you own a tavern. Everything we have is in this place."

It was still early in the evening—only around six p.m. Gus had arrived at the tavern earlier than usual that night. He took out a match and started to twirl it. Then he looked out the window at Moose River. The shimmer of moonlight on water was something that he never tired of admiring. He continued to chew his cigar and was soon lost in thought.

"You gonna light that big blasted thing or not?" Kate broke his trance.

"Oh hell, I dunno. Ha!" he responded gruffly. "I hope fishing is good this week. I'm off to a bad start this year. Losing Jimbo sure was a hit."

"How'd that young Denton boy do for you?"

"Oh, ya mean Thomas? He's a nice young man. Works hard too. Never thought a southern city boy would pick up deep-water line fishing so quickly. But he only sat in for me for a week or two. Then I picked up my new mate—Billy. As you know, Billy barely passes for help."

"You like the Dentons?" she asked.

"Sure. I mean they seem like respectable folks. Jenny... That girl is sure a sweet little thing."

Gus started to strike the match, then stopped, fidgeted with it, and dropped it on the table. "Heck, I would have liked to have had a daughter like her."

Kate smiled and walked off as a new patron came in. She greeted him with the offer of a drink. Gus drifted off, remembering how Jenny would come to the dock and see Thomas off the boat, then ask his employer if she could come aboard. Although the only girl around, she sure loved to hang out with the boys when the boat came to dock. Jenny would ask questions about the fish they caught.

God, can she ask questions, he mused. *Why do the fish bite the fake metal things? Where did the blood on the deck come from? Who caught the biggest fish? Are you going to actually eat those?* Gus started smiling, thinking of her endless questions. He would have her sit in the trolling chair and tell her great fishing stories as Thomas finished washing the deck down. Then she would leave with her brother. She would wave goodbye and tell Gus she would see him the next day. Sometimes, his harsh language and snappy tone got out of hand and hurt her feelings. Gus was not refined around little girls, or ladies, for that matter. But Jenny always saw past his gruffness into his heart and forgave him. He was basically a lonely man with a lot of history to share. *Yes, how nice it would have been to have had someone like her as a daughter*, he thought.

At the bar was the tall thin man, Pierre. Kate thought she remembered him from somewhere, but could not put her finger on it. The man ordered whisky straight up in a shot glass. His voice was careful, trying hard to conceal the accent. Kate was too sharp to miss it. *French.* She looked at his black jacket and black leather gloves and wondered: *Where in the hell did this guy come from? Polite enough,* she thought, *but still...something was not right about him.* He had pulled out a piece of paper, staring at a list of names, but kept it close to him at all times. Kate strolled back to the end of the bar where Gus was slamming down a drink and still chewing his cigar. Finally, he struck the match, lit the cigar, took one puff, and let the smoke out slowly.

"What's eating you tonight, Gussie?" Kate asked with genuine concern.

"Kate..." he paused. "I know it's only been a short time since Jimbo died, but...do you know if he was doing drugs, or smuggling, or anything?"

Kate drew close, and bent over the bar to make sure the conversation stayed private. A good bartender understands the importance of respecting the confidentiality of her regular patrons. She was in the business, after all, of selling false security through intoxication. Despite their long-time friendship, Gus allowed his eyes to wander down to Kate's more than generous assets, now scrunched between her arms as she leaned on the bar. Then he continued.

"I hadn't told anyone before, Kate," he said, unburdening himself to her, his eyes still fixed lower on her body than even he thought proper. "It's to do with some damn sphere thing."

"What are you saying, you old fool?" she said, then reached over, gripped his chin, and turned his face up, making him meet her eyes. "What sphere?"

Pierre sat nearby in his retro black glasses. He finished his drink and was about to place his gloves back on his hands, when suddenly, something made him pause. Something he had just overheard. He continued to slide the gloves over his powerful fingers, but his movements were now slow and deliberate as he tuned in to the conversation he was eavesdropping on.

Without turning to face Kate and Gus to his right, Pierre Laroux was suddenly oblivious to everything around him but the conversation the two were having.

"Hush! Damn ya, woman," Gus erupted. "Aww hell! It's probably nothing."

A few minutes later, Pierre stood up from the bar and walked out. He took out his cell phone and connected with his wealthy employer only twenty miles away.

"Oui. He said, a *sphere*... Non. Nothing more. Non... It was the way he said it, Monsieur... I understand... I will follow him until we know... Merci... Bonsoir."

* * *

The small, determined woman walked up the spiral staircase. She stood about five foot and a few inches and tipped the scale at an even 112 pounds. Her jet-black hair was pulled back in a tight ponytail and her face was heavily made up. There was a cruel curve to her lips, further enhanced by the dark purplish lipstick that defined them. A small boy squirmed relentlessly under one arm; Jacob badly needed a nap. In her other hand, the woman clutched papers. Nearing the top of the staircase, she spotted Michelle, the younger housekeeper, and handed the child to her in the manner of a quarterback dishing a football to the star running back. She could hear her uncle talking to someone—probably Pierre—in the upstairs library. She didn't bother to knock as she entered his world.

"Here it is, Uncle," she said without hesitation.

"I don't care! Keep following him. We need to know," Jean Pilloud was barking into the phone as he waved Becky in and motioned for her to sit.

* * *

Becky placed her hand over her mouth, realizing she had interrupted his phone conversation. Her face flushed as she sat down in the nearest chair, and her small body sank deep into the plush leather. She truly admired her uncle and often fantasized that she had been born into *this* family instead of her own. She was, after all, a much shrewder businesswoman than his mousy daughter who lived overseas.

"If it is the sphere... Reclaim it... Yes. By whatever means you deem appropriate!"

Placing the phone softly back into the cradle, Jean turned to his niece and his tone dropped in intensity like turning a dimmer switch on a light fixture. "Sweet Rebecca..."

"I have it, Uncle Jean," Becky grinned, as if she had a trophy in her possession. "Look: the second closing. Done!"

"And in what fictitious name did we close the second property?" he inquired.

"Jackman Family Trust," she winked at him.

"Good. That makes two. Now if Pierre can get that Denton woman to realize what a generous offer we've made her."

"Where is Pierre, Uncle Jean?" she asked with more than passing interest. Since leaving Bear, Becky had become increasingly involved in family dealings and had become interested in her uncle's "go-to guy".

Jean had forbidden Pierre from seeing his niece; he understood better than anyone what a dangerous man Laroux really was. Some things were best left secret—even within the family.

"Pierre is on an important assignment for me, dear," Jean explained. "We'll see him for dinner tomorrow. Now, where's Jacob?"

"With Michelle." She brushed off the question swiftly. "Was that Pierre on the phone with you as I walked in?"

"You need not concern yourself with such matters. Now...where is Jacob? I do wish to show him my new hunting dog. Please bring him to me."

As Becky complied and left the room, Jean Pilloud, President of Kokadjo Timber Company, studied the documents she had delivered to him. Sure enough, the second cottage had been purchased. Becky was an asset to his company. His own daughter had never amounted to much in life. This had disappointed Jean immensely. All Jean Pilloud's wife had been able to provide him with was a mild-mannered daughter. He would never have a son to carry on the legacy of the great Pilloud lineage. Certainly, his Green Peace-obsessed daughter wasn't going to get his hard-earned fortune! Liberals! Jean grimaced at the thought of what his own flesh and blood had become. Becky and Jacob would inherit his wealth, not his own daughter. *Let her rot in France with her mother!*

Turning the pages of the documents, he could see that his niece had carried out his instructions to the letter. She was organized and efficient. In time, Pilloud might just get all of those pesky owners off the historic peninsula so he could bring his ultimate plan to fruition.

* * *

Dr. Wayne closed the door to his office and locked it. It was getting late, and he had two university stretch vans, full of students' gear, set to go to Kineo in the morning. The combined archeology and geology trip had been a success with the students earlier this summer. Les and Max had made several startling discoveries during their two-week stay. The younger professor was excited about returning. Laura's son had sent him photographs of some paintings he and his siblings had discovered on the cliffs of Kineo. His research on the characters puzzled him. Then there was the awkward stirring he felt when he thought of Thomas's mother—Laura.

Walking out into the hallway, he shut off the lights and started for his car. Then something caught his attention. He turned around and saw that a light had been left on in Room 212, where the graduate assistants had office space. It looked like Rob Landon had left his office light on. *Strange*, thought Max. *But then again, things have not been the same between Rob and me since the last trip.*

Landon had gone back to being publicly cordial to Dr. Wayne after the "episode" on the mountain. Yet, Max could not shake off the feeling that the young man was hiding something.

"Evening, Rob," Max said, walking through the door to the grad students' office. "Dang, son, it's late. We leave early in the morning. Whatcha doing?"

At the sound of the professor's voice, Rob quickly slipped an object back into his lower desk drawer. With the young man's back turned to him, Max could not quite make what it was, but the furtive gesture immediately placed Max on high alert. More importantly, it triggered the memory of the last time he had seen Rob act this way—on the summit of Kineo. *What was it that he was hiding*, Max wondered.

"Yeah, Doc. I know. Was making sure I had everything i needed packed to go," Rob replied.

Max hesitated, pondering whether he wanted to open up a can of worms this late. It was a mistake not to have questioned him days ago.

"Anything you want to discuss, Rob? I mean, you know, from our last trip?"

"Oh, you mean about… Well dang, Doc," Rob fumbled briefly, rising to his feet. "I know I got carried away in that volleyball match and all, but I won't an ass this year."

The two men faced each other. The younger man's breezy smile could not quite disguise his underlying deceitfulness. Max's face was expressionless. He considered pressing the issue.

"It's all good, Dr. Wayne. Come on. I'll walk you out."

Max grinned reluctantly and elected to let it go for the time being. It was too late to get into it and they had to get up so early in the morning.

"Don't forget your backpack Rob."

"Right." Rob hesitated and glanced down at the lower drawer thinking to himself, *Great. Now I have to get here 30 minutes early than the rest to get the gem sphere.* Then looking at Max, "See you in the morning…"

"Bright and Early," Max replied. He walked to his car, unlocked it, and watched the young man slide into his yellow Mustang.

Max drove off first in his silver Saturn, then pulled around the block as soon as he could, checking his mirror the entire time. Seeing that Rob had not followed him, he parked in the lot next to the building and snuck back to the side door to confirm that the student had actually left. The parking lot was clear. No yellow Mustang. Max bolted from his car, slipped his keys into the lock, and jogged up the stairs to Room 212.

He looked back over his shoulder with a feeling of emerging paranoia as he opened the door to Rob Landon's office—Graduate Student Assistant: Geology.

"This is silly," Max scolded himself. "Geesh, I'm a professor!"

He made his way to Rob's desk and hesitated a second or two as he thought about the implications of snooping in one of the graduate student's drawers. His fingers tightened on the handle. He gave it a big yank and opened the lower desk drawer.

27

Gus went to bed early that evening. It had been a tiring day. He was getting too old to work so hard for so little. Rummaging around in his bedside table, he found an old bracelet that his wife used to wear. Gus had kept it in this drawer for years. He hadn't really thought of getting it out in a long time. Looking at the bracelet, he noticed that it was silver. He thought of Jenny Denton. *Didn't she have on a silver ring on her fingers the other day? Sweet little Jenny. How was it that the little gal could overlook my annoying habits?* There were certainly many vices that Gus had developed over the years. So many, in fact, that his wife had got tired of his lifestyle and left him one winter for a more sensible and stable man from Bangor. A businessman. *College-educated bastard!*

Gus looked at the silver bracelet and placed it on the top of his nightstand. Then he lay back on the bed and looked up at his ceiling. Life wasn't so bad. He had a metal roof over his head, albeit with leaks that allowed a few drops of rain in from time to time. He owned his own trolling boat with two four-stroke Honda engines that kicked out a total of 400 horsepower. And he had the latest bottom-sensing deep-trolling equipment.

Still, he felt a bit cheated in life. A sense of loneliness and incompleteness pervaded his evenings, sending him often to the tavern for a bottle and the company of his friend, Kate. He and his wife had never had kids. Thomas and Jenny were such fine kids. Gus wondered if he would have made a good father. Picking up the silver bracelet again, he thought of innocent little Jenny. *She might like this damn thing.* It would look better on her wrist than sitting in his drawer. Tomorrow, he would give it to her. He could picture her smile at him and giving him a hug as though he were a favorite old grandpa.

Gus went to bed, thinking of the things he had been. A sailor. A fisherman. A soldier. A husband. A drunk. Things he should have been. Things he could have been. *Why were all the good ones like Kate already taken*, he lamented to himself. *Amazing how whiskey brings out the philosopher in me.* He continued to daydream.

His mind went on wrestling with life's many disappointments until he felt himself succumb to sheer fatigue. He had to get up early the following day to set the boat up. He had clients from Michigan to entertain. The previous day, he had hooked a ten-pound brookie; and the day before that, he had hit a twenty-pound togue. Gus finally fell asleep, dreaming of being out on the big seas, owning a swordfish boat, and chasing the really big fishes off the coast of Maine.

Outside, a figure in a black leather jacket crept around the old fishing camp from the right. Gus's dog caught the scent and went investigating. Milo emitted a few low warning snarls, then slowly approached the intruder. Pierre held out a ziplock baggie, slowly withdrew a piece of meat from it, and tossed it over by the old basset hound. Milo gobbled it up without hesitation. Gus, in his drunken stupor, had forgotten to feed Milo again.

Pierre talked to the dog in a soothing voice and sent another morsel flying his way. Soon, Milo and the intruder were friends. Then suddenly, the dog began to feel queasy and tired. He staggered off to a corner where his legs buckled under him and he crashed, sleeping the rest of the night away, his senses bludgeoned into oblivion by the drug with which the meat had been spiked.

Pierre had no problem entering the old wooden residence, since Gus, like most Maine folks, did not lock his house at night. This rural area simply did not have any crime to speak of; everyone trusted his neighbor. Pierre, unfortunately, was not a neighbor. The intruder stole through the kitchen like a cat stalking an unwary mouse and heard Gus snoring loudly in the other room. *This was going to be easy*, Pierre thought, *perfect. The boss does not like complications.* Methodically, he opened every drawer to every piece of furniture there was in the house, but discovered nothing of interest. He wanted to get in and out as fast as possible.

Pierre slipped into the snoring man's bedroom, wondering if the bedside stand might contain the item he had come for. Slowly, he crept alongside the bed, still measuring the depth of Gus's snores. Yes, the old fool was out stone-cold drunk. Pierre could smell the stench of whiskey on him. This was just too easy for a professional of *his* caliber. Pierre noticed the silver bracelet still lying on the stand and snatched it up. Then he slowly slid the upper drawer open and began groping inside as quietly as possible.

Gus rolled slowly to the side so his face was only two feet from Pierre's hand. The snoring stopped momentarily and the intruder paused, remaining utterly still and calm as he watched the other man to make sure he did not inadvertently awaken him. Killing people was always so messy. He was paid to resolve problems with minimum fuss, leaving no evidence. Snuffing people out was the very last resort and only in the most desperate of situations. This was a routine item-extraction mission.

Once Gus began snoring loudly again, Pierre reached inside the drawer and moved some papers aside. Then his fingers bumped into a soft cotton bag with a large, heavy object inside. It felt like a large glass ball. *There it is*, he thought. Slowly, he began hoisting the glass sphere out of the bag, rubbing it gently.

Oui, oui, this is it—no doubts at all. The boss will be pleased at yet another task handled impeccably.

Pierre had pulled the obsidian sphere free from the drawer when, suddenly, he felt a surprisingly powerful hand clamp down on his wrist.

* * *

Thomas lay sleepless in bed. He had sent the letter to Dr. Wayne, along with the photographs and sketches of the painting from the side of Mt. Kineo, but had not heard from him since. Earlier, when he and his mother had called Dr. Wayne at the university and described the painting, the professor had sounded excited. Thomas knew that he would be arriving in the morning and the thought of the painting's possible historical significance kept him wide awake.

When the boy had first mentioned the subject to his mother, he was surprised by the eagerness with which she had offered to help him find Dr. Wayne's address at the university and contact him. She had even helped mail the information to him. The professor had ended up calling Laura back when he received the package, but did not ask to speak with her son. Thomas had asked his mother what Dr. Wayne had to say and been informed that the professor was very perplexed about the painting and had to research its significance. Laura had received no further details. *Apparently*, Thomas thought, *the phone call between my mother and Dr. Wayne devoted more time to social chitchat than to the important issue at hand—my discovery.*

* * *

The struggle had been a valiant one. Pierre was actually quite taken aback by the old man's strength, given how overweight he was. Although the Frenchman was an expert in the martial art of Aikido, finding himself in the awkward position of having to hold a valuable glass sphere in one hand, while the other was trapped in another man's vice-like grip was not a situation he had anticipated. Aikido employs effective self-defense techniques which use the aggressor's momentum to advantage and reverse that energy against him, usually breaking bones and tearing ligaments in the process. Gus was not an attacker in motion. He was a startled, semi-intoxicated, and livid seaman, his fingers locked in a death grip on some idiot's wrist.

Pierre had considered clunking Gus over the head with the obsidian sphere, then thought better of it. His stolen treasure which looked like glass to him, might shatter on impact. In this brief moment of indecision, Gus had rolled out of bed and faced the dark, thin intruder.

"Who the hell are ya?" the seaman roared, his breath spewing the combined smell of cigars and alcohol from earlier in the evening. "What the hell ya want?"

Still clutching the guardian stone, Pierre considered his options silently. The very next moment, Gus's hands had lunged around his neck, placing him in a painful chokehold.

"Remove your hands...sir...and I'll explain," Pierre coughed out with difficulty.

"You came for the black sphere, didn't ya?" Gus growled. "I knew it! I can tell by your tiny wrist and Frenchie accent that you ain't much of a man! You better tell me what the hell's goin' on before I break your scrawny pencil neck in half!"

Pierre suddenly turned cold as ice. Irritated with himself for being careless enough to compromise his mission, he slowly raised the hand holding the sphere.

"Here, then," he choked out. "Just take it."

With the intruder apparently putting up no resistance to Gus's mighty grip, the seaman let down his guard. Without thinking, he released the other man's wrist to accept the sphere. A sudden twist, followed by an upper arm knocking Gus's hand away from his opponent's neck served as the prelude to a series of quick jabs that struck the seaman in the sternum, throat and groin. Gus never regained consciousness.

28

Early the next morning, three white vans pulled out of the parking lot of the University of Maine. It was still dark, but dawn was not far away. Each van carried that septic, institutional look that all fleet vehicles bear when mass-purchased at a bargain rate. Professor Les Mongeau drove a stretch van carrying, primarily, his geology students, while the white van that Dr. Max Wayne drove carried his archeology students. The third van was filled with supplies and equipment. Rob Landon had volunteered to pilot the "supply wagon", as Gary Micnick called it. Julie Walters had agreed to accompany Rob in the third van. The young man was quite happy with this arrangement; Julie was bringing some climbing gear that would come in handy and he needed to talk to her in private. But could he trust her? Rob was not sure if he should tell her why he needed the gear.

The Kineo trip earlier in the summer had allowed primarily graduate students to join up. But its resounding success had persuaded the professors to open it up to both graduate students and top undergraduates from each program. Rob was completing his work under Les Mongeau in geology while Margo had just been accepted in the doctoral program in archeology under Dr. Wayne.

This had caused a bit of friction between the two departments. Margo had originally transferred to the University of Maine to complete her Master's in geology under Dr. Mongeau. She had completed the program, but lost interest working under the pompous, often sexist professor from Louisiana. Through the joint program field trips, Margo had to got to know Dr. Wayne rather well and found his archeology and Native Populations Studies program much more interesting than the subject she was involved with. The research on Kineo, in particular, combined her two academic interests and provided the grounds for the transition she needed to move away from her connection with Les Mongeau.

Les was quite the chatterbox in the lead van talking to the young and attractive Tonya Collins, who was making the trip as one of the "undergraduate stars". Tonya was one of those girls who dumbed herself down for the guys, but was certainly no dummy. She wore dazzling outfits and talked of shopping and getting her nails done. Her blonde hair was so perfectly colored and teased that she often looked like a catwalk model. The graduate students did not take her seriously and figured that she survived off of extra credit. They could not have been more wrong about Tonya; there was nothing unintelligent about her 4.0 GPA, 1470 SAT, and 149 IQ.

Max drove the van that brought up the rear of the academic procession. The red-haired jokester, Gary Micnick, chose to sit in the back of the van next to poor Margo McKinnon who was doing her best to ignore his unrelenting stream of snide comments. Even though she did not appreciate his humor, the rest of the passengers in the van laughed out loud as he played to his audience, doing wonderful imitations of both Dr. Mongeau and Dr. Wayne. Since Julie and Rob were not around to defend themselves, they became the next target of his sophomoric impressions. In the front seat, Max seemed to be off in another world. He was still thinking about the purple sphere he had found in Rob's drawer the night before. He was also bothered by one of the photos of the wall painting that Thomas had sent to him. None of it fit. Then he suddenly realized who he should call when she awoke.

* * *

As the sun appeared on the horizon, hours after the fateful visit of the strange man in the black leather jacket, the old basset hound shook off his drowsiness and began to howl. Still a bit queasy from being drugged the night before, Milo could, nevertheless, sense something was very wrong inside his master's home. He continued to howl as flames began to engulf the small home along the fisherman's cove.

It had taken two hours for Pierre to remove evidence from the rooms and call for assistance from the Pilloud estate. But he had subsequently set the delayed fuses and made his getaway by boat at 4:10 a.m.. At 4:30 a.m.—time for the delayed fuses to set off—but his assistant, Boxer, realized that he had connected one of the ignition wires improperly, and the mighty fire he had arranged to set off had not ignited. Pierre was furious and had sent Boxer to manually start the fire.

The Frenchman's assistant, one of Pilloud's estate guards, was not a particularly competent covert operator. It was nearly five a.m.. There was barely time to complete the mission and return unnoticed. If the idiot screwed up this task too, he might consider disposing of his assistant as well.

"Don't screw it up this time!" Pierre warned Boxer in a menacing voice.

The Frenchman watched from a safe distance. He was not happy about sending this amateur back to the scene of the murder in the early hours of dawn. Finally, at 5:05 a.m., his assistant returned, rubbing a large sore place on his upper forearm where he had burned himself badly. The two men watched the fire roar into a furious blaze. By 5:30 a.m., the remains of any incriminating evidence Pierre may have failed to remove were consumed by a hungry inferno with a voracious appetite.

* * *

Kineo: nine a.m.

Patricia Wellington was an elegant old woman of seventy-six whose smart sweaters and scarves made her look younger. Although she had been born in Canada, her family was proud of its British lineage. She had a remarkably sharp wit and a keen memory. Patricia had chosen to stay in the Rockwood-Greenville area, even though most of her family and children had long since moved away. The Wellington name had once been a very distinguished one in the Kineo area. Now Patricia lived alone in Greenville in a beautiful old Victorian home on a bluff overlooking the east side of Moosehead Lake.

Today, she was on the *Katadhin*, the steamship from Greenville, where she had enjoyed a nice breakfast before heading to Kineo. Patricia was one of the leading philanthropists supporting the historic ship and the local historic society. The old relic from an earlier period of Moosehead Lake history was more than just a fancy boat for tourists. Patricia enjoyed riding the *Katadhin* to Kineo, because it reminded her of who she was, who she had been and of what Kineo had been.

Attending the Kineo docks, Dougie caught the bowline and securely tied it to the metal bollard in order to pull the large steel and wooden ship snug against the piers. Patricia disembarked from the ship and walked over to him. She told him that she might end up staying on Kineo longer than the *Katadhin* was visiting (typically an hour for the tourists) and wanted to know if his shuttle service would be available to take her back to Greenville if she missed the boat. Dougie informed her that the Kineo shuttle only took passengers back and forth between Rockwood and Kineo. If she wanted to get back to Greenville, she would have to get back to the *Katadhin* on time.

Gently placing her hand on Dougie's shoulder, Patricia slipped him a twenty and suggested that he personally ensure that she was back on the steamship "on time". Dougie, who was very familiar with the Lomax way of providing incentives, graciously accepted the tip and assured her that if he failed to get her back on the *Katadhin* in time, he would personally shuttle her all the way back to Greenville.

"Where are you going, ma'am?" he asked politely, wanting to be confident to know where to find this sophisticated lady when the time came.

"Try the Dentons' bed and breakfast, son. If I am not aboard in one hour, I will be there."

Then Patricia began walking along the crushed stone path to Cottage Row. This was a path she had taken more than a thousand times in the past.

* * *

"Becky, damn it!" Bear exploded on the phone. "He's my kid too. I've a right to see him!"

"Of course, Brutus darling," Becky retorted with venom, "but *not* today. You'll have to schedule an appointment to see him tomorrow."

"No. Today is *my* day. We agreed. I'm tired of this crap!"

"Aww Bear," she mocked him. "You know the order says you must schedule an appointment at least forty-eight hours in advance and *you* didn't now...*did* you? Let me fetch Uncle Jean's attorney and let you two boys work it out. Bye, Honey Bear."

Before Becky could hear Bear's explosion of expletives, she had closed her cell phone. Bear paced the room, debating what to do next. He lacked the legal connections he used to enjoy once. Ever since the incident that had implicated him in the affair involving Becky's conniving uncle, his relationships with professionals had deteriorated. He wished Laura had lived next door—he would have asked for her advice. But she had her own issues to deal with. Slamming his huge fist down on the table, he glared out the door and decided he was going to take matters into his own hands today.

"Screw Becky Pilloud and her evil bastard uncle!" he muttered.

* * *

The first knock on the door sounded confident. One snappy strike, then a long pause, followed by another, slightly louder knock.

"Mrs. Denton, are you home?"

"Hello," responded a little voice from within. "I'm Jennifer. Who are you?"

"Wellington. Patricia Wellington, young lady. Is your mother home?"

"Oh, hi!" Jenny had recognized the name. "Come in. I'm just making cookies for guests upstairs. Mom's downstairs."

"Oh, I see." Patricia Wellington had a very serious topic to discuss with Laura, but the sweet and innocent voice of the cute thirteen-year-old briefly distracted her from her agenda. She stepped inside and looked around curiously. "You know who I am, dear?"

"Why, of course," Jenny giggled. "I know *everyone*! You used to own the Goldman place that burned to a crisp. And you made those calls to my mom that made her stare off into space afterward."

"I did? I see." Patricia Wellington studied Jenny's face. There was nothing mean or cynical in her comment. The young teenager was simply describing it the way she saw it.

"Mind if I have a seat while you summon her?"

"Not at all," Jenny beamed and took her hand. "In fact, you must sit in this chair. It's my favorite and it's sooo comfy! I recommend it to all my guests."

Jenny quickly strode off to find her mother down in the basement with Rix. Patricia repeated Jenny's words to herself..."Mom's downstairs." *Oh no! This may be worse than I thought.*

She looked around the room and was impressed with all that Laura and Rix had done with the old cottage. Constructed in 1906, it had the architectural character of the late Victorian Queen Anne style. It had once been a beautiful summer cottage. Then with Kineo falling on hard times, the structure had been allowed to fall into total disrepair. The last time Patricia had been in this cottage was over thirteen years ago. Some furnishings were still needed to make it all work together, and Laura's curtains did not match the period of architecture. *Oh my, the curtains clash with the pattern in the sofa upholstery, but...Laura is young*, Patricia thought to herself, *and all and all, she has made admirable progress. A shame that she would have to abandon it all now...*

"Hello Mrs. Wellington," Laura said, interrupting Patricia's silent critique of her remodeling efforts. "We finally meet." She approached the haughty-looking woman. "No, please stay seated. To what do I owe this honor?"

"Mrs. Denton. I will be brief and to the point."

"Yes. You always are," Laura quipped.

"Your family is in danger. It would be best if you sell this place and move on."

"Okay, Mrs. Wellington! I'm tiring of your mysterious warnings. We love this cottage and we're not selling it. So now, what did you come to tell me?"

Patricia sighed. "I had heard you were stubborn. But that is fine. I will tell you my story, Mrs. Denton."

"Laura," corrected the other woman.

"Fine. Laura," Patricia continued. "And for God's sake, call me Patricia, then. I owe you explanations, but I warn you, this will take some time."

Laura sent her kids outside. Rix came running up from the basement, shouting, "Laura, I found it! I found it!" Then he saw the two women sitting there in their chairs, looking like they were in an Indian stand-off.

"Oh, sorry...didn't know you had company."

"Rix darling!" Patricia raised her voice as he turned away. "Don't you remember me?"

"Ya'll know each other?" Laura looked confused.

"Everybody knows everybody in these parts, Laura." Patricia smiled knowingly at Rix. "Why don't you sit with us, Rix Kraft? What I am about to tell Laura may involve you as well, since you are, undoubtedly, the one digging around in her basement."

Rix and Laura shot surprised glances at each other.

"Yes, I know about the secret basement," Patricia Wellington continued. "Be careful what you seek on Kineo. You may not always enjoy what you find."

29

Moosehead Lake; Afternoon, of July 2, 1999

"Kate and her husband made a positive identification from the remains," Deputy Harris informed Larry Magleton. "They're pretty upset. I'm going to drive them home."

"Go," Larry dismissed her with a wave of his hand.

"It looks like an accident," Deputy Carlson said to the sheriff.

"Yup. I agree. Take the body away and get these nosy people out of here," Larry ordered.

"An accident?" Bronson Thurman said incredulously. "An *accident?*"

"Calm down, Bronson."

"I know what it looks like, but both Gus and Jimbo by fire? Come on now! You know this is suspicious."

"Could be a coincidence," Larry muttered unconvincingly.

"Damn it, Larry! I know you don't believe that. Why is it you never act on your instincts? I know you feel it. Are you deliberately avoiding the facts here?"

"Shut up, Bronson!" the sheriff snapped back, his fingers balling into a tight fist.

"You wouldn't be reckless enough to hit me, Larry," Bronson told him sternly. "I'm twenty years your junior and could clean your clock—I'm mad enough at you right now to actually do it too!"

Larry's face turned fire-engine red, but he considered Bronson's warning, uncoiled his fingers, and turned to walk away from the brewing altercation.

"Don't walk away from me, Sheriff. I want to know what's up with you. Now!"

Larry stopped dead in his tracks. He shook his head and spun around to face Bronson.

"Jimbo was in deep trouble… You're right about that," Larry admitted. "I did check out your theories. You're a good investigator, Bronson. *Too* good, maybe. Jimbo was tied to the Pillouds, and that is not a family we want to mess with."

"But they may be implicated in more than just arson, Larry… We're talking possible premeditated murder!"

"I know, damn it! Stop tellin' me *my* job, fireman!"

"You're gun-shy, Larry, and have been since the day you took this job," Bronson said in a baiting tone. "What gives?"

The other man looked at the burned-out ruins of Gus O'Malley's home and marina and the red warning tape strung up by his deputies.

"Poor bastard," he mumbled. "He was a decent guy, they tell me. A good fisherman. A military vet. Did you know that? Gus served in the Navy."

Bronson just looked at Larry, then sat down on the edge of the concrete wall—one of the few structures that had survived the incineration. His eyes never left Larry's. Not for a moment.

"Okay, okay! Let's get away from this friggin' smoke! It's pollutin' my lungs," Larry complained, then followed Bronson back to the fire investigator's sport utility vehicle.

"When I was a *real* cop back in Massachusetts—working the metropolitan area—I had a couple of bad experiences," Larry begun. "A few years back—me and my partner were on patrol. A young kid saw the squad car and began running from us. He hadn't done anything wrong as far as we knew, but he sure ran from us as if he were guilty as hell. We pursued him on foot and called it in. But I got separated from my partner. The last thing he yelled to me was, 'Larry—you got my back.' What he meant was: be ready to shoot the S.O.B. if he doubles back."

"Okay, so what happened?" Bronson prodded him.

"The little shit doubled back, caught my partner off-guard, and knocked him to the ground. His revolver went skidding across the pavement. The kid pulled a knife on my partner as he scrambled to his hands and knees for his revolver. He blocked my partner's path to his weapon, began talking trash, and flashed the knife in front of his face. And that's when I ran up and told him to drop the knife."

"Did he?"

"I was sure he would. Hell, I had a gun! But he didn't. My partner saw the look in the kid's face and knew the delinquent was going to try suppin' stupid. He yelled for me to shoot the little bastard."

"Did you?"

"Hell, no! It was just a knife. I had no indication he was going to use it or why he was even running from us. He seemed scared and he saw my gun. But..." Larry took a deep breath, "I was about thirty-five yards away, when I stopped and ordered him to drop his weapon. I didn't have the best angle and the kid was next to an alley."

"Why didn't you get closer?"

"I tried! My mistake was already made: I had stopped short and made my presence known before I was in position. Really stupid of me. He...he suddenly, without warning, sliced my partner in the neck, then ran down the alley."

"Good God!"

"I didn't shoot. I just stood there, shocked, and watched my partner clutch his neck. I...I hadn't thought the kid would do it—it made no sense."

"The world often makes no sense, Larry."

"The boy cut him bad. The neck wound was deep and near the carotid. He nearly died. When he got out of the hospital, he was fuming. Wanted me off the force. The division's psychologist labeled my hesitation "buck fever". It was my first experience of choosing between violence and reasoning. I blew it. No one wanted to be my partner after that. I was taken off patrol duty for a couple of years. After a few years, I proved myself and earned the right to another chance. But the stigma never left me. I worked hard to sharpen my reflexes and vowed I would never hesitate like that again. I would cover my next partner's back and die if I had to."

"And there was a next time?"

"Yeah…eventually. Finally, a new partner was assigned to me—an eager rookie. We patrolled the safe part of town and had no incidents for the first year. It was a cakewalk assignment. My new partner trusted me and wasn't worried about my past reputation. Then, during our third year together, fate reared its ugly head and ruined my life."

"You didn't lose this partner, did you?"

Larry heard the comment, but did not acknowledge it. He stared off into the distance. Bronson remained quiet, but stared intently at Sheriff Magleton.

"Call came in—an incident in the bad part of town," Larry began. "A car chase. The driver was pulled over for a bad brake light, but fled. He tried to outrun the unit. We were dispatched to join in and provide back-up to the units in pursuit. They cornered him in a tough part of town—a run-down crack neighborhood, two miles from our quiet patrol area. In the car was a young man and his girlfriend. Once trapped, he fled his car, with officers in pursuit."

"Sounds familiar."

"Yeah. And he lost the pursuing officers and stumbled into my back-up position. My partner chased him and the suspect emerged out of an alley, came up to a sky-blue Buick, and fumbled for the door handle. My partner ran up and told him to stop. My colleague did not have his weapon drawn as I arrived from the other direction. The young man snarled at my partner to back off and reached into his coat. It looked like he was withdrawing a weapon. He pointed it at the cop. I couldn't believe my partner hadn't drawn his weapon and started thinking about the buck fever comment."

"You allowed him to kill your partner?"

"Damn it, man! No! That's when I unloaded three rounds into him. Two struck him in the chest—the other in his head!"

"Bravo, Larry!"

"Yeah—I was a real friggin' hero this time," Larry looked down. "Fate… An old black woman on her front porch screamed as the young man collapsed to the ground—dead. The keys to his sky-blue Buick, strung on a big, solid vanity chain, slid from his inert fingers."

"Wait. You said he ran from *his* car."

"No. He ran from *a* car. His *girlfriend's* car! He ran down the alley to where his own car was parked. He had taken out his keys to unlock it."

"My God! You mean you shot a man for pulling his keys out on your partner?"

"Yup. No hesitation this time, Bronson. Shot the poor bastard dead."

"Why was he running? He had to have done something wrong?"

"Yeah…he ran," Larry said cynically. "The stupid bastard ran."

"I don't get it."

"He had recently been given a three-year prison sentence, but was let out for good behavior. He and his girlfriend had a few ounces of pot on them that night. If he had got busted with the pot, he would be back serving the rest of his time—plus a few years. He thought he could outrun us."

"Stupid!"

"There's more. The old lady watching from her porch was his aunt. She ran down from the porch and screamed that this *white* police officer had shot her nephew "for doin' nothing". She showed my partner that all her nephew had in his hands were keys.

"They played the race card on you too?"

"The neighborhood erupted into violence over the incident. Rioting, looting, fires…
Good God! Civil rights activists came from all over to parade me around as another racist cop
with an attitude and a gun. The force received damaging press and Internal Affairs lived with
us for months. Politically, it was a nightmare for the force. Once the newspapers got hold
of the story, I was portrayed as a two-time loser. Hadn't protected my first partner when I
shoulda… Had killed an innocent kid when I shouldn't have."

"Larry, I didn't realize…"

"No one knows, Bronson. Keep it that way. I had to leave the force and move away. I
could only get jobs that paid half of what I had been making earlier and started working the
midnight shift at crummy locations as a security guard. You know, jobs where they hire old
men who aren't allowed to carry a gun. And dejected cops like me."

Bronson just shook his head.

"Finally, after ten years, I moved to Maine and started my life over. Found a sleepy little
county where there are no murders. No drug dealers, racists, hypocrites, activists, or media
attention. Got my confidence back and became a respectable sheriff. Now this crap! I'm not
happy about it one bit, Bronson. I liked it boring around here, okay?"

"Okay, Larry. I'll cut you some slack. But this is still a case that needs to be broken—
with or without you. I sympathize with your run of bad luck, but we can't turn our backs on
this arson and now…possibly murder. We have to take this one down."

"I know. We will, Bronson," Larry muttered softly, but sincerely. "But sure you want
to with *me* as your partner?"

"Look, Sheriff. You're a fine lawman. Perhaps a bit too cautious. But I'll work with you
on any investigation. And I trust you with my life. Your luck has changed, Larry. I am confident you'll react appropriately, if and when the time comes."

                                    * * *

"My family has shared a close and unique relationship with certain natives," Patricia
began to slowly explain. "Our ancestors were originally from England. They belonged to an
earlier generation of English settlers. Some settled in what is now New England, others in the
English-dominated areas of Canada."

"What do you mean by *natives?*" Laura asked.

"Indians," Patricia replied. "In particular, the Iroquois nation. One of their tribes—the
Mohawk—hold a special significance where my personal heritage is concerned."

"You mean the guys with the funky hair thing?" Laura asked.

Patricia paused at the comment, neither amused nor annoyed by the description. She
had an agenda to carry out and her focus remained steady. With her beautifully styled silver
hair and regal posture, the older woman was beginning to command more serious attention
from Laura and a modicum of credibility as she continued to speak. Patricia Wellington had
not only been involved in a considerable part of Kineo's history, but was well informed

about it too. Laura began to think of Dr. Max Wayne and how he would have loved to talk to this historian.

"Yes, Laura, the Mohawk were the tribe of Iroquois with the characteristic scalplock," she explained. "They were the largest group of Iroquois living on Kineo. Before the arrival of our ancestors in the New World, there were...only twenty thousand or so of these people. But by the late sixteen hundreds, wars and diseases introduced by the Europeans had virtually wiped out the Mohawk. From what I have read, no more than eight hundred of them survived."

"I hadn't realized that," Laura said somberly.

"Most Americans don't," Patricia said in a wry tone. "Nor Canadians, for the most part. The truth underlying the decimation of these people is glossed over in history books. Laura, as a woman who is clearly self-confident and used to taking charge—oh yes, I know about you—you would be interested to know that the Mohawk—unlike other native peoples in the area—had a matrilineal social structure."

Laura's interest seemed to grow keener, while Rix appeared confused.

"What do ya mean, Pat? The ladies were the bosses?" he asked.

"You appear surprised, Laura, but it's true," Patricia Wellington continued, ignoring Rix for the moment. "The *women* owned all property and determined kinship."

"Well, no wonder their society crumbled! Ha!" Rix joked. He was hoping a bit of male chauvinistic humor would break the tension in the room.

Patricia rolled her eyes and gave him a dismissive look.

"The primary function of men was warfare," she went on.

"Big surprise there!" Laura said sarcastically.

"And breeding, I hope?" Rix joked again. Seeing that the woman were clearly into this discussion and his comments were not going to get a rise out of either one of them, he slumped back in his chair, almost as if he were sulking. The room became temporarily quiet, while everyone digested the exchange of comments.

"How do you know so much about the Mohawk, Patricia?" Laura finally said, ending the silence.

"Because," Rix interjected, "she's one of them!"

"Nice guess, Rix, but not quite," Patricia corrected him. "But I do have Iroquois in my bloodline. A lot of Wellingtons do. I am part Cayuga, but others in my family married Mohawk. Anyway, while the Europeans shared a role in drastically reducing the native population, they were at loggerheads with each other. The French, for instance, were fighting the English for territorial rights, although they shared their foe's antipathy for the Mohawk. In the early sixteen hundreds, there had been skirmishes between the Mohawk and the French, and the Dutch had rushed to the aid of the natives because they shared a common distrust of the French."

"Fine history lesson, Patricia. What does this have to do with us?" Rix asked abruptly.

"Hold your horses. I'm getting there. Laura needs to understand the background."

The younger woman gestured at Rix to be silent so that Patricia Wellington could continue.

"Many wars were fought between the Mohawk and other native tribes over the fur trade, with European settlers pitting themselves against each other by taking sides with various natives. The Beaver Wars lasted seventy years, with violent fighting between the tribes for control of the European fur trade. The other Iroquois tribes remained allies of the Dutch, as the Mohawk fought many other tribes in the area. The French allied themselves with the Huron and the Abenaki."

"Who are the Huron and the Abenaki?" Laura inquired, wishing now she had spent more time listening to Dr. Wayne when he was telling her kids about the Native Americans in the Kineo area.

"Other native peoples important to the area's history," Patricia answered. "But those groups were all Algonquin. They spoke a language that was different from that used by the Iroquois. They had a different culture. Their *men* ruled the roost."

"Hmm, now those groups I like," muttered Rix, clearly miffed at being left out of the conversation.

"Most of the native peoples that spoke the Algonquin language spent most of their time supporting the French," Patricia continued, unperturbed. "There were many peace treaties, as control of the fur trade bounced back and forth from one European nation to another and from one native tribe to another. A period of complete chaos ensued in America. Many wars were waged between Iroquois and the Huron. When the Huron were defeated in the mid-sixteen hundreds, the French fur trade declined. The Iroqouis became the main players in the area and could have held sway for a long time, had their Dutch allies not been overrun by the English in the late sixteen hundreds. My ancestors were part of that period in America, having arrived in New York and Massachusetts."

"I'm afraid I'm not really following all of this, Patricia. Besides, I'm thirsty. Would you like a drink?" Laura asked sweetly.

"I sure would," responded Rix.

"By all means then, Rix, please bring Laura and yourself something to drink, while I continue."

Patricia fixed him with the commanding look she had acquired and perfected over the years as the president of several ladies organizations and community service groups. Rix recognized it as his cue to go and slowly stood up, murmuring he knew where the ice tea was. Laura thanked him, then turned back to Patricia, who looked at her watch and appeared anxious to get on with her account.

"The British shrewdly made their own treaty with the Mohawk. British traders from Massachusetts exploited the opportunity to trade with the powerful Iroquois nation. The Mohawk tribe, in particular, worked well with our English ancestors. With little remaining French opposition in the area, the Mohawk, as small a group as they were, successfully drove the remaining natives from many areas," Patricia continued.

"For many years, the alliance between the British and Iroquois worked well for both parties. They jointly defeated the Wampanoag uprising in King Philip's War in the late sixteen hundreds. Later, with the outbreak of King George's War in the mid-seventeen hundreds between Britain and France, only the Mohawk supported the British. The Iroquois League of Nations remained neutral. By now, the other Iroquois tribes had developed mixed feelings about the British and could easily have switched sides to help the French. In the mid-seventeen hundreds, the Mohawk remained steadfast in their allegiance to the British, even as their sister tribes and other Canadian Iroquois formally declared war on the British colonies. Captain Wellington of the English Army used the Mohawk as scouts and warriors against the French, but was killed in combat in seventeen forty-eight."

"No doubt, a relative of yours?" Laura conjectured.

"Indeed."

"I'm no history wiz here, Patricia, but aren't we getting near the point where England was fighting the American colonizers and not the French?"

"Yes. Once the French and the English were done fighting, America's Revolutionary War broke out. Both the British and the Americans tried to enlist the support of the Iroquois who had historically favored the English-speaking people over the French. The Iroquois League considered the arguments advanced from both sides in the white man's war. Although they recognized the new United States in 1776, their decision was to still remain neutral during the conflict. The Mohawk, however...my dear Mohawk," she sighed and looked out the window reflectively. "The Mohawk remained loyal to the British and thus, in the end, picked the losing side."

Rix entered the room and handed each lady a tall glass of ice tea. Then he sat down quietly on the sofa beside Laura, sipping from the glass of tea he had made for himself.

"Thank you, Rix," Laura said as Patricia rambled on.

"Ultimately, the American colonists raised arms against all of the Iroquois nation and went on a rampage. Intoxicated with their new freedom, the victorious Americans burned dozens of settlements and towns. The Iroquois named George Washington 'Caunotaucarius'. In their language, that means 'the destroyer of towns'."

"Really?" Laura looked surprised. "And your family?"

"Ironically, my English family ties died out with Captain Wellington, but some Wellington settlers who had remained in New England and were loyal to the colonists stayed back here to raise families in the northeast, particularly Maine. Other Wellingtons moved into English-controlled Canada."

"Those whose sympathies lay with the English?" Laura ventured.

"Correct," Patricia responded. "The Iroquois nation, however, never recovered from this fresh round of slaughter."

* * *

"It's so nice to hear from you, Max," Dr. Mary Chase said with genuine enthusiasm. "When are you coming down to Massachusetts to have dinner with Ralph and me?"

"Oh Mary, you know I'd love to enjoy Ralph's cooking again," Dr. Wayne replied. "But I need to pick your brain here for a minute, and I'm not able to..."

"Do you have company, Max?"

"Righto."

"No problem, Maxie. We'll chat about old times later. What can I do for you?"

Dr. Chase was a noted anthropologist and historian. She taught at Harvard and was a leading expert on Native American history and culture.

"What native tribes used highly polished stones as part of their rituals in the northeast?"

"Slow down, Max... What did you find?"

"I'm not exactly sure, but it appears to be a stone. A mineral...purple... Gemstone quality. It is very round."

Mary considered what Max had described so far. "Is it a perfect sphere?"

"Quite."

"Hmm..." she considered the possibilities.

"It was found on a site that historically had encampments of the Red Paint People, but that makes no sense at all."

"No, no, Max... No way could it be them."

"I know. I just meant the site is known for the Red Paint People and... Well, much later, various peoples who spoke the Algonquin languages—the Abenaki, in particular, but various Iroquois tribes as well," Max continued.

"Max, none of that correlates with any of the northeastern tribes we've studied. Let me think...hmm... Was the sphere about three to four inches in diameter?"

"I'd say yes. In fact, I'll bet it was exactly that."

"You don't know? You don't have it in your possession?" she asked, surprised.

"Um, Mary, it's complicated... But no, I don't have it with me. Please stay with me anyway. So do you know of a culture that used a three to four inch spherical gemstone?"

"Purple gemstone you say, Max?"

"Yes, it appeared so."

"Only one?"

"Yes. Why?"

"Max, let me get back to you. I need to think. I remember reading about a secluded culture of Indians out west that used volcanic glass in a symbolic manner to delineate the lines of territory between rival tribes. As I recall, however, they used only black glass—you know, obsidian, not purple gemstones. It was always used in a geometric arrangement, forming a circle or triangle."

"How far out west? What period of history?"

"Far, Max. Like the fourteen hundreds to sixteen hundreds. It was natives that lived in Arizona and New Mexico or something. Nothing like this has ever been reported in the northeast. Frankly, I don't remember which group it was. I'll have to check for you."

"Please do, Mary. It's important. But does it sound improbable that such stones were exchanged freely between tribes across the Mississippi back then?"

"Let me look into it, Max—I'll call you."

"Thanks, Mary. Give my regards to Ralph. 'Bye."

* * *

Bear could no longer suppress his anguish. She had cut him in the deepest and ugliest way possible. Rebecca had all the money a woman could want. *Why did she need to control Jacob too?* He had the day off and wanted to see his son. Bear looked forward to taking him on a boat ride to the north end of Moosehead Lake to spot moose feeding in the shallow headwater marshes.

The more he thought of how Becky had ignored him and his feelings, the more enraged he became. Bear was not a man you wanted to tangle with. His emotions were concealed beneath a thin veneer of impassivity that could easily be scratched and peeled off. Now he jumped into his boat and powered it to the Rockwood docks. He was on a mission now, and failed to obey the "no wake zone" signs, as he bumped hard against the bulkhead. Several locals saw this and began to go over to reprimand him, but the look on his face discouraged them immediately from intervening.

Bear jumped into his Jeep 4X4 and sped off. He was heading away from Rockwood to the Pillouds' 20,000-square-foot compound overlooking the northwest shore of Moosehead Lake. As he drove to his destination, Becky's last taunting words reverberated in his mind: "*You know the order says you must schedule an appointment at least forty-eight hours in advance and YOU didn't now...DID you?*"

Bear's Jeep Laredo raced along, exceeding the posted speed limit by more than twenty miles an hour.

30

Moosehead Region in the 1700-1800s

During the 1700s, the white colonizers swarmed across the land like locust feeding upon grain fields. During one of his many adventures in the Midwest, Kajo had witnessed such a plague of insects first-hand. Before he died, he had warned the natives on Kineo that the white invaders would come from every direction and consume all of their resources like the locust. His prophetic words now echoed in the minds of the elders as they watched the advance of the light-skinned Europeans with their modern firearms that could shoot deadly lead balls into the flesh of game and man.

Most of the native tribes fled from the area. The remaining ones gathered and decided that they needed to vacate Kineo after hiding the flint chamber and Kajo's sacred burial site from the invaders. They hoped that some day, when the white man had been driven back to where he had come from, they could return. In the meantime, it was important to ensure that the secrets of Kineo did not fall into his hands. The remaining group of guardians began to carefully conceal the sacred entrances to the mineral-rich inner chamber. They mined as much of the Kineo flint as each of the tribes could haul away. Then in 1750, the three table monuments with the three guardian spheres were all buried and concealed inside Mt. Kineo, preserving the fragile balance of unity between the descendants of the three depleted tribes.

Anxious that the white man might eventually stumble upon the entrances and desecrate their sacred grounds, the elders hurriedly worked to camouflage their burial grounds, trying to blend them into the landscape as much as possible. They also developed an ambitious plan to further guard against the invaders. Each tribe would send forth trusted guardians of the chamber as agents into the white man's society. *What better place to watch your enemy's moves than within your enemy's camp?* The legend of the Cow Moose and of Kajo the Trader would be spread by word of mouth among the remaining guardians and from generation to generation of trustworthy elders. The survival of their cultures depended upon it. The great curse could not be contained; they wondered if it might be unleashed on the invading Europeans and colonizers.

It wasn't until the late 1700s, however, that the non-indigenous people completed their invasion of the Moosehead region. The white man came primarily to exploit the abundant timber. In 1764, surveyors from Massachusetts explored the area and began mapping the resources. After 1776, the natives watched the rebellious colonists stake their claim to their new possession as they successfully defeated the Europeans to form their own country. But it wasn't until 1824 that a settlement of white people began to be established in Greenville, leading to the beginning of the rapid growth of the timber industry in the Moosehead region.

This swiftly expanding industry would become an important aspect of Maine's history and economy and lead to the Moosehead region's growth and prosperity. Over ninety percent of the state's nineteen million acres became timberland. The cutting of timber in Maine actually began as early as 1631, with the industry making inroads into the Moosehead region much later. The West Branch watershed of the Penobscot River was a vast area north of Moosehead Lake that had abundant resources to exploit. Woodsmen earned their living in this region as early as 1828, before the Great Northern Paper Company took over the area. As timber operations spread, steamers began plying on several lakes, including Moosehead. Roads were constructed to provide easy access into the heart of the wilderness, where the precious timber lay.

The mysterious loss of the steamship, *Piscataquis*, on Sept 12, 1883, was one of those events in history that would mark the birth of a local legend. While the tourist industry began to flourish on Kineo, no one would have imagined that a shipment of stolen Confederate gold reserves from a war settled only two decades earlier could be in the possession of a tiny band of scattered natives. Surprising the French Canadians and the greedy English soldiers in an ambush had not been a problem. With the European invaders having grown overconfident from their success in subduing the natives in the area, that part had been remarkably easy. Stealing the Europeans' precious mineral had been immensely gratifying. The theft would provide significant wealth to the culprits. The pressing concern of the moment was to find a suitable place to hide it from the other native peoples, the white settlers, the double-crossed Canadians, and the northern Federal army.

There was only one logical place, reasoned the guardian descendant. It had been approximately 130 years since the last of the tribes mined Kineo flint. The great gift from the Cow Spirit Moose no longer bore fruit for his people who had now been either assimilated or driven away. They would sneak the white man's gold back to the hidden inner chamber on Kineo, from where it could be retrieved when they were ready to do so.

Six Iroquois men devised an ingenious way to transfer the pirated treasure up Mt. Kineo and conceal it where no white man would ever find it. The gold was cleverly hidden deep in the inner mining chamber next to its Iroquois side. The Abenaki and Mohawk Guardian descendants only checked their chambers once a season at best. They never did learn about the yellow metal prized by the white man that had been concealed right under their noses.

The six Iroquois men kept their heist a secret. They had not expected Major Pilloud to survive the attack on the *Piscataquis*. The major himself was astonished to be still alive. His anger continued to seethe as he lay in the hospital in Bangor, recovering from his substantial injuries and exposure to the frigid water. A conniving man with little conscience, Major Pilloud was not a person one would want to double-cross.

Eventually, he and a few well-armed colleagues set out for the North Country on a lead that promised to reveal the whereabouts of the Iroquois that had betrayed him. It took only two weeks for them to track down the guide who had led the ambush on the steamship. He was killed in the shootout that followed and some of his surviving accomplices were captured.

Three men were killed in all and the rest injured. Among the survivors was a former guardian of the inner chamber. He refused to talk even under intense torture. The will of the last two Iroquois men had been weakened, if not broken from witnessing the torture and fate of their companions. While some useful information was beaten out of them before they died, not all of it could be extracted. Major Pilloud was furious at his associates for failing to acquire all the information. One of the Iroquois had disclosed that the gold was hidden in Moosehead Lake, "but you would have to find the three guardian spheres to locate the place where it rests," he had added. The other had revealed with his final breath that "the angered Spirit of the Cow Moose will rain down fire on all of you and your descendants". Major Pilloud would serve out his lifetime trying in vain to solve the puzzle of the three guardian spheres that held the key to the secret hiding place for his Confederate gold. While his descendants would not inherit the treasure, the major did manage to bequeath to them the legacy of his obsession for finding it at any cost.

Late Afternoon, July 2, 1999

"The ties to the Mohawk remained strong in my family," Patricia continued. "My grandfather married an Iroquois. Although his wife wasn't Mohawk, she was of the Cayuga tribe. Grandpa had made a fortune from the timber industry, and they moved into the Moosehead Lake region. Kineo was their vacation retreat during the glorious years of the great hotels."

"This is the part of your family history I've always wanted to understand," admitted Rix, his interest beginning to quicken.

"My parents became an integral part of Kineo. By the age of thirty, my father had become an officer of the Great Northern Paper Company. This was around 1920, the period during which my family began building our summer cottage on Kineo. Not over here on Cottage Row, mind you—that area was still part of the hotel and reserved for *special* guests—but down near the end of Kineo Cove."

"That's the structure that was recently destroyed by fire?" Laura probed carefully.

"Essentially," the other woman answered. "The place expanded over the years. The Goldmans changed it radically when they took ownership of the Wellington place."

"Patricia," Laura interrupted. "This is all very interesting, but you still haven't told me how this has anything to do with us, and I have to attend to some guests upstairs. I don't mean to be rude but—"

"Are you familiar with the legend of the Polish princess who died on Mt. Kineo?" the older women interrupted her.

"Yes. A little."

"Oh, this ought to be good!" Rix mumbled contentedly. "Now where you taking us, you crazy woman?"

"Hush, Rix!" Patricia's snappy tone expressed both affection for Rix and the sort of reprimand one reserves for a talkative child. Then she continued.

"The princess died a few years before my family had started construction of their cottage. There was turmoil on the island following her apparent suicide. In fact, some Mohawk descendants my family knew were deeply distressed and behaved strangely after she was gone. My father told me that several natives had combed the bottom of the cliffs of Kineo for several years thereafter without revealing to the locals what they were looking for."

Rix stood up abruptly and began to pace the room. Something about this story sounded too familiar. His mind flashed back to the time he and Bob had had their encounter with the crazy old Indian lady.

"I was born in nineteen twenty-five," he heard Patricia say. "The Wellington Cottage was complete by then, and my family enjoyed their summers there. I would hear my father talk about how Kineo was 'cursed'. A beautiful place to visit but…something odd and mysterious was going on. There had been so many fires that had burned down the great hotels. One of my close Mohawk friends confided to me that those fires were caused by a curse. The desecration of gravesites and the disappearance of a precious guardian stone had only made things worse."

Rix felt a knot in his stomach grow to the size of a grapefruit. It was time to go. He began to head for the door, turning back to say goodbye to Laura, but Patricia suddenly raised her voice. "Sit down, Rix!"

The sharp, commanding tone raised the hairs on Laura's arms. Something in Patricia's voice told her there was a much larger piece of the puzzle she knew nothing about, and somehow, it involved Rix.

"You and Laura were poking around down in your basement earlier, weren't you?" Patricia asked, already knowing the answer. "Don't you want to know *what* you were fooling around with?"

Neither Laura nor Rix replied. The latter reluctantly came back into the room and hovered by the sofa.

"Sit," Patricia repeated. "Sit, Rix. Please. This affects you too."

Rix sat down next to Laura once again. His face was drained of color. Laura could see he was half-terrified.

"Although I remained close to many natives," Patricia Wellington went on, "most had been forced to leave the Moosehead area. Between the eighteen eighties and the nineteen thirties, they had largely kept themselves aloof from the wealthy guests staying on the island. Essentially reduced to the status of second-class citizens, the natives would be hired from time to time to assist the resort guides during fishing and hunting expeditions, although they were, undoubtedly, the better woodsmen.

"My father, of course, was more sympathetic to them because his mother was Iroquois. As tourism grew in the area, the company he worked for began forcing the remaining indigenous people out. Before the fortunes of the resort went into a tailspin, something happened to my family that I am unlikely to forget. It was the summer of nineteen thirty-nine. My older brother and I were hiking with my dad near the upper base of the cliffs of Kineo. My brother begged Father to recount us the story of the Polish princess' bizarre suicide. The way most locals tell it, it is a gruesome tale—as you may know."

"So my daughter tells me," Laura acknowledged. "She seems to know the story quite well."

"Father showed my brother the exact spot where her body had been discovered. Finding the topic utterly distasteful—as a well-bred young lady should—I wandered off from their macabre discussion and walked though a dense, wooded area adjacent to the large boulder field near the base of the cliffs. I had strayed off over a hundred yards from my father and brother and sat down to rest on a large boulder. Bored on my own, I just happened to be poking around with a stick in a crack in the large boulder, when I spotted it… Inside the crack lay the missing guardian stone!"

* * *

Bear arrived at the Pilloud residence compound and was immediately intercepted by one of the guards. "Brutus!" the man said. "You shouldn't be here!"

"Really?" Bear said sarcastically, walking up to the much smaller man. "I suppose if I come up to see my son, you're gonna stop me?"

"Look man, it's my job!"

"Yeah, you work for a prince of a man. Sorry, sport. I *am* going to see my boy."

Bear turned and began to walk past the guard. The latter whipped out his two-way radio and clicked the transmit button. Bear stopped, looked at the guard, and shook his head. The guard froze in his tracks and began to estimate his speed against Bear's if he had to flee. Bear walked back to the man and snatched the radio out of his hand before he could even tell his colleagues upstairs about the crisis at hand.

"I don't think you really want to do that now, do ya?" Bear asked, tossing the radio into Moosehead Lake. "Now scram—unless you wanna get hurt."

Bear proceeded to the rear of the house where he heard the distinct sound of a dog's metal chain collar rattling around the stone wall beyond his range of vision. The giant snatched up a two-by-four stud that maintenance men had left propped up against the wall. No sooner had he acquired a firm grip on the potential weapon, than the Doberman Pinscher appeared around the corner, greeting the huge intruder with a ferocious, fang-baring snarl. Without a moment's hesitation, Bear brought the full force of his wrath down upon the dog, striking him squarely in the back. The board snapped in half with a loud crack, breaking the dog's spine. The Doberman collapsed, let out a brief whimper, and did not get up after that.

Tossing aside the broken half of the board he had been holding, Bear proceeded up the stone stairs.

"Dobie?" he heard a guard calling down. "You hear something? Dobie...?"

"Yeah! Me!" Bear announced, rounding the flight of stairs and catching a glimpse of the guard at the top of the landing.

"Bear! What are you doing here? Where's my dog?"

The two men immediately engaged in a furious scuffle, with the larger, more driven one throwing the guard against the French doors, causing the glass to shatter. Behind him, he could hear the first guard yelling up to warn his colleague that Bear was here and in a rage. But it came much too late for the winded second guard who was now staggering to his feet and attempting to extricate himself from the jagged edges of the broken glass door. Bear grabbed him by the collar and flung him down the stairs where he crashed into the first guard up to assist in the apprehension of the intruder.

"Back off! I just want my son." Bear bolted into the house and ran up the grand stairwell.

Pilloud appeared at the top of the stairs to investigate the noise he had heard of shattering glass. Becky gasped when she saw Bear and the look of determination on his face. She thought back to her earlier taunting of this gentle giant, wondered if it had been such a bright idea after all, and called out in panic for Pierre to come to her aid. Bear came up the stairs, looking like an angry version of the beast after which he had been nicknamed. Pilloud ducked quickly into his study and tried to deflect with a wave the attention Becky was drawing to his whereabouts. Rebecca continued, however, to desperately call out for Pierre who, unbeknownst to her, was unavailable at the moment; he was out on another "special errand" for her uncle.

Opening the door to Jacob's room, Bear found his son and snatched him up in his arms. "Come on, boy," he said, his voice gruff with emotion, "it's my day to see you."

"Daddy!" wailed Jacob, "I missed you!"

"Me too, lil'guy. I got a neat day planned for us."

Pilloud emerged from his study, grabbed hold of his niece, and forced her to back away. He knew Bear would not harm the boy. If he walked out of the house with Jacob, Pilloud would have him locked up for a long time. Becky could barely keep from screaming at her uncle, but he kept his hold on her, gave her a hard shake, and commanded her to get a grip on herself.

Bear emerged from the boy's room, cradling his son in his arms. Tears streamed down his cheeks. Becky glared at him, her eyes filled with disdain and hatred.

Pilloud calmly said to the Bear, "You know you will not get away with this. Your life is mine now!"

Bear ignored the other man, hurried down the grand staircase, and threw open the front door, avoiding the shaken guards who were still disoriented after their nasty tumble down the back entrance stairs. The two guards suddenly burst, with pistol drawn, into the room where Pilloud stood with Becky, looking at thier employer for direction as they saw the front door left wide open. Pilloud looked at the guards and shook his head. Bear's arrest and incarceration by the authorities would be far more rewarding and a neater solution than having him shot on the Pilloud estate in front of his innocent little nephew who would, no doubt, be traumatized by the sight of his father being murdered in cold blood.

"Let him go and call the police," he calmly stated to the guards. "Bear is mine now. I own his ass!"

His confidence now buoyed by the Smith and Wesson cradled in his hand, the larger of the two guards, Boxer, looked back toward the open door, a bit disappointed. His little taste of revenge would have to be postponed.

* * *

"What was it you found?" Laura asked curiously, while Rix held his breath.

"A large black sphere," Patricia answered mysteriously. "It was so beautiful. I had to keep it. I mean...I knew it was something that should be returned to the Mohawk. But it was so mesmerizing!"

Rix buried his head in his hands. Laura gazed out the window, wishing Max were here to hear all this nonsense and decipher it for her. She was beginning to fidget at the thought of the guests she had to check on upstairs.

"I remembered my father telling me how the natives had scoured the mountain looking for a lost stone sphere," Patricia continued, oblivious to Laura's impatience. "We all thought they were mad. Finally, one of the older Mohawk fishing guides that trusted me explained more than I would have cared to know. Apparently, the Polish princess had been riding a horse up on the mountain one afternoon and had dismounted to take a brief nap. She was hidden from view as she rested peacefully. A native Indian had quietly walked passed her carrying a beautiful sphere. One of the guardians of the sacred place on Mt. Kineo, he had, unfortunately, been drinking. Distraught over their land being usurped by our kind, many of the natives had begun drowning their sorrows in cheap liquor. This particular guardian had taken the sphere out of hiding and considered holding onto it. But observing the object in the sunlight, he realized how great a spiritual significance it held for him. According to local legend, the sphere had been placed in the heart of Mt. Kineo by Kajo, a powerful shaman from a faraway land. The intoxicated guardian now decided to return the sphere to its hiding place, as it was one of the markers of the sacred site where Kajo was supposedly buried. Such reckless behavior by this drunken guardian in the middle of the afternoon was unthinkable. The fool! The rules were clear. Never be seen on Kineo. Never tend the spheres during the day. Only visit the chambers at night, under cover of darkness. But the man was not in his senses. He was spotted by Princess Radziwill who noticed the sphere in his hands."

"This is certainly not mentioned in the local history books! So what happened?" Laura inquired tensely.

"Followed him at a distance, she watched him sneak into the Mohawk secret entrance tunnel where it had been kept. When he finally crawled out empty-handed, she knew he had left the sphere somewhere in the small crawl space. After he had covered the secret opening and departed, she stole in through the entrance, found the sphere, and removed it."

"Oh, I don't like where this is going!" Rix said in a voice filled with dread.

"No. You shouldn't. What I'm about to tell you is something I have never told a soul. Concerned about the trouble that their drunken colleague might get himself into, two additional Mohawk ventured up the mountain only to discover the princess with the sphere in her possession. Outraged, they gave chase. The princess mounted her horse and, in her panic to get away from the angry natives in pursuit, rode too close to the narrow cliff edge. Her horse stumbled and the sphere went flying over the edge. The foliage of the trees below somehow broke its fall and the sphere landed on the ground, intact. How it ended up where I found it…I have no idea."

"The princess…so did she really jump? Was she carrying a letter from a jilted lover?" Laura asked, knowing how disappointed Jenny would be in Patricia's version of the folklore.

"A letter from her lover? Perhaps. But did she commit suicide? Ha! What do you think, Laura? Is *any* man worth that type of end? Especially when you have the privilege of being royalty. I think not. The cliff edge simply gave way under the combined weight of rider and horse. At the site of the mishap were two very bewildered and furious Mohawk. They bounded down and searched for the sphere, worried that the white man might find it first and appropriate it."

"Oh my!" Laura gasped.

"You know, Laura, there have been many fires on this accursed island. Some were natural. Some were the outcome of insurance fraud by business owners overextended in debt. But many were my native friends—trying to drive the tourists and white invaders off the island."

"You mean the early fires in the eighteen hundreds?" Rix asked.

"That's right, Rix. But the natives had actually stopped the practice by the time Princess Radziwill visited Kineo at the turn of the century. They were a disorganized, demoralized, and defeated group of people. This traumatic event involving the princess had, however, shaken them. They had very strong beliefs about how the spheres maintained a balance between the spirit world and the material world and how this special relationship was at the source of the unity among the three tribes. I never fully understood it. I just accepted it. Their life was so simple and pure. Once you study it, you realize what an amazing culture they had before we stamped it out of existence! Until I found the sphere, I didn't realize that the myth of the Circle of Three Tribes wasn't actually a myth; it was a real place—a physical location of spiritual significance to the natives. The old Mohawk shared the truth about the princess' demise with me, knowing I was sympathetic to his peoples' cause. He hoped I would help them."

"Oh my, Patricia! Did you tell the old Mohawk that ya found the missing sphere?"

"Of course not! I was too afraid to make that confession. They would not have forgiven me for meddling in their spiritual affairs. They would have chased me over the cliff as well. That I am sure of."

"So you hid it!" Rix sounded appalled.

Patricia Wellington slowly nodded.

"And what about the old witch-like lady that scared the crap out of me and my brother when we were kids?"

"Ha! She is no witch, you idiot! She is one of the last remaining guardians of the spheres, the gatekeeper to the Circle of Three Tribes. She's the very last of the surviving line of Mohawk guardians. She was likely responsible for setting fire to several of the structures on Kineo— perhaps even our family cottage—in her lifetime. I guess it was fair justice that someone finally burned my family's old cottage to the ground. Serves me right. I never told anyone."

"I don't think any native Indian burned the old Wellington place down, ma'am," interrupted Dougie who now stood at the door, ready to take Mrs. Wellington back as prearranged.

"Dougie! How long have you been standing there?" Laura asked, startled, inviting him in.

"Not long. I didn't mean to eavesdrop on your private conversation. I shouldn't say anything. It's just that… Oh hell! You all know that Jimbo was a good friend of mine. And I know he found that damn thing too—that black sphere at your place, Mrs. Wellington. I'm also sure it was no native guardian, or whatever you call them folks, that…that…killed him. And I've seen the old Mohawk woman you spoke of."

"Do you realize what you're saying?" Rix jumped in.

Laura slumped in her chair, overwhelmed by the bizarre inflow of information. Patricia sat quietly, considering what Dougie had just said, uncertain as to whether she should continue.

"Look," Dougie said, "just forget it, all of you. This island is as beautiful as it is mysterious and cursed! C'mon Mrs. Wellington, let's get you home."

And as quickly as he had appeared, the young man left, with Patricia in tow. Rix and Laura sat on the sofa in silence for ten minutes. Finally, Laura jumped up; she knew what would make her feel better. She picked up the phone and called Professor Max Wayne.

PART FOUR

The Chamber

32

"Rob, I don't see why we should stray so far away from the group like this."

"Look, Julie. It's fine. The professors said we had a couple of hours of free time after the last dig. C'mon."

"Yes, I know. But most of the other guys are eating lunch or practicing volleyball. You know, a lady has to eat."

Rob looked at Julie Walters, bent forward and gave her an unexpected peck on the forehead. When he spoke again, his voice was soft, but impatient. "I promised to show you something, remember, that you would find more exciting than a bagged lunch?"

"Oh, you mean the gemstones you told me about in the van?"

"And the fun place to climb down to. You still got your gear with you?"

"Sure. In my climbing backpack. But Rob, shouldn't we tell one of the professors where we're going...for safety reasons?"

"No! Oh no, Jules. No way! You'll understand once we get there. Trust me. Now come on, I need your help to rappel down the wall over there with me."

"No, Rob, wait. You need to tell me more. Dr. Wayne will be..."

"Okay, fine! Here, look at this." Rob yanked an object out of his day pack and began to carefully unwrap the cloth from around it. He then held the large, perfectly sherical and highly polished gemstone up to the sunlight and smiled at Julie.

"It's purple!"

"It's pure amethyst."

"You found it in here?"

"Oh, Jules, yes...and so much more! I didn't have a good source of light with me or the supplies I needed to really explore inside. I need you, Julie. Please come with me."

As the young woman fell in with Rob's plans, she couldn't help but wonder what she had gotten herself into. Max would not like this. The image of Dr. Wayne shaking his head in disapproval made her pause as she watched Rob pull some debris away from a crevasse in the side of a cliff wall. Rob looked back and motioned for her to hurry along. Julie let out a long breath, knowing subconsciously that this was not a good idea. But the image of the purple sphere that had piqued her interest drew her along like a magnet. As Rob held out his hand to help her drop down through the tiny opening to the entrance, he looked back in the direction from which they had come. *Not a soul around. Nobody watching this time. thank God.*

* * *

"Max, I know all this sounds crazy. I'm sorry to bother ya when you've only been back for a day and have so much work to do with your students."

"It's fine, Laura. I am glad you called. I saw you from the golf course as we were unloading yesterday, but I was really tied up... I had planned to stop by to say hello."

"It was all I could do to keep Thomas and Jenny from bustin' down your door to see you yesterday. I told them they had to give you a day to settle in."

"It would have been fine. Really. Well, I'm glad you kept my cell number. And I have reason to believe what you're telling me. And it's not all that crazy. I've a lot to tell you too. I can be there in say, fifteen minutes. Okay with you?"

"Yes please, Max. This really has me bothered!"

"Don't worry. I'm coming," Max assured her confidently.

He flipped his cell phone closed and looked over at Les who was staring at him with a disapproving frown.

"I suppose that call means that our scheduled combined dig will be delayed while you court the Denton woman?"

"No, Les. It isn't like that at all."

"Hmm," Dr. Mongeau grunted, sucking on his pipe and inhaling deeply as he pondered the latest development.

"Laura Denton has information that's very relevant to our findings on Kineo. But there's some sensitive material I should screen...in person. Look, Les. Can we talk about this later? I really have to go now."

"I can see that, Dr. Wayne."

* * *

Rix had boated off Kineo in search of his brother so he could share all that he had learned that day. So much of their confusing past was coming to light so quickly. Laura was making a quick run through the cottage, checking to ensure all her guests were doing fine. They appeared to be off on an excursion to Greenville. *Good. Now where are my kids?* Laura found Brandon up in his room, playing Game Boy. Normally, she would insist he put aside the toy and go outside for some exercise. It was a sunny day, after all, but she had too much weighing on her mind to care at this moment. Bounding down the stairs, she found the rest of her brood outside on the porch. Thomas and Jenny were there with Amanda and Tiffany. All were in swimwear and carrying towels.

"Mom? You mind if we take the Lomax's boat up to Big Duck Cove to jump off the rocks?" Thomas asked politely.

Laura looked at the four kids, thinking how nice it was that they were all getting along so well. It was curious, though, that the older Lomax girl was actually interested in hanging around with the other three. She started to wonder if she had misjudged the brat. There was no time to sort through all the emotions and questions going through her mind right now. Jenny and Amanda looked so cute together—all smiles and eager to go swimming with their two older siblings as chaperones. Thomas looked so mature. Tiffany looked surprisingly mild-mannered and totally unthreatening in a simple midcut wetsuit, instead of the tiny bikini Laura had expected her to wear.

"Thomas, are you driving?" she finally said, answering her older son's query.

"Yes, Mrs. Denton," Tiffany replied on his behalf. "Seems Daddy trusts Thomas with our Sea Ray after he proved himself seaworthy with Gus this year."

"Even got Dougie's approval to pull the girls wakeboarding and skiing, when he's not available," Thomas added with a proud and infectious smile.

"Okay, go ahead then," Laura said. "But be back before dark and be careful with the Lomax boat."

As the four teenagers left on their golf cart, Laura had little time to reconsider what she had given them authorization for. For Bear came running up the path carrying Jacob in his arms and a look on his face that told her that things were about to get even crazier around the Denton place real soon.

* * *

"My God, Rob! What *are* these?"

"I told you there would be some really interesting artifacts and minerals in here!" Rob picked up the large chunk of solid metallic stone that was part of the table supporting the original sphere he had removed on his previous trip to Kineo and held it close to his flashlight. "I think the cradle was sculpted out of chalcopyrite. Look at how it glistens. Fool's gold."

"Is this where you found the sphere?"

"Yes. Resting in this cradle, on top of the chalcopyrite."

"Unba…friggin'…believable! What does this all mean?"

"No clue. I couldn't see past this area before. I needed more light. Let's keep exploring."

"Look, Rob! There's another tunnel on the other side of the inner chamber. Can we check it out?"

The two students crawled through the opposite tunnel and found another smaller side tunnel. Julie found a second table of rocks, capped with a small mantle sculpted from but another thin layer of fool's gold. A stone table, holding an amazing spherical gemstone.

"Look at this one! It's beautiful. It's pink! Can I keep this one?"

Rob moved over to Julie and noticed she was holding a pink sphere in her hands that was three to four inches in diameter. The look of excitement on her face reminded him of how he had felt last year, when he found the purple sphere. *Look at her! Ripe with gem lust and in the throes of treasure hunter's disease!* But for Rob, things were starting to come together. He sensed there was a much larger find inside this chamber.

There must be something much more valuable in here than the spheres themselves, Rob thought to himself. *The spheres are simply a kind of "marker" for something more significant. But what?* The answer had to be inside the central chamber that they were carefully crawling around in their bid to find the other side tunnel. The spheres marked the entrances of at least two, maybe three tunnels, all leading to *this* very central chamber. Rob focused on the deep pit in this chamber with near vertical rock walls. These were, for the most part, slick surfaces of exposed rhyolite, where water from the saddle just above their heads had seeped into the fractured area and thick ice formed every winter. After being subjected to years of pressure from the expanding trapped ice, the rock had split away, leaving these large surfaces. There was evidence that people had taken pickaxes and enlarged the chamber over many years. Spent rock was piled along the edges and made up portions of the tunnel ceilings.

Rob and Julie searched the third tunnel and discovered that it too had a table with a chalcopyrite cradle to hold another sphere. In this entrance tunnel, however, the cradle was empty and the sphere missing. Crawling back to the main chamber, Rob became obsessed with the layout of the central chamber and studied it intently, while Julie continued to polish the dust off the pink sphere that she maintained was hers to keep. He did not bother to respond to her assertion. Rob was no longer content finding mere mineral spheres in the fissures around him. He was confident that the very fact that three separate tunnels all led directly to this deep central chamber was of greater significance than he had realized earlier.

Three ways to sneak into the central chamber, Rob observed, *and each one identified by a stone table created to hold one of the three highly polished gemstone spheres. The cradles supporting each of the spheres were made from chalcopyrite. I see other minerals and many implements and Indian artifacts everywhere. Dr. Max would freak out if he could see this place.* But there was more. He could *feel* it. *Why all this fuss and secrecy? What was the significance of the central chamber?* A sort of deep fissure here that descended from the central chamber looked as if it had been mined for many years. The old wooden ramps and catwalks that had once provided easy access were now all dilapidated to the point of being hazardous. The bottom of that fissure had to hold the answer.

"Julie, get out your climbing gear," he said. "We have to go down this fissure. Oh, and you can certainly keep the pink gemstone sphere. I already have a purple one."

"Oh my, Rob! When you promise a lady excitement, you do deliver, don't you! What do you think it's made from?"

"I'm not sure. It looks like it could be made from a huge chunk of rose quartz."

"Okay now... Wow! See all these paintings and symbols? Do you realize how Dr. Wayne will react once he sees this?"

"Hey Jules, remember this is *our* discovery for now. Just yours and mine. We'll include the others at the proper time."

"Yeah, yeah, whatever, Rob. Come on, let's rappel!"

＊ ＊ ＊

"Bear, what have you done?" Laura asked, opening her front-porch door and fearing she knew the answer. She took Jacob gently by the hand and told him that Brandon was up in his room playing Game Boy. Her younger son came down eagerly and took the little boy back upstairs to show him his latest game. Although Jacob was younger, Brandon always enjoyed entertaining him. Bear sat down next to Laura on the living-room sofa. He looked as if he had been crying.

"I lost it, Laura. I couldn't take it anymore. That bitch was toying with me. I took matters into my own hands."

"Bear? What did you do?"

* * *

"Call Toonie in Rockwood and have him meet us," Sheriff Larry Magleton ordered. "And get the fire inspector on the road as well."

"You want them both to meet you?"

"Yes! That's what I said!" Larry barked out impatiently. "At the Rockwood docks. Tell Toonie to have his patrol boat ready. The mail can wait. Oh, and tell Bronson he was right. I gotta go... Hold down the office here!"

Larry darted out of his office in Greenville and hopped into his vehicle. His secretary noticed that for the first time, he was moving as though impelled by a real purpose. Gus had been found dead that morning, his house burned to the ground. Now Bear breaking into the Pilloud estate. As Sheriff Magleton drove toward Bronson's office to pick him up, a call came in from the Rockwood-Somerset County representative. Deputy Toonie.

"Toonie heeya. What's up, Larry?"

"Toonie. I'm picking up Bronson. I have a little domestic disturbance thing to deal with on Pilloud's estate. You need to join us, since it's in your jurisdiction, but then, I think the three of us are gonna have to comb Kineo on a related matter. I'll need your help, even though Kineo is technically my jurisdiction. I know the jurisdiction issue is confusing, but all of this is likely related."

"Well, it's getting' late in the day, but nooo problem, Larry. Glad to be of service. I'll have my patrol boat ready at the Rockwood docks to take you to Kineo. You want me to meet you at the Pilloud mansion in ten?"

"I won't be there quite that fast. But ten-four."

"Oh hey, Larry? Um...you expecting anything that might warrant my bringing along my nine millimeter?"

"Cripes, Toonie! What'd you think? This is friggin' Rockwood!" Then after listening to the long, quiet pause on the cell line, Larry offered, "Look, Toonie. This is a routine deal. Just need some back-up with someone who knows Kineo and the people there better than I do. The Pilloud estate is really in your jurisdiction, but they called us in Greenville. Don't think Pilloud even knows that the Rockwood area has a deputy sheriff."

Toonie was hurt by the comment about Pilloud not knowing that he was the local law representative in the area. But he kept his thoughts to himself and simply agreed to work together with Larry on the two matters. He hung up the phone and started for the door, but then stopped. He moved back to his desk and pulled out his nine mm.

"I'm an officer of the law. I think you're gonna go with me, sweetheart," Toonie said out loud in the emptiness of the little post office. Then he hung a sign on his door, informing the public he would be back shortly, and rushed down the hill to ready his patrol boat for the Kineo investigation.

* * *

"Look Bear," Laura started, giving the huge man's hand a tender squeeze. "You have to give Jacob back. I know ya want to see him, but if ya don't fix this quickly, they'll put you in jail. You can't be a father to him in jail."

"I know. I know. It was stupid." Bear shook his head and wept some more. He could hear his little Jacob laughing with Brandon upstairs. He sighed deeply and looked at Laura. Even in this moment of total distress and pain, Bear could not help but notice how attractive she was. *Maybe in another time and another place*, he thought. *Maybe if I weren't a damn thug who beat up two guards and broke into an estate and forcibly removed my son? Damn. Stupid. Stupid.*

Suddenly Bear's expression became more perturbed. Staring out the window, he had noticed Dr. Wayne heading across the golf greens toward the cottage. Laura continued to gaze at her friend with sympathy, but the look of pity he saw in her eyes only galled Bear. He did not want to be a man who people pitied. Especially Laura.

"Looks like your boyfriend is coming. I should go."

"Who? Oh…Max? Oh geesh, Bear. He's not my…"

"Look. Will you watch Jacob for a few minutes? There's something I need to do."

"Sure, Bear, but you know the authorities are gonna come looking for ya. You have to return Jacob…"

"Please, Laura. You can call them for me."

Bear stood up and walked over to her. Laura stood up and faced him, worried as she recognized the desperation in his eyes.

"I can't bear to have my boy see this—to be arrested like a common criminal. You call the authorities and have Jacob returned to his mother. I'll turn myself in to Magleton, but I need a few moments alone."

He then wrapped his huge arms around Laura and gave her a long, emotional hug. Laura felt the tears well up, and she struggled to hold them back as the gentle giant wept onto the top of her hair. The door suddenly swung open with a partial knock, and Dr. Wayne poked his head around the corner.

"Laura. I'm here."

Laura turned and slowly let go of Bear who looked down, embarrassed. Max took in the scene, unconsciously holding his breath.

"Um, is this a bad time? I'm sorry. Maybe I should…"

"Max. Hush. Get inside here now," Laura demanded, her voice a blend of southern charm and purpose.

"Hi professor," Bear managed. "Nice to see you again, but I gotta go. Bye, Laura, and thanks."

He hurried past the professor without looking him in the eye. Laura followed him, but stopped when she reached Max.

"Bear, I'm so sorry," she said. "We'll take care of it."

The huge man did not turn around again. He kept walking and headed down the path along Cottage Row in the direction of Mt. Kineo. Max stared at Laura. He was both embarrassed and surprised that it bothered him so greatly to see her hugging the huge timber man.

"I thought you wanted...I thought you said...um... What was that all about?"

Laura said nothing. She stared out the window, watching Bear retreat.

"Laura...perhaps I should I go?"

"No, Max. Definitely not. I need you. We need to make a very difficult call to the authorities. But out of respect for that poor man, we're gonna wait a few minutes. In the meantime, you and I have a lot to discuss."

33

"Thomas! Look! Me and Amanda are gonna climb on this rock and do a cannon ball," Jenny cried out. "Look, guys. Look at the splash I can make!"

The thirteen-year-old let herself drop from the large boulder and flung her arms about, trying to keep her balance. They flapped back and forth like the wings of a big duck trying to land in water and she spun back awkwardly and hit the surface like a sack of potatoes. Not much grace, but certainly a lot of enthusiasm. Amanda immediately burst out laughing at the sight, synchronized with a painful smacking sound in the water below.

"Yow, that looked painful!" Thomas said to Tiffany who was sitting next to him. His sister slowly swam back to the rock, but not as eagerly as when she had launched herself. Thomas found himself smiling fondly at her, even though she was a bit annoying to be around. Her cannonball attempt was, all in all, quite hilarious.

"Oww!" Jenny protested as Amanda reached into the cold water and helped her out of Moosehead Lake. Thomas glanced over at Tiffany to see if she had found the cannonball flop as amusing as the rest of the group, but the teenager merely allowed herself an aloof smile. Her long wavy blonde hair was blowing in the breeze and she seemed more focused on Thomas than on the two younger girls in the water. Thomas did not know exactly why his stomach had started to twist in knots, but was sure it had something to do with Tiffany sitting so close beside him.

"Thomas! Tiffany! You guys gonna jump in too?" Jenny asked, as she climbed back onto the boulder where Amanda was preparing to make her own cannonball entrance.

"Yeah, Tiff. You coming in?" asked Amanda.

"Not this second. Tom and I are going for a stroll."

"We are?" Thomas asked.

Tiffany stood up and looked down at him with an expression that he had only seen once before—earlier this summer, when she had flirted with him at the old water tower. But this time was different. The look in her eyes was far more frightening—and exciting. As Tiffany held her hand out to help Thomas up, she barely noticed his face turning pale.

"Yes, silly," she said. "*We* are."

* * *

"Now Rob, be careful. Control the speed of your descent with your right hand—like this."

"Got it, Julie. I've done this before, you know."

"I know. But you tend to get careless when you're excited. Follow my instructions or I'm not taking you deeper with my gear."

"Yes, Mommy."

Julie Walters landed softly on the gravel-bottomed pit. She held the light so that Rob could see, then watched him execute a more abrupt and impetuous landing next to her. Julie helped him remove the belaying-rappelling device. She had taken the time to place several strong holds in the rock above with cams and wedge nuts so that they could climb out easily.

"Okay, beautiful. What do we have here?"

"Look! More of the same markings like we saw on the walls above with the three radiating arms and circles."

"I see that. Plenty of evidence they were mining deep down in here. See?"

"Those look like places where they were chipping out... Oh, wow! Look at this, Rob. Some very unusual grade of rhyolite here. Wow! Look at the conchoidal fracture."

"I see it."

"Look how sharp these breaks are. This could really slice you open."

"Would make for very tough tools and arrowheads, wouldn't it?"

"Oh yes. That must be it. Max would be sooo..."

"Look here, Jules! This isn't just an excavation site here. Someone has *buried* something here too."

* * *

"Thank you for delivering my package to me, Pierre," Jean Pilloud said. "While you were gone, there was an incident at the house and the police had to be called. We will talk about it later." Then he turned to look at the young man standing before him. "Hello, Douglas."

"What do *you* want?" Dougie asked. "Why did he bring me here!"

"Since you were Jimbo's close friend, perhaps you have information you've been withholding from me."

"I've told you guys all I know."

"Hmm. Well, Douglas. I don't believe you. Do you, Pierre?"

"Non."

"Pierre suggested, nearly six months ago now, that I let him *persuade* you to be more cooperative, but I wasn't ready for it then. Things have become a bit more urgent since. I've now authorized him to extract what we need by whatever means necessary."

"Dude, I really don't know!"

"Oh? You never realized that Junior is on our payroll? Don't look so surprised. Sure, he was also a good friend of Jimbo's, but well, you know there simply isn't enough work in the Moosehead area. A man has to pay his bills."

"What's this you're saying about Junior? He's our friend."

"So I understand. But Pierre learned that narcotics are Junior's special friend."

"You boys should stay away from that addictive stuff," Pierre added.

"A man will sell out his friends to supply his habit."

"I don't do that stuff!"

"Yeah, whatever, surfer boy. Junior heard Jimbo say he had found a gem-quality sphere while helping Rix over at the Wellington place. We need that sphere to complete a trade with some natives. We asked Junior to extract the sphere from Jimbo for a small cash reward. You would be surprised what a strung-out loser like Junior would do for us."

"After I got him hooked," Pierre added.

"All we had to do was deprive him of his supply for a few days. Then when he was desperate enough, we dangled a bag of coke and a few hundred dollars in front of him!"

"Dudes, you're twisted!" Dougie exclaimed, outraged.

"I suppose we are. Junior tried to persuade Jimbo to show him where he had found the sphere at the Wellingtons' by jacking him up with more narcotics. Junior himself was high at the time. There was an argument and a scuffle and, somehow, Jimbo overdosed."

"I don't believe..."

"Dreadful outcome, actually. His heart stopped. Junior accidently killed your pal, Jimbo. And we temporarily lost our only lead to the missing guardian stone."

"Look Mr. Pilloud...I never liked you when I worked for you. You're mean and corrupt, but you weren't like an evil dude. What's happened to you?"

"If we find and return the missing black sphere to the old Mohawk woman, we are told she may cooperate with us. We need to know where all of the spheres are supposed to have been preserved—a special place, hidden somewhere on Moosehead Lake where my great-great-grandfather's special belongings are believed to be safely stashed away."

Dougie's face had turned ashen. His former employer had become single focused on that old legend of the Piscataquis sinking with his lost inheiritance aboard, or as they were once told, and seemed willing to do anything to recover it—if it really even existed to begin with.

"Junior could not have done that to Jimbo!" Dougie protested. "It just can't be! The dudes were friends!"

"As you wish, you naive idiot. The scuffle destroyed things in the cottage and left behind evidence that could have implicated us. I had been patient far too long."

"Mr. Pilloud requested I make the evidence disappear," Pierre added.

"So it was *you* who burned down the Goldmans' cottage?"

"Surprised? Then you're a bigger fool than I had realized. You worked the scuba-diving mission with my men. You should have surmised what we were capable of."

"We found the black sphere, Dougie," Pilloud then suddenly baited.

"What? Where?"

"In a bedside table in Gus O' Malley's home."

"His place just burned down. Gus died when his house burned down!"

"Pierre is capable of anything, Douglas—for the right price. But the death of the old sailor was unfortunate. That has caused my time table for finding my inheiritance to become far more pressing."

"Time for a professional to speed things up, Mr. Pilloud?" Pierre interjected.

"Of course, Pierre. Do take over."

"Oui, Monsieur. Okay, Dougie. Es-tu prêt à mourir? Ready to die, are you?"

"Wait! The deaths of Jimbo and Gus were careless mistakes, but now, I'm expendable? Dudes…you don't have to do this. I saw the old Mohawk woman at the Goldman cottage. Why not have her show you where the secret hiding place is?"

"She has no idea about the hidden Confederate gold" Pierre offered more than he was allowed.

"Gold? This is about that fairy tale of missing gold? You still think that silly story of your grandpappy is real?…Dude…I mean you are out of …"

"It was the other tribe of Iroquois that stole the Confederate reserve, not the Mohawk, Pilloud responded, now showing some loss of composure and anger at Dougie. "Neither the Abenaki nor the Mohawk descendants know about it. All they're concerned about is to protect their sacred site and keep us whites from encroaching on it. They are a determined and proud people that did not betray my family. We don't want to mess with them."

"All I would need is a day at the hidden site to get Mr. Pilloud's family's legacy out. Then those old Indians can go on wasting their time guarding their sacred lands as long as they choose to."

"Enough!" Pilloud interrupted. "Show Pierre the spot. I need to get back to the house. I have guests arriving shortly." He looked at Pierre. "Keep Douglas in the boathouse and continue—as instructed."

Expecting Dougie to be intimidated into compliance, Pierre asked him, "Es-tu disposé à nous aider maintenant?"

"I don't do French, asshole!" Dougie snarled.

Standing motionless as he contemplated his next move, Pierre laughed out loud at the young man's words.

Pilloud has become insane, Dougie thought, *and this paid guard dog is a homicidal maniac.*

Bunching his fingers into a tight fist, Pierre expelled a hard burst of air from his mouth as his two lead knuckles made explosive contact with Dougie's sternum, sending him down on his knees. Clutching his chest and gasping for air, the young man wished Jimbo hadn't confided in him. He wondered how long he could feign ignorance with a man as ruthless and determined as Pierre. The latter rolled on top of Dougie and trapped him in a painful jujitsu hold intended to render him unconscious. The young man's body became limp as Pierre pulled out the rope and bindings from his dufflebag.

34

"So, Pilloud. From what I gather, Bear broke through your French doors in a rage, attacked your guards, and took off with your great-nephew?" Larry Magleton asked, a trace of sarcasm in his voice.

"You understood me correctly, Sheriff. You may talk to my assistants downstairs. That ruffian has homicidal tendencies. This trespass on my estate took my security personnel completely by surprise. Given the injuries each sustained from the encounter, you're not going to let the man go unpunished, are you?"

"Yeah. I'll talk to them in a minute," Sheriff Magleton murmured. "So where do you suppose Bear went from here?"

"To Kineo, of course!" snapped Bear's furious ex-wife.

"Quiet, Rebecca," Pilloud commanded. "These fine officers will bring him to justice. Bear may be impetuous, but he is not stupid."

Rebecca looked at her uncle with seething anger. She had overlooked a number of his shady dealings and participated in a few herself. *But using my child as bait*, she thought to herself, wanting to scream the words out loud. *His own flesh and blood—good God! His own great-nephew as a pawn?*

"So you think we should go check out Kineo?"

"Yes!" Becky replied indignantly. "His beloved Kineo. That damn rock! Of course he'll be out there on *his* property."

"Well, then, we'll check it out and..."

As Sheriff Magleton dished out the standard platitudes to Becky, the cell phone in Pilloud's pocket began to vibrate, then ring. He ignored the first ring, pretending to find the intrusion irritating, but then rolled his eyes as if to imply that he didn't really have much of a choice about answering the call. Glancing down at his phone, he was pleased when he recognized the number displayed.

"Sorry, I must take this call," Pilloud murmured, then said into the phone. "Oui... Oui... Bien." Continuing in French so that Magleton would not understand, Pilloud praised Pierre for executing his tasks so promptly. "It is too late now. Get the boats ready for tomorrow morning. I will call you when I am done here."

Then turning his attention back to the sheriff, Pilloud explained, "Some important business matters with the timber-operations people. Now I think you are finished here, apart from the statements you need from my employees. So we'll go downstairs, shall we?"

Pilloud escorted the Piscataquis County sheriff downstairs where, Somerset County Deputy Toonie and the state fire investigator were already interrogating the two estate guards. Bronson was doing all the talking. Toonie stood as tall as he could, his arms folded, trying to look important and authoritative.

"So how did Bear so easily overpower a well-trained guard like you, anyway?" Bronson taunted Boxer, the larger of the two guards.

"He jumped me without warning. A cheap shot. If that guy even thinks of… Well, if he ever sets foot around here again…"

Bronson watched the two carefully, studying their expressions as they talked. Toonie participated silently, trying to look intimidating with one hand inside his vest clutching his nine mm for comfort. The smaller of the two guards knew very well what was under his vest and wondered if the overzealous law officer even had the skills required to hit a target from twenty yards.

"Just seems like it would be hard to throw a man of your size and training down a flight of stairs," Bronson continued, trying to provoke Boxer.

"Look," the other man retorted. "My dog is dead. My face needs stitches. This arm may be broken. I'm heading to see a doctor in Greenville. Are you through yet?"

Bronson simply stared at the man.

"Good. Then I'm outta here…"

Bronson studied Boxer's swollen arm as he carefully tucked it back into the sleeve of his shirt.

Sheriff Magleton and Pilloud joined the investigators below. The guards' expressions indicated they were not enjoying the interrogation by the fire investigator. Bronson looked very confident. Larry's respect for him grew as he watched him work. The sheriff thought he would have made a good detective. Bronson followed the two departing security guards through the front door and suddenly let off a parting shot at the larger man's retreating figure.

"Oh and hey… One more thing."

Boxer bit his lip and grimaced. He did not want to field any more questions from Bronson. The man held his composure and turned slowly.

"Yeah. What?"

"That's a nasty burn on your forearm."

"Yeah…so?"

"From what, may I ask?"

"Pilloud asked me to burn some yard debris a couple of days ago."

"Did you have a fire permit?"

"Funny. Now may I go?"

"Sure… Thank you for your time."

Bronson walked back through the front door and noticed that Sheriff Magleton had been hovering near the threshold, listening. The fire investigator indicated to him with a look that he had all he needed for now. Toonie was rattling off some of the same questions to Jean Pilloud that he had heard Bronson ask the guards. Pilloud played along with the charade, although it was obvious to Sheriff Magleton that the man was dangerously close to overshooting his tolerance levels.

"Enough questions, Toonie. We're done. Thank you, Mr. Pilloud. You did the right thing by calling us instead of having your guards to apprehend Bear. We'll go get Jacob now."

"Good. Please do. This whole matter has been most unpleasant for my family and particularly for my dear Rebecca."

Once safely inside the investigator's vehicle, Larry turned to Bronson. "So what's with that burn question?"

"I've been investigating fires for years. I've seen many burns. The one on Boxer's forearm is fresh—not that many hours old."

"You thinking Gus?"

"Yup."

"Hey! What're you guys talking about?" Toonie asked from the backseat.

Ignoring him, Larry rubbed his chin and looked at Bronson. "Good work, fireman. Things are coming together."

"What's up, guys?" Toonie asked again, his hand stroking the handle of his nine mm pistol.

Larry turned to him. "We're about to find out. Your boat better be ready. To Kineo, gentlemen."

* * *

As Thomas felt Tiffany's lips slide across his own, he knew he was in for more trouble than he was prepared to handle. It wasn't that he didn't find her incredibly attractive. Far from it! Tiffany made his knees quake and his heart work overtime when she flirted with him. He simply didn't appreciate her arrogant attitude and snobbish princess routine. She wasn't the girl he wanted for his first romantic encounter...or as a girlfriend. She was far ahead of the point where Thomas wanted to be at the moment. So he pulled back and looked at the sky, then back at the boulders where the girls were still splashing around. "Look, Tiff. We really need to be watching the girls. They're my responsibility. The sky's looking bad. The weather may get rough on the way back."

"Oh snap, Thomas! You are so full of it! You're terrified of me. You're a big wus! Cute, but still, a wus."

Thomas frowned and expelled a burst of air. He turned suddenly and walked back to the girls. Gathering up the towels and empty cans of soda, he asked Jenny and Amanda to return to the boat. He looked back up at the dark clouds forming. Fortunately, there *were* some nasty thunderheads forming. His explanation for wanting to head home was actually shaping up to be quite plausible. It provided him the comfort level he desired as he second-guessed his decision to halt the evolving action back there with Tiffany.

"Aww, Thomas! Why do we have to go right now? I thought Mom said..."

"Jenny! I don't have time to argue with you now. C'mon, let's get back."

Tiffany sauntered up to the boat, her hair all tossed aside and her pout of annoyance directed at Thomas. Jenny missed the look, but Amanda caught it right away.

"Uh oh," she whispered to Thomas. "What'd *you* do? She looks unhappy. And when Tiff doesn't get her way…we *all* suffer."

"Sorry, Amanda, but we gotta go. It's getting late and I don't like the look of that sky."

* * *

Rob grabbed his geologic crack hammer and a chisel and began prying the boards off the chamber floor under which the wooden vault was buried. The construction of the vault dated back many years, but was clearly far more modern than everything else in the room. The boards were fastened securely with thick iron that the chisel could not pry away.

"Damn! We'll never get this open with a chisel and a crack hammer. We need more tools."

"We need to get back anyway, Rob," Julie reminded him. "If we don't, they'll come looking for us. We can collect the necessary tools tonight and try again tomorrow morning. Maybe early, before the first class dig."

"Good idea, Jules. Let's hide the two spheres down here and go back."

"Clip in, handsome. I'm going to show you the easiest way to climb out of here."

"On belay."

"Climb on, sexy!"

* * *

Larry and Bronson jumped off the boat as Toonie pulled the bow around with a gentle nudge to the bulkhead from his starboard bumper. Bear's boat was tied to a nearby cleat, as anticipated.

"Well, he's here somewhere…just as Rebecca thought. Tie your boat, Toonie. Bronson and I'll go to the clubhouse and get golf carts so we can split up and search the island for Bear and Jacob."

"Got it, Larry. I'm right behind you!"

Toonie's enthusiasm was infectious. With his legal authority severely limited, he never saw any real action. Lawman Toonie was enjoying every moment of this real manhunt.

"Toonie's a character," Bronson remarked to Larry as he hurried toward the golf clubhouse.

"He's eager."

"Yeah. But misguided enthusiasm can get someone hurt," Bronson added. "Okay. I'll go in and tell the golf-course manager what we're doing."

"Commandeer three carts while you're there. Here…put an individual radio in each."

The three men each went about their duties. Toonie had his boat tied quickly and jogged to catch up with the other two investigators. Bronson got hold of a cart with "No. 12" affixed on the side in black letters. *My lucky number*, he thought. Toonie chose No. 17, and Larry hurried outside the clubhouse, commanding the final cart.

"Toonie," Larry directed, "do a general sweep of the island. Ask anyone you meet whether they've seen Bear or Jacob. Radio us immediately if you learn anything. Do *not* attempt to apprehend Bear by yourself. I'm going straight to his property on Kineo. He's completed enough of the construction to be able to sleep under a roof. Bronson, you take the…"

"Larry, if you don't mind," Bronson interrupted. "I have my own hunch that I'd like to play out."

"Do tell, fireman."

"The Dentons' cottage. I hear Bear is particularly fond of the attractive widow that runs the place."

"Hmm…interesting angle. Go. Call me if you have anything."

* * *

Thomas had the Sea Ray near full throttle as he carefully studied the storm brewing from the northwest. There was fury building up in the sky. Tiffany refused to even look at it and validate his reasons for ordering everyone homeward. Amanda did gaze at the sky, however, and confirmed to Jenny that Thomas was right in turning the boat back for home in such a hurry. The sky grew dark and ugly within moments. It was one of those near dusk thunder-heads that roll in without warning and envelop Kineo in a wicked pall of darkness.

Lightning began skipping sideways across the horizon, but the clap of thunder was still far enough off. The first crash struck with a vengeance and the noise was so ear-splitting that even Tiffany had to turn and look back toward the source. She noticed the sky for the first time, and the wind caught her hair and tossed it violently from one side to the other. She snickered, then looked up at Thomas who was standing tall at the helm of her father's watercraft, looking more mature than his age, and staring intently ahead at the lake's turbulent surface. *What a shame*, Tiffany thought to herself and smiled. Thomas looked down at her as another lightning flash backlighted the sky behind her. She shook her head at him and he smiled and threw the throttle full forward. The Sea Ray found smoother water hugging Kineo's northwest coast and Bennington's boat accelerated to forty-eight miles an hour. Thomas realized that the storm, on a straight bearing for Cottage Row, was going to be fierce. He had to swing around a few islands, however, and hug their coasts for the smoother water. The storm had the advantage on them and was advancing rapidly.

"Looks like we're in for a harsh gale, ladies!" Thomas looked back at Amanda and Jenny. He then looked ahead to see Mt. Kineo coming into view for the first time, but was distracted by Tiffany sprawled out on the bow of the ski boat in her skimpy bikini.

"A nasty gale you say, Thomas?" she teased. "Hmm. You might have felt the full force of a hurricane, if you hadn't chosen to flee earlier."

Thomas could not quite process all of the meanings hidden within her supposedly witty innuendo, but knew from the way she tossed it at him that it was meant to make him feel inadequate once again. And she succeeded. He looked over at the Carriage Trail and saw what appeared to be a huge man moving swiftly along it. *Who would be crazy enough to head up there in this storm? It looks like Bear! Who else is that tall?* But the figure disappeared into a thicket of fir trees and Thomas began to doubt what he thought he had seen. He had bigger worries to concentrate on now. He could not dock the boat off the Benningtons' cottage, with the wicked storm chasing them directly from behind. The boat would need safer harborage.

"I'm gonna take your father's boat into Kineo Cove; this storm is gonna be a doozie."

"Father would certainly approve of your decisions, Thomas," Tiffany responded coyly.

Jenny looked over at the Denton cottage and noticed her mother out on their back porch with a tall man.

"Look, Thomas!" she exclaimed. "Isn't that Dr. Wayne on the porch with Mom?"

* * *

"I know, Max. It's crazy. These strange deaths that have taken place recently. Indian rituals, fires, spherical gemstones, guardian stones, or whatever you guys call them. Bear and Jacob. God! And look at that storm brewing over there. I shouldn't have let Thomas..."

"Hey, hey, Laura," Max comforted her, taking her hand in his. His eyes radiated a reassuring confidence. "Things will be fine. Thomas is a very responsible young man."

"I know, Max. But it's just that... Oh look! The boat. Look. Here he comes now."

"Told you they'd be fine," Max said with one of his characteristic grins. "Jenny and Amanda are waving at us."

The boat sped by the Denton dock as the dark, angry clouds continued to advance on Kineo. In the near distance, you could see black wisps of condensed vapor engulfing Farm Island. The downpour was spreading fast. Knowing her kids were about to dock in the cove, Laura felt a huge sense of relief. Her children would all be safely home in minutes now.

"We better get inside, Laura."

"Right. And Max...thanks for being here with me."

She gave his hand a tender squeeze and then stood up. Max opened the cottage door and held it for her. Laura smiled back at him and walked though.

"Now what about this situation with Jacob?" Max inquired. "You've got to call the authorities."

"I called Toonie at the post office. He didn't answer."

Suddenly, there was a knock at the front door.

"Mrs. Denton?" a man's voice called out. "Mrs. Denton? Anyone home?"

"Yes, coming!"

"May I?" Bronson said, poised on the threshold.

"Oh... Can I help you?"

Laura had never seen this man before, but he was wearing a uniform.

"I'm Bronson Thurman, the state fire inspector."

"Oh? Hello, Mr. Thurman. Pleased to meet you. Has there been another fire?"

"No. I'm sorry to intrude. I'm helping the sheriff with an investigation here on Kineo. Do you know Sheriff Larry Magleton?"

"No. I'm afraid I've not been pulled over for speeding in Greenville—*yet,*" she said with a twinkle in her eye.

Bronson could not help taking a liking to this woman. He now understood why Bear, a divorced single man, would take an interest in this attractive widow. As he looked her over, he suddenly noticed the tall athletic man standing behind her and was overcome with embarrassment at being caught checking out Laura. Bronson nodded at the man who now approached in a manner characteristic of a male protecting his territory.

"Max Wayne." Dr. Wayne extended his hand to the fire inspector. "So Toonie's with you here somewhere?"

"Yes, Toonie and Larry are both on Kineo. We're looking for Bear and Jacob. Have you seen them?

"Oh dear, Mr. Thurman," Laura said, "you may want to have a seat. I'll fetch Jacob from upstairs. Max will fill ya in on what happened today."

"So Jacob is here. And Bear too?"

"No. Just Jacob."

"Great. I need to call this in immediately."

* * *

"Rob, this was so much fun today! Thank you." Julie Walters gave him a kiss on the cheek and finished stowing their gear. "Look at the storm heading this way. Wow! The late afternoon dig must certainly have got called off. Maybe they didn't miss us, after all."

"Oh, they missed us all right, Jules. Max noticed for sure. Come on, let's get off this rock fast!"

"What's with you and Max anyway?" Julie asked. "Slow down, Rob. I could sprain my ankle jogging down this trail so fast."

"We've to get back, Jules," Rob said, breathing heavily from his exertions. "Did you leave the two spheres back where I told you to?"

"Of course."

"We can get them again tomorrow when we bust the wooden planks off that excavation vault and see what else is down there. If you consider the locations of the three cradles that held the spheres and draw a line between them, they triangulate the location within the central mining shaft where we found the vault."

"So you think the gem-spheres are markers indicating the location of the vault in the bottom of the mining chamber?"

"I don't think it is a coincidence."

"When can we tell Dr. Wayne and Dr. Mongeau about our findings?"

"Soon, Julie. Now keep moving and watch your step. This trail will be difficult, what with a dark sky and imminent rain."

As the two scrambled past the rock formation the Dentons called the Big Chief, a large figure, the size of a bear, silently crouched behind a big boulder. *Don't need to be spotted right now*, thought the man to himself. *Got to keep moving. They'll be looking for me soon.* Luckily, he knew of a place to hide in near the summit of Mt. Kineo, where no one would be able to find him.

Once the two university students had safely passed by his hiding place, Bear continued to climb. He had a lot to think about. His heart was heavy. All he could do was lament the fate of Jacob, his little lost cub. He felt intense bitterness toward Becky and her manipulative uncle, in particular. *He's an evil man. God will not look favorably on his life. He should be locked up, not me!* And then Bear's mind drifted off to someone infinitely more pleasant—Laura. *Damn! If only, in another time—another place—under different circumstances...*

Bear climbed into a small fissure in the side of Mt. Kineo that was off the south wall, about three-quarters of the way to the fire tower. The site was concealed by over a hundred years of tree and shrub growth. Bear had inadvertently stumbled upon the site one winter when he was hunting and had been caught unprepared in a fierce blizzard that he had had to ride out.

Today, however, the summer squall was fast becoming so intense, it might cause the investigators to postpone the search for Bear on Kineo. It was near dark and the lake was becoming dangerous. Larry gathered Bronson and Toonie together and informed them about posting a law officer at the docks that night to make sure Bear did not slip off the island in his boat. Toonie volunteered for first shift, while the other two investigators would sleep on one of the empty floors of the dormitory where the students were staying. The dorm was very close to the docks, in case Toonie required any timely assistance. The men would take turns relieving each other in their vigil over Bear's boat.

Sheriff Magleton called Pilloud and informed him that they had been successful in getting Jacob away. With the fierce lightning and gail force winds, however, he recommended waiting till morning to return the little boy to his uncle's estate.

"Yes, I see the waves rolling in my back cove," Pilloud agreed. "How's the water crossing Kineo?"

"Currently, three feet, Pilloud, but it looks like it is building steadily. I fear we'll have four to four and a half feet tall swells before long."

"My Rebecca is most anxious to have Jacob safely in her arms, Sheriff."

"I'm sure. But it's not safe to cross the lake with him tonight in this weather. Bear surrendered Jacob to the Dentons who own a bed and breakfast on Kineo. They've agreed to look after the little fellow for the evening, and you and Becky can pick him up at the Dentons' cottage first thing in the morning."

"Yes. We know the cottage. That seems reasonable, Sheriff. But is there a real threat of Bear returning to make off with my great-nephew again?"

"No. Bear has realized he screwed up. He dropped Jacob off with Mrs. Denton and asked her to take the boy back to Rebecca. Then he fled. He's a fugitive, but I don't believe he's dangerous."

"You mean you haven't taken that maniac into custody?" Pilloud's voice had risen sharply at the realization that only part of his plan had been executed. Bear ought to have been in custody by now. "I want that man in jail!" he demanded.

"He will be, sir. Don't worry. We know where he is and we're bringing him in. Jacob is safe for the night and I thought you should know that."

"Thank you, Sheriff. Rebecca and I will be there at six a.m., weather permitting, to bring my great-nephew home."

"Fine. See you tomorrow, Mr. Pilloud."

Hanging up the phone, Larry felt anger growing inside of him. He did not like Pilloud. He did not trust him either.

Back at the mansion, Jean Pilloud paced back and forth on his perfectly polished maple wood floors, furious that the authorities had not yet arrested Bear. And now their search had been abandoned temporarily because of the storm and the onset of darkness. He and Pierre debated risking the weather for Kineo, but realized it was a hard enough mission in good weather. They had much to do in the morning. In addition to picking up Jacob—something that would keep Becky occupied—Pilloud, Pierre, and Boxer would be taking Dougie up Mt. Kineo to finally resolve the mystery that had been plaguing them for so long.

The spheres have to be the key to locating the hidden gold that was rightfully mine, Pilloud said to himself, the thought running back and forth in his mind. He was the sole heir to the small fortune. Nobody would stand in his way. And then he would buy out the rest of Kineo and develop the land as his own private hideaway. Pilloud considered that if he really had to, he would have Pierre set fire to the remaining holdouts, like Mrs. Denton's. *To hell with all these pesky tourists, locals, and carpetbaggers!*

"Pierre. Come. I have one more thing for you to do tonight."

"Oui, Monsieur. I am at your service."

"Get word to that crazy old Mohawk woman that we will exchange information tomorrow afternoon on the summit of Kineo."

"And we will trade her back the missing black sphere?"

"Maybe. Let's see if Dougie can first help us complete the puzzle in the morning. If we are not successful, we will deal with the crazy old woman."

"She has no phone. It would be difficult to reach her tonight in this storm."

"That's why you are paid handsomely, Pierre."

"Understood. I'll be back in three hours."

Becky was still crying in her bedroom as Pierre collected his rain gear and left on his next mission. Pilloud watched from upstairs, then walked up to Rebecca's bedroom door. He could still hear her sobbing inside. *Oh well,* he mused, *a necessary series of events in order to fulfill my destiny. No need to bother an emotional mother tonight with news of Jacob's whereabouts. She would undoubtedly insist we risk drowning in Moosehead Lake to bring her son back tonight. This information can wait till morning when the lake is less dangerous.*

* * *

Having finally climbed down off Kineo, a rain-drenched Julie and Rob snuck back to the old dormitory only ten minutes after Bronson and Larry had called it a night. Dr. Mongeau was the first to spot the students and immediately scolded Rob for returning so late. The young man apologized for the delay, then pulled out of his day bag a large mineral crystal he had supposedly found in the inner chamber. He thwarted the professor's inquisition by inundating him with information about the mineral discovery, being careful not to disclose the specimen's actual location

"Well, if *I* had found a specimen like this up there," Dr. Mongeau said, examining the mineral carefully, "I suppose I can understand why you and Ms. Walters stayed out so long looking for more. But Mr. Landon, you do realize, don't you, that finding this particular mineral here is most odd. It should not be found on Mt. Kineo, is *not* found in this parent rock material."

"Of course, Professor. That's what excited us so much. Julie thinks it was left behind as a paleo-relic of one of the Indian groups that used to mine this area. Maybe it was a valuable trading item brought in by a visiting tribe in exchange for Kineo rhyolite?"

"Hmm. Indeed. An intriguing hypothesis, Mr Landon. Now both of you should get out of those soaking wet clothes before you get hypothermia. And get some rest. We will discuss Miss Walters's speculation with Dr. Wayne in the morning."

"Where is Dr. Wayne, by the way?" Rob inquired cautiously.

"I would hope he's back by now. He was visiting that young widow at the cottage across the fairway."

"I see. Well... Goodnight, Professor."

The weather remained inclement all night, with intense squalls rolling in and out. Bursting gusts of wind made the old building creak mercilessly. The boats tied to the docks slammed against the bumpers and many lines were frayed to near exhaustion. The creaking of her cottage and the howling winds kept Laura up most of the night. Finally around four a.m., the storm lost its intensity, and the sheets of pelting rain smashing against the windows softened to a steady drizzle that continued till dawn. Laura thought to herself just before she finally fell asleep: *I pray this apparent calm is not the lull before the storm.*

35

July 4,1999: six a.m.

Weather on Moosehead Lake at this time of year can be unpredictable. Although the lake had slowly vented its anger during the early-morning hours, there was still a steady drizzle of rain, and the temperature had dropped significantly. It was forty-four degrees outdoors, as Rebecca and one of Pilloud's estate guards raced across the lake in a boat to Kineo to bring back her son. Elegant North Face rainwear protected her long-sleeved sweater. With the previous night's gale-force winds having spent their fury, the swells in the lake rose no more than a tame eighteen inches.

Rebecca was on the bow of the lead boat, looking back at Pilloud's bodyguards. While the smaller man seemed to have retained a modicum of humanity, three years of service with her uncle invariably transformed most of his employees into heartless jerks—like Boxer, the larger bodyguard. *Am I any different?*

She wondered if she would ever be able to forgive her uncle for the way he had used her and Jacob. She was beginning to see a dimension to his self-centered and obsessive personality that she could no longer tolerate. *Maybe I should take Jacob and move out of the compound*, she thought. *But where would I get the money to raise him?* Rebecca contemplated the idea of giving up the lavish lifestyle to which she'd grown accustomed.

The Four Winns bow rider was the twenty-foot model powered by a 260-horsepower engine. It was obvious to Pilloud, following closely behind his niece in his twenty-six-foot cabin cruiser, that Rebecca was forcing his guard to push her slower lead boat to the maximum. Jean Pilloud didn't mind. He knew getting Jacob back was the most important thing on his niece's mind. He was more concerned with what was stowed away in his cabin below. Bound and gagged, Dougie lay there, closely watched by Pierre. No need for Rebecca to know about his primary mission on Kineo. He would allow her to return to his estate with Jacob by herself.

By 6:10 a.m., the two boats were tied to the dock behind the Dentons' cottage, and the entire Pilloud entourage had climbed the granite steps to the back porch.

* * *

Four hundred yards to the north, Rob and Julie began their anxious ascent up the Indian Trail with a backpack full of tools and supplies. Dr. Mongeau had given them permission to deviate from the class's morning itinerary for four hours, during which they were to search for further evidence of the trading gemstone hypothesis that Rob had presented to the professor the night before.

Bear was still on the loose. His boat was still docked in Kineo Cove next to the old dormitory. The law enforcement officers confirmed that nobody had seen him either the day before or this morning. Sheriff Magleton asked if the professors and their students would stay down off Mt. Kineo and keep a watch out for Bear during their archeological and geological digs that morning. Although Dr. Mongeau assured him with a dismissive wave that they would remain vigilant, he considered the request an inconvenience. *Matters of law enforcement were best left to law-enforcement professionals, not academicians.* He mentioned in passing that two of his students might already be on their way up Mt. Kineo. Dr. Wayne, for his part, simply nodded at Toonie and Larry. He was preoccupied with other matters. Turning to Les, Max inquired about Rob and Julie's whereabouts and was told about their discovery of the amethyst discovery and the young man's conjecture about its significance. Max realized instantly that Les had been duped. He looked up at the face of Mt. Kineo and thought he detected the two tiny figures climbing along the cliff edge.

Rob, what are you up to now, he mumbled to himself.

Max filled his backpack with gear and called off his morning lecture at the excavation site near Sunset Beach. The sky indicated there would be more rain anyway, and he was piecing together his own theory about the spherical gemstones. Dr. Mary Chase had called Max back with the results of her research on the native Indians using spherical gemstones as ritualistic markers. The information confirmed what he had suspected—that the finds were completely at odds with the practices of the native peoples in this region. But then again, the carved specimen of amethyst was not indigineous to these parts. Rob and Julie had a clear forty-five-minute head start on him and were probably near the top of Mt. Kineo already.

"Margo and Gary. Over here, guys. Now!" he demanded.

"What is it, Professor?" graduate student Margo McKinnon asked with an eager-to-please smile and a gaze that held the professor's own.

"Yeah, Prof—wassup?" Gary Micnick joined in.

"Don't have time to explain, guys. Gary, I'd appreciate you not cracking on me." Max turned suddenly and looked directly into Margo's captivated eyes. "Margo. You're the seniormost of the lot. Assemble the archeological students and, if weather allows, finish the site work on the east cove. If it rains, then take the others to the dorm basement and start keying out fragments. Gary, I expect you to ensure that nobody gives her the business. I gotta go for a few hours. That's it. Thanks."

As Max turned purposefully to leave, he was oblivious to Margo's long and affectionate gaze lingering on his retreating figure.

"We'll get it done, Dr. Wayne," the young woman called out a bit awkwardly, a moment too late for him to catch the words. "You can count on me."

Max headed straight across the golf course in the direction of Laura Denton's cottage.

* * *

"Thank you, Mrs. Denton, for watching over Jacob." Rebecca Pilloud's voice sounded weary and tense. "I'd like to take him home now."

"I completely understand, and believe me, it was our pleasure to help. Jacob is a sweet lil' boy. Brandon enjoyed entertaining him. When things settle down, he is more than welcome to come and visit us again."

Rebecca managed a smile, but it lacked warmth. Outside, Pilloud and Boxer stood on the porch. The former thanked Bronson for finding Jacob so quickly. With the grilling the fire investigator had subjected him to at the Pilloud estate fresh in his mind, the bodyguard refused to acknowledge his presence.

Clutching Jacob in her arms, Rebecca boarded her boat and signaled to the smaller guard to pilot her back to her Uncle Jean's compound. Dr. Wayne continued toward the cottage with a look of grim determination. Placing his hand on Bronson's shoulder with sudden authority, Jean Pilloud attempted to steer the investigation back to Bear.

"Go find your sheriff and track that maniac down," he said.

"I assure you, sir," Bronson replied, "Larry will track him down this very morning. He's still on Kineo, and we'll find him."

"Yes. And Boxer here will be happy to assist in the search."

"No, thank you, Mr. Pilloud. It's best to let the proper authorities do their job. But I will certainly let Larry and Toonie know you offered."

"As you think best, Mr. Thurman," Pilloud said, his reply sounding a bit too rehearsed for Bronson to accept at face value. "Well then, sir, I'll be getting back now to comfort Rebecca."

Laura stepped onto the porch, still somewhat shaken from all the disconcerting developments she had been witnessing. But the sight of Max heading straight for her porch reassured her.

"Bonjour, Mrs. Denton," Pilloud murmured, bending to kiss her hand. "We appreciate your assistance in this matter."

Then, as suddenly as he had arrived, Jean Pilloud left through the back screen door to his boat, idling below.

From where he stood on the back porch, trying to keep one eye on the Sea Ray and the other on his employer leaving the cottage, Pierre had been observing Bronson Thurman's face for telltale signs. But he found the man he had sized up as a potential adversary surprisingly difficult to read. Pierre then scanned Laura Denton's face and found it as transparent as an open book. He saw no reason to speak to either, having dismissed them as inconsequential—insignificant prey, unworthy of pursuit.

Pierre then noticed the tall athletic professor enter the cottage and head toward Bronson and Laura. *Now there is a guy that would be fun to take down*, he thought to himself. Then realizing that his employer had nearly reached his boat, he spun around abruptly and hurried after him.

"Oh, Mr. Thurman. I just don't like those people," Laura confessed in a shaky voice.

"You shouldn't."

"Laura? Is everything all right?" Max asked, shaking Bronson's hand.

"Oh, Max. It's good to see you. Those Pillouds are sooo..."

"Yes, indeed," Bronson agreed.

This morning, there seemed to be a change in the equation between the fire investigator and Max. Nothing like interacting with the Pillouds and being at the receiving end of their overbearing ways to put things squarely in perspective. Max and Bronson realized they were allies.

"Laura, I don't have time to talk to you about all that's going on, but I need to climb Kineo," Max told her. "Rob and Julie are up..." he paused, uncertain as to whether Bronson could be taken into confidence.

Sensing the awkward pause, the fire investigator turned to Dr. Wayne.

"It's okay. I'm not a cop. Just a fire investigator. But if you need to talk to Mrs. Denton privately, I have to go anyway."

"I'm sorry, Mr. Thurman," Max said apologetically.

"No, it's fine, really. Hey, but be careful with your students this morning. Bear is still on the loose. I'm pretty sure he is harmless...but who knows?"

"No, I agree. I'll have all my students off the mountain today, and I am bringing the other two down right now. But thanks. Good day, Mr. Thurman."

Max watched the other man walk away from the porch and out of earshot before attempting to speak to Laura again. Laura found herself using those few moments to sneak in a long look at Max and wonder why she was so attracted to this man, that too under such stressful circumstances. *I should be thinking about poor Bear and Jacob—what is wrong with me?* Wishing she could reach out and give Max a tight embrace, she found her brief reverie cut short as he turned to her with an anxious expression.

"Look, Laura. Two of our students went up Mt. Kineo very early this morning. I think they stumbled onto artifacts of historical significance. I fear they are disrespecting..." his voice trailed off.

For a moment, she thought she saw him choke back a rash of emotions. She wasn't sure if it was anger, grief, disappointment, or all three.

"With the Bear thing going on and..." Max managed, before relapsing into silence.

"Does this all have something to do with the guardian stones and the excavation in my basement?"

"I'm sure of it. Rob has that amethyst sphere. And I know he is up to something. Anyway, keep your kids away from Kineo this morning. I'll come see you when I get back."

Laura suddenly reached out and squeezed his hand. "Be careful, Max. I have a bad feeling."

He squeezed her hand back, then turned to face the responsibility before him. Tightening his backpack straps, he headed toward Mt. Kineo. The cold wind blew across his face, and he began to curse himself for not bringing warmer clothes. No time for that—he had to get up there quickly.

Thomas was in the kitchen, pouring a bowl of cereal and preparing to plant himself in front of the TV. His attention was drawn to a weather report from Bangor. The report said that the front that had moved in last night had stalled and some additional bad weather was on the way for the Moosehead Lake region over the next two days. *Lots of rain and some very heavy gusts expected.* Thomas wanted to go check his geo-cache on the nearby island, but realized that boating was out today. He got up and took his bowl of cereal to the porch where he found his mother watching Dr. Wayne hike off in the distance. The steady drizzle began to pick up.

"Dang! There's going to be more rain," Laura mumbled to Thomas as he stepped outside to join her.

"Actually, Mom, the TV just forecast bad weather again. Lots of rain and wind. Two days' worth."

"Oh no, Thomas! That poor man is heading up Mt. Kineo without rain gear. Go collect a couple of raincoats and fetch the golf cart. See if you can catch him and give him what he needs to stay dry."

"Sure thing, Mom. I'm on it!"

* * *

"Julie, hurry up! We don't have a lot of time."

"Slow down, Rob. This type of scrambling on weathered rock isn't safe in dry weather— it's downright foolish in rain!"

"Jules, Jules, chill, babe! Don't you wanna see what's behind the wooden planks? We gotta get down that pit again, open the vault, then climb out quickly. You know Professor Max will be on our tail soon."

The two students shed their raingear at the inside entrance of the tunnel crevasse. Then they each adjusted their equipment packs, turned on their flashlights, and began making their way through the entrance tunnel. It took only ten minutes to reach the central chamber and rearrange their equipment for the rappel down into the pit. Julie noticed for the first time that the chamber contained a small ledge that completely encircled the room. Small wooden bowl-like objects were spaced evenly along the ledge, with Native American markings painted on the wall behind each.

"Max would love to see this!"

"Forget Max!" Rob snapped, "We've got to get down there now."

"Rob, what's it with you and Max? I swear you're like… Whoah Rob, whoah! Do not go down that way! Here, let me lead this route."

"No Jules, I got it." Rob clipped into his rappel with reckless abandon. Julie noticed he had not properly set his anchor for his short descent and was not paying attention to details.

"No, Rob. Stop! Let me fix your set-up."

"Sorry, sweet cheeks, gotta descend," he smirked as he leaned over the pit edge and began to let out rope. "Hurry, babe! I need ya to hold a light for me at the bottom."

"No Rob! Wait!"

* * *

With Pilloud, Pierre, and Dougie on board, Boxer, the large bodyguard with an unforgiving memory and an axe to grind, carefully throttled the boat around the far side of the island and docked without notice at the private fishing cottage on the northwest side of Kineo, next to the Indian Trail. He carefully edged the boat under the roof of an old cantilevered structure anchored to the shore, far away from the winter's destructive force of expanding ice. As Pilloud and Boxer unloaded supplies, Pierre cut several branches off a nearby aspen tree and used them to cover the watercraft's exposed stern.

"Good enough, Pierre. That provides sufficient cover to camouflage it from passing boats. We have work to do. Bring Douglas up from the cabin and *motivate* him to participate on our little scavenger hunt, will you?"

"My pleasure, Mr. Pilloud."

Meanwhile, Boxer was dispatched to scout ahead for Bear—an assignment he was eagerly looking forward to. Bear was now proving to be a hindrance to Pilloud's operation. They needed to find him and turn him over to the law before they could have a free run of Mt. Kineo, undisturbed by either Bear or the authorities. Pilloud was too close to his prize to take undue risks.

Certainly, this cold rainy day is my day of destiny, Pilloud thought. *We must drive these intruders away from my family legacy, buried somewhere within this historic mound of rock.* Although the mere thought of harming Bear or even killing him gave Pilloud a feeling of disturbing pleasure, any such incident would only draw unwanted attention from the authorities. Better to simply capture the rogue and turn him in, or scare him down the mountain into the waiting arms of the law. *Heck, maybe we'll get lucky and that idiot with the itchy trigger finger—Toonie, was it?—will accidentally shoot Bear dead.*

Pilloud had spent a lifetime trying to locate the Confederate gold that his great great grandfather had confiscated. That gold was rightfully *his* now. *Forget Bear. This is about claiming my inheritance. Then I will rid the island of these pesky cottage owners and proceed with my huge development plans.* Pilloud considered how he could melt the gold, sell it, and use the money to fund the condominium development. His timber company was losing money and he foresaw the ability to make millions on tourism-development by exploiting all of Kineo. *I'll sell the timber business or let Rebecca have it,* he concluded.

Dougie emerged from the cabin, his wrists bound and blood dripping from his nose. On his face was fear, alternating with anger and despair. He stepped off the boat with some prodding from Pierre, who meticulously wiped the blood from his own knuckles.

"I don't like the American pig's blood on me," Pilloud's deputy announced with distaste, yanking the duct tape from Dougie's mouth. There was a piercing sound of tearing flesh as the skin on Dougie's upper lip split wide open. The young man valiantly resisted flinching from the pain, but did take the opportunity to spit blood from his mouth in Pilloud's direction.

"Now Douglas, is that any way to show gratitude to your former employer?" Jean Pilloud taunted. "Ha! Enough amusement—show us what we came to see. We know Jimbo told you more than you're letting on. Take us there now!"

Pierre shoved the handle of his hunting knife into Dougie's back and ordered him to begin the ascent up the Bridal Trail. Although it was a little longer than the Indian Trail, it was much easier to climb in the rain and lay out of the visual range of the cottages on Kineo. It was a steep hike, but it required no scrambling. Allowing one's hands to be free would ensure the equipment could be taken up Mt. Kineo in far less time. A rapid ascent to the former volcanic mound was crucial.

It was now nearly six-thirty a.m., and Pierre noticed the storm gaining in intensity as he dragged Dougie up the mud-covered trail. The rain began to pelt down harder, and Dougie could feel it stinging the back of his neck. With mud now sliding down the incline, the Bridal Trail was proving to be a well-chosen path for Pilloud's expedition. The Indian Trail, on the contrary, would have been treacherous for hauling up equipment, because the rhyolite had been worn smooth over the years by the tramp of hiking boots and snowmobile scarification.

Dougie slipped and, with his hands tied behind his back, was unable to regain his balance. He crashed to the ground and lay motionless in a deep puddle as his head struck a rock. The mud seeped his eyes, and he began bleeding from a gash in the side of his skull. Cold and merciless, Pierre hauled the dazed prisoner to his feet and pushed him along. Pilloud said nothing, but was clearly pleased with his henchman's handling of the brief delay. The rain began to sting harder. A crack of thunder sounded in the distance. All were protected by raingear except Dougie, who was already chilled to the bone. Pilloud wrapped his North Face rainwear tight around his body and summoned his third man on the two-way radio.

"Anything, Boxer?"

"I think so. At the junction of the Indian Trail and the Bridal Trail, I found some boot tracks that would be a size sixteen."

"Bear?"

"I would think so. But the rain has worn the trail away. I lost the tracks a few minutes ago. He has been this way recently."

"Find him and chase him down to the authorities. Call me when you have him and do *not* shoot him! We don't need noise attracting the authorities. I want Bear down alive and all these people away from Mt Kineo while we are complete what *we* are here to do."

"Understood." The disappointment in his voice was all too apparent.

"You better understand, Boxer. Or you'll have Pierre to answer to!"

* * *

"Okay, Toonie. We're doing this together—my way. No hot-dog stuff. You see something, you call for back-up. No guns. Bear's a decent guy. A bit confused, but we can talk him down. But careful. He's huge and distraught and may try something foolish."

"You think he'd kill himself?"

"I've seen it before, Toonie. I have reserve deputies arriving at the dock in a few minutes. We'll send 'em up to assist the search and capture. For now, we take two carts. You take Deputy Russell and his hound dog up the hill with the old water tower. If you don't find a trail, take the dog across the talus pile. I'll meet you up the mountain. You take the Indian

Trail. I'm going to check out Hardscrabble Point and make sure there's no sign of him there. I'll then work my hound along the water and take the Bridal Trail on the way back.

"Oh, man! The Indian Trail will be a bitch!"

"You're local, Toonie—you know it best."

"It'll be a muddy mess in this rain!"

"Keep in constant contact with me by radio. Got it?"

"Yeah, Larry. Got it."

Toonie felt his hand slide down the handle of his nine-millimeter sidearm; it felt comforting. He ran his finger and thumb around the brim of his brown hat. As he relished the pride his uniform provided, Toonie began to care less about climbing the Indian Trail in the downpour. Rubbing the brim of his hat, he let the rainwater bead off and stream to the ground at his feet. He congratulated himself for his wise selection of headwear in that day's dismal weather. He clipped his radio to his utility belt and set off, grinning proudly.

* * *

"Dr. Wayne, stop!" Thomas called out.

Max was so intent on his mission, he had already covered most of the distance down the Carriage Trail before the boy could locate the raincoats and dry clothes, load the golf cart, and catch him.

"Hey! Mom had me bring this to you."

Drenched from the cold stinging rain, the professor ducked under the covered golf cart and stripped off his wet shirt. Then he put on the synthetic Columbia long-sleeved fishing-wear shirt and sweater that Thomas had brought him. Finally, he slipped on the raincoat and zipped it up all the way. He shivered a little as he wiped the rain off his face. Then he nodded to Thomas in gratitude. The boy escorted Max the rest of the way to the trailhead in the Denton golf cart.

"Did Laura send you to rescue me?"

"Yeah. Sorry, Dr. Wayne."

"Tell her, thanks. But I'd like you to go home now. No point in both of us getting soaked."

Thomas kept driving till he reached the talus pile and parked the cart.

"I'd like to go too, Dr. Wayne. I've nothing else to do on a rainy day. Maybe you could use a hand."

Max did not like the idea—the weather was steadily getting worse, and he might be in for an unpleasant confrontation with Rob Landon. But Thomas was a mature kid. Max might actually need someone to go back and get help if his students foolishly got themselves into trouble.

"Well. Okay, Thomas. But you must do as I say. Listen carefully. If I ask you to go back, you go back. Hear me?"

"Got it, Dr. Wayne."

"Righto. Let's scoot."

* * *

"Damn, Rob, why can't you men ever listen!"

"I know," Rob said feebly, his voice reduced to a desperate whimper. "Gimme a break... This hurts!"

"You probably *have* a break! You fell nearly fifteen feet! I'm coming down to check you out."

"Okay, Jules. Just throw the bag down to me first." Rob was panting heavily. "I still want to see what's under these boarded doors."

"Rob, you're being ridiculous! You need help. I'm coming down. Here's your bag of supplies on the rope. Don't try to do anything foolish until I get down there."

"Right," he groaned, "Pass the bag down."

"Watch your head—the bag is heavy. I'll then rig to rappel down and assist you."

"Thanks, Jules. You rock! Damn, my leg is really starting to hurt!"

The bag of equipment slowly slid to a stop about three feet from Rob's left leg. The young man wasted no time in opening it and getting out a crowbar, a hammer, a chisel, and a battery-operated hand drill. Driven by adrenaline and the raw excitement of expecting a marvel behind the well-secured door panels, he immediately went to work, trying to open the doors to the floor vault.

The wood was very old and thick. The fasteners and hardware appeared to be old and, in some places, rusty. *Whatever they buried inside here was sure meant to stay inside*, he thought. Julie began rigging for a safe descent to rescue him. Outside, the rain continued to pelt the mountain, and wind speed had increased substantially. Neither Julie nor Rob was aware of the worsening weather conditions. No sounds from the world outside could penetrate the thick walls of the ancient mining chamber.

Rob managed to remove much of the historic hardware that had been standing in his way. He was less successful as he tried to break away a support with the chisel and the hammer. He then tried the crowbar again, and the door began to lift a little, but not enough to see inside. Exasperated and impatient, Rob placed both legs under the structure and pushed it up with all his might. The door moved up nearly six inches. Then a terrifying snap echoed inside the pit as the door sprang back like a coiled spring and smashed Rob's injured leg against the side of the vault. The young man's weakened tibia fractured all the way under the stress and he rolled onto his back and screamed out in agony, letting out a stream of expletives.

He was beginning to feel faint at the very moment that Julie slid skillfully off her rope next to him and detached herself from her rappel line. Dropping to her knees, she pulled out a knife from her equipment bag, and slit Rob's trousers open. As she examined the injury, Rob's face became pale and lifeless.

"No, Rob, no! What were you thinking? This looks bad. It's a serious fracture. If the fall didn't mess you up enough, you sure finished it off with that last stupid stunt!"

Rob said nothing. The pain was excruciating, and he knew he was screwed. Although the door he had tried to pull off had slammed back shut, the impact had wrenched the other door off its remaining hinge and it now stood askew. Part of the vault was now open. Rob realized he could finally peek inside and see what it contained. But he was so faint with pain that he simply clutched the side and waited. He contemplated lifting himself up high enough to look inside for a second before his eyes rolled back into his head and he lost consciousness.

* * *

Earlier that morning, Bear had awakened from a disturbed night. He knew he had to turn himself in. He had decided he would take himself down the mountain as soon as it stopped raining, when he heard the two students talking in hushed tones. He was instantly alert; why were they were climbing Mt. Kineo that early on a rainy, miserable morning? He debated whether he should follow them or hike down the mountain to face the authorities. *Oh hell! I can turn myself in later. What are these students up to?* He began tailing the two. Bear realized from their careful, surreptitious movements that they were anxious to remain undetected. They were quite unaware that a much more experienced woodsman was maintaining a safe distance from them.

Bear reached a little-used side trail off the Indian Trail, where he had seen the students remove branches to uncover another hidden side trail. He carefully moved the branches aside as he had seen the students do only minutes before his arrival. He was amazed at how cleverly the entrance to the side trail had been constructed with the intention of keeping strangers off it. It was orientated along a minor side trail about twenty yards off the Indian Trail. The fact that this stretch of the Indian Trail provided a sudden, spectacular view of Moosehead Lake from the cliff served as a ploy to draw one's attention to the south exposure and away from the clandestine route in the opposite direction which offered no views. Moreover, the debris of dead branches made that spot uninviting and the path virtually invisible. Bear wondered how regularly the pile of debris was checked and rearranged to ensure complete obstruction to that path. Even as an expert outdoorsman, he would have likely missed this side trail, had he not been closely following these two students.

Advancing along the tiny path, he noted it was no more worn than a typical animal trail. Deer scat along the path offered further evidence in support of his assumption. *It was a game trail, wasn't it? But then, where had the students gone, if not along here?* Bear wondered briefly if he was about to intrude on a little lovers' romp in the downpour, but then remembered that both were carrying a lot of equipment with them. *No, this was something infinitely more suspicious.*

The trail continued to narrow until there was hardly any discernible path. Scratches marked Bear's skin as the undergrowth sprang back at him and lashed his face and arms. His large body kept becoming entangled in the foliage. Before frustration could set in, Bear summoned his most developed outdoors skill. He stood perfectly still, the way he had learned to do so adeptly as a hunter in the deep wildernesses of Maine. All he could hear was the sound of the rain and the wind. He focused more intently. He had, after all, the most acute sense of hearing among any of the humans he had ever met. Some had even teased him for possessing the ears of a wolf. He needed to distinguish between the sound of the wind and the rain and the distinctive sound of humans harshly violating the purity of the wilderness. Finally, he heard it. Faint though it was, he heard the sound of a metallic object striking a rock face—behind him. He had come too far.

Quietly, Bear retraced his steps and discovered a tiny opening formed by a crease in a large boulder face. The sound came from behind the boulder. The rain began to fall harder once again, and he knew if he didn't slip into the crease, he would likely lose the sound altogether. Bear was not interested in staying in the rain any longer anyway. He carefully approached the opening, exhaled, and stuck his crippled leg in first. *Dang, this crease is narrow!* The enormous man imagined himself being as thin and flexible as a serpent, and was astonished when he deftly slid inside the opening.

* * *

"What more do you know about the guardian gemstones, Dougie? Pierre asked harshly.

"Do tell us, Douglas. I'd hate to see you beaten again," Jean Pilloud added sardonically. "Are they up here?"

"I've told you all I know. Jimbo found the black sphere at the Goldman cottage under the old flooring."

"But we know the natives' legend of how the Polish girl lost it from above."

"I don't know anything about that. This is as far as I can take you."

"Oh, I don't agree, Douglas. Pierre, do use your powers of persuasion with the poor boy's head. I suspect his memory can be stimulated."

"As you wish, sir," Pierre responded in a soft, chilling tone.

36

Toonie's hound was not able to discern Bear's scent around the old abandoned water tower. The postmaster wondered how effective a hound's olfactory system was in rain anyway. The dog was hard to control on the leash and kept pulling Toonie around eagerly, sniffing at anything and everything. But still, he had not found a scent that matched the sample they had provided the dog to track the fugitive. *Maybe the sample wasn't good enough?*

Either way, it was time to track through the steep talus pile as Larry had ordered. *No, not ordered,* he thought to himself, *requested of him. The Deputy of the Rockwood area does NOT take orders from the Sheriff of Greenville. I am the local Sheriff representative of Somerset County, for Christ's sake!*

"Toonie, anything?" the radio broke his concentration.

"No, Larry. Nothing. I'm 'bout to head through the talus pile...You?"

"Nuttin' at Hardscrabble. Headin' your way. Up Bridal next. You got Indian, remember?"

"Yeah, yeah. I remember. And it's rainin' harder now, you know."

"Ten four."

"Kiss off!" Toonie told off his radio speaker bravely although the transmit button was no longer depressed.

* * *

Thomas studied the tall professor as he easily strode up the first series of rhyolite steps carved into the outer edge of the Indian Trail. Even with the rain pounding them and the trail now a turbid stream, the athletic professor effortlessly climbed through the maze of rocks, roots, and slick mud. Thomas had been impressed with this man from the day he met him. He was smart, strong, and kind. He wondered if Dr. Wayne fancied his mother. He *seemed* to. Thomas was fairly confident that his mother had taken notice of Professor Max as well. He continued to ponder over the two adults as he struggled to keep up with Dr. Wayne on his aggressive ascent.

"Going too fast for you, bud?" Max asked, looking back at the winded teenager.

"I can keep up with you!"

"Think so, huh? You can go back and wait at the cart if you like or..."

"Heck no, Dr. Wayne! I'm right behind you."

Max considered the teenager's contagious enthusiasm. "Righto! Then be careful in this slippery chute and let's go!"

* * *

Growing increasingly concerned, Julie knew that she had to climb out of the mining pit, leave Rob lying there, and bring back help. The fracture in his leg was quite serious, and she feared he might go into shock. She could not help peering into the partially opened vault and was startled by the sight of the skeletal remains of a human covered in pelts from animals and a string of turquoise beads draped around its skull.

"Crap!" she exclaimed. "We just disturbed a native Indian burial site. Max will be furious!"

Still out cold from the pain and trauma, Rob did not hear her. Climbing quickly up the pit wall and over the lip of the chamber wall, she unclipped herself from the belt, tucked her carabineers away, and stowed the rope quickly on the floor.

"I'll be back with help soon, Rob. Hang in there."

Julie ran as fast as she could through the narrow passageway. She had advanced only fifteen yards before her head struck a low passage overhang, sending her tumbling to the ground. Raising herself to her knees, she bent down and felt the throbbing in her forehead and a small trickle of blood. Once the pain had subsided enough to allow her to refocus on the task at hand, she reached into her backpack and found her Petzel headlamp and climbing helmet. Wiping bloody strands of hair out of the way, she strapped the headlight around her helmet and turned the light on.

Julie studied the very low overhang of the entrance passage to the main chamber. She had forgotten how little clearance the entrance offered a brave explorer. She needed to hurry for help, but she also needed to be more careful. *I'd be no help to Rob unconscious.* She carefully crawled through the narrow passageway.

When she finally made it out of the tunnel, she was greeted by weak daylight up ahead. The filtered light was a welcome sight, even if the thunderstorm outside had reduced visibility to a great extent. At least she could see without using her headlamp. Julie began running carefully through the final passage maze and was only about twelve yards from the crevasse opening when she felt a large arm suddenly swing around her body and neck and bring her to a complete halt. She was in the unexpected embrace of a person with unimaginable physical strength.

37

"You little punk!"

"Good, Pierre. Hit him again."

"I'll never tell you, crap!"

"Enough of the pleasantries, Mr. Burelli."

Pilloud's expression suddenly turned vicious. He looked at Pierre and gave him a nod. The Frenchman, in turn, gave Dougie a menacing stare.

"I'm beginning to tire of your insolence," he told the young man. "Let's see how well you wakeboard with a broken knee."

Before Dougie could deflect the blow from the mercenary, Pierre had taken the ferry captain's legs out from beneath him with a swift, well-placed kick. As the young man attempted to regain his balance even as he fell, Pierre swung around again and kicked him in the kidney. Dougie collapsed, hitting the ground with full force. Pilloud watched expressionlessly, as his highly paid pit bull wasted no time in inflicting as much damage as he could to their helpless victim.

Before going to Quebec, Canada, Pierre had lived in France and Algiers for a while. There he had trained in the French Special Forces and picked up more Aikido, Jujitsu, Karate, and kick-boxing techniques than he required to be effective in dishing out pain when he felt so inclined. Martial arts skills were not intended as tools of torture or to facilitate interrogation. It required a mental shifting of perspective for a trained military man to assume the role of a successful mercenary. Had Pierre remained in the Special Forces instead of offering his military skills for hire, he would have been hauled up for abusing the revered martial-arts tradition in this manner. Now having to handle this stubborn surfer boy and his smug responses, while the freezing rain soaked him to the skin, was all the Frenchman needed to metamorphose instantly from soldier to hired killer. Shifting into psychopathic mode was something that his conscience was quite comfortable with. Jean Pilloud had witnessed this personality change before and it frightened him as much as it excited him.

"Don't kill him, Pierre. At least—not *yet*."

The mercenary had Dougie's right leg pinned awkwardly behind him. With one swift, calculated move, he twisted the limb in a direction in which it had not been designed to move naturally. The sound of knee ligaments tearing was so sickening that even Pilloud grimaced. Dougie screamed in pain and began lashing out with his fists at Pierre. The first swing actually caught the other man by surprise and split his cheek open under his right eye. The next few swings missed their mark as Pierre applied his knuckles directly to Dougie's sternum, knocking the air out of his lungs. The Frenchman stood looking down at his hapless victim, then glanced back at his employer.

"Don't worry. He'll live," he said.

"Dude, you suck!" cursed Dougie in a pitifully broken voice. "Kill me! I don't care! Kill me! I'll never tell you shit!"

"Hmm," pondered Pilloud, looking down with distaste at the broken bundle of flesh and bones spitting blood from his mouth and writhing in pain. "I guess we will just have to see if your other little buddy feels as inclined to absorb pain, Mr. Burelli. What was that sweet little girl's name, Pierre? You know—the one you saw Douglas frolicking with in the lake?"

"I believe her name is Amanda," responded the other man.

"No! no! You leave Amanda and her family out of this!" Dougie implored.

The distress in his voice told the two men all they needed to know. *Jackpot! We know your weakness, and we will have what we want from you now.*

                                    * * *

"Let go of me! What do you think you're doing?"

"What do you think *you're* doing?" retorted the imposing giant. "And what the hell are you doing sneaking around in *here*?"

"We're university students looking for archeological relics and geologic minerals. Rob's hurt real bad. He's inside there. He needs a doctor."

"He'll need more than that if he disturbed artifacts or tampered with an Indian burial site on my island!"

Outside the crease in the mountain, two other pairs of eyes watched the developing action on Mt. Kineo. They too were drenched in the cold Kineo rain, but seemed totally immune to its numbing effects on the body and mind. They had their own mission to fulfill. The older of the two signaled to the other to flank around to the side passage and be prepared to take evasive action if the big man spotted them. The younger observer, although much stronger and more eager to use violence, if necessary, carefully sized up Bear from a distance and thought to himself: *It would be best if this large man were allowed to pass in peace. As long as he does not interfere with our plans.*

Bear took the trembling girl's hand, feeling pity for her. Her look of distress and panic explained much of what he needed to know. "Let me go back with you and see if I can help your friend," he offered.

"No! There's no time. He's becoming hypothermic, losing consciousness, and heading into shock. He has a bad bone fracture. Now trust me—he's screwed and time's of the essence."

"Okay, sweetie. We'll fetch him some help. Trust me. The authorities are not far away. Let's go find them."

As Bear helped Julie move through the final few yards of the tunnel toward the exit, he thought he heard the faint sound of another human somewhere in the tunnel system. He didn't have time to process what this might mean. Julie was in no mood to sit and discuss odd sounds in the distance. She felt responsible for the accident, since she was the experienced climber and should never have let Rob rush ahead of her.

The young woman ran purposefully down the hidden path from the outer crease, with Bear struggling to keep up. She was not concerned this time with covering her tracks and placing the brush back as they raced closer to the Indian Trial. Bear slipped in the mud and lost his balance temporarily, allowing Julie to get further ahead of him. She busted through the low hanging underbrush out onto the Indian Trail and immediately became disoriented. Which route should she take? Rain pelted her face and strands of her hair stuck to her cheeks as she caught her breath, waiting for Bear to catch up. Then hearing his huge frame crashing through the same underbrush, she knew he had caught up with her again, and bolted off down the Indian Trail—this time, in the right direction.

Bear lost sight of her momentarily as she raced down the second glacial carved ravine on the south side of the Mt. Kineo cliff face. Then suddenly, he heard voices ahead.

"Hey! Who the hell are you!"

* * *

"Toonie, what's your ten-twenty?" the radio crackled.

"Strugglin' through the damn talus pile, attached to a most annoying hound, Magleton! How about you?"

"Heading up the Bridal Trail and I have tracks. Recent ones."

"You got tracks?" Toonie's voice was both surprised and disappointed. *Damn, he finds the trail of the bandit.* "How many tracks?"

"We got three, no…four sets here. Real recent. Copy?"

"Copy. Any with a huge footprint?"

"No. One set heads toward the junction with the upper Indian Trail and the other three sets stay close together. Their stride is slower and they're moving in a group."

"Who'd be heading up Mt. Kineo in this weather?"

"I dunno. Students, maybe. The islanders certainly know well enough to stay away. How soon can you get over here to cover a potential exit down the Indian Trail?"

"Hell, Larry! In this rain? Over this talus? Talus, my ass! Some of these rocks are the size of a school bus!"

"Okay, okay. Just do your best and hurry."

"Ten-four."

* * *

Max was rapidly nearing the junction of the Indian and Bridal trails. He rounded the corner of a large granitic feature that had several steps conveniently carved into it by the action of water. This made the ascent a less harrowing one in such dreadful weather. Rounding the hairpin curve at the top of the last step, he looked back to check on Thomas. The boy's pro-gess was fine, but from his new vantage point, he could see over the side of the cliff and down the face of Mt. Kineo to the talus pile below. There he saw a police officer, dressed snugly in black rainwear from head to toe and a large sheriff department-issued hat. *Good. We have the local authorities coming our way searching for Bear*, thought Max. *If Rob and Julie are in trouble, I could use their help.*

* * *

When Bear reached the location where he thought he had heard voices, he saw some-one threatening Julie and recognized the man at once. The latter was backing her out onto a ledge of rocks overlooking the face of Mt. Kineo. This was one of many spectacular scenic vantage points on the Indian Trail—at least on sunny days. But with the rain and mud slosh-ing around at her feet, lightning crashing in the distance, and the terrified student staring down the 700-foot drop—the vantage point seemed, in Bear's eyes, more like the boundary to hell.

"Okay darlin'," said the man holding Julie in his vice-like grip. "Whatcha running from? Huh? You see Bear up here? You look like you seen a ghost."

"Let me go!"

"I know a guilty face when I see one. Tell me whatcha running from up here? You seen Bear?"

"Right behind you, dirtbag!" the big man's voice boomed out over the sound of the rain and thunder.

Boxer turned sharply, a smile of sadistic delight appearing on his lips as he saw Bear. Then he seized Julie and pulled her out near the cliff edge.

"Been lookin' for you, Bear," Boxer said. "Remember me?"

"You're the big sissy I threw down the steps at Pilloud's place, right?"

The smirk on the big guard's face vanished, only to be replaced by a look of mortification that quickly morphed into fury. He twisted Julie's wrist forceably and sent her to her knees in pain below him.

She let out a whimper. "Mr. Bear? Help me, pleeeeeease!"

"Let her go, you goon!" Bear ordered, enraged. "It's me Pilloud wants."

"Actually he wants all of you down off of his mountain. Now!"

"Let the girl go. I planned on surrendering peacefully anyway. This does not involve the students."

"I've been ordered to help bring you all down. With force if need to."

Bear moved toward the large guard unimpressed. Boxer's cheap, inadequate rainwear was unequal to the task of protecting him from the heavy rain. With his body chilled to the bone, he pulled his gun out with is free hand and pointed it directly at Bear. The gun shook in his trembling hands and his thoughts were increasingly irrational.

"I said I'll come peacefully. Move away from that young lady!"

"Stop right there, Bear, or I swear I'll shoot you!" Boxer began to shiver uncontrollably from a combination of excitement, fear, and the cold.

"Pilloud certainly did not tell you to shoot anybody. Walk away from her *now*!"

Boxer knew that Pilloud would be furious at him if he did not successfully take advantage of the situation and immediately bring down two of the people his boss needed off the mountain. Julie huddled in the mud at her captor's feet. Bear continued to advance on the guard who now seemed confused by the sudden turn of events which made the threat to his well-being from his huge opponent imminent. Boxer lowered his revolver and fired off a warning shot into the ground near Julie's feet.

"Stop!" I will shoot"

The image of his son's innocent smile flashed before Bear. All morning, he had been visualizing his ex-wife testifying against him in court. Now remorse, anger, a renewed purpose, and absolution from Almighty God whom he had spent much of the morning praying to for forgiveness—as the good Pastor Davis had taught him—were uppermost in his mind. Bear suddenly broke into a run and charged at the other man. In that precise moment, their fate was sealed.

As he hurled his enormous frame into Boxer's body, tackling the stunned guard in a manner that would have made Dick Butkus envious, another thirty-magnum round exploded from the gun. The two men crashed to the ground and Bear's forward momentum drove both men very close to the ledge, As they wrestled for position and possession of the firearm, Boxer realized he was soon to be over-powered by the man he despised and tried to force the gun barrel against his foe's head. Bear countered by doing what Boxer least expected—he drove the bodies of both clenched men with his powerful legs over the ledge. Bear's eyes fixed on the look of bewilderment on Boxer's face that would fast turn to one of horror as the guard realized he was on a death trip to the bottom of the talus pile 600 feet below, locked forever in the other man's unyielding grip.

During the last few moments of Bear's brief existence, his mind was filled with images of Jacob, the pride of his otherwise pitiful life.

Looking up, startled, at the sound of two bullets being fired in rapid succession, Toonie saw the falling men crunch abruptly into a large boulder only twenty yards from him. The gruesome sight caused him to collapse to his knees, while his hound ran free to investigate the splattered mass ahead of them.

* * *

"What the hell was that?" Larry bellowed into his radio. The silence on the other end was maddening. "Toonie? Status?"

Static hissed from Sheriff Magleton's radio as the postmaster tried to respond. No words were audible.

"Toonie. Repeat. Sounded like shots?"

"Yeah."

"You okay?"

"Yeah...gimme a second." More silence at Larry's end of the radio was not received well as Toonie finished throwing up.

"Tell me what's goin' on, Toonie. *Now!*"

"Two shots fired from up above. Two bodies came down. They're both here at my feet...or what's left of them."

"Bear?"

"Affirmative... The other one looks like Pilloud's estate guard. The big one we questioned at his mansion."

"Can you tell if the shooter is one of them or still up above?"

"Negative."

"Damn! Okay, Toonie. Call for back-up. Get an investigative team out here on the double. Alert Bronson. I'm gonna follow these tracks. Keep in constant radio contact."

"Ten-four."

Larry Magleton felt a knot inside twist so tightly he could barely breathe. He had a dreadful feeling about this situation. The relentless rain suddenly petered out and an abrupt calm settled over Kineo. Larry had a sense of déjà vu—as if he had played out this scene before. Although he could not remember the ending to the movie, he knew one thing without a doubt: he was not destined to be the hero in a story with a happy ending. His sense of duty tugged at him, and he shook off his initial hesitation. He had three sets of tracks to focus on. Larry resumed climbing.

* * *

"Thomas, you hear that?"

"Yeah, whoa? Was that lightning striking twice?"

"I dunno, Thomas, but it sure sounded like a gun to me. Maybe you should go back and wait for the deputies to get up here. I'm responsible for my students. I've got to continue."

"Dr. Wayne, I think I ought to stay with you..."

"No way, Thomas. Your mother would kill me. I'll be fine. Go back now. The rain has stopped too. You can hurry. Go!"

"Okay. But be careful, Dr. Wayne. Don't do anything crazy up there."

Max Wayne assured Thomas he could handle himself. But even as he uttered the words, he wondered if the gunshots had been fired by Rob or *at* him. *Surely that stupid kid hadn't brought a gun along? He's obsessed and misguided, but he isn't unstable. Or is he?*

Max bounded up another set of vertical scrambles cautiously. His movements were deliberate and powerful, like a mountain lion in pursuit of its prey.

* * *

Julie's legs trembled uncontrollably and nausea threatened to overtake her as she deliberately averted her face from the spot where the two men had tumbled over the cliff. *Bear saved my life! Rob. Poor Rob. What the hell is going on?* She began to cry hysterically as she climbed off the vantage point from where the goon had nabbed her. *Who was he anyway? What did he want? Why was he willing to kill Bear to force me and him off Mount Kineo?*

Blood oozed from her left knee through a large tear in her climbing leggings. Although the rain had stopped, the cold had chilled her to the bone, and now she was shivering uncontrollably. Hypothermia and adrenaline created a confusing concoction of biochemical reactions in her body. Julie knew Rob would die if she didn't get help soon. The temperature had already dropped by twenty degrees since the storm first began to vent its fury and Julie feared that if she were affected by hypothermia, she would be in no position to help her classmate.

* * *

Climbing over another slab of wet rhyolite, Max found, to his relief, a nearly level trail he could easily jog down. Turning a corner, he spotted Julie recklessly climbing off the Indian Trail and heading down in his direction. He immediately realized she was in trouble. She was too skilled at rock climbing to be stumbling so carelessly down a steep, but technically simple scramble section. Running up to the base of the wall, he held up his arms and guided her trembling body into a warm, paternal embrace.

"Dr. Wayne!"

"Julie, you okay?"

"No! Some man threatened to kill me and this huge man...he's called Bear...threw himself over the mountain...and Rob's leg is messed up...he's in shock..."

"Whoa Julie, slow down. It's all right. I'm here now. Tell me about Rob. Tell me everything. Slow down and take a breath."

Julie struggled with her words. She was frightened by the violence she had just survived, panicked about Rob's plight, and slipping deeper into hypothermia with each second. Her lips were blue and her hair hung down in her eyes, wet and bloody. Her skin felt clammy and cold to Max.

"Look at you, girl!" Dr. Wayne said. "You're going to freeze. We need to get you into dry clothes quickly."

Max reached into his daypack and found a spare shirt. He began to strip Julie's thin, soaked cotton outer layer off her, as she shivered uncontrollably. After forcing a dry sweater over her head and getting her clenched fists through the sleeves, he took off his raincoat and wrapped it around her. Holding her closely to give her as much of his body warmth as he could, Max began to rub her arms and legs frantically to stimulate circulation.

"Damn, Julie! You know better than to get yourself into a situation like this!"

"We can't go down, Max...not yet! Not without Rob."

"If I can't get your body core warmed, Julie, I'm taking you down and coming back for Rob. Hypothermia can be fatal."

"I know. I know!" her teeth chattered as she spoke. "But we cannot leave Rob. We can't—he's broken up bad."

"What happened?"

"He found this vault inside a hidden tunnel where prehistoric Indians had mined rhyolite in a deep chamber. He found some crazy gemstones as part of their cave system."

"So that's where he found that sphere of…"

"You knew about it?"

"Partly. Rob's acted strange ever since he found it."

"But there's so much more, Max! He thinks there are valuable minerals and archeological relics in this sealed chamber we found. He was attempting to open it when he had an awful accident. His leg broke right through. He's in shock."

"Damn fool! Why didn't he tell us? Why didn't he have us help him? Why…"

"Oh, Dr. Wayne. I begged him to, but he was so…"

"Obstinate." Max suggested, then let the matter drop. "Hey, what were the shots I heard?"

"From the strange man who tried to kill that huge island man. He fired twice, but Bear kept coming at him and took him over the side of the mountain with him. He saved my life!"

"Good God! We're way over our heads here, Julie. Do you have the gear you need to get Rob out of the chamber with my help?"

"Probably not," she sniffed. "I have some basic gear with me, but it's not right for this rescue."

Max could see that she was still weak and having difficulty forming her sentences. She was still shivering.

"You seem like you're stabilizing, but you're still on the fringes of losing it, Julie. I'm taking you down. We'll get the proper equipment and have the deputies help us. They're on Kineo right now, heading up. They're here looking for Bear."

"Thanks for rescuing me."

Julie squeezed Max tightly and gave him a kiss on the cheek which made him blush. Then as she began to feel faint again, she closed her eyes. Max continued to rub her arms back and forth, but urged her to keep on her feet and start down with him.

"Not so fast, you two!" a menacing voice with a French accent barked out. "Mr. Pilloud wants to hear more about the chamber where your student friend is guarding *our* possession."

38

Toonie was unable to reach Bronson with his two-way radio, and his cellular reception was poor on the island. The other support personnel would begin assembling immediately to join the deputies on Mt. Kineo. Toonie climbed across the talus and down to the boulder field, taking a shortcut through the striped maples and quaking aspen until he had run right into the abandoned water tower. His golf cart was only a quarter mile down the slope. He raced to the nearest cottage to ask if he could use a ground line to reach Bronson. But nobody was home and he continued down Cottage Row.

Toonie had always wanted to be involved in something important and exciting, but the sight he had just witnessed of the two men splattered on the rocks was not the kind of action he was looking for. He was still feeling nauseated and shaken when his golf cart came across Laura Denton standing outside her cottage in the drizzly weather. As she stared up at the formidable cliffs of Kineo, the look on her face was one of desperate anxiety.

"Mrs. Denton, may I use your phone?" Toonie asked. "It's an emergency."

"Of course! What's going on? Where's Thomas?"

"Ma'am, I haven't seen your son, but I can tell you we have a real mess up there, and I need to call for some help immediately."

Laura handed him the phone. Listening carefully to Toonie's end of the conversation she contemplated jumping into her golf cart and going out in search of her older son. *But then again*, she thought, *Thomas is with Max, and Max can handle himself. Still, were those gunshots I heard a few minutes ago?* Then a horrifying realization struck her.

"Oh my God! Bear? Did you guys shoot Bear?"

"No! Not us, Laura! Look, I'll fill ya in, but give me a second. I have to… Oh. Got him now… Hang on… Bronson? That you…?"

"Yeah," the fire investigator replied. "Find him yet, Toonie?"

Bronson listened intently, stunned at the news the postmaster gave him.

"Bear? Good God! Right… Sure I can help. I can get there in the next hour."

"Sheriff wants you now!"

"All right—in twenty. And Toonie, get Larry some back-up!"

"Already called in, along with the coroner and a crime-scene team."

Hanging up the phone, Toonie handed the receiver back to Laura who stared at him inquiringly, impatient for answers. Only a mother could have worn that expression of acute concern.

Moved to pity, Toonie turned to her.

"Laura, I know Thomas. He'll be fine. If he's still up there, we'll bring him down safely. I promise you that. Yes, those were gunshots you heard. One of Jean Pilloud's guards fired a weapon at Bear."

"Pilloud's men?"

"Yes. That's what you heard earlier."

"Anyone injured?"

"Now listen, Laura. I have a crime-scene team arriving by floatplane and back-up deputies by boat. It's too rough for the floatplane to land near the water on the west side by the Indian Trail. The plane will have to land in Kineo Cove. I need your help. Stay off the mountain. Use your carts and help shuttle the team from the Kineo docks to us. The crime-scene team needs to be dropped off at the water-tower site, while the back-up deputies must be shuttled to the Indian Trailhead. Thomas will be fine. I'll bring your son to you. I promise."

"But...but..."

"Laura. I don't have time right now to discuss this further. Larry's up there with Pilloud and needs my help."

With that, Toonie turned and hopped back into his golf cart.

"Toonie!" Laura called out, "Dr. Wayne is up there with my son too. I want them *both* back safe!"

The postmaster read the earnestness in her eyes and nodded in agreement. Then his golf cart sped off, back to the Indian Trail.

* * *

Thomas had only worked himself about 100 yards back down the Indian Trail when he suddenly stopped. *This feels all wrong.* He knew he should go back the way Dr. Wayne had instructed him. But his gut told him he should stay. He couldn't leave Max. *What if Max needs me?* Slowly, Thomas Denton began retracing his steps, scrambling back up the trail he had just descended. He promised himself he wouldn't do anything stupid, his senses hyper-alert to every sound, smell, and sight. His mother would be furious if she knew what he had just decided to do.

* * *

"Well, Douglas... Doesn't seem we need you anymore, after all."

At a single nod of consent from Pilloud, the manic mercenary flung Dougie to the ground. The young man's knee throbbed with pain, as did a dozen other places where Pierre had inflicted injury. Dougie made no attempt to resist or complain. He was already resigned to the inevitable—that once Pilloud finished with him, he would be killed and disposed of somewhere his body would never be found.

He had guided them up this way to mislead them. He didn't really know anything about secret chambers, hidden Confederate gold, ancient artifacts, Indian burial grounds, and so on. All he knew was that his friend, Jimbo, had found a strange sphere that he had carefully protected while he was alive. The sphere had both scared Jimbo and fascinated him. He had spoken of how obsessed Pilloud was about finding three gemstone spheres that somehow were the key to locating something of extreme value to him. He knew, however, that Jimbo had found his sphere in the Goldman cottage, far below the base of the cliffs.

None of this made sense. He only knew that he had promised Jimbo to keep quiet about the sphere. Dougie was loyal to his friends. All he cared about now was preventing these maniacs from harming the innocent little Lomax girl. Amanda was like a younger sister to him. He was willing to keep this charade going as long as it took to protect her. But now he was spared further agony. Dr. Wayne and the graduate student apparently knew far more about what was going on than he did. They held the secret to the location of the chamber that Pilloud sought. Dougie looked up from the ground and noticed the smirk on Pierre's face.

"You may dispose of this liability, Pierre," Pilloud instructed. "Quietly. No gun."

The mercenary approached Dougie and ordered him to his feet. The young man complied despite his aching injuries. His expression was that of sad resignation. Pierre led Dougie to wall of rock with thick conifer understory. He pulled out his hunting knife and considered his options. He knew how difficult it was to carry a dead man back to the boat. Then he noticed Dougie's expression morph to one of hope.

"You aren't thinking that you can take this knife from me, are you?"

"No… But dude, I think I can choose to die on my own terms."

Dougie suddenly flung his injured body using his one strong leg and headed toward the wall. There was nowhere to escape except over the edge of the wall of fir trees growing from steep ledge directly below them. Pierre watched, stunned, as Dougie made a desperate leap to freedom by launching himself off the side of the ledge and grabbing the nearest tree, a young fir. He clung to the side of the undeveloped young trunk as it bowed low toward the talus, bent by the weight of his body. The tree swayed wildly with his every struggling motion, as he tried to cling to it like a squirrel. Pierre ran up to the edge and inadvertently dislodged a large rock that bounded over the edge and struck the ferry captain as he was desperately attempting to climb down the young, unstable tree. The mercenary heard Dougie let out a pathetic groan before he disappeared from view.

* * *

The open space had grown very dark. Rob's flashlight battery had nearly spent all of its stored chemical energy trying to brighten the large, damp chamber. Apparently, Julie had left the small backpacking light lying next to him, with the lamp switched on. Numbness enveloped his entire body; yet, he felt strangely chilled. He could hear voices. *One? No, two. A man and a woman. My rescuers? How long have I been unconscious? Julie back already with help? I'm so tired. I just want to sleep.*

He had not been able to see inside the vault, although he thought he had successfully busted open one of the wooden doors that concealed its mysterious contents. He did not want to share this discovery with anyone. He had only included Julie because of her climbing gear and her skills. *Who are these people in here?* Rob could not make out their faces in the dark, and they moved so quietly. *Why aren't they helping me?*

The woman's voice sounded old and crackly. She was giving orders to the man, but her words were unintelligible. *Is she speaking another language?* Rob wanted to sit up to see better, but weakness prevented him from moving. It was all he could do to keep his eyes open. Suddenly, he heard a loud snapping sound as the remainder of the vault's wooden frame gave way. As quickly as Rob had regained consciousness, his mind succumbed to the strain of anticipation and he passed out again.

* * *

"Pierre?"

"He's gone, sir. He jumped over the side of a steep ledge."

"Well, is he dead?"

"I would think so. But I didn't see him land. Even then, it was a nasty fall. He certainly will not be going down to get help. Shall I go down and verify?"

"No. There's no time for that now. The sherriff certainly heard the gun shots earlier. You can dispose of the body later. Nobody knows he is up here and nobody will find him down there. We need to finish what we initiated today."

"Good God!" said another male voice, "you forced him to jump!"

"Surprised, Professor?" Pilloud said, casting Max Wayne a contemptuous glance. "Now that you know how serious we are, I suggest you cooperate fully or you may have to share the young man's destiny."

He turned to Julie Walters with a pleasant smile. "Now take us to the chamber, Miss."

"It was you who shot Bear!" Max accused Jean Pilloud.

"Unfortunately, that pleasure was denied us. Now Pierre, do discourage this gentleman from meddling further in our affairs."

"Shall I deal with the professor, sir?"

"Hmm? No. Since we appear to have lost Boxer, we might need his assistance in extrication of my rightful inheritance. And we have no time to waste."

"Boxer was sloppy. A liability."

"Without doubt, Pierre. No matter. We have the professor, and I'm sure he'll be useful to us, as long as he bears in mind what we can do to his young girlfriend here if he doesn't cooperate."

Julie began to weep again. The trouble they were in seemed like a bottomless pit. She had just witnessed men die and wondered if she would have to witness Dr. Wayne's murder as well. Rob would be left to die of shock. If only she had told Max about all of this earlier, when she had had the chance.

"I'm so sorry Max," Julie cried softly. "This is all my fault."

"No, it's not, Julie. We'll be fine. Just let these gentlemen find what they are looking for and everything will be all right."

"Excellent advice… Um…Max, was it? And Julie, correct? Now let's get this over with. Continue."

Max pondered the possibilities and tried to estimate how far the deputies were behind them and how long it would take them to catch up. They had heard the shots. It was just a matter of time and they would be up here too. He had to delay finding the chamber, but without arousing Pilloud's suspicions. He had no way of communicating all of this to Julie without the other two listening in. He had to take the chance that she would understand.

"Okay, Julie," he said. "I'll take them to the chamber. I'll lead so that Pierre can hold you hostage. That way, Pilloud, you know I will not try anything foolish. Please. I don't want to see anyone else hurt."

"Fine plan, Dr. Wayne. Now move!" Pilloud ordered.

* * *

Unbeknownst to Pierre, Thomas had been slowly gaining on the action above him. He had heard the odd sounds of a man struggling in trees above him and knew the sounds came from the direction where he had left Dr. Wayne. Climbing up the ridge where he had seen Max disappear in his quest to find Rob and Julie, Thomas reached a point where he thought the sounds had come from. Something caught his eye just below him: a male body tangled in a mass of blueberries, with one leg turned at a gruesome angle behind him. Nausea overwhelmed Thomas as he recognized Dougie. The young boy could not climb down from the ledge to see if he were still alive. Douglas lay utterly still, unresponsive. Although Thomas had never seen a corpse before, he was sure that the ferryboat captain was dead.

Given the hideous injuries Thomas's father had sustained in the accident that took his life, he had been cremated so that his mangled body would not have to be on display for the benefit of the mourners at his funeral. Thomas had not seen his father's body. Seeing Dougie lying there, he was reminded of the traumatic day when he had his siblings had been informed of their father's gruesome death. Shaking off the unpleasant memory, he realized that nothing in his life had prepared him for this moment: contemplating a corpse, that too of someone he had known and admired. *How did he fall like that*, he wondered. *Is this related to the gunshots I heard?*

Thomas was suddenly consumed with worry about Dr. Wayne. Thinking quickly, Thomas grabbed some of his hiking tape out of his backpack and tied a long strip of plastic pink ribbon to the location where he had seen the body of Dougie. Despite his conscience telling him that he should not go forward, he ventured on, moving himself ahead of the spot where the body lay. He quickly found four sets of fresh tracks in the wet mud and began following them.

Sheriff Larry Magleton was quickly converging on the same location. He stopped after his strenuous ascent, hands on hips, and stole badly needed gulps of air. *I am so glad I stopped smoking,* he thought. Then looking ahead in the mud, he noticed footprints heading in every direction. Apparently, this was a place where a lot of characters had converged and significant action had taken place. The tracks led to a high ledge where he saw boot prints in the mud and across the rock edge. Then his eyes fell on the pink flaggin tape that Thomas had tied below him. He worked his way down slope to where the tape was hanging from a small tree and then noticed further below him the body. Discarded like a useless carcass, Dougie's body violated the purity of Kineo's fir trees and blueberry underbrush. Dropping to his knees and drawing his gun, Larry felt adrenaline race through his blood vessels as his fury mounted. He carefully looked around to see if those involved were still in the vicinity. He saw and heard nothing—apart from the eerie moan of the wind. Larry then pulled out his radio and called Toonie for the status of the back-up deputies.

Magleton instructed the postmaster to send a deputy up from the lower ledge at the trail fork to check on another body. He explained that he would not, without risking injury, be able to descend to the spot where the person lay to check if he were merely uncon-scious. Larry then told Toonie to look for the bright pink survey-tape ribbon that marked the spot where the body could be easily identified by those approaching from below the ledge. Toonie acknowledged the instructions and directed the personnel from his position to assist Larry Magleton accordingly. Larry put his radio away and continued uphill, wondering what Pilloud had to do with all of this. Below him, the fingers of Dougie's left hand began to move slowly.

* * *

"So this is why they invaded our sacred chambers!" the young man yelled up at the old woman after successfully prying open the other vault door.

His elder looked down at him below, securing the rope tightly so that he could climb back up when he was done.

"Surprised?"

"I am. They desecrated a burial site and hid it here?"

"Greed drives the most foolish of men. Exploit resources and then move on."

"So the legend of the sinking of the *Piscataquis* was true."

"It appears that the Iroquois renegades did seize the white man's valuable cargo. Ha, ha, ha! And all those years they wasted scouring the bed of the lake!"

"But the Iroquois hid it here? In the abandoned mining chamber? This is where Kajo is laid to rest. The turquoise string. See it on him! Is this *him*?"

"No, dear. Kajo would not be buried in a vault like that. His bones would have been placed to rest ceremoniously covered by the pelts of beaver, not moose, and his most pre-cious personal artifacts would be buried with him. The renegades may have found his jewelry down here and put it on the remains of some trapped miner."

"Why would they…"

"To discourage anyone opening the second vault door. A superstitious warning to stop."

"But…but you had me pry it open."

"Ha! Why yes, I did. Because I know better. I knew that's not Kajo. Shine the light diretly on the body...See?...Kajo was said to be a very small man. The bones of the person in the vault that you are showing me belong to someone much larger. But Kajo is buried in here somewhere. I am sure of that. And it's better that we remove those accursed bars from his chamber so that he may rest in peace."

"They must have known this is sacred ground. I would have looked down here. I've never climbed down to this lower level in my life."

"Nor I," added the elder. "We were too busy tending to the guardian stone and ancient relics in the tribal tunnels. Just staying hidden from the white invaders all of these years was difficult enough."

"How long do you think this wooden vault has been down here?"

"Since the late eighteen eighties, when the renegades confiscated the soldiers' gold. All were killed before anyone could figure out where they hid it. But today's events are in our favor. If we rid this sacred mountain of its cancer, the pests that climb all over it will surely leave."

"They will never leave, Grandmother. Never. It would be best to take this gold and use it to buy the island from the white man."

"Oh, no! This evil stash might infect us! We are *not* like them!"

"We can discuss this, Grandmother, but not now. We don't have the supplies to remove the bars and Pilloud will be coming soon. But I have an idea. Please, Grandmother—help me back up."

"What about that injured student in the corner?"

"Hmm. We do have him to thank for stumbling across the vault."

"Then let the Great Spirit of the Cow Moose decide. If he lives, he will be rewarded for finding the hidden vault that plagues Kineo. If he dies—it's his punishment for desecrating these sacred grounds."

"Agreed. Now I must climb up. We must move quickly, Grandmother."

✳ ✳ ✳

"You're stalling, Max. Why aren't we there yet?"

"Just a little further, Pilloud."

"Maybe you're not trying to get us there. Maybe Pierre needs to get better acquainted with this young lady?"

The mercenary allowed a smile to play around his lips and looked Julie up and down. "Just give the order, sir."

"No! We *are* near it!" the student cried out. "Here, I'll guide us the rest of the way."

Pierre released his grip on Julie, allowing her to proceed, satisfied that his point had been made. The young woman moved toward Max, catching his glare of disapproval. He had been hoping to stall a little longer to give the deputies more time to intervene. His delaying tactics were a delicate balancing act, for he had to ensure no one would get hurt. *If Julie gives them what they want too quickly*, Max considered, *our usefulness to Pilloud will be over. Then we will certainly be disposed of.*

Julie strode past Max without looking him in the eye and assumed the lead, redirecting the party and pointing them in the right direction. She marched up to the hidden side trail and indicated the way to the central mining chamber. Still numb with cold, she looked weak and exhausted. Max felt regretful for having shot her a hostile look. She could have died from hypothermia earlier and still appeared terrified by the events that had overtaken them. Maybe if she hadn't volunteered to help right then, Pierre would have lashed out at her to prove a point. In any case, the speculation over how far they could push it was over. Julie was going to lead them right to the inner chamber, and Max could only hope an opportunity to turn the odds in their favor would present itself very soon.

39

"Jenny and Brandon, listen up! I'm not going to repeat myself. Run over to the golf course, get some carts, and take them to the docks now."

"You mean, just take them?"

"Yes, Jenny. Drive them to the docks and wait for the sheriffs' boats to arrive."

"But shouldn't we ask permission?"

"Jenny, for once in your life, please just do as you are told without asking further questions."

"Where you going, Mommy?" Brandon asked hesitantly.

"See that floatplane up there? I'm going to the cove to direct them when Matt lands. Make sure the deputies get those carts as soon as they arrive. Now go!"

Laura hopped into the Dentons' back-up cart and sped to the cove where the floatplanes usually landed. She could see her two younger children sprinting across the fairway to the pro shop to get extra carts for the arriving deputies. In the distance, two boats, with a number of law-enforcement officers and other emergency personnel on board, were racing through the "no wake" zone. Laura couldn't keep nightmarish possibilities from crowding her mind. *My oldest boy is up there somewhere. Why hasn't Thomas come down off Kineo? All he was supposed to do was catch up with Max and hand him the extra clothes and rainwear.*

Despite her fears, knowing Max was up there calmed her somewhat. *That man is confident and smart. But damn it! Once I find Bronson, I'm going up Mt. Kineo myself to make sure Thomas gets down safely.*

Young Matt Kowalski landed the old Cessna floatplane smoothly in the cove and let it idle up to the bulkhead. Bronson jumped out and began unloading the extra equipment requested by Sheriff Magleton. Laura swung her cart to within three feet of the bulkhead and waved anxiously for the fire investigator to hurry. Matt immediately recognized her and gave her a friendly wave. But Laura was too preoccupied to acknowledge his friendly greeting.

"I'm your ride, Bronson. Hop in!"

Bronson Thurman quickly collected the equipment he needed, leaving the rest for the arriving deputies, and threw it in the back of the cart. Before he had even finished lowering himself into the passenger seat, the wheels began to spin in the mud and gravel and Laura was speeding down to the boat docks. She spotted her other two kids as they arrived with the carts borrowed from the golf clubhouse. The first of the two outboard boats pulled up to the bulkhead at the Kineo docks. A female deputy from the sheriff's office jumped out and appeared to be in charge.

"I'm Deputy Harris."

"Laura Denton. Toonie asked me to make sure you got these carts. I'm to take Bronson to the Indian Trail where he can hook up with Sheriff Magleton. Toonie is on his way on foot right now to assist him up Mt. Kineo. Your medical team is to be taken to the talus pile area where the...the two men fell from the cliffs."

Jenny immediately realized that her mother was near tears and put her arm around Laura. Neither she nor Brandon had been informed of Bear's demise.

"What's the matter, Mother?" Jenny inquired, "Mom?"

Shaking her head and clearing the grief from her mind, Laura ignored her daughter and stared straight at the female deputy. "My daughter here can lead you to the starting point of the trail where the accident occurred. Do *not* let her go with you up that trail!" Laura turned to her daughter. "Jenny, ya hear me? You're to come back home right away."

"Yes, ma'am. But what's wrong?"

Deputy Harris knew exactly what Laura Denton meant. She looked at her with understanding and assured her, "Don't worry, ma'am. Your daughter will be escorted back home by one of my deputies. I will personally see to that."

"Thank you, Deputy Harris. Now Brandon, run home and wait for Jenny. I'll be back in a few minutes."

"Now, can you escort me to the trail where the sheriffs are?" asked Deputy Harris.

"Yes. As soon as you have all your gear loaded onto your cart, you can follow us."

The second boat landed, and the men and women in it jumped off and picked up their gear. Within sixty seconds, Jenny was leading a cart with medical investigators and forensic examiners to the top of the upper fairway trail where the abandoned water tower was located. The other cart carrying her mother and Bronson was on its way to the Indian Trail, with another cart filled with deputies following right behind.

"What's in your bag, Bronson?"

"Medical supplies. I am more than just a fire examiner. Started my career as a fireman and EMT. I am still pretty useful with triage."

Laura gave him a brief smile and swung a tight corner around the last golf hole. Bronson thanked her for the ride, then suggested she return to the cottage as soon as she had dropped him off. Laura shot him a look.

"My son is up there, Bronson! I should already have been up there looking for him. You're lucky I even stopped to pick you up!"

The fire examiner did not venture to utter another word as they raced toward the old Carriage Trail that bordered the mountain's western edge.

* * *

Thomas heard voices ahead and slowed down. He saw a group of people, including Dr. Wayne and one of his female grad students—Julie. He remembered the girl; he had thought she was quite pretty. Two men were walking with them; both carried handguns. The older of the two appeared to be making the decisions. The other man was tall and thin, but fit and wore wire-frame glasses and heavy black clothing, right from his wool cap down to his boots. Constantly scanning the landscape, he looked on edge. There was something of the soldier in his bearing, in the manner in which he carried his firearm and moved through the desnse forested terrain. *He is a man to fear*, thought Thomas. He knew he would have to be extra wary of this man. *What are they doing with Max and Julie?* The boy decided to drop back, making sure he maintained enough distance from the figures ahead to remain unnoticed.

Suddenly, the group disappeared around an abrupt bend in the trail. Thomas waited a few seconds to make sure that they had advanced a little further, then crawled up to the blind corner. He was suddenly overcome by panic at the danger he might be in. If the man in black had aleady spotted him, this would be the perfect place to ambush him. Thomas proceeded cautiously through the narrow, overgrown trail, worried about losing the group altogether. They appeared to be heading off-trail. Thomas could not afford to wait any longer. He had to move through the blind corner if he weren't to lose Max. Peering around the corner, he could see nobody at all. *Dang! I lost them. I was too cautious!* He considered the idea of jogging down the trail a little further, then had second thoughts. *No! They shook me off back there. Could they have known I was following them and purposely changed direction to throw me off-track? Or is there something about that trail that can confuse people?*

Thomas slowly retraced his steps and examined the vegetation carefully. He studied the mud, hoping to find tracks. Then he saw footsteps that seemed to disappear into some brush that had been pulled to the side. Thomas expelled his breath to calm his nerves, proceeded cautiously for about fifty yards, and sat down, willing himself to remain perfectly still. He could hear people moving in the bushes off to his right. The side trail was so hemmed in by vegetation it was impossible to walk through without brushing against dense undergrowth that left the skin scratched and burning.

If I can hear them move, they can surely hear me too the moment they come to a halt! Finding a cluster of rocks that rose nearly thirty feet out of the brush, Thomas realized he could clamber up from the back without being seen and reach the top. From that vantage point, he could scan the underbrush and notice movement of any kind. Climbing swiftly and silently, he reached the top of the rock outcropping and peered down, just in time to see Max duck his head through a crease in the mountain wall about forty yards away.

Thomas was about to jump down from his perch and follow the group again, but his intuition held him back in time. Sure enough, in a couple of minutes, the tall, thin man in black emerged from behind a tree; he had been bringing up the rear and had paused to ensure they were not been followed. Watching his movements that resembled those of a hound dog on point using all its senses to protect its rear flank, Thomas shuddered at the thought of what would have happened had he impulsively followed the group and been caught by this man. Meanwhile, the man had turned slowly to inspect the rock on which Thomas was perched. The boy quickly ducked and huddled on the other side as the man began methodically trailing his gaze up the rock. *Dang, this guy is good!*

After about ninety seconds, Thomas peered around the rock again; the man was gone. *Had he followed Max into the crease? Or has he spotted me and is heading this way right now? Dang, I aint waitin' around to find out!* Thomas climbed down from his perch and ran the way he had come. *I know where they are. I'll get help. I'm way out of my league with this guy.*

* * *

Having sat in the post office for years sorting mail, Toonie was not in great physical shape. The climb up the Indian Trail was taking a toll on his heart and respiratory system. He stopped to take deep breaths and radio down to the docks below to ensure that the back-up deputies had arrived and were being shuttled to their assigned destinations. Everything was coming together surprisingly well. Deputy Harris was directing Bronson to go up and inspect the body that Larry had reported discovering earlier, and the main team was heading for the talus pile where Bear and Boxer had fallen to their death. Then he checked to see if Larry was still pursuing Bear's assassins. *Nothing but silence.* He tried again, but only heard static. Toonie couldn't decide if the sheriff had turned his radio off or was in trouble. He reached down and unholstered his nine millimeter, making sure it was loaded, with the safety off. Then he took one last deep breath and began climbing up the steep trail again.

* * *

"Superb, Julie," Pilloud commended. "Now keep moving forward through the tunnel."

As the student obeyed, Max studied the excavated walls of the tunnel that led in from its entrance in the mountain's hidden crease. He could make out the bare outlines of paintings and inscriptions on their surfaces whenever they were momentarily illuminated by the flashlights that Pierre, Julie, and Pilloud carried. *If only I could have a flashlight*, he thought. Or if they would just stop for a moment and give him a light, he could decipher the writings. He recognized a few words in the Algonquin language.

Soon, they were passing one of the three tables of rock, located at the junction of the main chamber with the three tunnels, that had held the now missing guardian stones. Julie explained that this was where she and Rob thought all the large spheres had originally rested. Even Pilloud stopped to look at one of the marker tables and rub his fingers in the perfectly sculpted bowl that was shaped like a semi-sphere—the exact size of the guardian spheres they had sought earlier.

Markings on the wall indicated the Circle of Unity, with the radiating spokes from the central hub that represented the central chamber. Pilloud watched Dr. Wayne's intense interest in the markings and began to wonder if he knew anything about the symbols and writings in the chamber that might help to locate the Confederate gold.

"Move, woman!" barked out Pierre, addressing Julie.

"No, wait, Pierre," interrupted Pilloud. "I want to know if Dr. Wayne can explain the significance of this chamber."

Max fought off the urge to tell the man what he really thought of him as he contemplated his options. With the deputies hopefully not far behind, any delay would buy them more time. While the urge to teach others about indigenous peoples had always been close to the professor's heart, wrapping his hands around this man's neck and choking the life out of him seemed a much more attractive proposition at this moment. He brushed back the thought.

"I can make out some words," Max replied. "To understand all of it would take weeks. If I were not concerned for Julie's safety, all my focus would have been on these paintings and inscriptions."

"Well, you may be in luck. If we're unable to find what we're looking for in the lower chamber, you may be of some additional use to me—especially if the writings in here can help us solve the puzzle in this room."

"What is it exactly you're looking for?"

"That need not concern you at this time, Professor. Pierre is right. We must proceed swifly now. There will be others up this mountain soon, trying to stop my from claiming *my* rightful family inheritance."

Julie led the group by crawling through the narrow twenty-yard tunnel. It ended in the central mining chamber and contained no Paleo-Indian writings or markings. It simply emptied into a vertical shaft that required a relatively easy descent, achieved with basic chimney movements.

"How the hell do you think they retrieved minerals from the chamber if they had to use this narrow access tunnel?" Max asked his student.

"Rob and I found a larger vertical shaft, wide enough to accommodate a pulley system inside the mining chamber. I assume they rigged some sort of mechanical leverage system like that. This appears to be the pathway that led the workers to the chamber."

Max wondered if he had ever read about Indians of that era devising a pulley system. *Probably not till much later, when they had began trading with the white man in the region.* "How did Rob fall inside here then?" he asked.

"Oh, well... The fact is, we didn't know about this vertical shaft when we first descended into the mining chamber using climbing and rappelling gear. Had I not been forced to look for another way to get Rob out, I would most likely have not found this way out at all."

"Then you can rig a pulley system for us, can't you, to extract some heavy items from the chamber through the main mining area?" Pilloud asked, a steely note of command apparent in his tone.

"Yes," replied Julie. "I can. If you give me time to get additional equipment, I can do that for you—but only if you agree to help me get Rob out of here!"

"Making demands now, Miss Walters? Pilloud laughed. "What do you say, Pierre? Want to help her lift her boyfriend out of the chamber—or would you rather just finish him off?"

The Frenchman simply shook his head. Banter and distractions of that kind were an annoyance to him. If Rob awakened, he would likely begin to moan and whine about his leg. Pierre would certainly favor extermination.

Suddenly, Max spotted Rob near the corner wall. He and Julie ran over to him and felt his pulse; its beat was perceptible, but weak.

"He's experiencing hypothermia," Julie said in a tremulous voice. "Looks like he's going into shock from the injury. If we don't get him out soon, he'll die!"

"You better get to rigging the pulley system. You don't have much time," warned Pilloud.

Julie pointed to the location where Rob had tried to open the wooden latches on the floor vault. Pilloud walked up and rubbed his hands together. He could feel his heart pounding in his chest. The greatest moment of his life had finally arrived. He would soon see if the legend of his grandfather was true and whether the gold from the Confederate Treasury was indeed buried here.

"Pierre. Break that door open."

The mercenary approached, inspecting the doors cautiously to ensure they were not booby-trapped. Then he noticed that they had already been forced opened.

"Looks like your boyfriend has already succeeded in opening the safe," Pierre commented.

Julie remembered seeing skeletal human remains from above when the other door hatch had been jarred loose and wondering who they belonged to. Then Pierre nodded at Pilloud, reached for the wooden doors, and gave them one mighty jerk. Both hatches opened unexpectedly and hit against the wall nearby with a thundering crash that echoed throughout the chamber and its feeder tunnels. Inside the vault, next to the bones that Julie had seen earlier, were neatly stacked bars. As the beams of the flashlights bounced off them, Pilloud realized with greedy delight that he had found his long-lost Confederate gold at last.

* * *

Thomas continued to run down the trail, mindful of the most secure places—between the white pine roots and the slick rhyolite—where his feet could land without skidding. The mud got the better of him on one steep section, and he crashed to the ground and bruised his knee. There was no time to tend to his wounds. He bounded up and began scrambling down the steep rock ridge on all fours. As he squeezed through a narrow passage in the rock, the throbbing in his left knee seemed to grow more intense. Jumping down the last four feet of the descent, he spun around, and began to dash across the next twenty yards of nearly level ground—a small reprieve before the most strenuous section ahead. Rounding a corner lined with small spruce trees, he nearly crashed headlong into Sheriff Magleton, who stood his ground, weapon raised. Fortunately, Larry recognized the Denton boy and lowered his weapon in time to brace himself for the impact.

"Whoaa, son! It's Sheriff Magleton... Who's up there?"

"Sheriff? Oh good!" Thomas panted. "They're up there...two of 'em with guns... They've got Dr. Wayne and his student...Julie." Thomas continued to gasp for air. "You need to get up there quick... But you better have help."

"What gives, son? Tell me quickly!"

"One man...dressed in black...wire glasses...wool cap...tall dude...he's dangerous!"

"Pilloud's highly paid help, no doubt. Wait here. I'll check on the status of my back-up..." Larry grabbed his radio and called Toonie. "Toonie? Where the hell are ya?"

"Behind ya... This trail's killing me!"

"How far back?"

"I'm at the junction of the Indian and Bridal trails."

"Damn! Where are our deputies?"

"On their way, about fifteen minutes behind me..."

Sheriff Magelton looked at Thomas with a very grave expression. "Okay, son. Tell me how much time you think they have up there."

"Sheriff, it's bad!

"Okay, let me think... All right. Take me to where you last saw them. Then run as fast as you can back down to Toonie and lead him to me ASAP! Can you do that for me, son?"

"Yeah. Sure can, sir."

"Good. Make sure Toonie has back-up deputies right behind him. This isn't the way we should be doing this. But let's go."

* * *

"Bronson. I know this trail better than you do. My son and I hike up it often. Let me lead."

"No, Mrs. Denton," Deputy Harris answered for Bronson. "My deputies and I will lead. But you can advise us on the shortest way to join our officers above."

"Fine. Is Jenny on her way back?"

"I'll confirm. Just a second... Tim? You get her back yet? Okay, fine, I'll tell her... Mrs. Denton, they're nearly back at your cottage now."

"Great! Thanks, Deputy. Thirty yards ahead of us is a shortcut we normally don't take— it causes erosion. We try to keep the tourists off it, but...well, that way!"

Bronson looked at the deputy and gave her a smile. Both were impressed by Laura Denton's level-headedness. Deputy Harris had, in fact, connected with Laura the second she met her. As the only female deputy in a very male-dominated profession, her rapport with other women who showed courage and ambition was instinctive and instant. The same qualities in her own personality had enabled Deputy Harris to rise through the ranks to be the second-in-charge behind Larry Magleton—a somewhat old-school cop, but a decent lawman, nonetheless.

Deputy Harris and Laura finally reached the junction where Bronson could go down with his medical gear and check on Dougie. If they continued on the main trail, they would soon be too high above him, like Larry had been. Bronson followed Laura's instructions and peeled off through the woods, while the others kept climbing the main trail. At the top of the ledge, Harris found the pink flagging and yelled down to Bronson, directing him to the spot where Dougie lay. Laura looked down from the ledge and grimaced when she saw the awkward angle of the young man's broken leg.

"Status, Bronson?" Harris called down to the fire investigator.

"Found him. Checking..."

"Well?"

"I have a pulse!" Bronson announced, astonished. "He's alive."

"Stay with him and get the rescue team up here to him now. We're moving ahead."

* * *

"Pierre, give it a tug."

"As you wish."

The mercenary pulled at the rope with both hands, testing the strength of the riggings and their ability to hoist weight up and out of the chamber. Max feigned interest in the rope and pulley system they had rigged up, but his entire focus was on the number of steps he would need to take before he lunged for the pistol that Pierre had laid down on a rock. Pilloud stood ten feet away, directing the action, his gun held ready. *Still*, Max thought, *Pierre is the real threat. He is unarmed at this moment, but he sure looks like he could use his hands as lethally as any weapon.* Julie crouched down against the chamber wall and shivered. She placed one hand on Rob's forehead and wiped her tears away with the other.

Pierre nodded back to Pilloud when he was confident of the load capacity.

"You did a fine job rigging this, Julie," he said in sincere praise of her abilities. "I couldn't have done better myself, and I am very good with ropes. You may learn that soon enough."

"How many gold bars are there?" Julie asked.

"Haven't counted them yet," Pilloud responded. "Why do you care?"

"Well, I'm wondering about the weight we are about to lift on my rigging. Those bars certainly look heavy."

"Each bar should weigh about twelve point four kilograms, or—as you Americans say—around twenty-eight pounds," Pilloud informed her.

"Then I would not try to lift more than three or four bars at a time."

Pierre nodded in agreement and glanced at Pilloud, while Max eyed the gun.

"Professor, I wouldn't think about trying that," the Frenchman warned, having followed the direction of Max's gaze. "You'd be dead before your body touched the cavern floor. Stop eyeing my gun and take a load of gold to the rigging, will you? You too, Julie."

"I will keep my gun pointed at these two while they load my inheritance," Pilloud offered. "Go to the top and make sure the cargo it is unloaded and organized for distribution up there."

"Agreed. But have the girl work the rope. I want the professor busy loading the bars. I don't trust him."

"I have them covered, Pierre. Go climb that service shaft now."

The mercenary shot Max a look that sent chills down Julie's spine. She knew he had every intention of killing Dr. Wayne once the heavy lifting operation was completed. Pierre had identified the professor as a potential threat to the operation. Julie herself might be spared long enough to serve as a hostage to ensure they got down Mt. Kineo safely.

"So, Pilloud. You know the deputies are coming," Max commented, continuing to load the cumbersome bars onto the rigging harness. "They couldn't have missed hearing the shots."

"Yes, Dr. Wayne, I know. That was a most unfortunate decision on Boxer's part. Makes it critical for us to get the gold out of here quickly. We have our escape planned quite well. They will never guess what we were doing up here. Nor will they ever know how we disappeared."

"Once we get your load out of this chamber, how do you expect to get it out of the *smaller* connecting tunnels? And even if you do, it'll take hours to carry it down the mountain. Especially since you are a man short. That'll give the deputies enough time to find you and discover what you are really doing up here."

"I see. So you advise me to simply give up then, huh? Surrender? You think me that stupid, Professor? You don't think I have every detail planned meticulously in advance? Now start loading faster!" Pilloud placed the barrel of his gun at Rob's temple and cocked it. "You know, perhaps I need to blow this poor boy's head off just to remind you what a sick bastard I really am!"

"No, Pilloud!" Julie yelled from her position on the rope. "We're working as fast as we can. You promised to leave him alone."

"And you promised to help me. So hurry, or your friend is no longer part of the deal."

"Here, Julie," interrupted Max. "Hook the rope on the anchor line there, and we might be able to get all the remaining six bars on the rigging this time. If we both pull the rope from here and Pierre does so from the top—I think we can hoist the rest up in one last lift."

"Now that's the team spirit, Dr. Wayne. Proceed," said Pilloud, delighted at the news of their improved progress.

* * *

"This is amazing, Thomas! I would have never found this side trail in such dense woods without your help, son. Now go get Toonie. Run!"

"Sheriff?" The boy looked back at Larry before scrambling down the path. "Please make sure Dr. Wayne doesn't get hurt."

"I'll do my best, son... Now go!"

Thomas began following the circuitous trail through the tangled underbrush. He had left Larry Magleton twenty yards from the crease in the rock—the spot where he had seen the man in the black wool cap disappear. His heart continued to beat uncontrollably. He hoped the sheriff would get there in time.

40

Larry stole up to the side of the mountain with the large crease opening. Above the entrance to the tunnel, he saw three straight lines and a pair of crow's feet drawn with red paint. Studying the old Indian painting for a moment, he thought: *Probably says, stop right here, you white idiot. Armed bad guys inside. Wait for back-up. Ugh! I wanted to be the small rural county Sherriff working in a peaceful little town in Maine. Who needs this?*

Larry reached down to his utility belt, pulled out his flashlight, and flipped the switch on. *Here goes...* He held his gun out in front of him, the flashlight, unlit, in his other hand. *No need to alert anyone in here by showing my beam yet.*

He turned sideways and eased his left foot and arm into the crease. Expecting to feel someone grab him, his entire body tightened up. Nothing happened.

Okay, that wasn't so bad. God, I hate tight spaces! Sliding in all the way, Larry let his flashlight light up only the floor in front of him. He wormed his way forward about twenty yards, then stopped to listen for sounds. He could hear nothing. So he continued past more ancient paint markings in the tunnel.

* * *

"You two have performed well!" Pilloud complimented his hostages. Then walking over to Rob Landon, he kicked him in the side. There was no response. Pilloud looked at Julie. "Unfortunately, my dear, it looks like your friend is dead—or close to it."

The student looked at the man with loathing. She refused to believe Rob was dead.

"He has been unconscious for the entire time we've been here," Pilloud went on. "To demonstrate that I'm a man of my word, I'll leave him here for the police to try to revive and rescue him."

"Assuming they find him!" Julie shot back. "How the hell will they do that? No one else knows about this hidden chamber just under the surface of the mountain."

"They will, Miss Walters—when Dr. Wayne leaves us to inform them about it."

"You mean, you'll free Max to do that?"

"If he fulfills one last request."

Julie remained silent, speculating about the nature of such a request. She looked to Max for answers. His face was impassive.

"It's as much as I can do, Julie," Pilloud said. "I promised I would spare your friend if you cooperated. I've kept my end of the bargain. Now I need you two for one final task. Then I'll free Max. If he is fast, he can seek help—maybe in time to save your friend. By the time this all goes down—we will be long gone… Look, I agree Boxer didn't behave like a gentle-man, but my instructions were to bring Bear down alive. I did not want anyone harmed. I just wanted all you meddlers off this mountain. I'd waited years for this opportunity. It was so close I could taste it. Boxer was incompetent and let his anger get the better of him. For that alone, he deserved to die. This Confederate gold is not some historical artifact destined for the museum. It is mine. It has always been with the Pilloud family. Once I have what is rightfully mine, I have no reason to worry about the law."

Max said nothing. Rob was no threat. He had been unconscious during the entire ordeal and had witnessed nothing. But he would never be found by the authorities unless someone escaped from this place and reported his presence. *None of us will*, Max thought to himself. Still, he had managed to buy some time and hoped the deputies were closing in on Pilloud. *I just hope Thomas made it safely back to his mother. Laura… Sweet Laura. She must be desperately worried by now.*

Max and Julie complied with Pilloud's instructions and climbed up the service tunnel to the central chamber. Pierre had arranged the gold bars into neat, low stacks in an enclave of the upper chamber—ready for transport. Little did he know, however, that a pair of eyes was watching him carefully from a side tunnel.

"Finished, sir," he told Pilloud. "Contents ready. Phase Two?"

"Indeed, Pierre. You confirmed the bar count?"

"One hundred, even. Should be around twelve forty kilograms, more or less."

"That is all?" Pilloud asked, crestfallen.

"It will be hard to move it out of here, as it is."

Pilloud's financial problems had made him greedy to the point of desperation. He had been hoping to find 200 to 300 bars.

"You know how much that is worth, Pierre?"

"Non, Monsieur. That is more your concern than mine. I am paid the same, regardless of how much we find."

"Well, this gold is worth no more than sixty-three million or thereabouts and I need more than that!"

Pilloud turned and looked at Max. "Okay, Dr. Wayne. Although your police friends may be coming up Mt. Kineo to look for you and the students, they have no idea where you are. The hidden entrances to the chamber could take days to locate, if ever. I know that the mark-ings in here are what the indigenous folks refer to as the 'Unity of Three'."

Max was surprised by Pilloud's knowledge of the paintings and of Indian folklore, but refused to offer any information. He looked past him as he listened silently.

"Oh, yes. I've done my research too, Professor. Achieving my life's ambition to locate the gold depended on understanding the natives in the area. The larger circle represents the inner chamber here. We forced this bit of information out of an intoxicated Abenaki several years ago. The radiating lines from the circle represent the three concealed entrance tunnels that lead to the main chamber used by each of three historic tribes. We only recently came to suspect that we had been searching for the missing gold in the wrong location. The key was to find the location of this hidden central mining chamber that no surviving native seemed to know about."

"Or was willing to protect with his life," Pierre added.

"We discovered that there was one old woman that still knew of the location. We were going to *negotiate* temporary access to the chamber in exchange for the one missing guardian gem-sphere. We understand that she was desperate to restore the historic markers to their original resting places."

Max remained strangely quiet. He listened carefully to the facts that Pilloud eagerly spouted and kept a careful eye on Pierre at all times.

"The Mohawk tunnel supposedly opens out through a natural cleft in the wall to a concealed portion of the northeast face of Mt. Kineo. You know the cliffs shown in every tourist postcard. The Mohawk later constructed another concealed emergency exit tunnel when more modern tools became available. If we can find that tunnel, we will be able to haul my gold to that hidden entrance and be on the other side of Kineo—away from the police and other trespassers. But we are not sure how to find this tunnel exit from the inside of the chamber."

"Sounds like you could use some help in reading these markings in here?" Max said, baiting Pilloud.

"By all means! But do it quickly."

"Max!" Julie interrupted. "Rob had this theory that the guardian spheres were more than mere tunnel markers. He thought they were used to help triangulate the exact position of the wooden vault in the inner chamber floor. See the small wooden cradles along the ledges? They're like the hours on a clock face."

Max considered Julie's words and began reading the writings on the walls that he could decipher. Suddenly, his face lit up with excitement as he realized that Rob had been onto something important.

"Pilloud," Max said urgently, "do you still have the black sphere?"

"I do. In the black storage bag over there, by Pierre's feet."

Max ran over and picked up the perfectly formed obsidian gemstone that had been crafted on Kajo's instructions and climbed up the ledge where one of the wooden bowls rested. He read the lettering above the bowl before reverently lowering the sphere into its depths. It fit perfectly.

"Julie, go back down and bring me the pink and the purple spheres that you and Rob have in your gear bag."

"Have you figured out the puzzle of the gemstone spheres, Max?" Julie asked with intensifying interest.

"My God... Rob was right!"

Julie rushed up and handed Dr. Wayne the other two guardian spheres as Pierre and Pilloud watched eagerly. The Iroquois symbols above the bowls indicated to Max which bowls to place each gemstone sphere into. Once he had completed the task, he had Julie help him tie small guide ropes between the rested spheres. And they did indeed triangulate the exact spot below, deep in the inner mining chamber where the wooden vault had been placed.

"Clever stalling on your part, Professor," scoffed Pierre. "But we've already found the wooden vault with M. Pilloud's gold."

"Thanks to Rob!" Julie added scornfully.

"So how does this help us locate the secret Mohawk exit tunnel?" Pilloud asked impatiently.

"Don't you get it?" Max said excitedly. "The black sphere is the Mohawk guardian sphere. When removed from the entrance tunnel cradle and placed in here in its proper wooden cradle, triangulating the vault, the vault and the sphere form a unique direction bearing."

Max pointed along the bearing and Pierre crawled over the ledge and up to the side of the rock, investigating with his flashlight.

"M. Pilloud," Pierre said, "this is truly amazing! There is another cleft in the rock. A tiny entrance hole I would not have given a second glance. But it appears to lead to two more tunnels opening out into the central chamber here."

Thinking about the Mohawk exit tunnel Pierre had found from the bearing Max gave him, Julie felt that this escape plan did not make any sense. "Yeah, fine, Pilloud," she barged in. "But like Max said, how are you gonna get the gold down from there? That exits where the cliffs of Kineo go vertical!"

"More than vertical, Julie. The wall is actually undercut there," Pilloud laughed, having organized every detail of the elaborate removal plan. "I suppose that a seven-hundred-foot drop would be a problem, wouldn't it it?" he taunted.

Julie was revolted by his smug arrogance. Max simply wondered how Pilloud had figured out a way to overcome that 700-foot obstacle.

"Both exit tunnels have fallen into disrepair," their captor explained. "According to the intelligence we paid for, both would require significant debris removal before they are fit for use. Both end up near the northeast cliffs. But only one of them—the emergency escape tunnel—exits onto a precarious precipice located on the northeast Kineo cliffs where the mountain had crumbled away, leaving the undercut below it. It seems if you drop a rock from the edge of the cliff, it will free-fall seven hundred feet and straight down into the depths of Moosehead Lake. This is so uniquely treacherous a spot—and, therefore, secure from enemies—that only a crazy Mohawk warrior would dare to climb around it. Your new task, Dr. Wayne, is to interpret these native symbols and tell me which of these two tunnels is the one I just mentioned. As I'm sure you understand, we just do not have enough time to clear debris from two tunnels. So Max, which tunnel it it?"

Pierre suddenly seized Julie, and pulled her close to his body, his left arm trapping her neck in a stranglehold. Then looking back at Max, he said, "Okay, Professor. We are running out of time. You heard my employer—impress us with your knowledge of Indian cave writings."

* * *

"Toonie, this is Deputy Harris."

"Go ahead."

"I've deployed two groups of deputies. Smith and McMahon are coming up the Bridal Trail to prevent someone circling back on us. I'm coming up the Indian Trail with Carlson and Mrs. Denton. Thurman is back, attending to that young man—Dougie—until the medical team arrives."

"Good. Have you seen Denton's son up there?"

"Negative."

"You hear from my boss yet?"

"Negative Harris. And frankly, it concerns me. Larry has gone radio silent."

"Damn. Ten-four."

Then Harris turned to Laura sincerely and offered, "I'm sorry, Mrs. Denton. No word on Thomas yet."

Laura felt a pit yawn open in her stomach. The thought of her son being in trouble was agonizing. The good news was that Thomas had to be with Max. The professor was smart, strong, and resourceful. She kept reminding herself of that fact before proceeding with the deputies.

Below the ledge, Bronson made Dougie as comfortable as he could and waited for the medical team to arrive. Seemingly minor bits of information whirled around in his head as he sifted through the findings from his fire investigation. He was beginning to put things together, establishing a connection with the Pillouds and their nefarious interests. He recalled the hidden camera that showed Rebecca Pilloud at the bank and the suspicious money exchange that had followed. Bronson could read people very well. Pilloud was a dangerously treacherous man. The deaths of Bear and the estate guard were also a disturbing development. Bronson turned on his radio and contacted Deputy Harris to share his concerns.

"Okay, I understand. What are we getting into, Bronson?" Harris inquired, aware of the concern in his voice.

"I don't know for sure, but I have a bad feeling about this."

Deputy Harris shared Bronson's apprehensions.

"Keep me posted on Dougie's condition, and if you have further thoughts about the recent developments, let me know."

"Ten-four, Harris. And…be careful."

Deputy Harris holstered her radio and looked at her team with determination. "Carlson…Take point and be alert."

"Yes, ma'am. I'm on it."

* * *

"Well, the symbols here are Algonquin…and the symbols over there appear to be…oh, hell! I'm not that good with more recent native languages. There are others that are much more…"

"Do your best, Professor! Lives depend on it."

Pierre tightened his grip around Julie's neck, making her gasp for air. Dr. Wayne shot the mercenary a look full of rage. Having taken note of the reaction he had evoked from the professor, the Frenchman smiled contentedly. He wondered how long he'd have to wait before taking Max down. He was looking forward to it. He had grown bored with a mission that had, so far, turned out to be soft. It certainly hadn't generated the excitement he was used to on other assignments overseas.

"Well, Professor? I suggest you get this right," warned Pilloud.

"I know the main tunnel there was Abenaki or some Algonquin group similar to it. These two entrance tunnels are both Iroquoian. The dialects of the tunnels are different. I can't guess why there would be two Iroquoian tunnels, but there were certainly many bands in the Iroquois nation. I presume one of the bands—most likely, the Mohawk—had their own tunnel, because they tended to be the most excluded of the five nations."

"Good, Dr. Wayne—now which tunnels are Mohawk?"

"Clearly the one that that Pierre discovered off my bearing."

"And he said there are two tunnels off that Mohawk tunnel. Which is the one that exits directly into the face of Kineo's undercut cliffs?"

"Step aside, Pierre, so I can see the markings inside the cleft."

The mercenary reluctantly yielded his ground to the professor who immediately looked at the symbols in the rock where the Mohawk tunnel bifurcated into two very narrow pathways.

"These symbols represent bravery and altitude. The higher you stand on a mountain, the closer you stand to the Spirit World. The Mohawk cherished precariously high places. It was, for them, a test of manhood. These four lines of symbols describe various tests of manhood... Well...I think they do."

"Let's hope you are right. Continue into the tunnel, Dr. Wayne, and I will follow you. I am obviously not in the shape you are. So do not proceed too far ahead. Julie will wait here, with Pierre as her special guest. If I don't make it back, Pierre, shoot her."

"Understood," came the reply.

At Pilloud's words, Julie began to struggle in Pierre's arms, a move he countered by pinching a key artery in her neck. Instantly, she went limp and fell to the ground, unconscious. Pierre had work to do; there was no time to babysit this young student, pretty as she was.

Max was already into the tunnel, with Pilloud following, his pistol ready. The professor had interpreted the Mohawk symbols as best he could, but had no clue whether he had actually selected the right tunnel. His specialty was the much older native peoples, such as the Red Paint People. Realizing that he couldn't afford to upset Pilloud, he had lied about his ability to translate the inscriptions on the wall. *Oh well,* he thought, *I have a fifty-fifty chance that I picked the right tunnel.*

Meanwhile, the pair of eyes that had been watching Pierre moved closer to the main chamber. Creeping toward the Frenchman, the owner of the eyes entered the central chamber behind him. Pierre was clearing away the rocks from the tunnel where Max and Pilloud had removed obstacles and tossed them out to him. Then, without warning, the owner of the eyes was upon him. The mercenary turned instantly, swinging his left leg in a swift sweeping motion that took his attacker's legs out from under him and caused him to fall to the ground with a thud, sending a cloud of dust up into the air. With his pistol pushed against the side of the man's head, Pierre watched him shake his head and draw a deep breath.

"Damn, you *are* good!" the Frenchman complimented the man. "I'd been keeping my ears pricked up for your arrival, but didn't hear you until you were right upon me."

The attacker did not respond. Instead, he sneezed twice. Then he laughed at Pierre and said, "My grandparents taught me well, did they not?"

"I *am* impressed. But I could have killed you in a split second."

"Clearly, my friend. But now, I suggest we get busy. Pilloud will be back soon."

"Did you bring the mining cart?"

"Yes. It has been fitted with large balloon wheels and a harness that we can attach to the mule."

"Did you get the abandoned shaft cleared?"

"Yes. As soon as you called me. It was tough. Grandmother was nearby when the signal came through. Fortunate, how things turned out. My people searched for Major Pilloud's gold over decades before giving up. We had no idea it was hidden here. No native would have dared to hide it in here. Very clever. I'll get the cart."

"Hurry. I figure it will take the professor and Pilloud fifteen minutes to crawl out the tunnel, signal the boats, ready the catch line, and return through the passage."

The young Native American did not reply. He was already scurrying through the tunnel, back to where his equipment was stored.

* * *

In another entrance tunnel, a man crouched near the main chamber and listened attentively. He had crept just close enough to catch a glimpse of Pierre stacking a pile of rocks when he noticed another man sneak up on him from the opposite tunnel. Startled, Larry backed up a few steps to make sure neither man could see him.

What on earth was that scuffle about, the sheriff wondered. He recognized the voice of the Frenchman that Thomas had warned him about. *My God, he has lightning-fast reflexes!*

Larry now realized that Dr. Wayne had left through the other tunnel with Pilloud. This might be his best chance to surprise the Frenchman with the gun. The sheriff had noticed that the female student was unconscious on the floor. *What is so damn important in this chamber worth killing people for?* Larry had noted that the other man the Frenchman had wrestled with appeared to be unarmed. *Toonie is still minutes behind me. But if I wait longer, I may be contending with three men and two hostages. Damn! Think!*

Magleton inched back to the opening between the main chamber and the tunnel. He could see Pierre lifting heavy rectangular object off of the floor near to the entrance of the tunnel the third man had just gone through. This was his best opportunity. It was either act now or await reinforcements.

* * *

"Deputy!" Thomas yelled, observing Toonie scramble up the next tier of rocks. "Deputy Toonie! Here!"

The postmaster looked up and was relieved to see the boy. Toonie had always admired him. He knew Thomas well from all the times the boy had taken the family boat across Moosehead Lake to Rockwood to collect his mother's mail. He could now call Deputy Harris and tell her the boy was fine.

"Harris…got him! Yes, yes. He looks fine… Let me find out what the situation is… Give me a second…"

"Toonie. Up here! Sheriff Magleton needs you now!"

"Give me the situation first, Thomas—I need to call it in. I have back-up help on the way."

"Sheriff Magleton can't wait… They have hostages."

Having climbed this path for the second time in ten minutes, Thomas was out of breath. "They have Dr. Wayne and his student…Julie… They have…guns." The boy put his hands on his knees and bent over, looking as if he might throw up.

"Here, Tom." Toonie tossed him a Nalgene bottle with a quart of water as he reached the top of the rise. "You've done well, son. Can you take me to Larry?"

"Yes… Just a second… I need to catch my breath."

Thomas took a few quick breaths, then gulped down the water, spilling about a third of it down the front of his rain jacket.

"Deputy, you read?" Toonie barked into his radio.

"Go, Toonie."

"I'm going to have Thomas take me ahead to Larry. I'll send him back to bring your men up. The boy says Larry needs assistance now—he can't wait!"

"Copy. Be careful, Toonie, and get Thomas down quickly!"

"Ten-four."

On the other end of the radio transmission, Deputy Harris explained the situation to Laura and Bronson. Laura could see how important Thomas had become to this operation and was very proud of her young man. Still, she was aching to see him safely down. Deputy Harris assured her that in Toonie's own words, Thomas was out of harm's way. Laura knew her postmaster well and trusted him. She knew he would look after her boy, as if he were one of his own. Renewed with hope and purpose, the four of them picked up their pace as they scrambled up the southwest shoulder of Mt. Kineo.

* * *

Max could see light ahead in the tunnel. There was not much rock debris to remove along the way. *Daylight.* As he approached the exit, the tunnel narrowed so that he had to drop to his knees from a stoop-walk motion and crawl on all fours. He wondered if he had chosen the right tunnel. As he crawled to the exit, he poked his head a few inches out of the rock and looked around. *Nothing,* he thought. *Something feels odd—just clouds and air?* He inched forward a little more so he could free his entire head and realized he could now see straight down. *Oh my God! That's a long way down*! Emptying out through a vertical wall of cleaved rhyolite, the opening had a very tiny ledge to secure one's feet upon. Max saw two twenty-four-foot boats idling far below them. The lead boat had a large steel bin in the middle filled with some light-colored, textured material.

Suddenly, he understood the plan. *Pilloud is clever indeed. They're going to position the boats directly underneath this exit shaft and drop the gold bars somehow directly into the boat below. The large bins must be padded to withstand the weight of the falling bars and cushion them from the impact. The large rope Pierre carried must be to rig a direct descent line to the bins.*

"Well, Max? Are you as smart as they say you are? Did this tunnel exit where it needs to or do I shoot you?"

"You'll be pleased, Pilloud. Unless of course, you were looking forward to shooting me?"

Pilloud grinned in approval at Max for retaining his sense of humor in the face of formidable odds.

"How did you know, Pilloud? If you didn't know where the Confederate gold was hidden, or where the ancient tunnels were, or how this tunnel emptied out into the side of the cliff overhang, how could you put together your plans so quickly for this getaway?"

"Excellent query. I've carried out some archeological research on my own, Dr. Wayne. When we realized the gold was not trapped inside the sunken *Piscataquis,* I began working through the puzzle of the gem-spheres that guarded the secret mining shaft and studied the history of the island's native peoples. I had Pierre introduce himself to some of the living descendants of Kineo's old guardians. He can be very persuasive, as you surely realize by now. He extracted crucial information out of one such elder—a keeper of the Circle of Unity. Although we never found the secret locations of either the central chamber or its entrance tunnels, we discovered a diagram on a leather hide that the guardian possessed. The diagram showed a schematic of the inner-tunnel system. Pierre was able to get this 'volunteer' to explain the general relationship of the Mohawk entrance/exit to the cliff below us."

"This could have been an amazing archeological-anthropological find, Pilloud."

"True. But I claim what is mine. My great great grandfather's prize! A band of renegade Iroquois robbed him of it and hid it in the bottom of the inner mining chamber. And they hid the treasure at the gravesite of a very important spiritual man—Kajo, a shaman of sorts. Quite sacrilegious on the part of the Iroquois, I must say."

"Yes. I saw the skeleton back there. But I didn't make the association. This man, Kajo, was apparently revered by his people. There was a lot of writing and symbols in the chamber about him spanning many generations of natives living on Kineo. "But still, how...how did you..."

"Ha! It seems that despite all their secrecy, the native peoples held the Mohawk and their climbing feats in awe. The old guardian man died without telling us about the hidden inner chamber, but he did boast of the exit tunnel in the side of the mountain. Had I been able to buy off the remaining lot of pesky cottage owners on Kineo, I would have hired a group of skilled rock climbers to rappel over the side of the cliff and scour the mountain's upper features till we found the hidden emergency exit tunnel."

"So it's you behind all the cottages being sold off!"

"These out of state investors do not appreciate what we have here."

"And Laura? Is it you behind the offers to buy her place?"

"Laura Denton? Ah, yes!"

"You know very well who!" Max's tone had become noticeably confrontational.

"I believe I struck a nerve there, Dr. Wayne. So you have feelings for the widow! She is quite attractive, I must admit."

Max stared back at Pilloud who was still inside the mouth of the tunnel, his flashlight trained on his hostage's face that clearly betrayed his anger.

"Ever meet her husband, Professor?"

Max continued to glare at his adversary.

"Not a particularly agreeable man, actually. I tried to get him to negotiate with me when he came up to claim his inheritance. He was not a co-operative seller."

Max did not enjoy this twist in Pilloud's discussion. Somehow, the topic of Laura having once had a husband did not make him feel any better about the situation he was in. Or perhaps, the thought that she had loved this man made him feel guilty about his obvious attraction to her. Either way, he wanted to steer Pilloud back to his boastful account of the intricate plot he had hatched to extract the hidden Confederate gold from the mountain.

"Fine, Professor," Pilloud said. "I will not pinch that nerve further for the time being. As I was saying... I wasted many hours looking at these cliffs through binoculars. Luckily, Jimbo found a missing gem-sphere and provided us additional leverage with the native guardians. Our goal was to use that leverage to extract more information from them, but then, your damn students began meddling in my affairs. I never expected them to stumble onto one of the secret entrance tunnels by accident and find another missing sphere!"

"Rob!"

"Oh, Dr. Wayne. Do not dismiss the meddling of your darling little Miss Walters. But no matter. We have it all now. And your students appear to be paying for their intrusion this afternoon, wouldn't you agree?"

"You are unbelievable, Pilloud."

"Believe it, Dr.Wayne—it is all true. Now get out on that ledge!"

"Hell, Pilloud, there *is* no ledge out here!"

"Sure there is...just not a substantial one," Pilloud laughed like a maniac. "Remember, the Mohawk wanted an entrance/exit that would discourage anyone but the bravest of warriors?"

"Yeah... Well, wait till *you* see this drop from here. I'm not going out there."

"I disagree. Remember, Professor—I have a gun pointed at you. I can still shoot you."

Max cursed under his breath, then began inching out further. The wind blew his hair into his eyes, but he dared not release his grip on the wall and use one of his hands to push the strands back. He had to exit headfirst. Freeing one hand and wedging it into the corner of a sharp chunk of fractured ryholite, he noticed the smooth edges that should have been much sharper and jagged. *I am not the first person to have engaged in this risky maneuver*, he was astonished to realize. *Incredible! I'm following the route of the brave Mohawk!*

Finally, Max could support enough of his weight to slide one leg out over the cliff and find a three-inch shelf below him to rest one foot. The wind blew again, and Max felt a twinge of vertigo seize him. He shut his eyes and clutched the side of the opening as Pilloud barked at him to keep advancing. Watching the athletic Dr. Wayne struggle for a foothold, he wondered suddenly if he himself would have the nerves to climb out on the ledge.

"Take your time, Max. I'm not eager to lose your assistance *just yet.*"

"That's reassuring, Pilloud," Max responded in a shaky voice, trying not to look down. Regaining his balance and his nerves, he used one hand to pull himself in the opposite direction, thereby creating enough support to slip his second leg around and out of the tunnel, while half of his body leaned over a 600-foot drop to Moosehead Lake below. Finally, he was able to get his entire body out and see clearly what he was being asked to do. He noticed that his knees were wobbly. He had just survived a terrifying exit that required strenuous maneuvers. Now all he could do was clutch the opening for support and edge along the wall till he found a widening in the ledge that would allow him a more secure foothold.

"Excellent, Dr. Wayne. Now takes these lines and sting a safety rail for others to come out there and have balance. Then keep moving sideways. I wish to inspect the escape route and signal my boat captains below."

As Pilloud studied the route intently, Max watched his captor carefully and considered his options. This was a very dire situation and the professor knew he was about to run out of time. Suddenly, Pilloud broke into his thoughts. A sinister smile played on his face. He turned slowly to Max and said in a matter-of-fact tone, "I had Laura Denton's husband killed, you know."

41

This was it—there might not be a better time. Drawing his weapon, Larry Magleton knelt and shouted at Pierre to freeze. Having already sensed the man's presence, the mercenary had slowly let his hand slip across the handle of his own handgun. For the time being, however, he simple froze, as commanded, and kept his back turned to the sheriff.

Larry had a very bad feeling about this man. It was the feeling one got after enforcing law in the inner cities. He wondered why he hadn't shot the suspect while he had the chance. *Dead men tell no tales.* But he couldn't shoot him in the back. Sheriff Magleton was not even sure if he could outshoot the superbly trained man in the black wool cap.

With one hand on his flashlight and the other on his county-issued pistol, the sheriff ordered Pierre to put his hands up in the air where he could see them. Struggling to keep his hand steady, Larry wished he did not have to hold the flashlight as well. His arms were tired from all the climbing and crawling he had had to do to get here. Observing the wavering flashlight beam, Pierre knew instantly that his opponent was exhausted. Without wasting a moment, the mercenary spun around, dropped to the ground, and pulled his gun—all in one smooth motion. Before he even landed, Pierre had fired off two quick rounds in the sheriff's direction. One bullet careened off the cavern wall, causing the rock to splinter into chips and strike Larry in the temple.

In response, the sheriff jerked off one futile shot into the central chamber, but came nowhere close to hitting Pierre. Then he backed into the tunnel for protection. Meanwhile, the mercenary had rolled away and ducked against the nearest wall, his gun pointed at the tunnel into which the sheriff disappeared. Larry tried to ease his arms out of the tunnel with his service revolver and flashlight ahead of him, but Pierre saw the beam of light easing forward and aimed at it. Another round ricocheted off the wall next to Larry's hand. Once again, fragments of rhyolite shards struck him—this time in the hand holding the flashlight, causing him to drop it.

Damn, this guy can shoot! Larry watched with frustration as his flashlight rolled out of the entrance tunnel into the central chamber. The larger diameter of the bell caused the flashlight to roll in a 180-degree arc until it had come to a stop, sending a beam of light shining directly back toward the sheriff, partially blinding him.

Great! He cursed himself silently for dropping his light. Realizing he was in a compromised position now, Larry hastily retreated, aiming his gun at the exit to the tunnel, in case the Frenchman foolishly rushed him.

Having noticed the flashlight blinding the sheriff and sensing his retreat, the highly trained mercenary sprang up at the opportunity and slid over to the tunnel opening. Then blindly pointing his gun into the opening, Pierre emptied his remaining clip into the tunnel.

He heard the unmistakable sound of hot lead striking flesh and the cry of anguish that followed. *Target down!*

His accomplice suddenly popped his head through the tunnel on the far side of the main chamber with the wheeled mining cart and yelled out, "You okay?"

Pierre looked back, frustrated. "Yeah. I'm good. But we have to hurry. That was likely the local law. Load the cart while I hold our position."

The young Native American loaded the cart, one bar at a time, till it was heavy, but not to the extent that he would be unable to push it along.

"I'll take this load," he told Pierre. "Once I get it through the smaller passageway, I can attach the cart to my mule and move it easily. Meanwhile, hold off other intruders who might make an appearance."

"I have my end covered. You do your bit…and hurry!"

On the floor near the remaining Confederate gold pile, Julie began to stir. Pierre listened, his ear cocked, alert to any alien sound that might herald the arrival of unwelcome others. From one tunnel came the sound of his accomplice moving sluggishly and noisily with a cart full of historic wealth. From the area near the remaining gold bars came Julie's groan as her foot slid across the dusty floor. From the original entrance tunnel came the gasps of a law-enforcement officer—obviously badly wounded—in retreat. He wondered how long he would last. Then he focused on the third tunnel, waiting to hear Pilloud return. *So much to concentrate on now*, he mused. *I love the action, the rush of excitement!*

* * *

"You did what?" Max asked incredulously.

Ignoring him, Pilloud looked down and signaled to the lead salvage boat. The man in the boat had binoculars and a walkie-talkie. Pilloud took out his own walkie-talkie and depressed the "send" button.

"I'm about to drop a rock," he said to the man below. "See where it lands. Adjust the distance accordingly so the boat is in place. I will then send the line down."

"You had him killed?"

Pilloud continued to ignore Max, while the boatman below waited for the rock to drop from the opening. The French Canadian had collected several rocks, dragging them through the tunnel in a bag tied at the end of a rope he had retrieved from Pierre's bag of equipment. He dropped the first rock, watching it gather momentum as it plunged down to the water below. The stone struck the lake's surface with tremendous force, sending up an impressive spray. *Ten feet off the port side.* The boat moved into position. The second rock fell.

As the boat closed in on the targeted point, Pilloud let another large rock loose. It plunged toward the boat and struck the side gunnel, ripping a huge gaping hole there before exiting through the hull into the deep cove.

"Jesus, Mr. Pilloud!" cursed the captain through his radio. "That could have killed someone!"

Then he moved the vessel three feet to starboard and three feet to aft.

The crew ducked, trying to shelter themselves behind any object they could find in the boat and escape being struck by the descending rock missiles. The damage the last falling rock had done to their boat had made them apprehensive.

"Get on real street, crew!" the captain yelled. "There's nothing on board that will save you from an object dropped from that height! So make damn sure it falls in the bin this time! Grab those anchor lines and adjust the boat's position, as requested!"

The crew moved the boat by pulling against the anchored lines. The captain had placed three deep anchors in the water to keep the boat in position so there would be no drift once it was anchored. The men hurried to patch up the hull so no water leaked in from the side-gunnel damage.

"Okay, Mr. Pilloud," the captain's voice crackled through the walkie-talkie, "drop the rope. We're in position!"

Jean Pilloud took out his final stone and tossed it aside. Beginning to flake the long 660-foot rope, he glanced at Max.

"This rope better land in the bin, don't you think? I almost sank one of my escape boats with that last rock."

Max shook his head at Pilloud, thinking to himself: *He is one crazy bastard!* He watched the man tie the rope to a tree growing from the side of the ledge nearby, then drop the other end. The rope untangled itself and sped its way down, the last forty feet landing with barely a "thunk" in the bottom of the steel bin. The four feet of packing material within it had absorbed the impact perfectly. The captain signaled a victory sign to Pilloud and his men cheered. The next drop would be the first load of the gold. It would be slowly lowered down the rope with the help of a descending device with a breaking mechanism that could be adjusted to match the weight of the cargo, thus preventing acceleration along the rope on decent.

Max took a deep breath, his eyes on his precarious foothold.

"Why did you have Laura's husband killed?"

"That should be obvious to you, Professor. He was uncooperative. You can tell immediately whether someone is going to be a problem. There was no way he would ever sell his inherited cottage. Especially after he discovered how I had driven his parents from Kineo! I figured I could burn the cottage down, like my father had done before me, to collect on the insurance. Or have Pierre arrange an 'accident' for Mr. Denton. There was no way a distraught widow would want to come up here and deal with all this. I planned to coerce her into selling and keep that particular cottage myself as an asset to work out of. I actually have some sentimental memories of staying in her cottage when I was a kid! I planned to have most of the other structures burned to the ground."

"So you really did have him killed! Good God, Pilloud! You're insane!"

"Well, technically, it was an accident, Max. Pierre is very good at making such arrangements."

"You have no conscience at all, you bastard!"

"That may be. But now you will help me."

"Sorry, Pilloud. You'll have to shoot me before I do anything more for you."

The other man frowned, then calmly connected the descending device. He did not want to draw attention to the cliff edge by firing his gun; nor did he want to waste any more time. *I could leave Max on the ledge*, he thought to himself. *But what if he somehow managed to work himself off the ledge, like the Mohawk warriors used to? He might get back to alert the authorities. Could he climb out and over the mountain in time to get help before Pierre finished passing all the gold through the tunnel to me? Not probable, but regrettably, possible.*

"Okay, Professor," he said finally, "this device can carry the weight of about five bars at a time. You will load them from where you stand. I will hand them to you as Pierre shuttles them to me. Try dropping one, and I will push you over the edge! Now come back off the ledge and assume your position at the rope."

"No way! I'm not helping you anymore. Shoot me right here, if you want to. Right now."

"Dr. Wayne. Do you really want to stay out here any longer? Take another look down."

Although Max refused to look down, the acids in his stomach were eating a hole right through him. He had a choice between two really unpleasant options. Pilloud started backing carefully into the tunnel. Max could do nothing out on this ledge but die; so he hugged the Kineo rockface tight and worked his way to the rope by the tunnel entrance, being careful about where he placed each step. Once he had reached the entrance, Pilloud offered him the first bar to load onto the descending device. Max reached for the bar, then suddenly realized that Pilloud had no intention of ever letting him back into the tunnel. It was now or never.

Recognizing the sudden change in the other man's expression and attitude, the French Canadian lunged forward to give him a shove, but Max had locked both hands around his captor's arm and pushed out from the wall. The sudden jerk caught Pilloud by surprise. He lost his balance, fell to his knees at the entrance to the tunnel, and tumbled forward. Had his legs not got wedged in a large crack at the tunnel exit, Jean Pilloud would have been pulled out of the tunnel and onto the tiny ledge below him.

Max clawed at the wall with his feet, trying to remain flush against the wall. If he lost his grip on Pilloud's arm, he would fall to his death. His opponent had his free arm wedged in a crack that was holding the weight of both men. He began twisting the arm to which the professor was clinging back and forth in an attempt to make him loosen his vice-like grip, but Max was strong and too motivated by a sense of self-preservation to let go of his only lifeline.

The professor finally obtained a foothold and used a tiny ledge below him to push up and over Pilloud's back, pinning him against the opening. As both men wrestled for position, Pilloud slipped further, and Max took advantage of the situation by advancing toward the opening. Both men struggled to capture the limited space available, while dangling halfway out of the tunnel exit, but Max was no longer the one verging on the possibility of sure death. Pilloud retained the apparent advantage of a gun, but he could not free the arm wedged in the crack to use it. Max had the advantage of superior strength. Suddenly, his captor let out a shriek of anguish, as he realized he could no longer support the combined weight of both men. And just as suddenly, both tumbled from the ledge into the void.

42

Thomas had grown ten years older in the past four hours. His heart was heavy, burdened with anxiety over Dr. Wayne. It had been an hour since he last saw the professor. He hoped Sheriff Magleton was with him now and the criminals apprehended. Toonie was following Thomas in a game-face trance. The Denton boy had been to the post office many times and had always thought of the postmaster as a gentle, happy man who liked to socialize and discuss hunting. Today, he looked like a hunter pursuing a lifetime quarry.

Toonie struggled to stay up with the more agile youngster. When Thomas suddenly turned and put his finger to his lips, the postmaster immediately drew his nine-mm sidearm, following the direction in which the boy was pointing. In a hushed voice, Thomas informed Toonie that the hidden path was just up ahead, but suggested that the older man advance along it very cautiously, keeping an eye out for the thin man in the black wool cap who had a gun and appeared very dangerous.

The postmaster took the lead as Thomas moved the brush back to fully reveal the entrance to the side trail. The boy walked about ten yards behind Toonie, providing him with whispered instructions as to when he should turn or slow down. In a few more minutes, they had reached the large rock formation from the top of which Thomas had spied on Pierre earlier. The boy listened carefully, but could not hear the movements of anyone ahead of them.

"Okay, Toonie," he said. "See the other rock formation in the distance? The crack on the left side of the rock goes back into some sort of tunnel. I've seen people disappear into it. Be careful."

"You've done well," Toonie said, placing his hand on the boy's right shoulder. "Go now and bring the reinforcements up here."

"I will, sir."

As the boy turned to leave, Toonie noticed a man stumbling out of the crease in the rock ahead. "Get down, Thomas!" he whispered.

The boy dove to the ground, as Toonie aimed his pistol at the rock seam and watched the man take a few tottering steps out of the tunnel before collapsing on the ground. It was Sheriff Magleton.

"Thomas! Sheriff's been hit! I'm getting him out of there. You need to go now! Run!"

Thomas had seen enough horror for one day. He took off, running for the deputies. He continued to worry about Max and wonder if he was safe. *Sheriff Magleton looked bad*, he thought. *Blood stained most of his uniform.*

For the third time that day, Thomas half-ran and half-climbed down the upper Indian Trail to seek help.

* * *

Pierre waited for his partner to return with the empty mining cart that could handle loads of up to 1200 pounds at a time. But a man could not push it through the tunnel with that kind of load. As a result, each load typically accommodated about twenty bars that should have amounted to just over 700 pounds. The last load had been relatively full and heavy, but the young native American was surprised how much faster he had moved the load than he had expected. The next load would hopefully take care of the remaining bars. With Pierre's help, the cart could be moved quickly through the third exit tunnel. *What is taking him so long? Is he double-crossing me?* Pierre watched his flanks to make sure that neither a lawman nor Pilloud entered the central chamber. *I have to protect the gold till the cart comes back. The lawman is surely dead. If not, he isn't likely to get far.*

Pierre was sure that he had hit the officer several times when he emptied his clip into the tunnel at short range. He had not actually seen the target, but had heard the shots striking tissue and the man crying out in pain. *No, the lawman is no longer an issue. But where the hell is Pilloud? Shouldn't he be back by now? Is it possible that the professor overpowered him?* The last thought brought a strange smirk to Pierre's face. Killing Pilloud was a prospect he savored, because he hated manipulative rich tyrants like him. That type of employer was the same anywhere in the world: smug, arrogant, and useless to society, except for the paycheck he provided to those he hired. Pilloud would be such an easy man to overcome. No challenge at all. *But Dr. Wayne,* he thought, *is a big man and fit. He would put up a decent fight. Yes, if the professor overpowers Pilloud and heads back through this tunnel, I'll welcome the opportunity to kick the intellectual's ass! After all, I got cheated out of my chance to kill Bear earlier. Still, no sign of Pilloud, Dr. Wayne, or my dark-skinned partner. Would that bastard actually try to take his half now and leave me in here to fend off the authorities?* Pierre became annoyed as he considered the possibilities, looking repeatedly at his wristwatch as he waited.

* * *

As Max tumbled off the concave cliff, his death grip on Pilloud relaxed automatically. The latter's eyes filled with shock and horror as he fell. Although he was a portly man and not particularly robust, he managed to grab the rope that had been rigged to transfer the gold to the boat and secure a handhold within the descending device. Max continued to tumble another twenty feet before he was able to catch hold of a small fir tree clinging to the side of a lower ledge. Holding on for dear life, he looked up to locate Pilloud's position.

Above Max, the once wealthy timberman held on desperately, as the descending device began to gather speed on its way down the rope. Before Pilloud could find and depress the braking lever, he had descended to near eye level with Max, about eight feet from the small tree that had temporarily saved the professor's life. Pilloud considered his options: did he have the strength to descend the entire length of rope to the boat below? Or could he use his hands and feet to climb back up the rope to the ledge? If he chose to descend, it would leave him no time to climb up Kineo again. He would lose his family's gold to the local authorities. That was *not* an option. He wrapped his feet around the steep rope and let go of the device so that he could climb up. He had managed to move up about ten feet when the consequences of abandoning his diet earlier that year hit him; his hands were unable to take his weight and he fell. On the way down, he instinctively reached out to grasp the rope line, but failed. His boat was still anchored exactly in the place where he had positioned it. He tried flattening his body and spread his arms, hoping to land in the packing material within the bin, but found it impossible to hold his position as his body tumbled though the air.

Below, a crewman had just climbed out of the bin after retrieving and throwing overboard the last rock that Pilloud had dropped, when another crewman shouted for him to watch out. The first crewman ducked out of the way and dived to the deck, and the others watched in horror as their boss missed the steel bin, striking the boat's recently wrecked gunnel like a torpedo at terminal velocity. The fiberglass imploded, leaving a gaping hole in the side of the vessel, and the boat shook violently under the impact.

Half of the boat's crew was thrown overboard by the unexpected collision, as the portside gunnel collapsed completely under the weight of Pilloud's body which was now partly impaled on the jagged pieces of fiberglass jutting out of the structure. The waters of Moosehead Lake rushed mercilessly inside the vessel as the structural members supporting the steel bin gave way and snapped. The bin plunged through the bottom of the boat's hull. The salvage boat buckled and slid under the surface of Moosehead Lake within seconds, washing away all evidence of this surrealistic catastrophe. The second boat hurried over to rescue the survivors.

* * *

High above the lake, Max continued to hold onto the small fir tree, but his weight had caused it to bend in half and point downward. The needles were also beginning to come loose from the branch and within moments, Max had lost his tenuous grip. He fell another ten feet, his body scraping along the cliff wall and dashing painfully against a great number of small firs, as he stretched out his arms and tried in vain to break his fall by grasping the branches that seemed to be passing by him at an impossible speed. However, the resultant friction did slow down his downward momentum as he continued to fall. His attempt to seize a more solid branch with his right hand merely resulted in him hitting his wrist so hard against it that the impact spun his body back against the rocks and slammed it into the side of the cliff.

Max felt as if he were experiencing the final moments before death took over, as he careened off a small outcropping of ice-carved stone and struck more tree branches projecting from the weathered ledge of rhyolite past which he fell. Once again, he tried desperately to grab one of the branches, but failed, because both of his hands were now raw and bleeding. As his body landed on top of a small conifer, it seemed that he would be given a chance. But before he could secure a hold, he had slid off the top and fallen another twenty feet, until his left arm made contact with a fairly sturdy branch and hooked onto it, the impact spinning him back a second time toward the great cliff wall.

As Max slammed into the wall with tremendous force, his left arm snapped on contact. His body bounced off, landing on a sloped section of rock on which grew several more stunted coniferous trees. His right foot caught in the crotch of a small fir tree with a bifurcated main stem growing precariously out of a crevice in the rock, snagging him so that he was hanging upside down as his head struck the cliff wall again, knocking him unconscious. To anyone who might look up at it, his now motionless body resembled a sleeping bat hanging from the roof of a cave. Although bruised and battered by the trajectory of his fall, Max had somehow survived the plunge of more than 100 feet and was now suspended 500 feet above Moosehead Lake.

* * *

A chillingly patient and calculating man, Pierre did not trust his Native American partner. It was, after all, a partnership of convenience. Not that a man like him trusted anyone. Placing your faith in someone could leave you stone-cold dead. That was why he had resigned from the French Special Forces. They had wanted him to be willing to die for his country. *Screw that! A man of my abilities and skills should be handsomely rewarded*, he would think to himself. If there was one thing he trusted, it was his own abilities. With the Confederate gold reserve in his safe custody, he could generate enough cash in the black market to set up his own business—shading dealings in Hong Kong, protecting business transactions in Switzerland, and arranging for the dispatch of illegal arms to the Arabs in his favorite North African countries. Pierre smirked to himself, remembering those wonderfully eager-to-please Czech ladies in Prague.

He was done waiting. The time had come to investigate what was taking his partner so long. He pulled out his flashlight and his special service pistol with the modified clip. Inside his gear bag, he found the awkward, but effective attachment to his sidearm that he now wished he had used when the lawman surprised him. He was screwing his silencer attachment onto the barrel when he heard the clattering of the mining cart. Quickly removing the silencer, Pierre shoved it into his inner jacket pocket from where it could be extricated more swiftly the next time he needed it.

"Where you been?" he asked his Native American partner.

"This cart was very hard to move, my friend!"

"Hmm… Well let's finish loading it. We're short of time."

The two men quickly loaded the remaining bars. Pierre asked how far it was to the end of the exit tunnel. Although it was important to move the heavily loaded cart out of the central chamber, it was just as crucial to protect their rear flank. Once the cart was in motion, it made a horrible screeching noise that echoed loudly in the tunnels. Someone could easily creep up from behind and take them without Pierre hearing the person approach. The mercenary had to be sure that Pilloud was not going to come up behind them and make trouble.

"Okay," he told the other man, "take off now. I'm going to check the tunnel where I last saw Pilloud and make sure he's not going to stop us from getting away."

"Well then, my friend. Should you not be fulfilling your part of this deal?"

"Don't you worry. He'll be dead before he knows what hit him. Then I'll seal our escape tunnel behind us by using explosives so no one can follow. Then I'll catch up with you and help you unload at the other end."

"Sounds like a good exit strategy, my suspicious Canadian friend."

"I'm not Canadian! I'm French! Don't confuse the two."

"Whoooa there! Sorry. I go now. See you soon, my friend."

Pierre watched the Native American struggle to move the large cart once again. The cart's axle and wheels had been designed for large loads of rock, with mechanically advantaged gears that could be adjusted. As the cart began to squeal and move away with the last load, Pierre looked at the diminishing light in the tunnel and muttered to himself, "My 'friend' my ass!"

* * *

"You okay, Sheriff? That looks serious."

"Damn it, Toonie. I could have taken him. I didn't get my shot off in time."

"It's okay, Larry. You rest now—our back-up is almost here. I'm going in."

"No, Toonie! That man in there is a highly trained professional. You'd be out of your league. He's dangerous."

"Ya think? Well I'm a true-born Mainard, Larry. He has no idea what he is messing with up here. Sit tight. I'll be back."

"Stand down, Toonie. Wait for back-up! Damn it, you stubborn Rockwood son of a bitch!"

Larry watched helplessly as the postmaster dashed inside the crease in the rock. He could feel the blood drain from his chest, and he was becoming increasingly dizzy. He snatched up his radio.

"Deputy Harris. Come in."

"Harris here, sir. That you, Toonie?"

"Get up here now! We got a problem. And send a helicopter—they're gonna have to fly me off this mountain or I'll bleed out."

"Sheriff, you hit bad?"

"Yep. Several times. And Toonie is playing cowboy ahead. I couldn't stop him. Too weak... Hurry!"

His last words were muffled and Harris could not raise him after that.

* * *

Julie Walters could only see blurred images before her. She was still damp and cold. She had spent so much time fighting off hypothermia that her body ached and she was completely exhausted. *Oh God, I'm thirsty! Where am I? No! Not still in this cavern? Rob? Poor Rob. Where's Max?*

She wiggled her feet and moved her legs back and forth, trying to get the blood to circulate in her lower extremities. A wave of nausea overtook her and she lay back down on the floor of the chamber. In the corner, guarding a side tunnel, was a very preoccupied assassin. She felt nothing but disdain for the man that Jean Pilloud called Pierre, a ruthless individual with no conscience. She would gladly crack him over the head with the metal end of her harness if she had the opportunity.

Finally, her eyes were able to refocus. She could see Pierre with his gun drawn, listening so intently for sounds from one of the entrance tunnels to the main chamber that he seemed oblivious to her stirrings in the other corner. Pierre's concentration was focused on the tunnel through which Pilloud and Max had disappeared. *Where's Max? He would certainly know what to do.*

* * *

The waiting was becoming intolerable. Pierre started entertaining the possibility of his employer not returning through the Mohawk entrance and escape tunnel. The tunnels reverberated with the minutest sounds and had Pilloud still been inside—alive—his movements would surely have been audible. Pierre could only imagine various scenarios. Logic dictated that someone—either Pilloud or Dr. Wayne—should have come back through the tunnel into the main chamber by now. The mercenary considered several possibilities. *Maybe they had ended up in a scuffle and the professor had overpowered Pilloud, but been shot in the ensuing fracas? Or...Pilloud had found a way to double back and double-cross him? Jamais! No way! The fool must have run into trouble with his ridiculous plan to lower the gold over the side of the cliff. No matter. My own plan is far superior anyway, and it doesn't include sharing any of the gold with you, Jean Pilloud, you filthy, arrogant Canadian pig! North Americans are all so full of themselves, basking in a land of abundant resources. Who wouldn't be successful here? Decades of stealing from the natives in a land ripe with opportunities. No wonder my third-generation Indian partner detests all of you! You're no survivor, Pilloud, you're an opportunist—and a poor one at that!*

Pierre decided there was no longer any need to be concerned either about his boss or about Dr. Wayne. He could now hurry back and join his partner and claim his share. *Maybe I should kill him and claim both shares?* The thought had crossed his mind many times, but timing and the right opportunity were factors that had to be taken into consideration. Pierre had recognized in the course of his professional life that those who had to tussle with irresistible temptations engendered by greed, including the best operators, invariably became sloppy and ended up ruining their well-planned schemes. *Best not get ahead of myself. I'll play that option by ear.*

Ducking to avoid the overhang, he re-entered the central chamber. Stuffing his Special Ops handgun into his pants, he reached into his duffle bag to remove the small plastic bag with explosive material, contact wires, and a timer that he had carried with him for this very moment.

Suddenly, catching a light beam heading his way from the tunnel on the far side of the chamber, he began retying the explosive bag. Then dropping the explosives into his duffle bag, he had just reached back down for his handgun when a voice echoed out from the other side.

"You there! Drop it and hold your hands up where I can see them."

* * *

Deputy Harris followed the utterly exhausted young Denton to the hidden side trail. Deputies Smith and McMahon had worked their way up the Bridal Trail and joined Deputies Harris and Carlson. Mrs. Denton greeted Thomas with a strangling hug and insisted he follow her immediately back down the mountain. The boy squeezed his mother back in a very tight embrace, but told her he couldn't leave.

"Not yet, at least," he added. "Max needs help. So do Sheriff Magleton and Toonie. I have to take Deputy Harris to them, Mom!"

There was little time for debate. Despite her maternal urge to grab her son and drag him home, she knew he had become a man, and he was right. She also felt a strong sense of responsibility toward the two local law officers—and Max, of course—and wanted to see if they could contribute in any way to their rescue. Laura and the four deputies, their guns at the ready, followed Thomas who, once again, began the arduous scramble along the edge of Mt. Kineo's southern face.

* * *

"Pardon?" Pierre asked calmly.

"Drop what's in your hands—*now!*"

"Certainly. Please don't shoot. There are some strange men in these chambers shooting blindly at people. I'm afraid my employer, Mr. Pilloud, was shot by your sheriff."

"What! Where? Sheriff Magleton is the one who's been shot!"

"Right. There was an exchange of gunfire in here. In the confusion, he may have been wounded."

"I saw Magleton outside. He said a man in black clothing and a wool hat had shot him!"

"I'm wearing dark pants, true enough. But as you can see, I neither have on a black wool cap nor a black shirt."

Pierre's black sweater and cap rested on a shovel handle near him where he had placed them earlier while loading the mining cart. A white thermal layer of polypropylene now covered his muscular torso.

He hoped Toonie would not notice the shovel right away.

"Well, just drop what's in your hands and get them up where I can see them!"

"Okay, okay! Just settle down. It's just a video cam. But I'll drop it. The bad guys you're looking for are down the side tunnel."

Pierre dropped the gun in his left hand to the ground behind his left boot so that Toonie could not get a close look at it. To deflect the postmaster's attention, he deliberately pointed with his right hand to the tunnel through which his Indian partner had left a few minutes earlier. Now that Pierre had safely dropped the object in his left hand, Toonie allowed his gaze to wander in the direction of the tunnel. This was the chance the mercenary had been anticipating. With lightning speed, he switched off the flashlight in his right hand and tossed it into the corner, plunging the area into darkness and causing the metal object to land and roll with a loud, distracting clanking noise several feet from where Toonie stood. Pierre threw himself on the floor, and snatched up his handgun as he rolled 360 degrees, managing to get his finger squarely on the trigger.

Instinctively, he aimed at the beam of light at the other end of the chamber and let loose with a double tap from his gun. Toonie fired at the moving target about twenty-four feet in front of him. A hot round struck the postmaster in the bicep, and the other bullet skimmed the side of his left cheek. One of Toonie's bullets embedded itself in Pierre's right shoulder, causing him to drop his gun. Snatching the duffle bag in his left hand, the mercenary scampered across the floor and headed to the exit tunnel through which his partner had disappeared several minutes ago.

With the bullet piercing his bicep, Toonie had dropped his weapon. He fell to his knees and pushed his body back into the tunnel for more adequate cover, looking on as the assailant fled with the duffle bag into the tunnel to his left. Toonie swore at himself for allowing the man with the French accent to shoot him. Grumbling in frustration, he groped around in the dust at his feet, searching for his nine-mm handgun until he found it. Cradling the firearm between his hands, he prepared himself mentally to pursue Pierre. The postmaster was infuriated now and wanted revenge.

During the intense exchange of fire between the two combatants, neither had noticed that the young woman in the corner had somehow disappeared.

* * *

"From this point on, it's dangerous," Thomas informed the wary deputies. "Down this narrow side trail. Your men should lead. I can give instructions about where to turn if they move slowly enough ahead of me."

"Bronson, you copy?"

"Yes, ma'am."

"Status?"

"Dougie is stable. Team arrived and will lift him out. I'm on my way to join you. You guys left an obvious trail—I'm not far behind you."

"Ten-four. Hurry."

"Out"

"Okay, now—Smith, you have the shotgun. You take point. McMahon—I want you to bushwhack your way through the brush on his right. Stay about fifteen yards off his shoulder. Be ready."

"Yes, ma'am."

"Carlson, you bushwhack your way along the trail fifteen yards off Smith's left shoulder. Dentons—you two stand directly behind me and we will follow Smith from fifteen yards."

Then Harris grabbed her radio again and contacted Bronson again. "Bronson—you got a gun with you?"

"Well, I wish I didn't," crackled his reply from the radio. "I'm only a fire investigator, you know. But yes, Carlson did hand me a firearm earlier."

"Consider yourself deputized. You hang back with Mrs. Denton, when you get here. You watch our back. Use your radio if you see anything."

"Ms. Harris," Thomas jumped in, "I can watch the approach of all the deputies from the top of that large rock over there. I used it earlier and could see the entire area, including the crease where the entrance tunnel begins."

"Good idea, Thomas," Deputy Harris concurred. "C'mon, Mrs. Denton, we have to get into position."

"Thomas, you be careful!" Laura commanded.

"Trust me, Mom. I'm fine. Dr. Wayne needs our help."

On hearing Max's name yet again on her son's lips, Laura's stomach suddenly became more restless.

* * *

"Deputy! I see him. Sheriff is down!" Thomas yelled out to Harris from his rocky perch.

Bronson caught up with Laura who pointed out her son on the rock. The fire investigator ran over to the rock and called in on his radio to Harris that he would take his radio up to Thomas. The vantage point on the rock offered a clear view of the dense Maine woodlands, tightly packed with spruce, fir, and white pine. Fearing an ambush with a wounded Sheriff as bait, Harris elected to wait for the fire investigator to reach Thomas. Bronson was out of breath, having run for so long to join the deputies.

"Confirm, Bronson?" crackled Deputy Harris's radio.

"Ten-four. Thomas is right. Officer down ahead. Another twenty yards down the path you're following. It widens out at the side of a large rock wall with a seam. I see Larry."

"Any sign of gunmen?"

"No ma'am, but I'm watching and have a great view from here."

"Carlson, Smith, and McMahon...be alert. You copy?"

Each deputy in turn buzzed in his 10-4. Each had heard Bronson's radio warning. All were in a somber mood. Whether you liked Larry Magleton or not—and certainly he could be sarcastic and abrasive—he was one of their own. He had gone in alone to take on the bad guys. To rescue decent people. Some bastard had taken him down. Not a man or woman in that group was going to stand for that. *Especially not with some foreigner shooting up respectable people in the backwoods of Maine! Not in Piscataquis County. Not in Somerset County.*

Upon reaching the clearing in front of the entrance crease, each deputy took position to cover the other. No ambush was going to happen on this wet, cold afternoon. Carlson reached the sheriff first and dropped to his knees to examine him.

"Where's…Harris?" mumbled Larry, raising his head feebly, but ready to let it drop to the ground again. He had bled so profusely it was hard to determine where he had been wounded.

"She's right behind us," Carlson replied.

"I'm here, Larry. What's the situation?" Deputy Harris had arrived and was standing near the injured sheriff, while two of the deputies covered the tunnel and surrounding area.

Thomas and Laura came running up to join them.

"Thomas, great job, son," Deputy Harris told him. "Now go back with your mom."

Larry managed a small smile for the boy before a grimace distorted his features again. Thomas turned back and put his arm around Laura who seemed deeply upset by the sheriff's condition.

"Toonie went inside the crack in the wall behind me," Magleton volunteered, coughing up blood as he spoke. "He needs help now. I heard more shots inside a few moments ago." He paused as blood bubbled up from his mouth.

Deputy Carlson was on the radio, with an urgent request for a helicopter to be dispatched to the summit with medical assistance. Bronson ran up next, carrying his triage bag, and began looking for supplies to stem the flow of blood.

"He's in way over his head," the sheriff said the moment he could speak again. "That tall, thin guy with the French accent is extremely dangerous. Don't trust him! It's dark and cramped there. They know you're coming."

"What's this all about, Larry?"

"I don't know… Something they found inside the mountain. Something they want badly. There's an incredible tunnel system in there that I had no idea about. Saw the man in black…loading something…looked…like…"

With that last gasped utterance, Sheriff Magleton fell silent and collapsed against Deputy Harris's chest. Three bullets had ripped through him from the full clip Pierre had emptied at close range. After a life tinged with regret, Larry no longer carried the burdens of his past with him. Deputy Harris wiped the sticky crimson fluid that had spattered her nametag and pocket and gently helped Bronson lay the sheriff to rest alongside the trail.

Then she said briskly, "Smith! Radio this in now! The body count is at least three and I'm one really pissed-off bitch! Bronson, this is no place for a fire inspector, a teenager, or a mother. Get the Dentons down from here. When that's done, lead the medical and investigation teams up here, once I declare it safe to do so. If things get worse and I call for more back-up, send it."

"That doesn't sound encouraging."

"It isn't, Bronson. Now get 'em out of here!"

"Gone."

Deputy Harris turned to her other deputies. "All right, gentlemen… Let's take these motherf……!"

43

It wasn't as if Pierre hadn't been shot before in his illustrious career. Such had been the inherent dangers of his Special Forces past. But this injury was different. He couldn't bring himself to believe that a poorly trained policeman had actually been lucky enough to hit him. A round had penetrated his shoulder and nicked a piece of his scapula. The amount of flesh it had ripped from his body made his injury far worse than any he had sustained in the past: it had rendered his entire arm useless. Pierre had also lost his gun in the exchange. He still had his satchel containing the explosives, however, and was more determined than ever to use them shortly.

Without a flashlight to show him the way, his head struck the overhang several times as he scurried along the tunnel. Using his uninjured arm, he dragged his hand along the wall, trying to interpret their texture, as if he were reading Braille. Since the heavy mining cart was slow-moving and his accomplice had not yet reached his mule, Pierre soon reached a point in the tunnel from where he could hear the loud squealing of the axles grinding under the stress of the load in its belly. If not for the gears, it would have been virtually impossible to budge. Pierre ran up to the cart's left side and began pushing with all his might.

"We must hurry. We have visitors."

"I heard shots."

"Yes, you did," Pierre responded in a strained, noticeably weaker voice. "How much further?"

"Just around that bend, the mule awaits."

"Fine! I'm going to set the charges here. This tight constriction should bring down enough rubble to block their advance. Keep pushing the cart!"

"Yes, my friend," the American Indian said, groaning, "I *have* been!"

By the time Pierre had packed explosives into several fissures in the tunnel and run the wires to his timer, he could see a light beam coming down the tunnel once again. It was Toonie.

Ha! I'll show you, you meddling little shit! Come closer! Bring it on!

Pierre set the last wire and estimated the time it would take for the postmaster to reach the explosives: about fifteen more seconds. Pushing the digital display to fifteen, the mercenary backed away and quietly retreated down the tunnel. He checked his synchronized watch display LED blinking in the dark passage. Four... Three... Two...

* * *

"Thomas!" Laura reached out and hugged her son as tightly as she could. "Son, no more heroics for ya today." Tears ran from her eyes, and he hugged her back.

"Thanks, Bronson, for your help today, but as Harris said—let's get the hell down now!"

"Mom, what about Dr. Wayne? He's still up here somewhere!"

"I know, hon. Let the deputies do their job. You've done all that ya can do."

"Do you think he's been shot too?"

"There's no reason to think that!"

Without another word, Laura abruptly averted her face. She did not want either her son or Bronson to notice the fresh tears that had begun streaming down her cheeks.

＊ ＊ ＊

Julie Walters continued to stoop and crawl-walk through the Mohawk escape tunnel. The passageway was getting narrower and there was virtually no headroom now. Then she saw daylight at the end of the tunnel. *At last!* Julie clutched her climbing-gear bag tight to her body, as she poked her head out of the tunnel. She looked down and saw the tiny ledge and rock outcroppings that camouflaged the precarious exit so that it was invisible from Moosehead Lake below. She looked to either side of her and failed to see any sign of Pilloud or her favorite professor. *Dare I call out his name,* she thought. *Where is Pilloud?*

Struggling out onto the ledge, she looked straight down. Even with years of climbing experience behind her, Julie felt queasy contemplating the dramatic vertical drop from this ledge. *Wow, that's a long way down!*

"Max? Max?"

She began by calling out his name softly, but as her desperation grew and she knew she wouldn't go back into tunnel where she might encounter Pierre again, these became shouts. *There is no way these men came out here and left this ledge,* she considered to herself. *The Mohawk may have been able to navigate around this formation to climb here, but I don't think either of these men could do it. Or could they?* She looked up at the rock face, examining the descent that would lead to this difficult tunnel route. *Wow! That's quite a tough descent without gear.* She started to climb up the treacherous route to seek Max, but then stopped and reconsidered. *No. This makes no sense.* She turned and looked over the ledge again, this time scanning the cliffs below her. Her gaze traveled along the concave undercutting and spotted a few fir trees growing out of the rocks a hundred feet or so below. And then she saw it: a tiny patch of yellow hanging from a small fir tree—the raincoat that Max had worn as he left with Pilloud.

＊ ＊ ＊

Toonie rounded a slight bend in the tunnel. His flashlight dimmed as its batteries began to fail. Something suddenly seemed wrong to him. The tunnel was too quiet. As he advanced steadily, he thought he saw a dim light reflecting off the tunnel wall ahead. Confused, he shut off his flashlight and let his eyes adjust to the dark. Carefully, Toonie took another few steps and recognized the steady beating of a red LED.

"What the hay?"

Toonie stopped; a voice behind him was calling out his name.

"Toonie! You down this way?"

Deputy Harris was now somewhere behind him. Holding his wounded left bicep, he felt blood ooze between his fingers and grimaced. Relieved to know he finally had back-up, the postmaster turned and headed back toward her.

"This way, Deputy!"

Toonie suddenly remembered the faint light he had just seen. He turned back in the direction from which he had seen a faint LED blinking. Then the blinking stopped. That was the last thing he remembered as the concussion wave ripped through the tunnel and blasted him off his feet.

✳ ✳ ✳

For the fourth time that day, Thomas climbed down the same steep section of the upper Indian Trail. This time, however, he went slowly. The previous times, he had been charged with an important mission—to get the good guys to the front line where the action was. Now, he felt he had abandoned the mission. All he could think of was Max. As for Laura, the closer home she got, as she escorted her son back, the more relieved she felt. Yet, her anxiety about Max ate away at her. Bronson could gauge from their expressions how deeply worried they both were. He had a gift for reading people. The fire investigator now used his radio and raised the investigation team still working the grisly deaths at the talus pile. He asked how things were proceeding below and was informed that it was a mess down there, with two bodies splattered all over the rocks. The investigation would be cumbersome, because the wildlife in those parts would likely further scatter the remains at nightfall.

"Well, if you guys hear anything about the others up above or...anything about Dr. Wayne or his student, anything at all, please call me ASAP."

"Ten-four. One thing you might be interested in: the other team got the young man—Dougie—to the floatplane with Matt, and he is on his way to the hospital in Greenville Junction for immediate care. He should be all right. They will transport him to Dover-Foxcroft from there."

"Keep me posted."

44

The golf cart with the most luxurious options on the entire island slid to a stop in front of the Denton cottage. Amanda and Tiffany Lomax stepped out and knocked on the door. The older girl had decided to join her father and sister on Kineo, after all, and her mother had allowed her to fly in to Bangor earlier this morning. Both siblings wore bright, beautiful outfits that their mother had purchased for them. Amanda asked Laura if she knew where Bennington was. She had slept in all morning and watched TV while it rained. She knew her father had been out jogging after the rain stopped. Dougie had offered to take Amanda boarding again when the weather allowed, but there was no Dougie either. The younger Lomax girl had not been able to reach either of them on their cell phones. Surely her father was over chatting with the Dentons. If not, Amanda hoped Jenny would know what was going on with all the sirens and law officers crawling all over Kineo.

It was unusual for Tiff to want to come along. She had said she wanted to ask their father something as well, but Amanda knew better. Her older sister was so transparent. She wanted to toy with Thomas some more, now that she was back on Kineo. There was no other game in town, and Tiffany couldn't resist the one that was available. *Heck, maybe she even liked him,* Amanda speculated. *After all, he is tall and handsome.*

Suddenly, the door opened and Jenny stood there, crying.

"Hey, what's wrong? Why you crying, Jenny?" Amanda asked, concerned.

"Bad things are happening up there on the mountain." Jenny pointed to the top of Mt. Kineo, but her anguished eyes were fixed on Amanda. "Mom is helping the police. We heard gunshots! Thomas is missing."

"Thomas?" Tiffany inquired with genuine concern. "Is he okay?"

"I dunno. But Mom looked real scared."

"You think Father's safe, Tiff?" Amanda asked her older sister.

"He's late getting back from jogging. Maybe we should go look for him?"

"C'mon, Jen. Come with us. We're going to look for Father. Maybe we'll find Thomas too."

"I can't go. Mom said to stay here. She was serious."

"Your choice, little girl," Tiffany taunted. "With all that fuss up there, we need to find our father."

"Let's all go," Amanda agreed.

"Oh, darn!" They've been gone so long! I'm worried."

"Thanks for the obvious, Jen, but we're out of here," Tiffany snapped impatiently.

"Wait! Wait...I wanna go too."

"Then stop your whining and jump in!"

* * *

"What the hell was that!" yelled Deputy Harris, her ears still ringing from the blast that had temporarily rendered her deaf and blown her hat right off her head. "Toonie, you okay?"

Her flashlight beam revealed nothing but suspended dust and debris ahead. The other deputies rushed up to Deputy Harris.

"Toonie... You there?"

The three deputies worked their way up through the rubble and debris. Meanwhile, Carlson had picked up the deputy's hat, brushed the rock debris off of it, and placed it back on Harris's head.

"You injured, Harris?"

"I'm fine, Carlson. But really pissed now! Someone set off an explosion, and I can't hear worth a damn now. Anyone hear Toonie reply?"

"No, but let me try," offered Deputy Carlson. "Toonie? Toonie, you okay in there...? No ma'am, nothing. Shall we advance up to where all the dust is?"

"Proceed...carefully."

The deputies picked their way cautiously through the debris of fractured rhyolite. The dust consisting of fine rock particles still drifting in the air had begun irritating the officers' lungs. Carlson began coughing. The fallen rock material had blocked much of the passageway in front of them, but the explosion had ripped a hole in the artificial ceiling created by the tunnel builders.

"Oh no! Looks like Toonie's buried in rubble!"

"Let's hope not. Quick! See if you can find him."

Right at the edge of the rubble pile, in the thick layer of dust and glass debris, lay a man's boot. Deputy Harris grasped the boot and shook it hard. The boot seemed to respond weakly with a slight tilt sideways.

"It's him here! He's alive!"

"Check his injuries. See if we can carry him the hell out of here without a stretcher. This pulverized rock suspended in the air can't be good for our lungs. Hurry!"

Fortunately, Toonie had turned back to Deputy Harris just before the blast. He had paused just long enough to save his life, without knowing that moving into the final bend in the tunnel, where the charges were set to go off, would have exposed him to the explosion's maximum impact. Pierre, now safely on the other side of the blockage caused by the rockfall, would have been disappointed to learn that his carefully timed explosion had not succeeded in taking the deputy permanently out of action. It had, however, allowed the Frenchman adequate time to escape with Pilloud's treasure.

Toonie had suffered a severe concussion wave across his body. He had been both blinded and deafened, and blood was running from his nose, eyes, and ears, compounding the damage inflicted earlier by the gunshot. Still, he was able to move on his own with some help from the others. There was no safe way to get the injured man out of the hole in the tunnel's ceiling, but at least the aperture provided some light to work by. It took the deputies ten minutes to escort the bewildered postmaster-deputy back to the stillness and safety of the central mining chamber.

* * *

Julie stood at the edge of the rock ledge overlooking Moosehead Lake. She could not believe her eyes. *That has to be Max down there. It's his raincoat. But is it just caught in the tree, or is it Max? Oh no, Max! First Rob, and now Max.* She had to do something. She looked down the cliff in front of her. This was no easy rappel, and climbing back up would be difficult. She had never attempted a route this technical. The route the Mohawk had used was doable, but the place where Max was caught wasn't even a climbable route without technical gear. The ryholite had actually sheered away from the cliff due to ice heaving and undercut it in a conchoidal shape. This would require very technical maneuvers.

The wind blew through Julie's sweaty, blood-matted hair as she slipped her climbing harness up her legs and over her shorts. She was determined to try. She had only carried one pitch of climbing rope with her into the tunnel, and was not sure if after securing the line from above, it would reach all the way to the fir tree where the yellow raincoat was snagged. She might have to slip off her rappelling line and free climb without protection for the last twenty feet or so. *This is ridiculous! This is crazy dangerous,* she told herself before calling out desperately once more time to the raincoat below.

"Max? Dr. Wayne? Please let it be you! Can you hear me?"

Silence. After another brief pause, she tried again. Still no response. Julie started to weep, but then shook off her grief and anger. She had to focus, if she were to attempt the rappel and descend. *Oh, what's the use? If that's him, he's surely dead. Why risk my life just to see him... him...dead?* As she pondered her options, she noticed the tree supporting the coat beginning to sway to one side. Then it moved again. There appeared to be something engaged in a sort of struggle with the branches.

"Max? Dr.Wayne?"

Julie heard a moan of pain. It was Max's voice. He was alive!

45

Despite his initial frustration at starting his running so late, Bennington had just completed a satisfying jog. *The bloody rain up here!* He had taken his frustration out on Kineo by pounding the trails a bit harder than usual. He had also opted for a route other than his usual one, because it added an extra two miles to his jog by running along the eastern peninsula through the wooded cart trails. He was winding down for his last stretch, approaching the hill that led to Pebble Beach—a very tricky section, because you could lose your balance on the loose gravel and steep incline. Slowing down to a near halt, Bennington walked the last twenty yards and stopped at the rope-swing tree, looking out up at the impressive vertical face of Mt. Kineo. Earlier, he had noticed some salvage boats against the cliffs (probably searching for the old sunken *Piscataquis* steamer again) and was surprised to see them gone. *Abandoned their search already*, he wondered, puzzled.

As he attempted to catch his breath, his eyes strayed again to the cliffs below which the boats had last been hovering. As he looked on, he was startled by the faint cries for help that drifted down from a distance. *But where were they coming from?*

* * *

Coming down the final stretch of the Indian Trail, the Dentons and Bronson Thurman passed a few more medical and rescue team members. The fire investigator stopped briefly to issue instructions and direct them to where Rob and the deputies were, then watched as fresh pairs of legs hurried up the trail. Bronson noticed that Laura had not stopped to wait for him. She seemed eager to get off the mountain.

"Okay Thomas," she said, relieved, "we're finally down off this cursed mountain. Here's our cart. Get in. Bronson, you going with us or back up again?"

"If you don't mind, Mrs. Denton, I'd like to check on the investigation team by the talus pile. Will you drop me off?"

"Certainly."

Bronson hopped onto the back of the golf cart and Laura headed down the old Carriage Trail toward the talus pile. Bronson's radio crackled with static until the voice of Deputy Carlson became audible.

"Bronson. You copy?"

"Go ahead."

"You down near the talus pile yet? We need that team up here now. More armed deputies as well. Can't reach the lower team. You copy?"

"Copy. Team on way."

"On the double."

"More trouble?"

"Trouble? Well we found the male grad student up here. He's busted up from a fall and in shock. Sheriff is dead, another deputy badly injured from an explosive blast. And we still haven't traced Pilloud, the dangerous Frenchman, the college professor, or the young woman. Other than that, all is just fine!"

"Good Lord!"

"We're still in a hot zone. Keep folks off the mountain. I repeat: the mountain is not secure yet."

"Ten-four."

Turning to Laura, Bronson said, "Sorry, Mrs. Denton. Still no word on Dr. Wayne or his female grad student. But they did find the male student—Rob. He's alive, but in pretty bad shape from a fall."

*   *   *

The cart full of teenage girls traveled down the cart trail toward Pebble Beach. The Lomax girls knew that their father liked to end his daily jog down at the beach overlooking Kineo's inspiring vertical face. The golf cart sped down the hill and Bennington's daughters were relieved to recognize their father near the rope swing. His body language, however, was one of focused intensity as he stared out across the cove toward the big mountain.

"Father! Father!" cried out Amanda.

The golf cart slid to a stop next to Bennington.

"Hush, darling, please. Just listen…"

The puzzled look on his face was troubling. Amanda had seen this look before and knew not to disturb him now. At least they knew that he was safe and not involved in any of the mayhem on the mountain.

"What are you listening for?" Jenny blurted out.

"Shh, Jenny, please!"

Then they all heard it. It was the sound of someone pleading for help across the cove. The voice sounded desperate. The voice, barely audible, came from somewhere high up on the cliff face.

"Father," Tiffany finally interrupted, "you should know that there's been a shooting up there. Police are crawling all over the mountain. The professor and some students are missing. Thomas is missing too."

"Hmm. And somebody is in major distress up there. We better go report this to the authorities."

"Who could be caught up there?" Jenny asked. "That looks like a very dangerous place to be stuck."

"Indeed, Jenny," Bennington responded solemnly. "Somebody with rock-climbing skills, I would suspect. Now hurry, let's go."

* * *

"Nicely done. The mule did well. I see you have the horses here already."

"Yes, my friend. See? We make a good team—you and I."

"How much weight can these horses carry in their saddlebags?"

"Enough, friend. I brought enough. They're tied together and well trained. The first load has already been distributed. Now let's empty this cart and load the remaining horses there."

"So this is what took you so long? Loading the horses?"

"Of course, my friend. I couldn't leave the gold in the mining cart. We needed the cart for the second load."

"Okay, keep loading. We'll split it up when we get down to Hardscrabble Point."

"Yes, there are plenty of places to hide the horses along the outer trail, if needed. Our boat arrives in thirty minutes to take us to the mainland. Then we can go our separate ways."

Pierre noticed that the young native man's demeanor had changed since he had been out of the tunnels. There was something that he was not saying. Pierre suspecting a double cross from that native, kept his eyes on his partner as the two men quickly unloaded the mining cart and filled the saddlebags to capacity. Not trained in handling horses, Pierre volunteered to walk behind the last one, while his partner led the animals down the mountain using an old side trail cut by his ancestors—another of the secret trails used for many decades by the guardians of the spheres. The pathway was circuitous and descended steeply through many sections of broken rock on the north side of Kineo, where no one ever ventured.

Pierre pulled out his cell phone, hoping to get reception. He could only receive one bar. He kept trying. Then no bars. *Damn!* Finally, about five minutes from Hardscrabble Point, he was rewarded with two bars—enough to hit the preprogrammed dial feature that would alert his own contact boat by sending it a GPS signal. It would not be long till his actual lift arrived. The only thing left to do was to get all the gold safely to Hardscrabble Point. Then he'd kill his partner and confiscate all of the Pilloud Confederate gold. Finally, the plan was coming together.

* * *

At this point, yelling for help seemed futile. Even if someone heard Julie, he would not be able to help her. She managed to descend a portion of sheer wall that was nearly impossible to access. A rescue team here would need to know about the historic tunnel systems that had remained a well-guarded secret for all these years until their discovery that day. It would also have to find the exact tunnel that led to the ledge from which Max had tumbled. Moreover, appropriate technical gear would be required to rappel down from the top of the mountain and sufficient protection devices for the ascent back up with an injured man. Things did not look good for Max. He might be dying, as far as she knew. She had to continue on her way down to try and save him somehow.

"Max, stop struggling," Julie called out. "You could fall out of that tree. Just wait! I'm almost there."

"Julie? That you? Ughh."

"Hang on, Max. I'm at the end of my rope. Oh, boy... Now comes the hard part."

Max was trying desperately to focus on the image in front of him, but hanging upside down for so long now, he felt faint again. Sweat and blood drained into his eyes and obscured his vision further. Finally, by blinking several times, he managed to clear it long enough to look down and comprehend how screwed he was—dangling hundreds of feet above Moosehead Lake, his broken foot wedged between two tree stems, and his raincoat snagged about his shoulders. *I wish I hadn't looked down. Ugh!*

Overcome by a bout of vertigo, Max closed his eyes and took deep, slow breaths, trying to calm his nerves and block the pain from his mind. When he finally mustered the nerve to open his eyes again, there before him was the most beautiful angel he had ever seen—Julie Walters in her sweaty white tank top and climbing shorts, sliding off of her rappel line just twenty feet away. Max watched as she scaled the vertical wall to get to him...*oh my God, without any protection!*

"Julie, no! Julie, it's too dangerous. Go back!"

"Too late, Professor. I'm too close now to turn back."

With those words, Julie suddenly summoned the courage to make three final athletic moves. Coordinating her strength and balance at precise moments, she flung herself against a rock next to the rooted fir tree. She then pulled a light-duty guide rope out of her backpack and tied it to the base of the nearest fir overhanging the cliff.

"Max," she explained patiently, "this rope is not meant to hold the weight of a suspended climber, but it should be fine for what we are about to do. Here. Catch this with your good arm and wrap it tightly around your hand and wrist. Then I'm going to use it to pull you horizontal."

"You're kidding, right?"

"No. Then grab this other tree and hang on, while I help free your trapped foot. Once you're free, jump onto my ledge and hold onto me."

"Righto!" Max gasped, trying to sound hopeful, but his voice was tinged with pessimism.

"I'm tying in to this tree to prevent us from tumbling over the side. Got it?"

"Julie, this is crazy. I'm too weak to do this," Max breathed hard and laboriously. "This is too dangerous. Go get help, instead."

Julie thought how sensible the words of her favorite professor sounded right then, as she glanced down at the lake far below her. She then contemplated the 160-foot climb she would have to make next—a very technical ascent up a treacherous concave wall, carrying a broken man much heavier than her. *This plan is crazy*, Julie thought to herself, feeling a bit overwhelmed and desperate. *I can't do all this!* She was famished, exhausted, and frightened. She looked into Dr. Wayne's face and saw him starting to pass out again. She threw the rope to him and it struck him in the chest.

"Just grab the damn rope, Max!" she yelled.

46

"Here's the trailhead to the water tower," Laura said. "It'll take you to the talus pile. We're going back to check on Jenny and Brandon."

"Understood. Let me check the radio once more. Want to see if anyone has an update on Max."

"Oh bless you, Bronson. Would ya, please?"

The fire investigator called in to the other teams, but there was no word on the professor. There was no reply either from Carlson or Harris high above. Deputy Harris and her men were still in the central chamber, busy extricating the seriously injured Rob Landon. Using the rescue ropes and gear they had brought along, the deputies rigged a lifting platform from one of the wooden doors at the bottom of the mining pit. They secured Rob onto the platform and began hoisting him to the top level of the central chamber. This deep inside the tunnel system, there was, however, no radio reception. Carlson had left earlier to send Bronson the request for another medical team, but he was back inside again, guarding the tunnels to make sure Pilloud's hired goons didn't come back to make more trouble. Toonie was resting and nursing his war wounds.

"She seems to be radio-silent still. I'm sorry, Mrs. Denton—at least no news is good news. I mean…"

"That's okay, Bronson," Laura replied. "I know what you meant and thanks. Okay, here's your drop-off."

"Thanks, Mrs. Denton," Bronson replied. Then he heard another golf cart racing toward them.

Laura Denton and the investigation team examiner turned quickly to see what the commotion was about. It was Jenny and three members of the Lomax family.

"Mom! Mom!"

"Jenny, what are you doing here? I told ya to stay home! Where's Brandon?"

"At home. Mom, we may have found Dr. Wayne!"

"Now Jenny," Bennington corrected. "We don't know who we heard up there. In fact, it sounded more like a woman's voice crying out for help. And why would Dr. Wayne be up there?"

"It *had* to be him!" Jenny insisted.

"Wait! Who heard what? You know, the female grad student—the Walters girl—is missing too," Bronson added.

"Somebody on the east face of Kineo was screaming for help! We were coming here to get the rescue people."

Jenny and Amanda were talking over each other, trying to explain the pleas for help they had heard from Pebble Beach. Bronson looked stunned. Laura did not know what to say. Thomas jumped off the cart and grabbed his sister by the shoulders.

"Jenny, where? Dr. Wayne? Has he been shot? Where is he, Jenny?"

"I don't know, Thomas!" Jenny burst into tears. "Up there."

"Take us there now, Jenny," her brother commanded, while Bronson and one of the medical team professionals boarded the cart with her and Amanda.

"No guys, you don't understand," Bennington interjected. "The only way to get up there would be to descend the east face from the top of Mt. Kineo."

"Oh dear God!" Laura muttered finally, realizing which spot they were referring to. "That's impossible! Nobody could be trapped on *that* face of the Kineo wall. There's nothing to hold onto. There's no way to even get stranded there."

Thomas looked at his mother, then examined the look of affirmation on Bennington's face. "It *must* be them, Mom. It must be the grad student and Dr. Wayne. We must get to them."

"But how?" Laura asked.

"It'll be impossible to locate their position from the thick underbrush at the top of the mountain," Bennington explained. "You'll have no reference up there, Thomas."

"Mom. Mr. Lomax. Just hear me out. The access must be from *inside* the mountain. That is why it seems impossible to be there. From within that crease, where the deputies went in. You know. I led them to the crease."

Benninton had no idea what Thomas was talking about. He looked to Laura for answers. She seemed to be pondering over her son's suggestion.

"We have to try!" Thomas said firmly and was surprised to see the resistance in his mother's eyes dwindling to nothing. In its place, he recognized resolve. Laura was in agreement with him! All of the rescue and medical people were now on top of the mountain or on their way, but they had no idea where Max and Julie were.

"Okay, Thomas." Laura turned to Bronson. "Get the rest of these trained professionals of yours. The three of us are going back up Mt. Kineo. Bennington, please take my daughter back home with you and make sure Brandon stays with her."

"Of course, Mrs. Denton. Girls—shall we?"

"Be careful, Mommy!" Jenny blurted out as she hugged Laura.

"We will be, dear. Now Bronson, call it in!"

* * *

"Well, my friend, here's Hardscrabble Point. My boat will be here any minute now. Let's divide up the shares."

The toothy Native American smiled confidently at Pierre who was still clutching his painful shoulder. The loss of blood and all the lifting were taking its toll on the tough Frenchman. This would be over soon. His own boat would also be arriving soon, but from twenty miles to the northeast. It was time for closure.

"Well, my native, um, friend," Pierre began in his thick French accent. "I have some potentially disturbing news for you."

"Oh? What is it?"

"You have generously decided it would be best if I took possession of all the gold."

"I have? And why would I do that?"

"Because it isn't much use to the *dead*." Pierre pulled a large hunting knife from a sheath and held it in the way he had been taught while studying the martial arts. "Don't worry. This won't hurt. You deserve to die quickly for being so helpful."

The Native American simply looked at Pierre, his toothy smile never abandoning his face. His perfectly white teeth were the product of living out among the whites for many years—a strange contrast to the native jewelry he wore, mostly for effect.

"Oh my friend, I'm not worried," he said finally. "You should not worry either. The real treasure of Kineo is the weapons-grade flint that my ancestors mined for all those years, not these gold-painted lead bars at our feet."

"What madness is this?"

"Ha, ha, ha! You did not know? You think yourself smart? You let others handle them or you would have noticed. Let me show you." The young native walked over to some bars that were in a separate pile on the ground next to a horse. He picked one from the pile and held it out for Pierre to examine. "See the emblem embossed on the bar? A sign of the Confederacy back in the American Civil War. Scratch it with your knife blade."

Suspiciously, Pierre snatched the bar from the other man and scratched the soft metal with his knife.

"This is gold!"

"Yes, my friend, so it is. As are all ten bars in that stack. These real bars were used to cover the phony load. Now use your knife on one of the bars from any of the other nine piles."

Pierre stooped down and picked up a bar from the pile next to him. It was heavy, but not quite as much as the one he had picked up earlier. However, its size and color were nearly identical to those of the first; but now in the daylight, something was very wrong. He looked back at his partner, wondering if this was a ploy to delay proceedings or escape, and began picturing his hunting blade slicing the other man's throat wide open.

"Look carefully at the seal embossed on the new bar in your hand," the Native American suggested. "It is very similar to the other one, but not the same. Someone tried to replicate the original."

"Bullshit!"

"Scratch it."

Pierre etched a line with the knife blade through what now appeared to be a thick coat of paint, whose color was meant to match that of the other bars in the first stack. The difference was so subtle as to pass virtually unnoticed in the darkness of a cavern or at night when clandestine activities usually took place. The color of the material beneath the bar's painted surface was a dark gray. *Lead?*

"You double-crossed me!" Pierre snarled. "How? Where is the rest of the real gold?"

"There is none. Don't you get it? There never was! The only gold is in the bars used to conceal the rest of the stash. Lead is cheap, my friend. It melts at one-third the temperature of gold. It would have been an easy way to exchange one for the other, and most people wouldn't even have noticed. Unless you had the two, side by side, and compared them, you wouldn't have known that the lead bar was far lighter."

Confused, outraged and still in great pain from his injuries, Pierre found himself growing increasingly infuriated by the smile that never left the native man's face.

"So there are only ten bars here out of the one hundred that are actually gold?"

"Yes, my friend. I did not realize it at first either. I was not sure how best to tell you."

"That means this elaborate operation was planned and executed just to...to...get six million dollars?"

"Apparently. But the value of the bars is not all that important, is it?"

"I think it's time to kill you."

"My friend, we were going to let you take half of the gold in the cover pile. Grandmother and I just want this disease off Kineo's sacred lands. You could have had three million for your troubles and we could cover our costs for the other half."

Pierre moved forward, knife raised to strike the young man.

"Pity, Frenchman. There was no need for it all to end this way...you didn't need to die."

"You're crazy," the mercenary said, shaking his head in disbelief. Then with knife pointed, Pierre lunged at the calmer man.

A look of utter surprise came upon Pierre's face, as excruciating pain erupted in the middle of his chest from a sharp object slicing deep inside of him. The Frenchman looked down at himself in disbelief. He had not been aware of the old woman stealing up behind him, ready, if need be, to protect her only grandson. The young man's toothy smile never faded as he nodded at the woman that few had encountered over the years—the one that Rix and his brother had called the "old witch". Using the ancient technology of a perfectly balanced spear, with a lethal tip crafted from glassy rhyolite, she had plunged it deep into Pierre's back, just as her ancestors had done on this very ground. The arrowhead had blazed a fatal pathway straight through his heart. Stunned, Pierre tried to confront the person who had impaled him like a human shish kabob, but the old woman kept a firm grip on the ancient family spear that she had possessed her entire life, preventing the gravely injured man from turning his body. With massive hemorrhaging in his chest and back, the life began draining quickly from Pierre.

"Meet my grandmother, my friend," said the Native American. "She was one of the last of the protectors of the spheres. A true guardian of the Circle of Unity. It appears you'll be taking a piece of the true treasure of Kineo with you...a piece of Kineo flint...to your afterworld."

Pierre had no idea what the man was talking about as he dropped to his knees. He felt his life ebbing away and a series of images flashed before him. He had always performed the dirty work on behalf of others for extraordinary amounts of money. He had been the man hired to "persuade" Laura Denton's husband into selling the old cottage the latter had inherited on Kineo and to arrange for his "accidental" death when he refused. The light faded from Pierre's eyes as he drew his last labored breath, the spear protruding from his back. The old woman released the spear with the Kineo "flint" imbedded in the Frenchman's heart.

* * *

A twenty-eight-foot cutty cabin pulled up to Hardscrabble Point and beached. Patricia Wellington looked over the boat's port side and yelled out to them.

"Well, come on! Load it aboard!"

"Most of it is counterfeit bars of painted lead," explained the young man.

"Splendid! It seems someone double-crossed Pierre before the Iriqouis double-crossed Major Pilloud. Who knows how far back? Major Pilloud? The Confederacy itself? No surprise to me! That is the nature of man, my dear nephew. And all of those bars of shiny metal are a curse to Kineo. Time to rid it of the curse," she said with a twinkle in her eye. "Place the gold bars aboard and leave the painted lead there for the authorities to remove. We don't want to dump lead into the lake."

Although heavy, the ten gold bars weighing nearly 300 pounds were loaded quickly into the boat. Patricia Wellington and her nephew waved to the old guardian of the Mohawk sphere. She waved back, holding the obsidian guardian sphere over her head, her traditional matriarch's tattoo prominently displayed on her upper arm. Her grandson had removed the important historic marker from the mining chamber when Pierre was preoccupied and taken it away in the mining cart. Now that he had placed it back into the hands of its rightful guardian, she smiled, knowing she could finally have her peace. He watched her from the boat as she picked up the reins on the pack of horses, which now stood freed of their burdens, and began to lead them long Kineo's north Island Trail. After they had covered a mile, she freed all of the horses in the woods, but for her old and faithful companion, Katobaquis, and commanded them to run wild. She patted her horse's mane and instructed him to take her home to Spencer Mountain. She did not intend to set foot on Kineo again.

* * *

Thomas had lost count of the number of times he had trekked up Mt. Kineo that day. His knees ached from the abuse, but he still climbed nearly as fast as he had that morning. His mother too seemed determined to keep up with him. Bronson could not help but admire the Dentons. Their courage, commitment, and devotion to friends and family were inspirational. The fire investigator radioed Deputy Harris of their intentions.

Harris was far from amused. "Didn't Carlson instruct you that no one comes up this mountain again till we say it is safe?" she said with asperity.

"Of course. But there's someone stranded on the east side of the Kineo cliffs, screaming for help. We fear it's Dr. Wayne and his student."

"All right, here's the deal. We're coming out of the chamber with Toonie and the other student. Both need immediate medical attention. The floatplane's ready on the west shore near the trailhead to pick 'em up. We're bringing up a hound to sniff out Pilloud and his men. I'll personally escort your group to the face when that's done. You all wait at the trailhead for me. Understand?"

"Ten-four."

"Good."

"I heard her," Laura said, looking back at Bronson as she continued up the Indian Trail. "You can go back and wait for her. My son and I are gonna find Max."

"Damn! Mrs. Denton, no!" He looked at mother and son bounding up the trail's step section and realized there was no stopping them. "Okay, okay. Hold up. Then I'm coming with you. I don't technically report to Deputy Harris anyway."

* * *

"Okay, Max... This is going to hurt."

"You mean...I finally get to...feel some pain now?" Max grimaced.

His foot and ankle were swollen badly from carrying his suspended bodyweight for so long, and his arms stung from the many lacerations they had suffered while grazing against the fir-tree branches when he attempted to break his fall. Julie pulled the guide rope taut and helped Max pivot his body to a near horizontal position so that his blood wouldn't flow back into his head.

"Owww! That actually *did* hurt more, Jules!"

"I know...hang tight. I'll tie this guide rope off now. This is really going to hurt. I'm going to free your foot from this tree."

"Careful. If you fall...you're gone forever."

"Yeah...I can see that!"

Julie attempted to lift Max out of the crotch in the tree, but he was too heavy. She couldn't get adequate leverage. He was hanging too far from the ledge and she had poor footing.

"I've an idea."

Julie reached into her climbing bag and found a fifteen-foot piece of strong webbing. She tied one end to one of the main stems of the tree in which Max was caught and the other to a small fir tree growing on the ledge. Remembering the way her father had shown her how to free a stuck automobile with a rope, she attached a draw rope to the middle of the webbing between herself and Dr. Wayne. Basic physics had not changed since her father had shown her the technique, and she was able to convert her eighty-pound pull to a 1600-pound force on the smaller tree stem that had trapped his ankle. The gap in the tree crotch widened and his foot worked free. Now Max found himself in the most awkward position ever—holding onto the tree with one hand and tied to another tree with a light guide rope.

"Okay Max," Julie said. "The fun part: I'm going to grab your back and yank you as hard as I can. You have to help me here. When you get to the ledge, you have to let go of the tree and grab hold of me. I've clipped my harness to this tree so I can't fall. But if you miss, I'm not sure that I can hold you if you go over the side. Understand?"

"Righto, Jules. Let's do this. I'm feeling faint again."

"One...two...three...launch!"

* * *

Nearing the section of the trail where the Chief's Head formation protruded from the mountain, Thomas and Laura could hear the voices of the deputies at a higher elevation, as the latter carried Rob down on a stretcher. On spotting Laura, Thomas, and Bronson, Carlson and Harris were livid with anxiety-fuelled anger.

"Bronson! I told you to stay down at the trailhead," Harris snapped.

"I know, I know. But I couldn't stop 'em. They wanted to find Max."

"I assured you we would look for the young woman and the professor, once we got Toonie and Rob down safely," she continued in a harsh voice.

Suddenly, Rob snapped out of his stupor, lifted his head slightly, whispered some instructions to Thomas, and passed out again.

"What'd he say?" Laura asked tensely.

Deputy Harris had rushed over to hear what Rob had to say, but he was unconscious by the time she arrived.

"He said he knows where Julie and Max went," Thomas told the others.

"Where?" three voices inquired almost simultaneously.

"Inside the central chamber. Follow the Mohawk tunnel to the end."

"Now how in the hell do we know which tunnel that is?" Deputy Harris asked exasperatedly.

"Max showed me some writings of the Mohawk. I can't read it, but I would recognize it if I saw it," Thomas announced with complete confidence. Then he reached down and picked up the gear bag that was attached to the stretcher. "Rob also said I'd need this."

"Great!" Deputy Harris barked out sarcastically. "Okay, Carlson, you and the other deputies and EMTs get Rob and Toonie down now. I'll escort these four and see if we can find the other two missing people." She turned to Thomas. "But young man, do exactly as I say. Understand?"

"Yes, ma'am."

Bronson grabbed an extra emergency-aid kit and had Laura help pack some additional supplies from the EMTs' medical bag into his backpack. "I may need this," he said. "I want to be useful till the EMTs can get back up to assist."

"We're wasting time," Laura said, urging them to hurry. "Son, take us to this central-chamber area now."

* * *

Max was finally free of the small fir tree that had kept him alive against overwhelming odds. His injuries were serious. The long gash on his face needed sutures. Several of his bones were broken. His arms were badly cut and he had lost much skin and flesh off his hands. Max also felt faint from having been upside down for so long. Now he teetered precariously on the edge of a narrow fold of rock, with Julie clutching him in her arms.

Clipped into the precarious east side of Mt. Kineo, the grad student pondered her next move. She knew that in his condition, Max had little strength left. Although he had never been one to give up, Julie knew he was near the end of his reserves. All he wanted was to collapse and fall asleep, and that she would not allow him to do. She held him as tightly as she could. He felt warm in her arms. Julie had admired him in lecture classes and even fantasized about what it might be like to hold him. She found it a bit disturbing, under the circumstances, to realize how much she enjoyed having him so close to her and chided herself sternly. *I have to concentrate. We could both die in seconds if I don't keep my wits about me!*

She allowed Max a few moments of respite to regain some strength. Then she began to talk him through the next maneuver. They were to slide around each other and she would clip him in safely to the wall, while she reclaimed the climbing rope that she had been forced to abandon above them earlier. She began preparing her mind and her equipment for the daring free climb back to the rappel rope still dangling about forty feet above her.

"Julie..." Max caught his breath and tried to focus on everything but the pain that seemed to overwhelm him. "Thank you. I owe you."

Julie looked back at him and smiled cheerfully for the first time in hours. *Dang! Even beat up, he is one handsome man*, she thought. "Well, I expect to get all 'A's this semester."

"Guess I could call this extra credit?" Max managed with a laugh that soon turned into a grimace.

Julie took a deep breath and began to probe the rock with her fingers to find the most secure grip before pulling herself up. The broken rhyolite edges were smooth and glassy. The lack of texture made the holds more difficult than she had anticipated. Finding what appeared to be the best beginning route, she began to move up the wall cautiously. This was going to be a tough climb and she herself was utterly exhausted by now. As Max watched her slowly ascend, a feeling of dread enveloped him. He had the utmost confidence in her judgment and determination, but this route was not going to be easy. Julie dug her fingers into some tiny fractures, their sharp edges tearing flesh off her knuckles as she levered herself up by her hands. She found a small chimey where she could push against the wall with her hands in opposing directions and rested long enough to find secure footing. Observing the muscles ripple in her back, shoulders, and arms, Max was impressed by his graduate student's strength. No rock-climbing expert himself, he knew enough, nonetheless, to realize that this route was an extremely difficult one, especially without protection, for someone of Julie's experience level.

The graduate student started to lose her footing on a hold, grimacing as the glassy rhyolite bit sharply into her pointer and middle fingers.

"Julie, to your right," Max directed, trying to guide her. "Five inches or so. Your right foot. There's a tiny nodule you might be able to smear..."

"I feel it!"

With one fluid motion, she smear-stepped the face with her right foot and shifted enough weight to let the pain in her fingers ease temporarily. *Only four more feet*, She thought, *you can do this. I climbed down this earlier somehow...come on!* She edged up to the rope, but resisted the urge to grab hold of it. *I must get up above it and then clip into my belt. Slowly. You're almost there.*

Julie had reached an elevation where she was above the rope and had a secure foothold. She slid the end of the rope back into the rappelling device on her harness and climbed far enough to pull the rope through and give herself some friction to hold her body weight. Then Julie rested back, placing all of her weight on the rope for a minute to relieve her aching hands, and burst into tears.

Max could see her body convulse with sobs. He said nothing. She had performed selfless acts of heroism to help him that must have been terrifying for her. Unfortunately, her rescue attempt was not over yet. She had to get *him* up—injured and exhausted as he was—to the descent rope somehow. It all seemed so futile. He wondered if Thomas had made it down all right. He wondered if Laura had her son safely in her arms. His pain began to dissipate as he drifted off, thinking of her.

✱ ✱ ✱

Deputy Harris and Thomas reached the historic entrance crease in the rock first. By then, Laura had given up trying to keep up with her more agile and fit son. She had stopped demanding that he stay behind the deputy for his safety. She was just glad to be ahead of Bronson who was not faring as well, having to climb the Indian Trail with sixty pounds of medical and rescue equipment on his back. Deputy Harris checked the immediate area. No sign of Pilloud or his ill-intentioned guards. No sign of anyone in the tunnel. In fact, she was unable to discern any sound at all.

"It appears they're all gone. We'll proceed cautiously. But I shall lead."

"I'm right behind you," Thomas replied.

Laura shook her head and followed close behind her son. There was blood along the walls and floor of the tunnel. Thomas and Deputy Harris did not seem to notice, but the slick, sticky feel of partially dried blood on her hands caused Laura to pause briefly. *What the hell? Blood from the deputies ahead of us?*

"You sure this is clear?" she asked.

"No, I'm not!" Harris replied, annoyed. "None of you should be in here. I'm using poor judgment allowing this. Feel free to turn back."

"We're going on!" Thomas replied defiantly. Laura was buoyed by her son's conviction. "Max has to be on the other side. Rob said so."

Deputy Harris reached the central chamber and inspected the room thoroughly with her flashlight. She studied the footprints in the sand and the pulverized rhyolite from the events that had taken place earlier. She quickly located the detonation-blasted remains of the tunnel leading to the west.

"This is the tunnel through which the Frenchman escaped and from where we removed Toonie."

There were other tunnels leading out of the central chamber over that way. Laura and Thomas were awestruck by all the indigenous people's markings and the strange stone-stacked tables that had been used to hold the guardian spheres. The boy followed the tracks up to the tunnel heading due north and stopped, rubbing his finger over the symbols on the tunnel header.

"This is it!"

"Are you sure, Thomas?" his mother asked.

"No doubts at all. This is not Algonquin. This is Iroquoian. And this symbol here... Max showed it to me once in a book. This is a symbol of bravery. The Mohawk were fearless of heights."

Well, obviously Thomas had paid attention to Max's words, Laura thought, smiling to herself. *I spent too much time paying attention to...just Max.*

Deputy Harris started to get the rescue ropes ready while Bronson got the emergency medical supplies sorted and ready for use. Thomas scouted ahead and found a second side tunnel with strange markings. The second Mohawk tunnel appeared narrower and would require more crawling. Harris caught up with the boy as he paused, considering which of the two directions he should take. Thomas had no idea what the symbols meant on these two tunnels and wondered which one he should enter.

"Look at the drag marks in the sand," Harris noted. "They went down this one!"

"It's going to be cramped in there," Thomas commented.

"Well then, the central chamber would make the best triage area if we find them and they have serious injuries," Bronson added from behind the two.

Deputy Harris proceeded carefully down the Mohawk exit tunnel, with Thomas close behind. What they were to see next would fill them with horror.

47

"Dr. Wayne…? Max? You doing okay?" Julie called down, her voice breaking with worry and fatigue.

"Hanging in there, Jules."

"Rob calls me Jules," she said to herself.

Max was too far below her to catch the words. "Sorry? Couldn't hear ya."

"Oh, nothing…" she responded, wondering how Rob was doing at this very moment. But then, looking back down at Max who seemed utterly exhausted, she felt awkward. At a traumatic moment like this one, her mind was on two men at the same time. One man she admired more than any she had ever known. He was sensible, intelligent, and handsome. But she was fully aware he was out of bounds. The other was unpredictable, exciting, available, and prone to foolish behavior.

"Hang tough Max—I will figure this out."

Max chose not to tell Julie how he actually felt. He was now in intense pain from his broken bones, as his body's natural painkillers—the endorphins—had expended their limited, but useful life. His body was now sending him urgent signals about its acutely traumatized state. He looked at his hands and then at the rope above. With so much flesh stripped from his palms, there was no way he would be able to grip a rope. He considered the prospect of climbing the sharp rocks with a broken leg and a dislocated shoulder. He also wondered what would happen if Julie didn't make it back. *Clipped into the wall of Kineo forever?*

Max didn't like losing. The thought of giving up and dying out here angered him. Especially after all the effort his overachiever student had gone to so far to free him from peril. He couldn't envision a way to help her at this point. The acute pain prevented him from focusing and he was exhausted trying to use his one good leg to support his entire weight on the miniature ledge. Every time he shifted even the slightest amount of weight to his broken leg, hot, angry shards of steel seemed to tear through his arteries.

Julie had nearly completed her ascent up the face along the pitch of descent rope. This was the most technical climb she had ever attempted. The stakes were very high, because she had nobody to belay her, in case she fell. At intervals, she carefully set protection that would be vital to assist Max up the wall. But first, she needed to climb up herself and get some additional equipment. *Another harness, more rope, and someone to belay us would be great*, she thought. *I wonder how far away Rob's equipment is?*

Julie fought to keep her increasing fatigue at bay. Lactic acid filled her arms and legs. She could see the ledge just above her now. She began to ponder if she could muster the strength to free climb to the top and be back on the ledge. *Enough with the self-doubt, Julie*, she chided herself, *it's not much further.*

Suddenly, a strange face appeared through the tiny opening of the Mohawk tunnel just above the ledge. It was Deputy Harris.

"Help me!" Julie implored.

"Oh my God! You must be the woman who was hollering for help earlier."

"Yes, over an hour ago. Thought... nobody heard me," Julie struggled to say.

"Someone did. You're lucky. Are you Julie Walters?"

Julie did not respond. She was too focused on her next two handholds. This was no place to get careless and fall.

"Julie?"

"Yes, that's me."

"Where's Dr. Wayne?"

"Below me. Hurt badly."

"Can you make it the rest of the way? That cliff face looks..."

"Yes, I think so... I've managed worse today."

"Be careful, girl... My God! Is that Dr. Wayne all the way down there?"

"I'm afraid so."

"How bad?"

"Bad," Julie responded, stopping just below the lip of the ledge to take one last breath before climbing up to join the deputy. "Broken leg and arm, dislocated shoulder, hands cut badly. He's bruised and lacerated everywhere."

"Dear God!"

"Is Rob...okay?" Julie panted and took another deep breath, waiting for the deputy's response.

"We got him down the mountain alive and he awoke briefly, but faded in and out after that. We brought his gear with us, in case we actually found you two."

"Great. Give me a hand then, will ya?"

The moment she reached the ledge, Deputy Harris gripped her by the arm and helped pull a very exhausted Julie to safety. Thomas was inside the tunnel, holding the deputy's ankles to make sure she had a strong anchor to pull the young woman up from. The moment the graduate student was on secure ground, Thomas released Harris's ankles and popped his head through the tunnel. He was relieved to see the grad student alive.

"Oh wow! You here! Max? Is Dr. Wayne alive?"

Exhausted, Julie simply nodded. Before Thomas had even located the missing professor, he turned back to the tunnel and yelled to his mother behind him, "They're alive!"

At that moment, the numbness that had gripped Laura for the past two hours suddenly dissipated. Suddenly, she felt invigorated. *He's here? He's actually alive?* She was surprised at how those unspoken words made her heart stir. She wanted to see Max right away and crawled quickly to catch up with Thomas who was now slowly working his way out out on the narrow ledge with Deputy Harris using the rope line rail that Max had strung for safety earlier. Laura stuck her head out of the tunnel and saw her son and Deputy Harris balanced on a thin rock ledge, several hundred feet above Moosehead Lake.

Laura observed the fierce effort with which Deputy Harris was holding onto Thomas and the rock wall. The two did not look safe at all even with Thomas gripping tightly to the makeshift safety rail. Laura's gaze wandered to Julie Walters, looking young and athletic, even if her tee shirt was soaking wet and she was unkempt, filthy, and worn out. At the sight of this pretty young woman who had spent the last harrowing hours with Max, Laura was consumed by a surge of jealousy. *How absurd and immature can I get*, she chastised herself. *What's wrong with me? Where's Max?* Then she saw him for the first time, far below.

Horror swept through her as she recognized the gravity of the predicament he was still in. She found herself falling to her knees in the tunnel, because she feared she might pass out. Max was more than 100 feet below her, clipped into a sheer wall. His body looked limp and beaten and bloody. Laura could not bear to imagine the consequences if he fell from the tiny bump in the wall where his grad student had attached him to keep him safe temporarily. Laura's legs began to tremble as she watched Julie and Thomas uncoil the second rope the deputy had brought with her and flake it out carefully along the rim of the ledge.

"Okay. This is how I see it. I'll rappel down, bringing the extra harness with me. I'll help Dr. Wayne into the harness and attach enough rope for a top belay. My only concern is how to get him to climb. He's exhausted and has several broken bones."

"Can we lift him up from here?" asked the deputy.

"Not easily. He's a big man and we have no footing for proper leverage. The tunnel is too narrow to work from. If we had more bodies, we could take some of the weight off his movements and help drag him over the tough places in the wall. It'll be difficult, but it's our best option."

"We'll need Bronson," Harris told the Dentons.

"What can I do?" asked Laura.

"Crawl back and get Bronson." Then turning back to Julie, the deputy asked, "How does this work?"

"As Bronson, Thomas, and you pull the rope, Mrs. Denton needs to take up the slack and wrap it around some kind of fixture—like that small tree beside you."

"Got it. Can we clip them in up here?"

"Yes. Secure everyone on the ledge to something that cannot be pulled down. In that bag are extra carabineers and some webbing. I need to head down now. Time is of the essence."

"Be careful, Julie," Thomas urged, filled with admiration for the graduate student that had been so sweet to him during many of Dr. Wayne's excursions on Kineo.

"Yes, Julie, do be careful," Deputy Harris added.

Julie chugged water from the bottle that Thomas handed her, smiled at him with a twinkle in her eye, and followed it with an awkward backward glance at Laura Denton. Then she slung herself with renewed confidence over the ledge once again.

* * *

The old Mohawk woman guided her horse to the end of the trail that circled Kineo's north perimeter. She was about to be exposed. She readied herself to bound quickly across the isthmus back to her mountain, east of Kineo. She looked up at the cloudy sky and thought about the day. It was still hours from dusk.

I'm far too old to continue playing this hide-and-seek game with these European descendants. So what if I am seen? I'm done guarding Kineo. We retrieved the missing guardian sphere. The cancer that Pilloud sought inside our mountain has finally been found and removed. But now we will have students violating our mountain for years!

She looked up at the top of Mt. Kineo and pondered all the wars that had been fought over the Kineo flint. She thought of the legend of the Trader—the great shaman that had rescued the native peoples from war with neighboring tribes and was buried within the mountain. She thought of the skeletal remains she and her grandson had seen that had been subsequently disturbed by the young students and wondered if it was one of her own people, or some other invader. She wondered about the turquoise jewelery she had seen earlier that had to have been worn by Kajo. The elderly matriarch then wondered if Kajo's remains had also been disturbed and that troubled her profoundly. *So much history on Kineo! So much had been learned today, and yet, so much had been lost. These tunnels must be permanently closed. Then I will be free.*

"Katobaquis," she patted her horse, "you're my dearest friend."

Katobaquis shook his head, acknowledging the attention the old Indian matriarch paid him. She then guided him up the rear flank of Mt. Kineo. She would pay her final respects to the mountain and find a way to permanently seal the sacred tunnels where she—and her ancestors before her—had faithfully protected the inner chambers. Her horse, getting along in years like herself, could no longer climb the steep and rugged back trail with ease. The northeast back trail to the top of the mountain was rarely used by anyone. The storms this winter had blown so many trees down across it that it made the final journey challenging for both rider and horse. This would be Katobaquis's last mission up Mt. Kineo as well.

* * *

Julie made the rappel descent much faster this time, using a longer pitch of rope that extended all the way to Max. She connected a safety line from the lead rope to him and back. Then she worked her way to where he was still clipped to the wall. Max continued to watch Julie in amazement. *My God, this young woman has determination*, he thought with admiration.

"Okay, handsome, time to go home," she quipped.

Max shook himself out of his daze and managed an awkward grin. He was not accustomed to being spoken to in such a manner by a graduate student. Julie then began to work the extra harness up his uninjured leg, but then began worrying about how she was going to slide it over his broken leg which had swollen considerably.

"This will hurt a bit," she said apologetically.

"Righto... But let's do it and get out of here," Max responded, the bravado failing to conceal his anguish.

Julie could see that the swelling was going to make sliding the harness up his injured leg extremely difficult. What was worse, she could see the broken bone pushing outward against the bruised skin. She would have to be very careful to ensure that the harness didn't rub against the bone. The distorted shape under his skin sickened her briefly. But then she refocused on the task at hand and began working the climbing harness up his injured leg.

Julie Walters had often fantasized about what it would be like to be in close proximity with her favorite professor, but this was not at all the way that she had imagined the scene. It was terrible seeing him in so much pain. She was as careful as she could possibly be, while Max tried concentrating on everything he could think of except what she was doing. He found himself willing himself to live so he could get off this damn rock.

It took several minutes to get the harness carefully fastened around Max, with all the straps properly secured. Finally, Julie was ready. She unclipped him from the wall and freed, Max swung back, suspended from the rope he held with his less injured hand in order to keep his position stable.

"Okay up there? Now pull!" Julie yelled to the gathering of rescuers. "Max, you have to use your good leg and take some weight off the rope. Dig your toes into the rocks near you. And when you are balanced and under control, grab a rock with your better hand and pull. They can't lift you on their own without some help from you. Not from up there."

"Righto, Julie. Got it!"

Deputy Harris, Bronson, and Thomas all began to pull Dr. Wayne's rope. Julie would, once again, have to use the shorter rope. So she had to climb up alongside Max without a rope yet again.

"Clip into my rope in case you fall, Julie."

"I'm not sure how secure the rope is that they are pulling you up with. It is working. Let's just get you up further and I will clip into my rope after a few more feet of free climbing."

"Be careful."

"Oh, believe me, I am!"

Julie found the route a bit easier the second time, although she was sure getting tired and hungry after this exhausting day. As soon as she had reached her line, she took a deep breath, clipped in, and sighed in relief. She smiled at Max who continued to grimace every time his badly injured leg or arm bumped against the cliff face.

Laura held the other end of the rope that was attached to Julie's harness. The graduate student had set up her rope so that the older woman could perform a top belay while she climbed next to Max and provided assistance when he needed it. Thomas quickly explained to his mother the technique for using her hands when belaying a climber. Laura looked down at the fit young woman that had spent this perilous afternoon with Max. Even under the duress of this heroic and risky rescue operation, it was obvious that Julie adored her professor. *A little too obvious*, Laura thought. *And now this twenty-three-year-old girl is relying on me to belay her up this wall!* She found the scenario both strangely surrealistic and bitterly ironic. *Stop it, Laura*, she admonished herself. *You're over-analyzing things. Stay focused on rescuing Max.*

Julie stayed very close to the professor and continued to encourage him to transfer as much weight as he could on his one good leg and arm. Max was in great pain, but tried to keep it from the young student. Whenever he took weight off the rope by putting weight on the rock face with his other, less injured leg, the rope would advance slowly and he would make some headway. Whenever he ended up having to touch down with both legs, the pain became so intense, he would rest back and the rope would stop advancing. During those periods when Max could not take any weight off the rope, the three at the top could only manage to hold his weight while he rested. There was simply not enough ledge to provide the three with the leverage they needed to offer Max more help in lifting himself up.

Progress was slow. Once again, Julie was overcome by muscle fatigue. Unfortunately, the water she had drunk before descending was no substitute for her body's craving for sugar. With her reserves nearly spent, she began experiencing cramps in her arms and legs.

"C'mon Max, keep going!" she urged him. "You're halfway there. You can do it!"

The professor recognized the utter exhaustion in her trembling voice. He hated himself for being such a burden. She had risked so much to get him this far. He had to fight through the agony. From deep within, Max found an inner reserve of strength that few could summon and pushed his body to its upper limit. Julie was suddenly re-energized by the boost in his energy levels and grew more confident that they would make it up the wall. Max blocked out all pain and quickly bounded another ten feet up the wall. The three rescuers at the top were surprised by the sudden progress in his movements and failed to take in the slack rapidly enough. Then without warning, his rope slipped from above, causing him to fall back five feet. In doing so, he hit his broken leg against the rhyolite wall. Max cried out in pain before blacking out. That would be the last rock-climbing step he would attempt.

* * *

The boat carrying Patricia Wellington and her nephew bounced periodically in the chop of Moosehead Lake. The young man stared at one of the gold bars that had caused so much turmoil on Kineo as his aunt piloted the craft toward Greenville. In a small cove next to the town, a covered boating slip and garage awaited their arrival.

"How much is it worth, dear?"

"I figure about six million. Each bar should be worth around six hundred thousand."

Patricia made no comment. It did not matter to her whether it was 200 bars valued at 120 million or only ten valued at six million. It simply was what it was. There were things in life far more valuable to her than money and possessions. Of the latter, she already had plenty.

"What are you going to do with it?"

"I have plans for it. You'll see."

Patricia turned to look at her nephew and the wind blew her gray hair across her face. She smiled at him, but again, said nothing. She was more worried about the fact that she would have to redo her hair, once they got back.

* * *

"Oh, no! Max!" Julie began to panic and looked up at the three on the ledge. "Pull harder!"

"We're trying—there's too much weight. Too much friction," Bronson responded, exasperated by his inability to help further.

"We can't get a good foothold here," Thomas added, his voice revealing his frustration as well.

"We can't lift him, Julie. We need more muscle," confirmed a very tired Deputy Harris. "Laura, can you let go of Julie's belay and help us here?"

Laura looked down at the worn-out and demoralized Julie Walters. *Is it safe to let go? Can you hold on,* she thought to herself, terrified about Max's condition. *What should I do?* She stared into Julie's eyes only forty feet below her now. The young woman looked defeated.

"Julie, are you okay by yourself? Can you hold on without the belay for a minute?" Laura asked her.

The graduate student didn't even consider the question. She was too drained from climbing routes that were far above her skill level and her fingers were aching as they dug into a small crack in the side of Kineo. She realized that her rescue had not been the best-executed or thought-out plan, after all. Julie had set a few protective anchors in the wall, but not as many as she needed to prevent herself from falling. In her hurry to descend to Max, she had failed to install enough cams. With the last forty feet left to climb, she noticed that she had not even laid any protection above this point. She had been careless. She looked up at Laura who was clearly more worried about Max than about the young woman at this end of the rope, and she understood. Julie realized why Laura Denton wanted Max safely up off the wall and into the cavern. *Who could blame her? Max is a great guy.*

Finally, the graduate student just nodded at Laura who started to let go of her belay line. At that moment, she noticed how Julie's arms and legs were trembling.

Damn! She's spent. That crazy girl is telling me it's okay to let go? She has nothing left. She's going to fall!

"C'mon Mom," Thomas prodded. "Julie can hang on by herself. We need another set of hands."

Laura looked down at the young woman once more and saw the resignation setting in on her face. Julie smiled up at her, as if to say: *Forget me. Let me fall. I'm done. Save Max.*

"No!" Laura yelled out. "She'll fall. I'll find a way to tie her off on something first. If I let go now, we'll lose her. And we're not losing anybody else today!"

"Do it fast, Mrs. Denton," Bronson cried out. "We could lose Max if one of us lets go here, and I know my arms are getting tired."

Just then, a strange voice cackled from behind them. It was the voice of anger, surprise, and wisdom.

"What are you doing here? Who dares to desecrate these sacred grounds?"

"What the hell?" Deputy Harris mumbled.

A very old woman with long white hair peered out from the tunnel. On her upper arm was an unusual tattoo—a large circle with three projecting lines, equally spaced, all connecting to three smaller circles at the ends of the spokes. She looked angry and half-crazed. Slowly and much more deftly than one would ever expect for a woman of her age, she slithered out of the tunnel. *Whatever was that*, Laura thought, *she could be seventy, eighty, or even ninety!*

"Who are you?" inquired Deputy Harris, her tone bewildered, as she still struggled to hold the unconscious Dr. Wayne in position below.

"Get off my ledge now, before I push you off!"

And she looks like she means it, thought Deputy Harris. *But if I let go of the rope and reach for my gun, we may lose Dr. Wayne.*

"I know who she is," said Laura Denton in a calm voice, inflected by her southern accent. "You're the ol' woman that the locals call some sort of Indian witch. A descendant of the great Mohawk tribe that used to live on Kineo. And now ya live over there, near Spencer Mountain."

The resentment on the old woman's face suddenly gave way to an expression of surprise. She started to speak, but Laura cut her off.

"I'm sorry 'bout being here," she said. "We didn't choose to be here. The evil men ya speak of forced my loved ones up here in search of somethin' in your damn tunnels. All I want is my friends and family off this damn cliff! Now will you help me?"

The old woman considered the situation carefully. How easily she could push them over the cliff, if she wanted to. *I could take at least a couple of them with me*, she thought, picturing the scenario in her mind. No matter. She was ready to die. But there was something admirable about this strange group of white invaders, all holding onto ropes on this precarious Mohawk ledge. The woman in the uniform looked like a leader—sure of herself, in command, and strong. She recognized the mother figure speaking to her as the woman that her stepdaughter, Patricia Wellington, had tried to persuade into moving away from Kineo. Patricia always spoke of Laura with great respect. The young boy looked strong, brave, and obedient to his mother. The old woman climbed further out onto the ledge and stood there, her long, white hair blowing in the stiff Moosehead breeze, as if she were the anointed matriarch of the mountain. She looked over and saw Julie Walters clinging for dear life on the side of the very treacherous east face, and then noticed a very banged-up and bloody professor dangling from the other line. She recognized Dr. Wayne and cackled.

"Ha, ha, ha, ha, ha! See what happens when you fool with the spheres?"

Taking advantage of the crazy old woman's momentary distraction, Deputy Harris glanced down to check how close her gun was holstered to her right hand. The matriarch looked back at Julie who still wore a defeated expression.

"My, oh my!" the old woman laughed. "This little beauty sure got herself into a tough spot! Yet, I see no fear." She was impressed that despite the other woman's dire situation, with her life hanging in the balance at this dangerous height, she clung bravely to the wall, unwilling to give up. "This young woman climbs Kineo like a Mohawk," the matriarch observed with grudging admiration.

She felt an unexpected sense of kinship with these people who were complete strangers to her. *They must be English descendants. Not French. They are allies of the Mohawk. I might have admired them in another time and place, but not here.*

"You must all leave now!" she abruptly announced.

Bronson watched this entire scene play out. He was a smart man and recognized that the old matriarch had softened a little, moved, partly, by the strength of the women around her. Bronson knew when to go with the flow. This was one of those times. "Deputy Harris, what would you like Thomas and me to do next, Ma'am?" he asked.

Before the deputy could respond, the old Mohawk guardian's demeanor morphed once again into one of indignation. With sudden vehemence, she cried out at Max. "You there! You're here to steal our guardian stones! To take our sacred flint and collect artifacts."

Hearing the old woman's voice begin to tighten with anger once again, Laura stood up, Julie's belay rope held tight in one hand, and looked her in the eye. "Dr. Wayne respects your culture more than anyone," she said firmly. "He lives to educate the ignorant about your proud people and teaches them to appreciate who ya were, and how ya lived. He teaches others how our ancestors ruined your lives. He's not responsible for what happened up here. It's that evil man, Pilloud, and..."

"And that nasty Frenchman," Deputy Harris interjected, completing Laura's line of thought. "That son of a bitch they call Pierre." Then she stared at the old woman, a look of determination on her face. "I promise you one thing: when I find that bastard, he's going to wish he had never set foot on Kineo!"

The old woman noted and absorbed the passion with which the other two had spoken. She let the last sentence sink in for a moment before smirking at Harris and Laura knowing that the deputy would not have that opportunity with Pierre. She did not acknowledge Bronson at all.

"Somewhere in your lineage...yes...somewhere, you *two* have Mohawk in your blood," she finally observed.

Just then, the rope began to slip through the very weary and slackened grips of Bronson, Harris, and Thomas.

"You'll never save your professor that way! Hang onto him," the old Mohawk woman commanded. "I'll help. Then I want you all out of here!"

As suddenly and mysteriously as she had appeared, the old woman vanished through the Mohawk tunnel back toward the central chamber.

* * *

Katobaquis was tied to a young sugar maple just outside of one of the three entrance tunnels to the central mining chamber. Several areas in these tunnels were too cramped to efficiently remove the flint once extracted from the rich inner core below. In later years, the three tribes had agreed to construct and share a more spacious route that could accommodate horses or mules. Since flint had not been mined for nearly 200 years, this "shared" mining route was closed by the guardians in the early 1800s. The trail leading to it had become so overgrown with vegetation as a result that even the guardians were hard put to locate it. Only two guardians of our era even knew of its existence; one of them was the old Mohawk woman.

Strolling out of the exit tunnel, she found her trusted horse chomping on some grass. She quickly untied him from the tree and searched inside her saddlebags for the ropes that she had used earlier to tie all the horses together. Finding them, she attached a rope to Katobaquis's harness, then led him through the underbrush to the old, abandoned mule tunnel that had been carved out of a large vertical fault in the mountain, thus allowing enough headroom for a horse and rider to move through it. Since, however, it was a bit claustrophobic for the large horse, Katobaquis would need a few gentle prods before he followed his mistress faithfully into the tunnel and, subsequently, into the spacious inner chamber.

"Good boy! Wait here. I'll be right back."

The old woman bent over again and moved in that crouched position down the old Mohawk emergency exit tunnel, crawling, at last, out to the ledge. Looking back at the tunnel, Thomas saw her approach. Strained by the effort of helping to hold Max's weight dangling at the other end of his line, the boy's hands were beginning to cramp and sweat dripped from his nose. The old woman tied one end of her own rope to the one held by the other three that had slackened a bit in her absence, causing Max to plunge some twenty feet further down.

"You will soon feel the rope being pulled from inside the Mohawk tunnel," the old woman announced.

"What's on the…the other end of your rope?" inquired Deputy Harris, panting from the strain of keeping her grip on the rope.

"Extra horsepower sister."

"Then let's have your horse…pull Max over the ledge…and all the way into the central chamber."

"Oh dear Lord, no, Deputy!" Laura protested. "With his broken leg and arm? That'll kill him!"

"It'll hurt like hell for sure, Mrs. Denton," Harris replied. "But he can't crawl on his broken arms and legs through that narrow tunnel. If we don't have him pulled through it, we'll never get him through in his condition."

Laura and Thomas stared silently at the deputy, trying to decide whether her apparently ridiculous idea actually made sense. As they debated the issue, the Mohawk woman crawled back the way she had come.

"She's right," agreed Bronson. "We'll never get him through that tiny opening. Besides, he may not regain consciousness to put in any effort on his own. Let the horse drag him into the central chamber. The tunnels on the other side are big enough for us to stretcher him out, but this one isn't."

Right then, they all felt the rope tighten. Katobaquis was beginning to pull.

"Okay, ladies and gentlemen," Harris said, "we have help. Now pull!"

Katobaquis and the three humans pulled the ropes taut. Thomas maneuvered the rope so that it rubbed across the instep of his hiking boot instead of grazing against the rock ledge. Max, now partly conscious again, was lifted higher along the rock wall until his face was visible to Laura just below the ledge. Inside the central mining chamber, the old Mohawk woman continued to urge Katobaquis to heave on.

"Come on, boy. Pull. This way. Pull, Katobaquis."

Laura gazed at Max as he was lifted up and over the ledge. He managed a pinched smile as his body slid past her, but his eyes betrayed the agony he was experiencing. Then he disappeared, head first, into the Mohawk tunnel directly behind them. Max was being dragged along on his bad shoulder, but no cry of pain emerged from his lips. He was beyond such futile outbursts. It was only when he passed out for a few minutes did he find a reprieve from the severe throbbing in his injured arm and leg.

Bronson had snatched up his medical kit and was the first to chase Max through the hole. Deputy Harris ran over to Laura and looked down at Julie. "We got him! Your turn!"

Julie smiled. "Climbing!" she replied faintly.

Well, climb! Laura thought. *I want to go see how Max is. Let's go!*

Deputy Harris asked Thomas to help his mother in getting Julie back up and over the ledge. Patting him on the shoulder, she explained, "I'm following Bronson to help with Dr. Wayne."

As the deputy crawled into the Mohawk tunnel, Julie continued climbing the wall. She found a small nut she had quite forgotten about after placing it only twenty-five feet from the ledge. She saw few places where she could secure her next handhold, but soon slid three fingers from her stronger hand deep into a crack in the rock and spread them out for full contact. Although a relatively good place for a handhold, it was at an awkward angle. Her other hand trembled as she reached across to pull the final protective nut and Thomas noticed how badly her knuckles were sliced open by the constant abuse from the edges of rhyolite along her climb. Julie pulled the last protective device from the mountain, clipped the tiny nut to her belt, and let her sore hand dangle for a few seconds to allow the muscles in her thumb to recover. *I'm out of here…finally*, she thought, looking up at Thomas and Laura for encouragement.

Then suddenly, her eyes went to her belay rope that had been pulled out of line earlier and was rubbing along an edge of rhyolite that erosion from last winter's freeze and fracture had exposed and dangerously sharpened. Portions of her rope had already frayed badly.

"Thomas!" she called out, "clear the rope from that knife edge!"

He looked down and instantly saw what she meant. Dropping to his knees, he tried to pull the rope toward him, but dared not budge it, as it was being pulled by Julie's weight still. He had noticed, moreover, that the rope's outer protective sheath had been worn away from the sharp edge by the final carabineer secured to the wall near his head that supported Julie's belay. The young woman was so exhausted that the belay line had not been advancing with the proper amount of slack to protect a potential fall. Laura, on the other hand, was keeping it taut the entire time to provide an upward pull while belaying. Julie needed that help as she managed the final strenuous moves that were above her level of climbing skill.

"Crap! The rope, Mom! Loosen the belay rope quick!"

"What? Why?"

"You're cutting her line on that edge. Take the weight off the line!"

Even though Julie knew what Thomas meant, she was too worn out to pause and think about the consequences of her line going slack and did not consider the tenuousness of her current hold. Laura held much of the other woman's weight in her arresting belay so that when she let the line suddenly slacken, Julie's tired legs took her full weight, without either foot having adequate contact with the wall. Both her feet slipped from her current perch, slamming her, face forward, against the wall. The three fingers she had awkwardly jammed into the tiny crack above broke with an audible snap as the full weight of her body placed an unnatural torque on that hand. Julie writhed in pain as she heard the sound of bone cracking. The only thing preventing her from plunging to death was her strong top belay from the carabineer set into the stone above, near Thomas. The full weight shift and small winging motion cut deep into the sheath of already damaged rope.

"Owww!" Julie's cry of pain was followed by a moan.

Laura thought it was the most pitiful sound she had ever heard.

"Get your weight off it now, Julie!" Thomas yelled anxiously. Using her left foot, Julie quickly secured a hold, obtaining some relief as part of the weight came off. But she needed a reliable hold for her uninjured hand, and struggled to find something along this section of glassy-textured rhyolite to grip. Tears streamed down her cheeks as panic overtook her. Exhausted, her fingers throbbing with pain, Julie felt utterly defeated. With her confidence gone, her remaining hold was beginning to loosen. She scanned the slick, smooth, wall face in search of a more secure hold. Just minutes ago, she had found one, but it was now out of reach. Desperate now, she thrust her free hand with the badly sliced knuckles into a deep crack below her and spread her fingers until her tender knuckles had made agonizing contact with every bit of cold stone surface area she could press against. This last-minute move came just in time, for her feet, still frantically exploring the face below for something to wedge themselves into, slipped again.

Several feet above, Laura and her son kept weight off the belay line, terrified that the rope would be sliced in half across the sharp edge. As Thomas looked at both the carabineer and the rope, an idea struck him.

"Can you hang on for a few seconds with those handholds?" he yelled down to Julie.

"Few...I think..." she muttered.

This was it. She could not hold this tenuous position for long. She closed her eyes and took a breath. There was no escaping her predicament. She screamed out a one-word expletive, then thought to herself: *This rope is going to slice into two and I'll fall to my death!*

Thomas recognized the despair in her eyes and the lack of assurance in her voice. He tied a short piece of some excess webbing from himself to the carabineer on the ledge to secure himself from falling. He hoped the purchase of the protective device would be strong enough to maintain both his own weight and Julie's, if need be. Then he leaned far over the ledge and reached down below the point where the jagged edge had gouged and sliced the line, and began pulling it up with his bare hands.

"Julie, I can take much of your body weight off the rope now. Climb!" he told her.

"Can I help?" Laura asked.

"Move the belay line off the edge over to there!"

Confident that the webbing would hold him, Thomas now pulled with all of his might. This took enough weight off to enable Julie to successfully smear the glassy portion of rock, ascend another five feet, and find a better place to finally obtain four points of secure contact. Laura moved the belay line over to a safer location.

"Okay Thomas," she said. "Done. We got good rope 'gain and I got her."

"Great, Mom!"

"Are we good now?" A hopeful Julie cried out.

"Climb on."

"Thomas…I…my fingers… Can you…"

"No problem. Just keep coming. I'll keep pulling ya till you make it."

"Let out a little more line, Mrs. Denton." The softly spoken, but confident words from the old Mohawk woman startled Laura. "Your son is a natural in high places. Mohawk blood-lines must run in your young man."

Laura Denton said nothing, but allowed the Mohawk woman to help her belay Julie, as she checked the security of the webbing preventing Thomas from falling upside down over the edge as he assisted the graduate student. By keeping much of her weight off her line, Thomas was able to encourage Julie past the last difficult ten feet up to the ledge. Thomas then clasped Julie's bloody hand, and helped her back up on the ledge.

"You OK?" Harris and Bronson asked together, clutching the trembling climber into their arms and pulling her securely beyond the safely line rail as she shook uncontrollably and sobbed. The young woman turned, smiled at Thomas in gratitude, and then looked back at the tunnel.

"How is Max?"

There was a scramble for position to be first off the ledge, but Bronson had already crawled through the tunnel—Max needed his medical attention immediately.

* * *

"You're gonna live, you tough son of a bitch!" Bronson assured him, pulling the profes-sor's eyelids open to check his eyes with a small light

"Pie…Pierre…where is he?" Max muttered. His eyes remained closed and his breathing was shallow, but he had regained enough consciousness to remember the danger the loomed in these tunnels.

"We don't know. Now get ready—this is going to hurt, Dr. Wayne," warned the fire investigator, playing out his role of an EMT. "I'm going to pop your shoulder now back in place, then set your arm the best I can. Then we're carrying you out."

"Righto. Do it!"

Julie Walters finished crawling through the Mohawk tunnel and appeared in the central chamber just in time to hear several stomach-churning popping sounds, followed by a groan of pain. Bronson Thurman had just forced Dr. Wayne's shoulder into place.

"Max!"

Julie ran and dropped to her knees beside him. She picked up his one good hand and hugged him, bawling uncontrollably against his chest. The professor felt awkward at first. But as her grip on his hand relaxed, he placed it gently on her head and stroked her sweaty hair in a comforting manner.

"I'm fine, Jules," he said. "You did well today."

Laura and Thomas appeared through the opening next. At the sight of Julie Walters clutching onto Max as if she would never let go, Laura was seized by the impulse to rush over to him as well. *To give him a hug? To tell him how worried I had been about him?* As Laura stood there contemplating her options, Thomas ran ahead and clasped Dr. Wayne's hand.

"You outdid yourself today, Thomas," Max said.

"Yes, Thomas," Julie agreed. "I owe you my life."

With those words, she kissed him on his forehead, bringing a bright red blush to teenager's cheeks, although unnoticeable in the dimly lit workspace of the circular balcony surrounding the central mining chamber.

"And I owe you mine," Max added softly, looking at Julie.

A bashful smile appeared on her face as the young woman continued to weep in relief.

Standing eight feet away, Laura smiled at the others, yet, felt disconnected. She wanted to plow through the group doting on Max and get to his side, but all she could do was stand there, silently counting her blessings and watching the others express their delight and relief that he had survived.

Max looked up and noticed an exhausted and dejected-looking Laura Denton standing by the Mohawk tunnel. His heart stirred immediately. Hers was the image that had helped keep him alive, when his body was urging him to give up. It was wonderful to see her again, and he wanted to sit up and hold her close, but was too weak to do so.

"Laura..." Max finally mumbled.

Before she could respond, however, Harris appeared with a sense of urgency, "So, Dr. Wayne?" she interrupted "What happened to that evil bastard—Pilloud?"

"Gone."

"What do you mean 'gone'?"

"Went for a swim, preceded by a long dive..." Max muttered. "I took him out."

Deputy Harris made no effort to suppress the unprofessional smile of glee that appeared on her face the moment those words sank in.

"He's stabilized," she announced. "Let's lift him and get him the hell out of here now!"

The makeshift stretcher that Bronson had fashioned out of old timbers in the cavern was lifted off the ground. The old Mohawk woman held Thomas back by the arm.

"Wait, young man," she said. "I have one final task for which I need your help."

Thomas called to his mother who appeared to be preoccupied at the moment with helping move Max's stretcher.

"I will be right there," he told her. "I'm going to help her with some gear."

Laura only half-heard the words, more concerned with getting Max proper medical care as fast as possible. They wound their way out of the original tunnel that had delivered them to this nightmare. Laura walked ahead of the group carrying a flashlight. Nobody paid attention to the old Mohawk woman and Thomas who had stayed behind at the top level of the mining chamber. As they rested the stretcher safely back down on the top of Mt. Kineo, Max shielded his eyes from the blinding sunlight with his one good hand. Bronson squinted until his pupils had adjusted to the intense light outside. He looked back at the tunnel.

"Who was that old woman anyway?" he inquired.

* * *

"Thomas. I'm an old woman. I need your help. Do you see that large mass of stone over the ceiling of the mining chamber?"

"Yes, ma'am."

"It has been there for thousands of years. See the fissures in it, where old ice floes worked their way deep inside, freezing and thawing and freezing again, eventually pulling it away from the mountain?"

"Yes, ma'am. I see it. It's spectacular."

"I need you to take this satchel quickly and stuff it up in that crack, as deep inside as you can reach. You'll need to climb that rock pile over there to get to it. I'll hold my light so you can see."

"What is in there?"

"Oh…something that was stolen from the chamber and left behind by Pierre. You need not know more about it at this time. But it must be hidden there—where nobody can find it. Just our little secret, Thomas. I trust you, you know? To hide it deep in the crack."

"Okay. Sure. Let me have it."

He was tempted to sneak a peek inside the sack, but saw the old Mohawk woman shaking her head in maternal disapproval. Thomas was enjoying the adventure anyway. He began climbing the rock pile and had to scramble in the poor light to the point where he could see the fissure near the ceiling. He used all the strength in his arms to pull himself up to the perch from which he could reach over to the crack, but it was about twelve feet above the level from which he had started, and a long way down below him to the bottom of the lower central mining chamber. He was about to place the satchel in the crack, as instructed, when the old woman spoke to him.

"Thomas. One more favor. Reach inside the satchel. You will feel a cord inside. Take it out and leave the rest of the contents inside."

"I feel it."

"Good. Let it dangle down from the satchel."

"Yes, ma'am."

Thomas pulled the long cord out and stuffed the heavy satchel as deep inside the rocks as he could, without toppling over himself. The thought of the fifty-foot drop to the mining chamber below kept him alert and cautious as he worked. He climbed down and approached the old woman.

"What is that cord for?"

"It is time for you to leave, Thomas. You were a big help. Thank you. It is time for you and your friends to leave this chamber. Below lies Kajo's final resting place. They should never have disturbed his final resting place."

"What are you going to do?"

"Ensure it remains his final resting place. Now go. Take Katobaquis with you and use him to get Dr. Wayne off my mountain! What was mine is now yours."

With that, the old Mohawk woman walked over the pit's ledge and looked down at the vault. She looked over to the cord, still hanging down from the satchel where Thomas had left it. She wondered if the amount of explosives in the satchel that Pierre had left behind would be enough to bring down the large slabs above and start a rockslide heavy enough to bury Kajo and the lower-chamber area forever. The cord hung down near the rim floor, but over the deep pit. She hoped she could reach it. She took out a lighter and flicked the tiny metal wheel, bringing to life, once more, the flame that had defined so much of Kineo's history. She noticed Thomas still standing there and turned to him.

"Go now!" she yelled at him. "Once this is lit, there will be little time to get out of here. Go, boy! Your work is done!"

As Thomas saw the old woman reach out over the open pit and struggle with the lighter to set the cord on fire, he suddenly realized what she was about to do.

"Oh, no!" he yelled. "Run!"

He ran as fast as he could to the exit tunnel from where he had seen his mother and the rescue team leave with Dr. Wayne. Before he ducked inside the tunnel, he turned back again to see the cord aflame, like a sparkler on the Fourth of July. The old Mohawk woman was nowhere in sight. *No time to worry about that*, he thought, and began running in a crouched position through the low-ceilinged tunnel, hollering all the way for the others to move fast.

* * *

The sound of the rescue helicopter arriving from Bangor made everyone feel optimistic. They all looked up and watched it closing in on their location near the top of Mt. Kineo. Laura was about to see Max fly off to the hospital. She felt frustrated that only her son and the graduate student could express their feelings about Max surviving his horrible ordeal. *I'm going to the hospital with him*, she thought, *I'll tell him what agonies I went through, seeing him hanging onto that cliff and...*

Suddenly, a deafening explosion was followed by pulverized pieces of rocks spraying out of the exit tunnel. Seconds earlier, Thomas had nearly reached the mouth of the tunnel and the force of the eruption knocked him clear off his feet. Laura saw him tumble out and ran to him. But by then, he had quickly bounced back on his feet, unharmed.

"What the hell was that?" she asked.

"I'm not sure, but I think that crazy Mohawk woman blew up the chamber to seal it up from..."

As the helicopter circled above, looking for a clearing nearby to land, Laura engulfed her son in a tight embrace, before he could complete his explanation, and asked him if he were injured.

"The old woman is not coming out, is she, Mom?" Thomas looked back at the smoke billowing out from the tunnel entrance.

"No, son. I wouldn't think so."

"She told me we could use her horse to get Max down, if we needed to."

"The helicopter is trying to find a place to land now. Let's go help. Are you sure you're all right?"

"A little hard of hearing, but other than that, sure, I'm fine."

Deputy Harris waved her arms at the helicopter pilot to direct him and he followed her to the tiny clearing nearby. Once the 'copter had landed, Bronson met the EMT who had arrived and explained Dr. Wayne's medical condition. Deputy Harris called in the status of the rescue to her deputies and informed them about Pilloud's end. Her deputies, meanwhile, had located Pierre and informed her now of the way he had died. The helicopter pilot asked Bronson if he wanted to ride to the hospital with them. Julie Walters tapped the fire investigator on the shoulder and told him she would escort Max.

"Who's this?" the pilot inquired.

"The young lady who risked her life to save him."

"All right. Climb aboard, hero. We need to go now."

Laura and Thomas jogged up from the tunnel area and watched young Julie climb into the helicopter. Bronson looked back and saw the forlorn look in Laura Denton's eyes. He started to close the door, then paused. His gaze dropped to Julie who was on her knees, holding Dr. Wayne's hand. The latter's eyes were on Laura. Suddenly, Laura approached the helicopter and looked at Max. He was fading again, but at the sight of her, his eyes twinkled.

"Julie. Switch out." Bronson demanded.

"Hey, we got to go. Who's this now?" the pilot asked impatiently, as the engines began to ramp up for take-off.

"Laura Denton," Julie shouted back to the pilot, struggling to be heard against the drone of the blades revving up. "She and her son saved *my* life!"

The graduate student looked out at Laura. She was not anxious to give up her seat on the helicopter, but as she saw Max smiling affectionately at the older woman, despite his pain, she knew immediately what to do. Squeezing the professor's hand, she gave him a parting kiss on the side of his face, then jumped down from the helicopter. Laura gave Julie's arm a comforting squeeze and smiled at her warmly. The helicopter took off with Laura sitting on the floor next to Max. He held her hand, closed his eyes, and fell asleep.

48

One Year Later; July 4, 2000

Pastor Davis smiled as he looked out into the crowd of familiar faces. The tiny Rockwood Community Church had never hosted so many people. The service was solemn, one year to the day after the tragic unfolding of events on Mt. Kineo that marred the 4th of July holiday last summer. Dougie sat on the front-row bench, his leg propped up on a stool. He had recently undergone his second surgery to restore function to his leg. He was back working with Bennington and would wakeboard again, but not this summer. He had no desire to ever fall from a tree again.

Over thirty people stood in the back of the log chapel, including Deputy Toonie with his freshly pressed uniform, holding his big deputy's hat in his left hand. The people of Rockwood now held him in high esteem for the impressive way he had handled the criminals on Kineo last summer. Fortunately, his bicep had healed nicely, although he still sported a nasty scar along his cheek where the bullet had ripped his skin. Toonie, however, wore his scar proudly, like a badge of honor.

Rix and Bob Kraft sat in the third row, observing the special memorial service for those lost on Kineo last summer, and gave their thanks to God for their own good fortune. The air-service business was booming, with more tourists coming to Kineo than ever before. Interest in the area had been revived, in part, by all of the publicity generated last year—a result of the unusual gun battle that had raged on the island, but more because of the amazing historic and archeological discoveries inside the mountain. New money was flowing into the area from other New England states, and Rix was getting more handyman work than he could handle. Of course, his favorite client, Laura Denton, commanded his special attention, as her bed and breakfast was already booked for the entire season.

Bennington had divorced his wife during the winter, and continued to spend a great deal of time on Kineo with his younger daughter, Amanda. Both preferred to spend much of that time over at the Dentons' B&B. Tiffany had opted to live in Paris with her mother. Neither had returned to Kineo since the events of last summer. The older Lomax girl often wondered how Thomas Denton had turned out, but was not interested enough to want to fly all the way to the backwoods of Maine, when she could shop to her heart's content and pursue men that were of a higher social status. Now in church, Amanda stood next to Jenny, sharing a hymnal, and giggled as she listened to her best friend sing a traditional hymn—a half-pitch off-key—at the top of her lungs.

Dr. Mongeau and several of Dr. Wayne's former and current graduate students were in attendance. Noticeable was the absence of Rob Landon, who had nearly died from his injuries last summer. Nobody had been surprised when he dropped out of the graduate program in disgrace. Pursuing her doctorate degree under Dr. Wayne's guidance, Julie Walters had become his most persevering research assistant and was helping him unveil the secrets of Mt. Kineo and what was left of its inner chambers after the explosion. Uncovering the rock that lay in the bottom of the mining pit was off limits as they all respected what the old Mohawk decendant was trying to preserve.

An anonymous donor had made a grant to the University of Maine, the most generous one it had ever received. It was to be used, as directed, for the study of native cultures. The grant had enabled the university to assemble a team of archeologists, native linguistic experts, historians, and geologists to study Mt. Kineo and its surrounding area. Of particular interest to Julie and Max were the artifacts and paintings that supported the legend of Kajo the Trader and the Circle of Unity. Julie was particularly interested in acquiring further knowledge and understanding of the guardian gemstones. She would often gaze at the gem-sphere she had once held in her hands and that was now safely protected under secured glass at the small museum on top of the mountain. Under the leadership of Dr. Wayne, the team had already made numerous interesting discoveries in other remote sites about much older indigenous peoples such as the Red Paint People—Max's other academic passion on the island. He considered himself fortunate to have the old dormitory again as the base of his research operations this year.

Rebecca Pilloud was horrified to discover what had happened that day on Kineo after she left with her son. The details of her uncle's conspiracy and malevolent intentions were repugnant, even to her, raised though she had been in a family that condoned dirty dealings. Arson, kidnapping, and murder were not crimes even Becky could overlook and guilt consumed her at the thought that she had been an assessory to much of it. Rebecca did not want her son, Jacob, to grow up to be like she and her uncle. Disappearing with Jacob after the authorities cleared her of direct involvement in her uncle's criminal operations; she exiled herself from the Moosehead region. Locals speculated that she had been wallowing in guilt and drinking heavily in a secluded compound outside of Quebec, but she never returned.

Pilloud's only daughter inheirited the Kokadjo Timber and Paper Company and stived to rebuild her damaged family name by re-establishihng the company under its new name: Green Timber Solutions. She had also become very involved in local philanthropy. Green Timber Solutions had donated a substantial amount of money to the State of Maine and the upper portion of Mt. Kineo had been granted a special preservation status, with a park ranger appointed to administer the area and deal on a daily basis with visiting touristst. The generous donation had helped set up, within a matter of three months, a small museum constructed from white pine logs.

Visitors would come by to admire the magnificent Native American relics, implements, and other fine museum-grade artifacts found by the university researchers and exhibited in the newly constructed Visitor's Center, named "The Bear's Den" in honor of the late Bear Pfitzheimer who had, in the end, been forgiven by the Moosehead region's locals and Kineo residents. Julie Walters frequented this structure often, quietly paying her respects to the man who had been responsible for saving her life so that she could devote the rest of it to the island he had considered his real home.

As the organist finished playing the final hymn, the gathering slowly made its way out of the small chapel. In the background, Mt. Kineo towered over Moosehead Lake, as it had for many thousands of years. The new owner of the island's rear portion was a mysterious trust made up of silent partners, who reportedly had some Native American affiliation. Although the mountain had been deeded as a special wildlife refuge, the University of Maine was granted an exclusive lease to explore and restore its inner tunnels and uncover its history.

Patricia Wellington, the only named trustee to the landholding, displayed her dedication to rebuilding the image of Kineo by hosting many educational programs for people to participate in and thereby enjoy the island's natural treasures. She would take time to discuss with the visitors the many fascinating things she knew about its history. Patricia had also had a new cottage constructed on the big hill in the meadow near the water tower, where she could overlook Moosehead Lake, Cottage Row, and live out her life as the gatekeeper to the trails to Mt. Kineo.

At the Rockwood Docks, her brand new twenty-eight-foot Sea Ray had pulled up and a toothy, well-dressed young man that Patricia called "her native nephew", jumped out and hurried across the lawn toward the log chapel to escort her home. As he approached silently, Patricia was still shaking hands with appreciative Rockwood citizens at the top of the chapel steps. Seeing her nephew moving across the freshly mowed lawn, she turned and looked for Laura and Max in the crowd.

She spotted the professor standing over by the table with the brownies and refreshments and talking to an animated Julie Walters, his assistant. In a beautiful green dress that showed off her figure to perfection and was quite a change from the casual field clothes she was normally seen wearing on Kineo, Julie looked like a different woman. Patricia was relieved that Dr. Wayne's injuries had healed well this past year and wondered how things were going between him and Laura Denton this summer. It seemed that they had kept in touch, although Laura had returned to Tampa with her family after the disasters that had taken place last summer. Patricia watched as Julie finished her conversation with Max. The young woman laughed at something the professor had said, then hugged him tightly. Then with a smile that glowed with admiration, she walked over to talk to Thomas Denton who was gazing with interest at an archeological implement he had placed in his pocket to examine after the service was over.

Hmm...that hug may answer my question, Patricia thought, disappointed. Then she noticed Laura walking up to Julie and Thomas. The younger woman gave Laura a big hug as well. Then as the latter whispered something to her son, he stuffed the ancient implement from the Red Paint People back into his pocket for later scrutiny. Patricia snickered at the frown the young man was unable to conceal from his mother. Laura then turned and approached Max. Their fingers interlocked the moment she reached him. He turned to her, smiled brightly, and planted a kiss on her lips that was eagerly accepted and returned.

Hmm...now that is more like it, thought Patricia as she continued to look over at them. Laura and Max felt her eyes on them and as they turned to acknowledge her, the latter gave them a little wink. The three of them smiled at each other in a knowing way. No words were exchanged; none were needed. Patricia Wellington's nephew strolled past the other memorial service guests and greeted his aunt on the steps. Then he took her arm to escort her down the log chapel's flower-lined walkway. Watching the guests move aside respectfully, Laura thought it was as if she were watching the departure of Kineo royalty.

The old Mohawk woman was never seen again. One popular rumor claimed that she had jumped from the ledge of the upper chamber to the lower one, just before the explosion, to ensure that the ceiling would collapse upon her and entomb her in the same spot as Kajo's burial site far below. According to another story, she had walked out onto the old Mohawk ledge one last time and leaped to a watery death in Moosehead Lake. Thomas hoped she had simply lit the fuse, escaped from the tunnels, unseen, and returned to her home near Spencer Mountain. The fact, however, that she had never returned for her horse made that particular theory untenable.

Katobaquis spent a month being pampered by Jenny who had always wanted to own a horse. But when the time came to drive back to Tampa, the Dentons realized that the old Mohawk woman was not going to be coming back for her equine companion and offered the old horse to Rix Kraft. The latter somehow took to the idea of keeping the "old witch"'s horse and treating him like a prize-show dog that would somehow keep him safe from the effects of both surviving local curses and the noxious effects, if any, of the previous summer's incidents. At first, it seemed as if the old horse might die without his old mistress; but he surprised the Krafts by actually taking to Rix. As time went by, a bond developed between the two.

Although Thomas did not like to admit it to himself, he knew in his heart how the old Mohawk woman's life had ended. Since her body was never found to support any of the prevailing conjectures, nobody would ever know the truth. Her role in the summer of cruel fires and tragic deaths on Kineo would establish her status as a legend, no less intriguing than the one of Kajo the Trader—the legend that she had grown up with.

No more mysterious fires would plague the historic island after that dreadful summer. Tourism blossomed once again, as it had in Kineo's glorious past. The greed and vendettas that had plagued the past three centuries of the island's history had come to an end and been replaced by the wonder of discovery. Everyone—natives, locals, and visitors alike—shared its amazing resources as the Spirit of the Cow Moose, her anger finally spent, forgave the mighty hunter for taking her calf from her.

AUTHOR'S NOTE:

This is a work of fiction, although the story is based on factual information from various historical sources, websites, and scientific texts. No footnotes have been used to mark the narrative's factual segments.

I wish to acknowledge the contribution of Karen Musser, Betsy Dasse, and Kathy Lundberg who spent hours reading through and proofing early drafts. I would also like to reserve special thanks to my supportive wife Karen who encouraged me to initiate the project and Mita Ghose for her detailed and insightful final editing. In addition, I was inspired by the many adventures of my children, and our friends, families, and neighbors, who shared their personal discoveries of Kineo with us. All the main characters are fictional and any resemblance to actual persons is purely coincidental, except where specified. Real-life characters woven into the text have been brought in from historical accounts for the sake of lending the narrative a different dimension and a flavor of authenticity.

This novel is dedicated to my wife Karen, sons David, Ben, and Daniel, and especially to my daughter, Sarah, who inspired the character, Jenny.

Partial Bibliography

Lee Sultzman's *First Nations/First Peoples* Internet site; various papers by David Sanger on Maine's archeological heritage and the Red Paint People, Moosehead Historical Society P.O. Box 1116, Greenville, Maine 04441-1116; *In the Maine Woods.*, Bangor and Aroostook Railroad Company.] 1931. pp 69-70 ; *Dictionary of American Fighting Ships, Vol. III, 1968*, Navy Department, Office of the Chief of Naval Operations, Naval History Division, Washington, D.C.; various books and publications by Dr. Everett L. Parker, Maine Department of Conservation and Maine Geological Survey; and an occasional referral from various geologic and ecologic references.